"I am *not* pursuing you," he said.

"And so you may ~~~~~~~~~~~~~~~~~~~~~~~~~~~ ld
have twice the f~~~~~~~~~~~~~~~~~~~~~~~~~~~ it! I
have a little mor~~~~~~~~~~~~~~~~~~~~~~~~~

For a moment s~~~~~~~~~~~~~~~~~~~~~~~~~

Shame burnt Thea's cheeks, and deep inside, coldness
spread, leaching through her, a slow poison welling up.
She fought it down, forcing herself to seem untouched,
unmoved.

"I suppose I must thank you for making your sentiments
so plain," she said stiffly. It didn't matter. It didn't! After all,
she didn't want him, or any man, to pursue her. The chill
spread further. *How* had he known?

Then, "Oh, damn!" said Richard. "I mean, I beg your
pardon, Thea. That was not at all how I meant to put it.
What I *meant* is that I am not on the catch for an heiress.
Any heiress."

Thea took a shaky breath. She had thought—for one
dreadful eternal instant—that he knew.

A Compromised Lady
Harlequin® Historical #864—September 2007

ELIZABETH ROLLS

A Compromised Lady

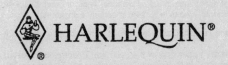

HARLEQUIN®

TORONTO • NEW YORK • LONDON
AMSTERDAM • PARIS • SYDNEY • HAMBURG
STOCKHOLM • ATHENS • TOKYO • MILAN • MADRID
PRAGUE • WARSAW • BUDAPEST • AUCKLAND

ISBN-13: 978-0-373-29464-0
ISBN-10:   0-373-29464-6

A COMPROMISED LADY

www.eHarlequin.com

Printed in U.S.A.

DON'T MISS THESE OTHER
NOVELS AVAILABLE NOW:

#863 KLONDIKE WEDDING—KATE BRIDGES

When Dr. Luke Hunter stands in as the groom in a proxy wedding,
he doesn't expect to be *really* married to the bride! Luke's not a
settling-down kind of man, but beautiful Genevieve may be the
woman to change his mind.

#865 A PRACTICAL MISTRESS—MARY BRENDAN

She was nearly penniless, and becoming a mistress was the only
practical solution. The decision had *nothing* to do with the look in
Sir Jason's eyes that promised such heady delights....

#866 THE WARRIOR'S TOUCH—
MICHELLE WILLINGHAM

Pragmatic, plain Aileen never forgot the handsome man
who became her first lover on the eve of Bealtaine, the man
who gave her a child without ever seeing her face.
Now that he has returned, how can she keep her secret?
The MacEgan Brothers

For Linda.
Who waited. And waited.
And then waited some more.
She even gave me another contract!
And for all the readers
who kept asking about Richard.
Thank you.

Chapter One

'David—he can't be serious! Why does he suddenly wish me to return after all this time? Nothing has changed! Nothing!' Thea dragged in a breath. 'I am still—' At the sight of her brother's taut mouth, the sudden tension in his clenched fists, she changed what she had been about to say. 'I am still of the same mind—I have no desire to return. What has changed Papa's stance?'

David's mouth opened and then closed, as though he too had thought the better of something. Then, 'I don't know, Thea. Not definitely. I have a suspicion, but since he didn't tell me anything beyond that I was to bring you back to town with me, I'd prefer not to say.'

Exasperated, Miss Dorothea Winslow stared at her brother across the confined gloom of their aunt Maria's parlour. If David's unannounced arrival in North Yorkshire from London had been unexpected, the news he bore was doubly so. She clutched the warm shawl closer, shivering despite the warmth of the fire crackling in the grate. Twenty minutes ago she had been knitting socks, a pot of tea beside her, quietly content and perfectly warm. Now the chill of the bitter rain gusting against the windows had seeped into her bones and the old panic stirred restlessly.

'Papa was more than happy for me to stay out of the way for the past eight years.' She added, 'He wouldn't even let me journey south to attend Mama's funeral. Why now, David? Don't tell me he wants me to be a comfort to him in his old age!'

David snorted. 'Hardly.' He stared into the fire for a moment. 'He is talking of a match for you, Thea.'

Her blood congealed, along with her forgotten cup of tea. *'What?'* Her breath came raggedly. 'But—'

David said, 'At Mama's funeral eighteen months ago, several people asked where you were. Remarked upon your long seclusion. Thea—burying your heart in the grave with your betrothed does not constitute a sufficient reason for not marrying. If people ask enough questions—' He broke off.

She steadied her breathing. 'I see.' *If people asked enough questions, someone might hit on the truth…*

He stood up abruptly and said, 'Our father fears the gossip. Which is at least part of the reason that he is essentially compelling you to come to London for the Season.'

'Compelling me?'

David nodded. 'He has instructed me to inform you that if you do not, you will receive no allowance at all.' His expression was grim.

Thea bit her lip. And then she gritted her teeth. 'I can still remain here with Aunt Maria.'

'He has already written to her—telling her that you are to come to London. Do you imagine she will defy him? She depends on his support.'

'But why? If I remain here—'

His grey eyes were flinty. 'As far as our father is concerned you have had ample time to recover from your…' He hesitated and then said, with an edge of violence, 'Your disappointment.'

Thea made a sharp movement and the now gelid cup of tea beside her crashed to ruin on the floor.

She ignored it.

'I see. Of course, eight years is ample time to recover from a *disappointment*.' She laid her hands carefully in her lap to prevent them clenching into fists. 'Especially a *disappointment* that never happened, according to one's point of view.'

He returned no answer to that.

'David, can't you—?'

'Damn it, Thea! Do you think I didn't try to talk him out of it?' David surged to his feet and prowled about the parlour, his movements jerky. 'I know this is not what you want, and if what I suspect is true, then in part it is my fault, but nothing would sway him.'

'And you aren't going to tell me?'

He shook his head. 'Better not.'

She shivered. There would be compensations. To hear good music again, visit Hatchards…and apparently she had no choice. But living in her father's house again…

'I suppose a chaperon has been arranged?' she said with forced calm.

David's mouth twisted. 'It is arranged that you should stay with Lady Arnsworth for the Season, and that she will chaperon you.'

Thea let out a sigh of relief, but said nothing; she merely knelt down and began carefully picking up the shattered porcelain. Aunt Maria was going to be most annoyed at the desecration of her best tea service.

Aunt Maria sat in a chair by the rarely lit fire as Thea packed later that evening. 'Certainly not, Dorothea!' she snapped, diligently folding handkerchiefs. 'Aberfield,' she continued, 'is obviously lost to all sense of decency and propriety!' She shot a hard glance at her great-niece. 'However, it is not for me to gainsay him; so, no, Dorothea, I will not attempt to change his mind.'

Along with her back, her lips were ramrod straight. 'Let us hope that your sense of duty to your family has increased in the past eight years. I say no more than that *I* have done my best to ensure that it should be so.' Her tone suggested that she doubted her best had been anywhere near good enough.

'But, Aunt—'

Miss Maria Winslow flung up her hand. 'No, Dorothea. Aberfield,' she proclaimed in the tones of one invoking a deity, 'is your father, and Head of the Family. It is not for me to argue with him. You will do as you are bid.'

No choice at all. With no money and no refuge, she was going to London. Thea laid her best gown, the dove-grey silk reserved for expected visitors, carefully layered in tissue paper, in the open trunk on her bed. She doubted very much that she would wear it again more than once or twice. What was adequate for the depths of rural Yorkshire would be despised in London. Thea stared at the gown. Three years she had been wearing it. Only yesterday when she had changed to greet the rector's wife, she had put it on with loathing, longing for something pretty, something *pink,* instead of the never-ending grey. Now it looked safe, secure. Anonymous. All of which were about to be torn from her.

In the corner of the post-chaise rocking its way down the Great North Road towards London, Thea sat straight and stiff, a book open and forgotten on her lap. David lounged in the opposite corner reading a newspaper. Outside, northern England fell away behind them, every mile, every hoofbeat taking her closer to London...

'I have been thinking, David.'

He looked up from the newspaper. 'I assumed there was a reason you hadn't spoken or turned a page in half an hour.'

She gave him a rueful smile. 'Was I being rude?'

He grinned comfortably and laid the paper aside. 'No. I'm your brother. It's not technically possible for you to be rude to me.'

Despite the roiling tension, she chuckled. 'Oh? You were used to be rude enough to me!'

'That,' he informed her, 'is different. Brothers exist only to be rude to and, on occasion about, their sisters. What were you thinking?'

Slowly, she said, 'Papa cannot want me quartered on him in London for ever—even at Arnsworth House.'

'No,' said David. 'He doesn't. He's counting on your marriage.'

She twisted her battered old gloves between her hands. 'It won't happen,' she said shortly. 'He may force me to London, but he still can't force me into marriage. If I do not marry by the end of the Season—surely once he realises—'

'Do you think,' asked David, his voice diffident, 'that you might, our father's machinations aside, find some fellow to care for? One who will care for you?'

Leaning forward, he reached out and covered her hand with his.

She couldn't help it—instinctively, she jerked back, every nerve jangling at the unexpected touch.

Very slowly David sat back, his eyes shuttered.

Silence grew and stretched. When Thea spoke it was as though the words dropped into an abyss. 'I hope to God that I don't.'

'Really, Richard! What were you thinking? Seventy thousand pounds! Of course it was snapped up! And after all my efforts to cultivate the connection, where were you? In Kent!'

With forced patience, Richard Blakehurst listened to the continuation of his aunt Almeria Arnsworth's tirade. He had heard most of the countess's diatribe before and this particular version had been running—with minor variations upon the original theme—for the past several months.

'I *wrote* to you, explaining the urgency! And now the wretched girl is betrothed! To someone else.'

With a silent prayer of thanks to a benevolent deity for this circumstance, Richard settled himself as comfortably as possible in an Egyptian-style gilt chair built for a female form rather than a six-foot male and cast a considering glance at the decanters gracing a console table supported by a pair of sphinxes. His cup of tea wasn't quite hitting the mark under these circumstances. It was weak to start with and Almeria had put sugar and what tasted like half a cup of cream in it.

No. It would be extremely bad form to dump the tea and stalk across the Dowager Countess of Arnsworth's drawing room for the brandy. Even if she was his aunt and godmother.

Sweet, weak tea and good manners were not much to fortify a fellow against a determined assault on his bachelor status. It had been bad enough before, but the betrothal last week of a major heiress to someone other than himself, appeared to have escalated the crisis in Almeria's view.

'After all, Richard,' she went on, 'if you are not to inherit the earldom, due to Max's *selfish* marriage, then you must be established in some other way and how better than—'

'*No.*' Before she could get into her stride again, he said, 'Almeria—I do not lack for money, so I have no need to marry a fortune.' The jibe about his twin's marriage stung. He added, 'And no one could be more delighted about Max's marriage than I am. He's happy. You must see that.'

His godmother's glare consigned that hope to Hades and beyond.

'He hasn't even come up to town this year!' she snapped.

Richard gritted his teeth. 'No,' he said patiently, 'because Verity is increasing. He wanted to stay with her. Braybrook promised to keep him abreast of all that takes place in the House. He will come up if he is needed.'

Apparently knowing that her other nephew, Earl Blakehurst, was not completely neglecting his parliamentary duties didn't help at all. Almeria's nostrils flared.

'Richard—you must marry. It is your *duty!*'

His *duty*? To whom? To *what*? Duty was reserved for heirs. He'd only just purchased his own small estate. Surely it wasn't quite that desperate!

He voiced the question. 'Er, Almeria—to whom do I owe this—?'

'The earldom!' she said, replacing her teacup in its saucer with a decided click.

Richard felt his jaw sag. The *earldom*? That was a bit much to swallow. With two brothers originally between himself and the blasted earldom, he'd never *expected* to inherit. Or wanted to. Especially not since it would mean the deaths of his brothers. Abandoning the tepid cup of syrupy tea, he limped over to the decanters and poured himself a glass of brandy. He ignored Almeria's obvious disapproval. A little early, but with Almeria in this frame of mind he needed more fortification than a cup of tea would provide, if he were not to deal her a resounding set-down.

Reseating himself, he sipped the brandy, and said mildly, 'Almeria, Frederick's death was a stroke of misfortune.' He resisted the temptation to emphasise *mis*. 'You can hardly fear the same sort of accident happening to Max! Besides, he is married. And Verity is on the point of giving birth to their first child. How the devil can it be *my* duty to marry?'

'It might be a girl,' said Almeria hopefully. 'In fact, I wouldn't put it past that…that *hussy* to present him with a score of daughters!'

'Verity,' said Richard between clenched teeth, 'is *not* a hussy.'

Almeria had the grace to look slightly abashed. 'Oh, very well, but even so, Richard—there is no guarantee there will be an heir!'

No, there was no guarantee. Indeed, given his twin's current state of terror over his adored countess's perfectly normal pregnancy, it was entirely possible that he'd already sworn an oath of eternal celibacy. Not that one should dismiss the risks. Childbirth was childbirth. Risky. But still…

As if reading his thoughts, Almeria continued. 'And childbirth—why, you never know what might happen!' she said hopefully. 'Really, Richard! You are being most unreasonable about this.'

Forbearance crashed into smoking ruin. He nearly spat out the brandy. 'Max is my twin, ma'am,' he grated. 'I have a considerable affection for both him *and* Verity. You can hardly expect me to be reasonable about a suggestion that I ought to be counting on her death in childbed!'

He noted Almeria's flush with grim satisfaction.

She recovered and rattled in again. 'But, Richard—'

He flung up a hand. 'Enough, ma'am! I've every intention of marrying.'

She blinked. 'But *who?* There were several eligible girls out this year, and they are, each and every one, snapped up, while you sat in Kent!' She counted the eligibles off on her dainty fingertips. 'Lady Sarah Wilding, Miss Creighton, the Scantlebury chit—' Her lip curled slightly. 'Trade, to be sure, but one hundred thousand! I suppose one can make allowances.' She glared at Richard. 'All betrothed! So whom do you have in mind?'

'How in Hades should I know?' he answered with forced

calm. Trust Almeria to take him literally! 'All I can tell you is
that I am not on the catch for an heiress!' Then, with fell intent
to end the conversation once and for all, 'Besides, you know
Max. He'll probably give Verity a dozen strapping sons in his
image.' He watched, fascinated, as Almeria's colour rose.
Judging by the peculiar sounds emanating from her, it was
entirely possible that she was actually choking. His baser self
stirred. 'I mean, it didn't take him long this time. They'll barely
have been married nine months.'

She favoured him with a look that would have felled a dragon
and said, 'I do *not* consider this a suitable topic of conversation.
And if you had the slightest regard for one who has only your
well-being in mind—' She halted mid-flight and drew a deep
breath. 'Well, that is neither here nor there. Now tell me, you
arrived yesterday; where are you staying?'

At the sudden change of tack, the back of his neck developed
a most unpleasant prickling sensation.

'With Braybrook, just for the moment,' he said. 'I mean to be
up for a few weeks though, so I'll probably take lodgings.' No
need to tell Almeria that in addition to the small estate he had
bought the previous year, he was in the process of purchasing a
small town house—she was likely to go into convulsions when
she did find out. Bloomsbury was not on her list of eligible ad-
dresses for a gentleman.

'And you mean to take part in the Season?' She sounded as
though she held out little hope in this direction.

'Actually, yes,' he confessed.

She blinked. 'Really? Well, then—you must stay here.'

Richard stiffened. 'Here?'

'But of course!' she said. 'Lodgings!' She shuddered in distaste. 'Quite ineligible. Of course you must stay here!'

He thought about it. He preferred lodgings. Much safer. He
knew the signs. Almeria was up to something. Something that
involved him.

Oh, for God's sake! As if he couldn't dodge yet another of
Almeria's matchmaking attempts! Even if it was compounded

by his own intent to seek a bride this year. Besides which, staying with Almeria, he might be able to give her thoughts about Max and Verity a happier turn. If she could see that he really didn't mind, had never considered the earldom his, then perhaps she would become reconciled to the match. Spending a few weeks at Arnsworth House would be a small price to pay for healing the breach in the family.

Taking a deep breath, he said with a tolerable assumption of pleasure, 'That is really very kind of you, Almeria, if I won't be in your way.'

She waved that aside. 'Of course not, Richard. Shall you be in for dinner this evening?'

Richard shook his head. 'No. I'm promised to Braybrook for the evening. I'll stroll back to Brook Street shortly and have my man bring my things over, if that's convenient.'

Lady Arnsworth looked like a cat drowning in cream. 'Perfectly. Myles will give you a latch key.'

Suspicions redoubled, Richard simply nodded. 'Thank you.'

She waved his thanks aside. 'Oh, nonsense, Richard. And you must not be thinking that I will for ever be expecting you to dance attendance. You may not have realised, but I will be chaperoning Dorothea Winslow this season.'

Richard stared. 'Chaperoning Thea? But…didn't she—surely she must have married years ago?'

Almeria's eyes opened wide. 'Dorothea marry? Dear me, no. Such a sad story… I dare say you will recall she was betrothed to one of Chasewater's younger sons?'

Richard remembered that only too well. At not quite seventeen, Thea Winslow had been betrothed to the Honourable Nigel Lallerton, third son of the late Earl of Chasewater. As a gentleman set for a career in Parliament, naturally he required a well-dowered bride. Thea had been it.

But Lallerton had died in a shooting accident.

'I assumed she'd recovered from her disappointment and married,' he said. He had been abroad himself for some years after that and had heard nothing more.

Almeria's metaphorical whiskers positively dripped cream. 'Sadly, no, Richard. Such affecting loyalty! Naturally one sympathises with her, but, goodness! It must be several years since poor Nigel Lallerton died.'

Richard stared. He remembered that Thea had retired from society after Lallerton's death. Understandable if her affections had been engaged. But never to marry? Had she then cared for Nigel Lallerton so deeply that she had retired completely from society after he had died? He'd not had much time for Lallerton, himself…a bully, as he remembered. He stepped back from the thought. The man was dead after all. And perhaps Thea had seen a different side of him… Still, never to marry…

Almeria spoke again. 'She cannot mourn for ever and I dare say Aberfield considers the time right…'

The sentence remained unfinished, but Richard had no difficulty filling the blanks: Thea Winslow could not be permitted to inter her heart or, more accurately, her hand in marriage, permanently in the grave. She must take a husband. Her father's political ambition required it.

'Of course she must marry,' said Almeria, echoing his cynical thoughts. 'Probably Aberfield would have brought her to town last year, had they not been in mourning for poor dear Lady Aberfield. 'Tis positively unnatural for Dorothea to waste her life because her first choice met an untimely end!'

Something about Almeria's airy tone of voice sent awareness prickling through him, like a hare scenting the hounds.

'Oh?'

She sighed. The sort of sigh that would have reached to the back seats in Drury Lane. 'Naturally Aberfield wishes her to make an advantageous match. Of course, Dorothea is not a beauty. She was used to be well enough, but at twenty-four she really is past marriageable age, and one must expect that the bloom has faded. Still, I dare say she will attract *some* offers.'

The prickle intensified. 'You are not envisaging me as an eligible suitor here, are you, Almeria?' he asked bluntly.

Almeria's eyes widened. 'Good heavens, no, Richard!' she exclaimed. 'Partial though I am, I cannot persuade myself that Aberfield would look on your suit at all favourably.'

'*My suit?*' Richard wondered if he had misheard. 'My *suit,* did you say, Almeria? I wasn't aware that I had one.' Under the circumstances he considered the even tone he achieved did him great credit.

'Of course not,' said Almeria crossly. 'How you do take one up! Naturally when Aberfield wrote to ask if I would chaperon Thea, I thought of you. After all, you were used to be fond enough of her.'

'She was a child, Almeria,' said Richard, striving to maintain his calm. 'I wasn't thinking of her in terms of a bride!' In fact, he'd been disgusted at the announcement of the betrothal.

Almeria waved dismissively. 'Oh, well. No matter. I understand Aberfield has already put out feelers. He is looking for a political alliance to a man of far greater substance, you may be sure.'

'How very sensible of him,' he murmured, tamping down a sudden flicker of anger at the thought of Thea being used as the glue in a political union. Again.

Apparently oblivious to the edge in his voice, Almeria went on to enumerate all the eligible men of rank and fortune who might reasonably be expected to have a chance of securing the daughter of an influential viscount. 'For you know, she will arrive in town this afternoon, and I must be prepared,' she said.

Again an odd flicker. This time of interest. Aberfield House was just across Grosvenor Square. Perhaps Thea would call. It would be good to see her again…

Aberfield House had not changed in the slightest in the eight years since Thea had seen it. Carnely the butler had a few more wrinkles, but otherwise she might have been stepping back in time. Thea checked her appearance in a pier glass in the hall as David knocked on the door of the library, reflecting on the futility of this even as she straightened her bonnet and tried to tuck a curl back into it. She was tired and travel stained, dusty from the journey. She wished that she could have gone to Arnsworth

House first to change and wash, but apparently her father insisted on seeing her first. Perhaps it was better to get it over and done with. Besides, Lord Aberfield would find fault with her appearance, or, failing that, with her very existence no matter what she did. Grimly she reminded herself that even if Aberfield House had not altered, she had. The despairing young girl who had left here eight years earlier was gone.

David's light knock on the door was answered by a loud injunction to enter. She did so, reminding herself to keep her face blank, her eyes downcast.

A swift glance located Lord Aberfield seated before the fire, one foot heavily bandaged, resting on a footstool. Thea uttered a mental curse: gout. He'd be in a foul mood.

David escorted her over to a chair. He smiled at her and cast a warning sort of glance at their father.

'Good afternoon, sir.'

Aberfield shot a glare at David. 'Took your damn time, didn't you?'

David looked amused. 'Next time I'll arrange winged horses, sir.'

Aberfield scowled and turned his gaze to Thea. 'Sit down. Hurry up. I've not got all day to waste on this. As for you, sirrah—' he turned to his son '—you may wait outside to take her over to Almeria Arnsworth. You've no more to do here.'

'I think not, sir,' said David calmly. 'I'll stay.' Grey eyes snapped fire.

'The devil you will,' said Aberfield. 'You've interfered quite enough. Writing your lying letters.'

A satisfied look of understanding came into David's face. 'So *that's* it. He *did* receive my letters before he died!'

'*Out.*' The softness of Aberfield's voice did not disguise his fury. 'Go to hell, sir.'

Thea blinked as she sat down. David's tones were as polite as they had been when he bid their father good day, and she didn't understand in the least what they were talking about. To whom had David written and what did it have to do with her coming to London?

Unable to quell his only son and heir's outright defiance,
Aberfield snapped his attention back to Thea. 'Get that mealy
mouthed look off your face,' he shot at her. 'You don't fool me,
girl. I know what you—'

'Enough!' said David sharply.

Aberfield's eyes bulged, but he said only, 'Suppose he's told
you already why I sent for you? Eh? Interfering cub!'

'No,' said Thea.

'No?' His colour rose. 'If I say he's an interfering—

'I've no idea why you sent for me,' she interrupted him.

'Don't speak over me!' he snarled. 'Surrounded by worthless
fools!' He caught David's eye and took a deep breath, evidently
attempting to control himself. He continued in bitter tones, 'Well,
he'll have told you that you are to go to Almeria Arnsworth for
the Season?'

She nodded. 'Yes, sir, but I don't understand why.'

He snorted. 'Aye. And well you might not! God knows what
I did to be saddled with you!' He caught David's eye again and
said, 'Everything's different now.' He swept up a sheaf of papers
from a wine table beside him and thrust them at her. 'Read
those—if you can! What a damned mess! Thought I'd made
things plain to the fool; but a few fairy tales, spun by—'

'I did what I thought right, sir,' said David.

An extraordinary noise burst from Aberfield, but he controlled
himself and said to Thea, 'David must needs meddle, blast his eyes!
I've no choice; but by God, if you're to marry, you'll marry as I say!'

Again she met David's eyes. This time he shook his head, his
expression faintly apologetic.

'Read them, Thea,' he said gently.

What had he done?

Leaning forward, Thea took the papers from her father,
forcing her expression to utter stillness, her hands to steadiness,
despite the shaking of her insides.

The first paper was straightforward enough—a letter from a
firm of London solicitors, assuring Lord Aberfield of their humble
duty and informing him that it was their sad task to apprise him

of the death in Bombay, some months earlier, of his brother-in-law, Theodore James Kirkcudbright. Thea bit her lip. Uncle Theo had been her godfather. She had been his heiress. Once.

She continued reading. The lawyers drew Lord Aberfield's attention to the enclosed copy of Mr Kirkcudbright's Last Will and Testament, which they believed to be rather different from the previous one. There were also two letters from the late Mr Kirk-cudbright: one to his esteemed brother-in-law, the fifth Viscount Aberfield, and one to his goddaughter, Dorothea Sophie Winslow, only daughter of the said Viscount Aberfield. They believed the letters would sufficiently explicate Mr Kirkcudbright's intentions and remained his humble servants, et cetera, et cetera.

Puzzled, Thea turned to the letter addressed to herself. Her godfather had not written to her in several years…not since he had written to express his shame and disappointment in her.

> My dear Dorothea,
> I shall be dead and buried before you read this, and can only pray that your brother has not been misled by his Partiality into overstating your comparative Innocence in the Affair your father related to me several years ago. You will understand that in reinstating you in my Will I have placed the strictest controls upon your inheritance, so that you are not placed in the road of Temptation again. It is not my intention to reward any Transgression, but to show my Good Faith, and give you the opportunity to redress the situation by making a good marriage.
> I remain your affectionate godfather and uncle,
> Theodore Kirkcudbright

David had persuaded him to reinstate her.

Her stomach churning, she turned to the letter addressed to her father—then hesitated. 'This one is addressed to you, sir—'

'Read the lot!' he said savagely. 'Damn fool! I told him! *Warned* him what you were—and he does this!'

Sick and shaking, Thea looked at the letter to her father. And frowned. She was to have two hundred a year? From her twenty-fifth to thirtieth birthday, unless she married with her father's approval in the meantime, after which she would have the rest of the income…that Mr Kirkcudbright understood from his nephew that not all the blame could attach to Thea…that Aberfield's foolish attitude… She risked a glance at her father over the letter. No wonder he looked apoplectic.

Her world spun and reshaped itself. Two hundred a year—her twenty-fifth birthday was less than three months away…she would be free. Independent. What happened after her thirtieth birthday?

She turned to the will. Apart from various minor bequests, the major one was to herself. And after her thirtieth birthday she received the entire income from the bequest.

Dazed, she looked up and met her father's bitter gaze.

'Well?' he said. 'God, what a coil! I *told* him what had happened! And he does this! Now there's no help for it—you'll have to marry! Almeria Arnsworth will find you a husband.'

'Only if that's what Thea wants,' interrupted David.

Aberfield ignored that. 'It shouldn't be too hard with fifty thousand to sweeten the deal.'

Thea dropped the papers. *'Fifty thousand?'*

Lord Aberfield snorted. 'That's about the figure. In trust, of course. Thank God Theodore retained that much sense, despite David's meddling. And believe me, I'll see that you never get more than the two hundred a year if you don't marry with my permission!'

Two hundred a year until her thirtieth birthday. Thea said nothing, retrieving the papers from the floor. It was wealth. An independence. And it would be hers in less than three months. All she had to do was to avoid her father's matrimonial plans until then. An odd crunching noise distracted her. She looked up. Aberfield was grinding his teeth.

'Don't get any ideas about setting up your own establishment after your birthday,' he warned her. 'You'll be married long before then. In fact,' he said, 'you'll be married by the end of the Season!' He looked triumphant. 'Dunhaven—he'll have you.'

'What!'

This exploded from David. 'Dunhaven? For God's sake, sir! Are you insane?'

Aberfield banged the arm of his chair. 'Who else would have her?' He cast a contemptuous glance at his daughter. 'No point being fussy at this stage. Thing is to get her married off.'

'Thea,' began David, 'you don't have to—'

She waved him to silence and lifted her chin a notch and considered Aberfield from an entirely new perspective—that of having a choice.

Playing for time, she said, 'I assume, then, that Lord Dunhaven is now a widower?'

'Just out of mourning,' confirmed Aberfield. 'And looking for a bride.'

Her mind worked furiously. Appearing to fall in with his plans would be far safer. Safer than outright defiance anyway. He had shown once before that there was little he would not do to force her compliance... If she allowed him to think that she would toe the line...

Calmly she rose to her feet. 'I shall look forward to renewing my acquaintance with Lord Dunhaven then. I won't keep you any longer, sir. I have no doubt that I shall be perfectly safe under Lady Arnsworth's roof.'

David's sharply indrawn breath told her that he had understood her meaning perfectly.

Aberfield's face was mottled. 'Just remember: this time, you'll do as you're bid. Don't expect me to protect you if you play fast and loose with another suitor!'

Her temper slipped its leash very slightly. 'Nothing, sir,' she said, 'could possibly lead me to expect anything of the sort.'

'Miss Winslow and Mr Winslow, my lady,' Myles announced. His eyes flickered briefly to Richard, with what Richard would have sworn was a look of amused sympathy.

So he'd been right. A trap. And Myles knew all about it. He wouldn't have been surprised had the dainty gilt chair he sat in suddenly sprouted shackles as Almeria rose and swept forward to greet her visitors.

Richard rose automatically as Thea Winslow and her brother came forward. Then he blinked in frowning disbelief. Could this be Thea? Dressed all in grey, not a scrap of colour, not a frill nor flounce relieved the drab, functional appearance of her pelisse and bonnet. She looked more like a governess or companion than an heiress.

Almeria said, 'Welcome, my dears.' She took Thea by the hand and leaned forward to kiss her cheek. 'Dear Dorothea, do come and sit down.' She led her to a chair, still patting her hand affectionately. 'I am sure you are exhausted after your journey. Shall I ring for some tea?'

Even her cheeks looked grey. A pang went through him. Did she still mourn Lallerton?

For an instant their eyes met, and shock hit him as her gaze blanked. She hadn't recognised him.

But would he have recognised her? The soft tawny curls were doubtless still there, hidden beneath the bonnet and cap. And her eyes—perhaps it was the grey of her gown, but he remembered them as more blue than grey. He remembered her face as vivid, expressive—not this blank mask with shuttered eyes. And she was thinner than he remembered.

He could have passed her in the street, even spoken to her, and not realised who she was. Yet now that he looked closely, in some strange way he did recognise her—as one sees the likeness between a waxwork doll and a friend.

The ache inside deepened. Had grief done this to her?

Thea's breath jerked in as she realised that Lady Arnsworth had a gentleman with her.

The gentleman had risen and regarded her with a friendly smile on his face. She lifted her chin a little. Surely he was familiar…tall, a spare frame, dark brown hair, his face lined a little…no, it couldn't be—

'I am sure you both remember my nephew, Mr Richard Blakehurst.'

It was. Richard Blakehurst. Lady Arnsworth's nephew and other godchild. Richard with his broken leg. As a boy he'd spent months here at Arnsworth House recovering after a riding accident that left it doubtful if he would ever walk again without the aid of crutches.

David was the first to speak, his voice coldly biting. 'Blakehurst. I didn't expect to see you here.'

Richard's eyes narrowed at this chilly acknowledgement. 'A mutual feeling, Winslow. How do you do?'

Eyes glittering, David strode forward and took the proffered hand.

'Servant, Blakehurst.' His tone suggested anything but cordiality.

Thea felt her cheeks burn. For heaven's sake! Surely David did not imagine that Richard could possibly have joined the ranks of fortune hunters? Or that he could pose the least danger to her?

Seemingly unconcerned, Richard turned to her.

Swallowing hard, she nodded. 'I…yes. I remember Mr Blakehurst. You are well, sir?'

The dark brows shot up. His eyes. She had forgotten how expressive they were. And she did not remember him as being quite so tall. Or the planes of his face to be so…so hard.

He inclined his head. 'Very well, I thank you, Miss Winslow. Delighted to meet you again.'

Panic flooded her as he came towards her, hand outstretched. He was going to take her hand. He would touch her. And she had stripped off her gloves in the hall…

Richard. This is Richard…you knew him as a boy… She forced herself to stillness. But Richard Blakehurst was no longer a boy. Tall, broad-shouldered—despite the remaining halt in his stride, Richard was a man…

Deliberately she lifted her chin. She knew Richard; he had been her friend—it wouldn't be too bad… Braced to withstand her usual panic, she held out her hand. A gentle vice gripped it. Her breath jerked in and caught as tingling warmth laced every nerve.

Their eyes met, his suddenly intent, even startled. She was

wildly conscious of the strength of his long fingers. They tightened very slightly, as though staking a claim, and an instant later released her.

The sudden silence seemed to hum with awareness as she struggled to understand what had happened.

Lady Arnsworth bustled up. 'Do sit down, dear Dorothea,' she said. 'How nice that Richard was here to meet you. It must be several years since you met.'

'Eight, or…or thereabouts,' Thea temporised, as she sat down. He had attended her come-out ball. Eight years ago, though his touch hadn't seared her.

'Of course,' said Lady Arnsworth. She turned to her nephew. 'Although I dare say, Richard, that you see Mr Winslow from time to time?'

'Not often of late years,' said Richard, resuming his seat.

Thea tried to listen, nodding occasionally, as Lady Arnsworth outlined all her plans for the Season, which were comprehensive to say the least.

Richard must be…two and thirty now, surely. He was about eight years older than she. He couldn't really be any taller than she remembered. It just seemed that way for some reason. She flickered sideways glances at him, trying to understand what it was about him that was so different to her.

Lady Arnsworth continued to expound her campaign. Almack's, of course. There could be not the least trouble in the world gaining vouchers…

Perhaps it was just that he was broader. Yes. That was it. He was a long way removed from the rather slight young man she remembered. She wondered if he still enjoyed chess… He had been a formidable opponent and she did not doubt that he was even more formidable now. Something about the calm self-contained gaze told her that. Still waters…

Only none of that explained why her whole body had seemed to shimmer and leap to life when he took her hand…

Lady Arnsworth preened a little as she listed the invitations they were likely to receive. Once people knew that dear Dorothea was at Arnsworth House, there would be invitations aplenty. And Lord Dunhaven had already left his card.

An odd choking noise came from Richard, and, glancing at him, Thea had the distinct impression that something had struck a jarring note with Mr Richard Blakehurst. His jaw bore a startling resemblance to solid stone.

A glance at David revealed his jaw in much the same condition, which was no surprise at all after what he had said about Lord Dunhaven as they crossed the Square.

Lady Arnsworth sailed on, listing all the more influential hostesses who would be *aux anges* to receive the Honourable Miss Winslow.

The Honourable, *wealthy* Miss Winslow. Lady Arnsworth didn't bother to spell that out.

Mr Blakehurst's fathomless gaze met hers over the rim of his glass. Thea forced herself not to look away, to keep her own expression blank... Richard had...had grown up. That was all. It had been surprise, nothing more. Nothing deeper.

Lady Arnsworth finished, 'I don't doubt we will be invited everywhere. Everyone will wish to make Dorothea's acquaintance, you may be sure.'

'Oh, without a doubt,' said Mr Blakehurst. 'How could it possibly be otherwise?'

Thea's gaze narrowed at the faintly ironic tone, as a spurt of annoyance flared, swiftly suppressed. Control. She could not afford to betray anything.

Lady Arnsworth shot Richard a quelling glare and turned back to Thea.

'Now, my dear,' she said, 'should you like to go up to your bedchamber and rest? Dinner will not be for some time, but perhaps some tea on a tray?'

Another strangled noise came from Richard, but, ignoring this, Lady Arnsworth smiled graciously at David. 'And I am sure, Mr Winslow, that you will wish to inform Lord Aberfield that Dorothea is safely with me. My nephew will see you out. I shall bid you farewell now.'

Chapter Two

There was something distinctly strained about Richard's voice as he assured Lady Arnsworth that he would not be in the least put out, but Thea had no time to ponder on it as she bid David farewell, and Lady Arnsworth led her from the room.

All along the upper hallway, Lady Arnsworth waxed lyrical about the joys of London. Especially for '…a young lady as well-dowered as you, dear Dorothea!'

Thea could not repress a chill, remembering how people clustered around heiresses. Gentlemen, smiling, pretending affection, while all the time… She pushed the thought away. She would manage perfectly well once she was accustomed.

Except— 'I…ma'am, I would really rather not have dozens of suitors tripping over themselves. After all—'

After all, what? What can you possibly tell her that would convince her you don't want a husband?

Lady Arnsworth opened the door to the bedchamber, an arrested expression on her face. *'Dozens of suitors?'*

It was as though the idea had never occurred to her.

Thea flushed. Was she that much of an antidote these days? 'Well, fortune hunters,' she said, following her godmother across the threshold.

A maidservant was already putting her belongings away.

'Fortune hunters? Oh, dear me, no! There will be nothing like that.'

And the sun might rise in the west. 'There won't?'

'Oh, no…now I am sure you will be perfectly comfortable in this chamber. And don't worry about fortune hunters. You may trust me to see to *that*. Why, the very idea! The maid will have your things unpacked in no time,' she said. 'And if there is anything you require, of course you must tell me.'

'Thank you, ma'am,' said Thea politely. 'Er, you seem very certain about the fortune hunters.'

'Ah, the girl has finished.' Lady Arnsworth flipped her hand at the maid. 'That will be all.'

The maid dropped a curtsy and left. Lady Arnsworth turned back to Thea.

'My dear, what a sensible girl you are!' Her ladyship was all smiles as she took Thea's hand. 'While naturally your circumstances will attract a certain amount of attention, you may rest assured that as your sponsor and chaperon, I shall be most careful to ensure that only the most eligible suitors are brought to your notice. Two, perhaps three at the most should be quite sufficient.'

Thea blinked as Lady Arnsworth patted her hand and repressed a shiver at even that simple touch. Two or three? What would her ladyship think if she knew that Thea didn't want *any* suitors?

She tried. 'As to that, ma'am, I have no thought of marriage. I…I find the whole idea…that is—' Her throat tightened.

Lady Arnsworth looked away and fiddled with her rings, turning them to better display the stones. 'Ah, yes. Your father did mention that—

'Of course, such things are not quite unknown.' There was something very odd in her voice, not quite distaste… She met Thea's puzzled gaze. 'Generally one does not approve, but under the circumstances—and your fortune is considerable. I am sure you need not worry.' She fussed with her cuffs, still avoiding Thea's shocked gaze.

Thea said nothing to this, but gripped her underlip hard between her teeth.

'Naturally your years of, er, mourning have given you ample time for reflection.'

'They certainly have,' said Thea, finding her voice.

Looking far more at ease, Lady Arnsworth said carefully, 'Indeed your feelings are quite understandable. I found the marriage act most unpleasant myself. But it is our duty. And once you have done your duty and provided the heir—and a spare, of course—if you wish it, most gentlemen will respect a lady's natural modesty and seek their pleasures elsewhere for the most part. Men, of course, are different. Very different. Now, I must change. I will be out this evening, but tomorrow we will have to do some shopping.' She cast a pained glance at Thea's travelling dress. 'Yes. A new wardrobe is of the first importance! I venture to suggest that you will feel very different when properly gowned!'

And with that, Lady Arnsworth whisked herself out of the room.

Staring at the closed door, Thea faced the fact that her father had told Lady Arnsworth the truth. Or at least the truth as he saw it. And she had the oddest notion that it had not been the fifty thousand pounds that had tipped the balance for Almeria Arnsworth...although that would certainly be the case with most of society. She felt sick to her stomach, thinking of the next couple of months to be spent in the full glare of society and its crowding, jostling throng...all of whom would turn on her if they knew the truth... From nowhere panic ambushed her, sinking familiar claws deep. Her stomach clenched, warding off the striking terror. She forced her body to relax, her lungs to draw breath steadily, blanking her mind. And as suddenly it was gone, a chill warning, leaving her cold and shaking, but free and rational. Free to wonder if she had been completely insane to imagine that she could do this.

As the drawing room door clicked behind Almeria and her houseguest, Richard throttled the urge to swear resoundingly. He could only marvel at the neatness of the trap, as he sat down. A trap compounded of his own good manners. The same good manners that would keep him from strangling his godmother when she returned. Very well, he was fond of Almeria too, and she was family.

'Quite a coincidence that you are here to greet my sister, Blakehurst,' remarked David in biting accents.

Richard's normally even temper flickered. 'Just so,' he said. 'Do take a seat again, Winslow.'

Perhaps he would strangle Almeria. Affectionately, of course. If he lived long enough. Judging by Winslow's narrowed gaze, there was every chance he might not.

'You are staying in town?' David asked, in deceptively casual tones. He remained standing.

Not deceived in the slightest, Richard said, 'I am. Here, as a matter of fact.'

The silence that followed this admission seethed.

Richard sat back and waited. Winslow's grey eyes resembled nothing more than twin blades.

'How very…convenient.'

Richard's temper did a great deal more than flicker. It smoked and curled at the edges. Winslow's attitude reeked of protective elder brother, although why he would imagine that Thea required protection from himself was beyond Richard's comprehension. And there was something else in Winslow's level gaze: scorn.

'Can I pour you a brandy?' he offered politely, damping down his temper.

Winslow declined. 'Thank you. No. I will take my leave of you.'

Richard smiled. 'Then no doubt I shall see you again. You will be calling on Miss Winslow, I dare say.'

'Most definitely,' her brother replied in clipped tones. 'If only to keep an eye on all the scaff and raff who cluster around heiresses.'

Richard blinked. Then anger welled up—it was a very long time since anyone had accused him of being a fortune hunter. And even then, at least he had been well aware of the chit's fortune! This time…

'No need to summon the butler. I'll find my own way out.' David executed a perfunctory bow and left.

Left alone, Richard said several things he had suppressed when Almeria left the room—and a few more for good measure. While he'd known that Thea must at least be respectably dowered, the term *heiress* suggested a great deal more. And while Almeria's penchant for dropping stray heiresses in his path had caused him considerable embarrassment on occasion, he couldn't recall that it had ever put him in danger of his life before. There had been a definite glint of gun metal in Winslow's eyes.

He took a deep breath. And then there was Thea herself. Something had wrought a change in her that went far beyond years. Far beyond the change from a young girl on the eve of her come-out to a young woman. Thea-the-girl had been exuberant, bubbling over with mischief. Thea-the-woman seemed half-lost in shadow…only there had been that flash of light when their hands met—as though something had awakened inside her.

And as for her blasted, hitherto unsuspected fortune—Winslow was right; it would have the fortune hunters out in force.

By the time Almeria returned to the drawing room, he had managed to reduce the situation to its proper proportion. Almeria was matchmaking. No more. No less. He rose as she sailed into the room, saying airily, 'I must have forgot to make clear to you that Dorothea will be my guest for the Season! 'Tis positively shocking how forgetful one becomes as the years advance!'

Despite himself, Richard nearly grinned. 'Quite shocking,' he said gravely. Not that he, nor anyone else, would dare suggest to Almeria that she was advanced in years. Although she must be slipping if she expected him to believe that all this had not been carefully prearranged.

Occasionally a little unsubtlety was called for.

He settled for being extremely unsubtle.

'Almeria—what the deuce are you up to?'

'Up to?' she said with a lift of her brows. 'Why should you imagine I am up to anything? Really, Richard!'

'Fudge,' he said bluntly. 'Don't waste your breath, Almeria. Instead, tell me precisely what is the extent of Thea's fortune. I was not aware she had one.'

Almeria looked a little conscious. 'Her godfather's fortune. *Not* the sort of thing one counts on, although he always intended to leave it to her, but after all, he might have married. And it is not a terribly big fortune as these things go, of course.'

The prickle at the back of his neck escalated into outright alarm bells.

'Just *how* not-terribly-big are we talking about here?' he pressed.

'Only fifty thousand,' said Almeria with an airy wave. 'And derived from *trade,* of course!' This last with a faint grimace.

Fifty thousand? *Only* fifty thousand? Hell and damnation! With that much at stake, it wouldn't surprise him to hear that Almeria already had the special licence in her reticule and a tame bishop in the back parlour.

The suspicion that he had stepped into a well-laid and very sticky trap was unavoidable.

But he could make one or two things plain.

'Almeria—let us be quite clear. Although I intend to marry, I am *not* in the market for an heiress, and—'

'Oh, for goodness' sake!' Almeria settled her skirts with a swish as she sat down. 'Naturally when Aberfield asked that I chaperon Dorothea, I thought of you—since you were going to visit me anyway...' She looked more than a trifle evasive.

'Was I?'

Richard couldn't recall his plans including anything of the sort. Almeria's summons to visit her as soon as he reached town had arrived several days ago quite unheralded. However, that wasn't to say that *Almeria's* plans...

She glared at him. 'Since I was *intending* to invite you—'

The moment she had an heiress staying with her—that went without saying.

'Richard, you must marry sensibly!' she said crossly. 'You need a wife, the right wife. Especially now that you have bought that property in Kent. One assumes you intend to get an heir!'

Wisely, Richard held his counsel. There was nothing to gain from encouraging Almeria. No matter how right she happened to be.

'And as for leaving these things to take care of themselves,' she said, returning to an earlier theme, 'I would have thought the danger of that was made plain by the appalling mess Max has—'

'Enough!' He controlled himself with an effort and said in a gentler tone, 'Almeria, I cannot possibly remain here if you are to criticise Max and Verity. He is happy. Does that count for nothing?'

Goaded, Almeria snapped, 'And how long can it last before she does something disgraceful?'

Enough was enough. 'Like what? Cuckold him? Is that what you mean?'

Her colour rose. 'Exactly!'

He shrugged. 'Then he would have to cope with it. In his own way.' Seeing Almeria's mouth open, he added, 'Just as our father did, in fact.'

Her mouth closed.

'Did you think I never realised? That summer I broke my leg and stayed with you here, I knew then.'

Almeria was scarlet. 'At least my sister was discreet!' she said furiously. 'I do not say that I approved of her behaviour, but she did not bring any disgrace upon the family!' With which she rose, swept past him and left the drawing room again. The door shut with the sort of controlled click that was a well-bred woman's alternative to slamming it. Settling back in his chair, he took a measured sip of brandy and muttered a few things that it was as well Almeria couldn't hear. What the devil was he to do now?

He had to wonder if every god in the pantheon had conspired against him. His laudable plan of reconciling Almeria to Max's marriage was clearly misfiring. Instead of accepting his own delight in the match, the mere sight of him was enough to stir up all her outrage at the ruin of his supposed expectations. Worse, she was now about to fling fifty thousand pounds' worth of heiress at his head. Although probably not with Aberfield's blessing.

In fact, Aberfield would probably succumb to apoplexy if he knew what Almeria was up to. A viscount, and a wealthy one at that, Aberfield didn't have a seat in the cabinet any more, but he wielded a fair amount of influence with those who did.

Almeria was howling at the moon. Aberfield would never accept a match to a younger son, remarkable only for living within his means, his fortune respectable but no more, and about as much interested in a political career as he was interested in succeeding to his twin's title—to wit, not at all. All Richard wanted was a quiet, private life improving his recently purchased acres and reading his books.

Nigel Lallerton was a younger son. He dismissed that as irrelevant. Lallerton had been set for a safe seat in parliament, supporting his father's interest. Not to mention Aberfield's interest. Lallerton's father, Lord Chasewater, had been an old political crony. No doubt the match was stitched up between them as mutually beneficial. It had probably been sheer luck that Thea had cared so deeply for Lallerton.

Stretching out his stiff leg, he considered his options.

If he returned to the country, Almeria would think it was because of what she'd said about Verity. Richard frowned. Max could look after Verity, but even so, he hesitated to expose his sister-in-law to any more of Almeria's rancour. Nor did he wish the rift between Max and Almeria to widen.

Besides, Almeria would be hurt if he left. She was actually fond of him, he reminded himself firmly. When he'd broken his leg, she had come up to town and had him to stay as soon as the doctors said his leg had healed enough for him to travel. Not that a twelve-year-old with a broken leg, wondering if he would ever walk again, had been precisely grateful for that, but nevertheless she had been kind to him. Buying him as many books as he could read, insisting that the kitchen made his favourite cake at least once a day. She had even put up with his dog, although she hated dogs in the house.

He grimaced. His own mother, while professing to be utterly devoted to her sons, had attended a succession of house parties that summer. He hadn't understood why at first...Almeria had taken over. Brisk, no-nonsense and frequently acerbic on the subject of his idiocy in trying to ride that damned hunter in the first place, but she had been there, while his own mother wafted through London several times between gatherings and recommended laudanum when she thought he looked *out of sorts*. She had invariably been accompanied by Lord Ketterley—he grimaced. Ketterley had seemed such a decent fellow...it had been Max, cynical, rebellious Max, who had worked it all out...

Almeria hadn't even complained when she discovered that he had inveigled Myles into playing chess with him. Her face when she caught them, though! Three days later she had appeared triumphantly with her other godchild, five-year-old Thea Winslow, announcing that *Dear Dorothea is come to stay as well, and she is most interested in learning to play chess...* The twelve-year-old Richard had barely choked back his disgust at having dear, *little* Dorothea foisted upon him. He'd taught her to play chess in sheer self-defence.

He found himself smiling as he remembered the little girl who had pored over the chess board, chewing her bottom lip with her untidy curls for ever falling into her eyes. Even at sixteen when she had made her come-out, her unruly curls had tended to escape their bonds. He'd teased her for it... He frowned as something occurred to him; there hadn't been a wisp in sight today. For all he knew, she might be bald under that ghastly bonnet. Not that he understood anything about fashion, but he could recognise an ugly bonnet when he saw one.

An odd thought came to him—could he help Thea?

Help Thea? An heiress?

Even an heiress needs a friend.

He grimaced. Almeria would be looking for every opportunity to throw them together. Was he really going to be so foolish as to assist her? A memory of grey eyes that should have been blue suggested that he was.

He sighed. It would probably be polite to inform Braybrook in person that he no longer had a houseguest.

* * *

Julian, Lord Braybrook, received the news that his guest of twenty-four hours would be departing, with a suspicious degree of *sangfroid*.

He laid down his pen, leaned back in his desk chair and said merely, 'Ah.' Not at all as though the news came as a surprise.

Richard eyed him warily.

'Food not up to standard, old chap?' enquired Braybrook in tones of polite interest. 'Bed unaired?'

Richard grinned. 'Indigestible. And damned chilly. How the devil did you find out so fast?'

'Thanks,' said Braybrook drily. 'For God's sake, Ricky! Are you mad? As for how I found out—I have just sustained a visit from the outraged brother!'

'Winslow?'

'She's only got the one,' said Braybrook.

Richard nodded slowly. 'I'd forgotten you were friendly. He's not been in town much the last few years.'

'No,' said Braybrook. 'But he recalled that I was also acquainted with you. You may imagine my surprise when he informed me that you were staying with Lady Arnsworth.' He shot Richard an odd glance. 'I was under the impression you planned to seek out lodgings.'

'It's not what it looks like,' said Richard, rather shocked to realise that his teeth were gritted.

'Of course not. And I do hope you will appreciate my discretion in not informing Winslow that your sojourn with Lady Arnsworth is of such recent date.'

'Dammit, Julian! I didn't even know Miss Winslow was expected when Almeria persuaded me to stay!'

'Then what did persuade you?' He flung up a hand as Richard glared at him. 'Oh, don't be a gudgeon! *I* know you aren't the sort to dangle after heiresses! I even did my best to reassure Winslow on that head; but I will admit to a very human curiosity about what possible cause you could have for staying with Lady Arnsworth!' He grinned. 'Apart from my unaired beds and the indigestible food.'

Despite his annoyance, Richard laughed. Damn. Telling Julian that in some odd way he was worried about Thea would have the fellow leaping to all sorts of unwarranted conclusions. Instead he fell back on his original reason for accepting. 'Almeria is still very bitter about Max's marriage, you know,' he said.

Braybrook looked rather self-conscious. 'So I hear.'

Something about his voice alerted Richard. 'Yes?'

'I had a letter from Serena,' said Braybrook.

Richard nodded. Serena, Lady Braybrook, was the previous Lord Braybrook's widow. Julian's stepmother. Almeria had long considered it her duty to keep the invalid Lady Braybrook fully apprised of her stepson's indiscretions.

'Yes?'

'Lady Arnsworth had written to her.'

Richard suppressed a grin at the irritation in his voice. 'Ah. Giving her advice on how to marry you off?'

Braybrook snorted. 'Precisely. Citing Max as a fearful example of what happens when a man is left to his own devices in the matter.'

'Annoying,' replied Richard, 'but there's nothing new in that. She said as much to me this afternoon. She's doubly furious because of the expected baby.'

The blue eyes narrowed. 'Maybe. Did she also express doubts about the child's paternity?'

'What?'

'No. I didn't think she'd have said that to you. Obviously you don't have to worry about it going any further, but she hinted at it in her letter to Serena.'

Richard swore. 'Is she still harping on that? She said something to that effect last year.'

'To you?'

'And Max,' said Richard grimly.

Braybrook's jaw dropped. 'That would explain why Max is at outs with her.'

'Exactly,' said Richard. 'Which is why I agreed to stay with her,' he went on. 'To try to convince her that Max's marriage has not consigned me to poverty, before she says something to create a permanent breach between herself and Max!'

A sceptical brow lifted. 'And questioning the child's paternity to his face hasn't done that already?'

Richard grimaced. 'Not quite. Max doesn't want a breach any more than I do, but if it comes to a choice between Almeria or protecting Verity—' He broke off. 'You know what he will do.'

Braybrook made a rude noise. 'Slight understatement there, Ricky. If it came to a choice between the entire world and protecting Lady Blakehurst, Max would consign the lot of us to perdition!'

Richard smiled. 'True.'

Braybrook looked curious. 'You know, Ricky—I've never quite understood just why Lady Arnsworth was so fixated on Max remaining single?'

Richard frowned. 'Max never told you?'

'I never asked.'

He nodded. 'It was my accident that started it. Mama and Almeria blamed Max for daring me to ride the cursed horse. Never mind that I was perfectly capable of saying no to him, he'd suggested it and therefore it was all his fault. Later, I was supposed to go into the army—Mama insisted that my leg made that unsuitable, and that Max should be bought a commission instead.'

'What else did they have in mind for him?' asked Julian.

'The church, if you can believe it.'

A most peculiar choking sound came from Lord Braybrook.

'Quite,' said Richard. 'I think he preferred the army on the whole. He was a damn sight better suited to it than I was.' He sighed. 'And then Freddy died not long after our father. And suddenly Max was the earl. But instead of demanding that he settle down and secure the succession, both Mama and Almeria decided between them that he owed it to me to remain single!'

'How very melodramatic of them,' observed Julian.

Richard snorted. 'I didn't take it seriously, but Max did. He always blamed himself for my accident anyway and Mama and Almeria had rubbed it in with a vengeance over the years.'

Braybrook's mouth twitched. 'And, of course, it's plain to the meanest intelligence that you yourself are bitterly disappointed in being cut out of an earldom,' he said drily.

'Bitterly,' said Richard, yawning. 'I've enough money for my wants.'

'And if you don't,' said Braybrook, 'you could always marry Miss Winslow.' He grinned wickedly. 'No point cutting off your nose to spite your face, you know. After all, she might be your perfect bride!'

'As long as her brother doesn't shoot me first,' said Richard sarcastically.

Unholy amusement gleamed in bright blue eyes. 'A risk, of course. Mind you, it would certainly calm Lady Arnsworth down to see you safely legshackled to an heiress!' He grinned. 'Proof positive that your game leg and Max's marriage have not combined to blight your life.'

'Oh, go to the devil, Julian,' recommended Richard.

All the same, the flippant advice niggled at him as he blew out his bedside lamp later that night, after walking back to Arns-worth House, as it had done all through dinner and numerous hands of piquet afterwards. A circumstance that had led to Julian relieving him of a vast, if imaginary, fortune.

In the best spare bedchamber, Thea Winslow was probably sound asleep…a thought that had made him very, very edgy as he'd tiptoed past to his own room… It had been a distinct shock to find a sleepy footman waiting up for him. He'd forgotten to keep his voice down as he told the man never to do such a thing again. He hoped it hadn't disturbed Thea… He pushed the re-curring thought of Thea away. Thea Winslow, sleeping peace-fully just down the hallway, was no concern of his. Or she ought not to be.

No point cutting off your nose to spite your face…she might be your perfect bride…

Leaving perfect out of it, he had always intended to marry. Marriage had always made complete sense—at some dim, un-specified future time. Apparently the future had arrived. With the purchase of an estate and a London house, marriage was becoming, if not imperative, then at least desirable. All he needed to do was choose the right woman—and of course persuade her that he was the right man. Yes, a sensible, intelligent woman with a sense of humour. She didn't need to be wealthy, just someone he liked and respected… His stomach clenched—someone who wouldn't view a child's broken leg as an interruption to her own life. Someone who wouldn't mind that her husband had absolutely no ambition to figure in society, but preferred a quiet life in the country with his books and acres, and was happy to remain there with him for the most part. Happy to remain, not self-sacrificing…not complaining that she had nothing to amuse her, and flitting off to yet another house party with her lover—he slammed a lid down on that; there was no point being bitter about the past, but you could learn from it. He added another criterion: honour. He wanted a woman to whom honour was more important than discretion.

Common sense firmly in place, he permitted his thoughts to turn to Thea. He liked her. He always had. She had always been blazingly honest as a child, and young girl, sometimes when it might have been wiser to dissemble a little. And she was loyal— if she had mourned Nigel Lallerton so deeply, he needed no further proof of that. What if she *were* the right choice for him? The sensible, logical choice…folly to discount her simply because of Almeria's entirely predictable matchmaking.

She was here in the house. It was the perfect opportunity to find out if she really would suit him. He caught himself—if *they* would suit. For all he knew, his bookish habits might drive her to distraction. Or his tendency to leave curls of shaved wood everywhere from his whittling. If their old childhood friendship could become an adult friendship and the basis for a successful marriage…an irritatingly rational voice suggested that perhaps he was being a little bit *too* rational about this, that perhaps he might look for a woman to love…after all, love wasn't ruining Max's life. Quite the opposite.

He rolled over and punched the pillow. That was all very

well, but if he hadn't fallen in love in thirty-two years, what were the odds of it happening now? A sensible marriage would be far more...sensible. Logical.

Safe.

His father had loved—and look what that had led to...a totally unsuitable choice. Max had been lucky. Damned lucky.

There could be no harm in spending time with Thea, and renewing their friendship. He liked that idea. What he didn't like was the memory of Thea as he had seen her that afternoon, all the old laughter and liveliness quenched. A feeling that was not in the least sensible stole over him...whatever had been responsible for the grey shadow in eyes that ought to have been blue— he wanted to remove it.

Hours after going to bed Thea lay waiting for sleep. Perhaps she should light a lamp and read for a while. The strange bed unnerved her...but it was so late. Surely she would sleep if she closed her eyes and emptied her mind. She had become very good at that over the years—keeping her mind utterly blank, refusing to allow emotion to creep in.

But now, back in London, among people who had known her as a child, a young girl—even though her body ached with tiredness, the thoughts and feelings held sleep at bay.

A little spark of anger flared in a dark corner of her heart, a corner she never looked into. From her father's point of view, her marriage now was an unquestioned necessity. She rolled over and thumped the pillow. She would *not*, under any circumstances, acquiesce to any match proposed by her father.

The little spark had caught, lighting up the corner. Thea shut her eyes to it, dousing it. She *wouldn't* look there. She mustn't. Better that it remained shadowed. Hidden from the light. If she permitted herself to feel anything again...anger, hurt...even love, she pushed them all away. Safer to remain calm. Unmoved. As untouched as she could ever be.

The news would be all over London that Miss Winslow, only daughter of Viscount Aberfield and heiress to fifty thousand pounds, was residing in Grosvenor Square with Lady Arnsworth. She would be sought out. Courted, flattered, every social distinction pressed upon her.

The thought sickened her.

Money bought acceptance; with fifty thousand pounds, as long as the truth remained a whisper, the past would be ignored by many. Not by all, but many including her own father.

She gritted her teeth. She didn't want that sort of acceptance anyway. Especially not from Aberfield. Uncle James had shown more understanding and affection for her than her own father. He had been prepared to believe her innocence and reverse his decision to disinherit her. Aberfield had reinstated her only because of the money. It was easier somehow to think of him as Aberfield, not Papa. It wasn't as though he wanted her as his daughter. All he wanted was for her money to secure a husband of benefit to himself.

A queer thought came to her—she doubted that her money would buy Richard's good opinion if ever he knew the truth. She could count on his honesty. She shivered, and drew the blankets closer. Why was she thinking of Richard anyway? How could she know what he had become? She hadn't seen him since her come-out ball.

The memory slipped past her defences. He had danced with her that night, laughing because her wretched hair was escaping, enjoying the ball as much as she, although he rarely danced because of his leg. He had danced with her twice, and then she hadn't seen him again until today.

She pushed the memory away. Richard would be revolted if he knew the truth; at best he would feel sorry for her.

She didn't want pity. She wanted nothing of anyone. She didn't need anyone—she could stand by herself. And in less than three months she would be free. Only…what on earth would she do with her freedom once she had it? She would enjoy it, that was what. And in the meantime she would enjoy herself now. Here. In London. She was not going to permit her fears to rule her life—she would not wait for her twenty-fifth birthday to release her, she would begin now. Tomorrow—no, it was tomorrow already. Today. She would begin today. She had put off enough tomorrows.

Thea arose early the following morning and dressed without summoning a maid—she could manage her short wraparound stays herself. Unsurprisingly when she went downstairs, she found the breakfast parlour empty. Having been out the previous evening, Lady Arnsworth would probably not arise until noon. Fully expecting to have to ring for tea and toast, she was startled to find a varied selection of food set out in chafing dishes on the sideboard, including, to her great surprise, sirloin.

Puzzled at this very masculine inclusion, Thea helped herself to toast, poached eggs and ham, and made a pot of tea from the urn steaming in the corner.

She enjoyed a leisurely breakfast, and afterwards sipped her tea with lingering enjoyment, wondering what she might do with her day. A day in which she might do precisely as she pleased.

Contemplating this rare treasure, Thea poured another cup of tea. She might take one of the maids and go for a walk. She could visit Hatchards. She might—

Stare at Mr Richard Blakehurst strolling into the breakfast parlour as though he owned it! At this hour! Swallowing her tea with difficulty, she realised that his limp was far less noticeable these days, more a slight halt in the stride than a limp. The harsh lines pain had etched in his face made him look rather forbidding.

Until he smiled his familiar crooked smile.

Which he was doing now, the corners of his eyes creasing in the way she remembered. His whole face lightened. She remembered that too, Richard smiling at her as he clumsily partnered her in a country dance. But he'd always been just Richard. An extra brother. Someone dependable. A dear friend. She didn't remember that she had ever thought of him as attractive…

'Good morning, Thea,' he said pleasantly.

She found herself smiling back.

Attractive? Surely not.

Oh, yes, he was. Even more so as his smile deepened in response to her own.

'Good morning,' she returned, confused. 'Er, Lady Arnsworth is not yet down, sir.'

His brows rose. 'Just as well,' he said, strolling to the sideboard. 'Or you would have to revive me with burnt feathers.'

A giggle escaped her at the image, and with a perfectly straight face Richard added, 'No proper lady leaves her bedchamber before noon, you know.'

Laughter bubbled up. 'Are you implying, sir—?'

'That proper ladies bore me,' he said, grinning. 'That's better. You should laugh more often. And stop calling me *sir*, Thea. It makes my teeth ache. Now, what have we here?' He lifted the lid of one of the chafing dishes.

She glared at him. 'A trifle early for morning calls, is it not?' she enquired. 'Especially when your aunt is still abed.' Better to ignore the implication that she didn't laugh enough.

He looked around, with a sudden frown. 'She didn't tell you?'

'Tell me what?'

The frown deepened. 'This isn't a morning call. I'm staying here too.'

'What!' Her teacup clattered into its saucer. 'Why?'

'Heiress hunting,' he said blandly, carving some sirloin.

'I *beg* your pardon?' she said icily.

'Absolved,' he said promptly. 'I'm sure you didn't mean to be rude.'

Her mouth twitched. She had forgotten his ability to turn the tables so neatly in any verbal sparring.

He helped himself to mustard, sat down and smiled at her again. 'Don't blame me. Curse our mutual godmother.' He took a mouthful.

'But why are you staying here?' she asked, refusing to return that annoyingly infectious smile. Smiles like that ought to be outlawed anyway!

He finished his mouthful and said, 'Because I have business in London and Almeria invited me.'

'Oh.' His business was none of her concern. 'Then—'

'I am *not* pursuing you,' he growled. 'And so you may tell your fire-eating brother! You could have twice the fortune and I wouldn't be interested in it! I have a little more pride than that!'

For a moment shocked silence hung between them.

Shame burnt her cheeks, and deep inside, coldness spread, leaching through her, a slow poison welling up. She fought it down, forcing herself to seem untouched, unmoved.

'I suppose I must thank you for making your sentiments so plain,' she said stiffly. It didn't matter. It didn't! After all, she didn't want him, or any man, to pursue her. The chill spread further. *How* had he known? Lady Arnsworth?

Then— 'Oh, damn!' said Richard. 'I mean, I beg your pardon, Thea. That was not at all how I meant to put it. What I *meant* is that I am not on the catch for an heiress. Any heiress. Unfortunately for us, Almeria has other ideas.'

Thea took a shaky breath. She had thought—for one dreadful eternal instant—that he knew. 'I…very well…' Then his remark about Lady Arnsworth's plans crashed into her. 'What do you mean, Lady Arnsworth has other ideas?'

He looked at her in disbelief. 'Thea—stop wool-gathering. Think—her goddaughter with a fortune of fifty thousand pounds; her godson and favourite nephew, a younger son with no expectations whatsoever—clearly a match made in heaven.'

Her eyes widened as that stabbed home. Oh, God! Why hadn't she seen it? No wonder Lady Arnsworth had assured her that there would be no swarms of fortune hunters! She took a couple of careful, deep breaths and met Richard's gaze.

He was looking at her oddly. 'Are you feeling quite the thing?'

She took a sip of tea. If she looked as shocked as she felt, then he had some cause for asking. 'Perfectly well, thank you, sir,' she lied. 'Er, thank you for your honesty.' At least he *had* been honest.

He frowned. 'Thea, if you think I am going to call you Miss Winslow and stand upon ceremony with you, then think again,' he said in rising irritation. 'And stop calling me *sir!*'

At this inauspicious moment the door opened and the butler came in with a coffee pot.

'Your coffee, sir.' His tones oozed reproof.

'Ah, thank you, Myles. That will be all.'

'Yes, sir. Very good, sir.' Myles placed the coffee pot before Richard and removed himself with all the air of a man removing himself from potential crossfire.

Thea met Richard's glare head on. 'Mr Blakehurst, you have been so kind as to make clear your position—mine is similar. I have no interest in marriage to you whatsoever. If you are concerned that your aunt wishes to promote a match between us, you may rest assured she will receive no encouragement or assistance from me. Good day. Sir. If you will take my advice, any familiarity between us will merely encourage any mistaken assumptions! In future I shall request breakfast in my bedchamber. It will be far safer for both of us if we are not alone together!'

She stalked out, leaving Richard contemplating his breakfast, furiously aware that he had displayed all the finesse of a cavalry charge. Nor had he made his position clear. Now that he thought about it, she had always been able to get under his skin with the greatest of ease, deflecting him from what he wished to say. And that knack she had of getting the last word was like to drive him insane.

But at least their argument had banished the shadows in her eyes. They'd been positively snapping sparks before she walked out. As though the waxwork doll had come to life or split to let out the old, passionate Thea… She was still too pale—or perhaps it was just the effect of the slightly too big, dull grey gown.

Muttering to himself, he poured a cup of coffee and stirred in several lumps of sugar. What really annoyed him was that in one sense she was right about them avoiding each other. The last thing Almeria needed was encouragement. She would be having a field day, dropping not-so-chance remarks about duty and commenting on all the advantages of the union—he paused, quite unable to think of any arguments Almeria would be able to advance in his cause beyond the purely mercenary ones. He didn't, however, let that fool him into believing Almeria wouldn't think of some.

He didn't want to avoid Thea. Why the hell should he? They were friends, and how the devil could he discover if they would suit if they were avoiding each other?

Chapter Three

Thea stared at the rose-pink gauze evening gown in the arms of the modiste's assistant. She loved pink and this was, without a doubt, at the very forefront of fashion, but... She gulped—it appeared to be missing its bodice...and the sleeves consisted of the tiniest scraps of gauze...but the way the light shifted on it...as though it were alive. Delicate embroidered flowers decorated the *rouleau* at the hem. Temptation flickered; involuntarily her fingertips brushed over it. So soft, so fine—there was nothing of it at all... She drew back.

'N...no. No, I couldn't possibly wear that,' she said cravenly.

'*Mais, mademoiselle,*' wailed the modiste, 'it is of the finest, ze mos' beautiful—*madame!*' She appealed to Lady Arnsworth who had stepped away to examine a dress length in softest blue merino draped over a chair.

Lady Arnsworth looked up. 'Excellent, Monique. Precisely what she should wear! With proper stays, of course.'

'But, Lady Arnsworth!' protested Thea, ignoring the reference to stays. She hadn't worn long stays in years. They were impossible without a maid. 'The bodice!'

'Bodice? What about the bodice?'

'It doesn't have one!' said Thea. The thought of appearing in such a gown, exposed to the gaze of all—her skin crawled at the thought of people, men, staring at her, leering. Touching her. No. It would be unbearable. But the gown really was very pretty…

Lady Arnsworth examined the gown. 'Dreadful the way some females flaunt their *charms,*' she said, subjecting the non-existent bodice to keen scrutiny. 'If charms one can call them when they are exposed to every vulgar gaze!'

Thea nodded.

'It is of the first importance that you should not draw attention to yourself,' continued Lady Arnsworth. 'But…' She hesitated. 'As an heiress, there will of course be those only too swift to be spiteful, whatever you do! It is a very lovely gown, Dorothea, but if you do not like it…'

Thea remained silent. That was the problem; she did like it. Very much.

The modiste, her mouth primmed in distaste, cast an affronted glance at Thea's grey dress, muttered something that sounded suspiciously like *sackcloth!* and issued a stream of voluble instructions to her assistant, along with the pink gown, which was borne away.

Sackcloth? Thea considered her current wardrobe. Her gowns were all grey…or brown. Discreet, modest, and…dull. No doubt any gowns provided by Madame Monique would be beautifully cut, and the material exquisite…but, did she really want them to be *grey?*

Sackcloth? She swallowed. That *was* the word that came to mind when she thought of her wardrobe. And there were probably some ashes about somewhere as well.

The old, rebellious spark, dimmed for years, flared. After all, she had never meant to dress in grey for the rest of her life. It was just the way it had turned out after…after Lallerton's death. There had been no money with which to purchase other clothes after her period of official mourning…decreed by her father, and enforced by Aunt Maria…even a pink riband for her hair had been burnt.

The spark ignited. How was shrouding herself in more grey helping her to enjoy herself? She took a very deep breath.

'If you please, *madame—*' she directed what she hoped was

a friendly smile at the modiste '—that pretty pink gown—I should like to try it on after all.'

Madame's eyes brightened. '*Mais oui!* But of course.' Now beaming, the modiste continued, 'The colour will be *ravissement,* of course. It will bring out the pretty colour in *mademoiselle*'s cheeks. We will put away *ces robes tristes.* One does not wish to cover oneself in sadness. The pink. *Oui*—the pink. And there are others, *mademoiselle!*' She rushed away.

Others? Thea gulped. What had she let loose?

No. She pushed the doubts away. She might feel alive again in the pink gown. A dangerous thing being alive, but the pink gown beckoned. She would enjoy the pink gown. As for the non-existent sleeves—well, she would be wearing long gloves. It would be concealing enough.

Madame came back, bearing the pink evening gown as tenderly as a babe. An assistant trailed behind, a rainbow of silks and satins cascading from her arms. Thea viewed it all with intense satisfaction.

Her gowns. Her choices.

Her life. To enjoy.

Lady Arnsworth gave an approving little nod. 'Excellent. Very sensible, my dear.'

By the time Thea left the modiste she had ordered an entire new wardrobe from the skin out, and was garbed in a new walking dress and a pelisse of turkey red. She still couldn't quite believe that she had spent so much money. And she felt completely different—just as Lady Arnsworth had predicted.

'That bonnet,' announced the other woman as she settled herself in the barouche, 'is an abomination. It always was, I dare say, but it is far more noticeable with your new clothes. We shall have to buy you a new one. Several new ones. Now.' She leaned forward to give directions to the coachman. 'And afterwards,' she said, 'we shall drive in the park.'

Her old bonnet consigned to a dust heap, Thea found herself being driven at a snail's pace through the leafy green of the park.

Fashionable London had returned to life after the festivities of the previous evening and their progress was impeded by the number of times the coachman was obliged to stop so that Lady Arnsworth might exchange greetings with her acquaintances.

Just as Thea had expected, no one seemed terribly surprised to learn the identity of Lady Arnsworth's companion; most remembered her from her first Season.

The carriageway was crowded, horses ridden by nattily turned-out gentleman and elegant women, weaving between the carriages, chatter and laughter filling the air as society preened itself. A show, she reminded herself. Like a peacock's tail. Nothing more. And she wasn't frightened of peacocks after all.

'Oh!' Lady Arnsworth's exclamation pulled her back. 'Goodness me—'tis Laetitia Chasewater. I dare say given your connection, Dorothea, that she will call. Nothing could be more fortunate.'

Thea's breath jerked in. The lady in question was seated in her own barouche on the opposite side of the carriageway a little further along. Elegantly gowned in soft grey, tastefully trimmed with black, the lady smiled and inclined her head.

'There...there is no connection, ma'am,' said Thea, her stomach churning. 'I should not like her ladyship to feel obliged—'

'Nonsense,' said Lady Arnsworth. 'Why, 'tis common knowledge that poor Nigel was by far her favourite child, and that she was very happy about the match between you. There! She is beckoning to you! Of course you must step over to greet her. Edmund...' she indicated the footman perched up behind them '...will attend you.'

Immediately the footman leapt down from his perch and opened the door. Thea dragged in a breath as she stepped out, bracing herself to greet the woman who would have been her mother-in-law. It would have been quite distressing enough without the awareness that a large portion of fashionable London had stopped in its tracks to view the exchange of greetings. Peafowl, she reminded herself, were harmless.

'My dear Miss Winslow,' said Lady Chasewater, with a sad smile, holding out her hand. Hesitantly Thea laid hers in it, and thin gloved fingers tightened like claws. 'How delightful to see you again,' said her ladyship. 'I think I have not seen you since, well…' The grey eyes became distant for a moment, before she went on. ''Tis all a very long time ago. I am glad you have come up to town again.' She patted Thea's hand. 'One cannot mourn for ever, my dear.'

No. One couldn't. Nor could one jerk one's hand away from an elderly lady.

Cold and clammy, Thea managed a polite response, her stomach tying itself in knots.

'And how does Aberfield go on? I understand him to be suffering dreadfully from the gout at the moment.' She did not pause for a response, but continued, 'I found some letters from him to Chasewater some time ago.' Her smile became reminiscent. 'After Chasewater died. Such memories as they brought back! All our hopes!'

Nothing in Lady Chasewater's languid voice betokened more than polite interest, but Thea's heart raced.

'Did you, ma'am?' she said with forced calm. 'I am sorry if it was distressing for you.' Of course Aberfield had corresponded with Lord Chasewater…it would have been unavoidable.

Lady Chasewater patted her hand again. 'Oh, no. Why should you regret what is past? I shall do myself the pleasure of calling on Almeria very soon. Now, I must not keep you.' And she gave Thea's hand another gentle pat as she released it.

'Good day, ma'am,' said Thea, relaxing slightly as she stepped back from the carriageway.

The barouche moved on and Thea breathed a sigh of relief, trying to quell the shivering that persisted despite the warmth of the sun and her new pelisse.

Upon reaching Arnsworth House again, Thea retired to her chamber to remove her gloves, bonnet and pelisse. Several dress boxes were already piled on her bed, having been delivered from the modiste's in her absence.

Not bothering to summon a maid, Thea set about unpacking them. These were only a fraction of what she had bought. The rest had required alteration, including the dusky pink evening gown which *madame* had promised would be delivered that same day, assuring Thea that her minions would not rest until it was done.

Thea could only gulp at her expenditure. In one afternoon she had spent ten times more than she had in the preceding eight years. And that was just at the modiste. She had—she was forced to admit—enjoyed it, once she had let herself go. Not that she wanted to fling her money about all the time. After this spree there would be no need. But, oh, it was lovely to know that when she dressed tomorrow morning there would be something pretty to put on. That—

'Ah. There you are, Dorothea.' The door had opened and Lady Arnsworth looked in. 'Do come down when you are ready. I have asked for tea to be brought to the drawing room.'

She looked critically at the new dresses on the bed and hanging over the back of the chair. 'Hmm. That will do for a start. Once a few more invitations have arrived, we shall think again. Do be quick, dear.'

Thea gulped as the door closed behind her godmother. *A few more invitations* sounded as though some had already arrived.

She hurried with the dresses. No doubt Lady Arnsworth had further plans to unveil for the Season. Balls, routs, dinners, soirées, making calls. All the activities of the social whirl. At least she had a day or two before she must plunge into it. Hardly anyone yet knew that she was in town, which meant she was safe for a couple of nights at least…

'Good God! That's…it can't be! Not the Winslow chit!'

Richard, whatever he'd been saying to Braybrook forgotten, stiffened as he heard the middle-aged matron's amazed tones ring out in the middle of the Fothergills' very crowded drawing room that evening. Forcibly he resisted the temptation to turn and stare her down. Whoever she was.

Instead he looked around for Thea. He found Almeria almost immediately, regal in purple, and…

The unknown female behind him continued. 'I had the most

interesting letter, my dear! Why, she was barely out when…' Her
voice dropped, and turning his head slightly, Richard could see
several be-turbaned matrons, feathers a-quiver, nodding and
casting startled looks at Thea as the knowledgeable one dis-
gorged her burden of gossip.

'And you say there was something more to it? Some indiscretion? I understood that story about her grief to be…' began
one. Damn it all! Could a girl not be absent from society for a
few years without the tabbies deciding that there must be 'something more to it'? Were their own hearts so withered that they
could not understand grief?

Another lady leaned forward, murmuring behind her fan. All
he heard was, '—*hurst!*'

'No!' Eyes popping, the first lady cast another, disbelieving
look at Thea. '*How* much? And Almeria actually has him staying
with her? In the very house?'

There were times when the mercenary tendencies of society
amused Richard. This was not one of them.

Braybrook caught his eye. 'People are so predictable, are they
not, Ricky? And, no, you cannot tell her off for it. Much less
demand satisfaction.'

Richard had to unclench his jaw before he could respond. And
Julian did it for him anyway.

'It should be entertaining to watch them all trying to work out
precisely how great an indiscretion can be glossed over with
fifty thousand pounds.' There was an odd snap in his voice.

'What indiscretion?' growled Richard.

Julian's brows drew together, and he nodded to another acquaintance. Then he said lightly, 'The imaginary one they are talking
about, of course, Ricky. And do, please, unclench your fists.'

Looking down, Richard was startled to discover that his fists
were indeed clenched. Since Julian hadn't even glanced at his
hands… He glared at his friend.

Braybrook raised a dark brow. 'Your voice, old chap. It always
gives you away.'

Behind them the matron continued, 'Well, I can't say I should

like the connection for Marianne, but—' a tinge of scornful con-
descension crept into her voice '—I dare say Aberfield can't
afford to be fussy getting *this* one off his hands; after all,
Dunhaven does need an heir.'

Her companion tittered in agreement.

All consideration of discretion crashed to splinters as Richard
spun and skewered the startled women with a glare that could
have felled a gorgon. He didn't waste time on words, merely
stared at them coldly as they flounced and muttered, before
hurrying off through the crowd. Dragging in a deep breath, he
turned and looked again…this time he found her.

Every nerve taut in shock, tension rippled through him. What
the hell did she think she was doing? No longer the grey mouse
who had snapped his head off at breakfast, but a vision in
shimmering rose-pink gauze. A soft, dusky shade—exactly
like…like something waiting to be plucked. He backed right
away from that analogy. The light brown curls were piled high,
a pink bandeau holding them in place, gold lights glinting in the
blaze of candlelight…but it wasn't the change in her appearance
that had fury simmering through every vein.

Aberfield had lost no time at all in offering his daughter up
on the altar of political expedience—Lord Dunhaven hovered
beside her like a dog guarding a juicy bone.

'Ah.' Braybrook nudged him. 'That is Miss Winslow over
there, is it not? In rose pink?' A brief pause and then Braybrook
added, 'With Dunhaven.'

'Yes,' Richard grated. Inside him something growled, and Braybrook's less-than-parliamentary remark about old goats went un-
answered—Richard was already forging a path through the crowd.

Braybrook blinked. Then his gaze narrowed. How very unlike
Ricky not to think a strategy through first. And while a full-
frontal assault might be sufficient, a little flanking manoeuvre
would not go astray.

Thea had completely underestimated the speed with which
news could travel through fashionable society. Any number of

people had seen her in the park and realised her identity. And of course all the people to whom Lady Arnsworth had presented her had been only too happy to mention their acquaintance with the latest heiress. Mrs Dallimore had been swift to bear the tidings to her sister, Lady Fothergill, who had dashed off a charming note assuring Lady Arnsworth that *of course* she would be delighted to welcome dear Lady Arnsworth's protégée to her little party that very evening.

In Thea's book, Lady Fothergill's assembly did not qualify as a little party.

She had forgotten what it felt like to be one of three hundred people squashed into one house. The roar of conversation, mingled with the half-heard strains of the small orchestra made it almost impossible to hear what was said to one. And the heat of all those bodies, the mingled aromas of perfume, cologne and overheated humanity, rose in an almost overpowering wave. Chandeliers and wall sconces blazed with wax candles, adding to the heat. At least this was only an assembly. There would be no dancing tonight.

Once that would not have pleased her at all. She had loved dancing. Loved the music, melody and rhythm sweeping her along in delight. Now she fought to keep a polite smile plastered on her face. And the knowledge that the following evening she was expected to attend a ball feathered chills down her spine.

People kept *touching* her, brushing by her. They couldn't help it, of course, in the press, but nevertheless her skin crawled and her stomach clenched, a solid lump of panic churning within. Each time she kicked her chin a notch higher and breathed with fierce determination. It was foolish, irrational—she *wouldn't* give in to it!

As various people greeted them, Thea's nerves began to steady, and she realised with an odd shock that, although she disliked the crowd, the fear of exposing herself was ebbing. She might be uncomfortable, but she wasn't going to faint or panic, even when one dowager went so far as to prod her with a fan, commenting that it was time and more that she did her duty. She shot a gimlet-eyed stare at Lady Arnsworth. 'And I hear you have that nephew of yours with you. Well, it might be worse!' and stumped off, leaning on a cane.

'Such a *dreadful* crush!' pronounced Lady Arnsworth in scathing tones, as the dowager retreated. 'Really, I wonder that Louisa cares to invite so many. I have not seen a single person I wished to see.' She smiled graciously, inclining her head at another lady. 'Lady Broome! How nice...yes. A frightful crush. I shall look forward to a comfortable cose later!'

Lady Broome sailed away into the seething silks and satins.

Lady Arnsworth shuddered. 'Vulgar creature! Her father was a merchant. I vow she smells of the shop!'

Thea remembered Lady Broome as a very good-natured, un-affected woman—not at all vulgar. And her own fortune, now re-spectably invested in the Funds, derived from her uncle's involvement with the East India Company. Perhaps Lady Arnsworth's sense of smell was selective...like her tolerance for other failings.

The gentlemen were no less assiduous in their attentions, several claiming to remember her from her brief Season.

She smiled and replied politely to their compliments, vaguely remembering names and faces from eight years ago. The smile was the important thing: vague, gracious, never direct. Let them think her cold, uninviting...

'Oh, goodness me!' muttered Lady Arnsworth, nipping at Thea's arm in warning with gloved fingers.

Thea recognised Lord Dunhaven at once. Slightly above average height, his powerful frame drew attention as he strolled towards them, his expression intent.

'Really! I did not think he could possibly be serious!' muttered Lady Arnsworth to Thea. Then, in far more gracious tones, 'Lord Dunhaven! How do you do?'

Instantly Thea was aware that although his lordship ex-changed polite greetings with Lady Arnsworth, all his attention was on her. Intent, knowing eyes looked her up and down. She stiffened her spine against the tremor that went through her as

Lady Arnsworth presented her. 'You recall Lord Aberfield's daughter? Miss Winslow, this is Lord Dunhaven.'

Thin lips curved in acknowledgement. 'Certainly, ma'am. I called on Aberfield earlier and he mentioned that she had arrived.' His gaze returned to Thea. 'Good evening, Miss Winslow.' He extended his hand with all the air of one conferring a signal honour upon the recipient.

Thea repressed a shudder, violently aware of her scanty bodice, as she placed her hand in his. She remembered Lord Dunhaven well; she had never liked him. Lady Dunhaven had always been casting nervous glances at him, agreeing with everything he said.

'How do you do, my lord?' She curtsied slightly as he bowed over her hand, and the odour of his pomaded hair sank into her. Her stomach roiled, but she lifted her chin. His lordship seemed inclined to retain possession of her hand and place it on his arm, but she withdrew it firmly. Something about Lord Dunhaven made her skin crawl, even through her white kid gloves. She quelled the urge to rub her glove as though it might be soiled. There was something about the way he looked at her—assessing, judging, as though she were a filly he contemplated buying.

'It is some years since you were in town, Miss Winslow,' he said. 'I will be happy to act as your guide in some measure. Aberfield was most anxious that your time in London should be spent profitably.'

Thea barely suppressed a snort. 'Really, sir? I am sure we can depend on Lady Arnsworth to ensure that my time is not wasted.'

'Yes, indeed,' said her ladyship. 'I have no doubt that—'

'Almeria! How lovely to see you! And Miss Winslow! How delightful!'

Whatever Lady Arnsworth had meant to say was lost as Lady Chasewater came up to greet them.

'My dear—I cannot tell you how pleased I am to see you again so soon—how much it gladdens my mother's heart.'

Dragging in a breath, Thea pinned a smile in place. 'Lady Chasewater,' she said with a smile. 'How kind of you.'

Something lit in Lady Chasewater's eyes, a spark deep within. 'My dear, you must not feel obliged to me. My poor Nigel— there! his name is spoken between us—let me assure you, he would not have expected you to mourn—now, would he?'

Thea shook her head. God help her, it was the truth.

'Of course not,' said Lady Chasewater. 'And I am so glad you have returned,' she continued, patting Thea's hand. 'People do say such foolish things, you know. But you may count on me to do everything I can. Perhaps if you were to drive with me in the park one day…'

Somehow Thea's heart kept pumping gelid blood around her body. Somehow she held herself still, mastered the frantic need to pull her hands away, and kept a smile frozen to her face as her voice fought its way past the choking blockage in her throat.

'Thank you, ma'am.'

Lady Arnsworth chimed in, 'Yes, indeed, Dorothea will be honoured. An excellent notion and so kind of you, Laetitia. It will do her a great deal of good to be seen with you.'

'Oh, tush, Almeria!' said Lady Chasewater. 'Why, she was to be my daughter-in-law!' Her gaze flashed to Thea. 'I would have been a grandmama by now. And poor Nigel has been dead these eight years, and no one ever speaks of him to me.' A sad smile accompanied these words. 'I know Dorothea will understand! I may call you Dorothea?' As she spoke, she released Thea's hands with a little pressure.

'Of course, ma'am.'

'And you will drive with me?'

A drive in the park. That was all. So why did she feel as though she were being manoeuvred to the gallows?

She lifted her chin. 'Thank you, ma'am. That will be delightful.'

Lady Chasewater inclined her head. 'Excellent, my dear. I shall send a little note round. Now, if I am not much mistaken, Lord Dunhaven wishes to stroll with you, Dorothea, and is wishing me elsewhere.' She cast an arch smile at his lordship, who smirked and disclaimed.

'Aberfield must be pleased to know that Dorothea is drawing such distinguished attention.' She rapped his lordship on the arm with her fan. 'And so pleasant to see you again now that your period of mourning is over. I am sure we *all* hope to see you happy again very soon.'

Lacing her farewells with another gracious smile, she glided away through the crowd.

'If you would honour me, Miss Winslow?' Dunhaven extended his arm, and Lady Arnsworth cleared her throat. He accorded her the briefest of smiles. 'Your ladyship has no objection?'

'Of course not,' said Lady Arnsworth, although Thea had the distinct impression that she would have liked to rattle off several objections.

As they strolled, Lord Dunhaven presenting her to this person and that, Thea could almost feel the whispers eddying in their wake. Faint smiles, half-hidden behind fans, betrayed a cynical acceptance. And as they proceeded she felt colder and colder from the inside out, as though the chill leached from somewhere deep within. She kicked her chin a notch higher, and told herself that a few people sliding away through the crowd at their approach meant nothing, that the speculative sideways glances were mere curiosity, nothing more.

Lord Dunhaven appeared not to notice, as though such things were beneath him. Instead he regaled Thea with an exact account of all the various improvements he had undertaken at his principal country seat, the refurbished stables, the rearrangement of the principal apartments.

'I should like very much to show it all to you, Miss Winslow,' he said, after telling her how his new billiard room was laid out.

Before Thea could do more than skim over all the possible ramifications of this, she prickled with sudden awareness as a tall figure came up beside her. She turned sharply and warmth flooded her, dispelling the growing chill.

Richard, immaculately turned out in utterly correct evening garb.

'Good evening, Miss Winslow. Servant, Dunhaven.'

Thea blinked. Anything less servant-like than Richard's

clipped tones would have been hard to imagine. He sounded as though he'd swallowed a razor blade made of ice. Even his bow held an arrogance that reminded her all at once that he was after all the son of an earl, one of the damn-your-eyes Blakehursts: assured, at home in the *ton* for all his scholarly nature.

The contrast between the two men was startling. Very few would have described Richard's evening clothes as stylish, but somehow the comfortably fitted coat over broad, lean shoulders had a greater elegance than Dunhaven's tightly fitted and, she suspected, padded coat. Dunhaven dripped with expensive fobs, rings and a very large diamond blazed in his cravat. Richard's jewellery consisted of a pearl nestled quietly in his cravat and a plain gold ring.

Dunhaven looked his disdain. 'Ah, *Mr* Blakehurst, is it not? How surprising to see you here.'

A spurt of anger shot through Thea at the sneering tone, but Richard merely looked amused.

'Is it, Dunhaven? I assure you that I overcome my boredom with this sort of thing quite regularly enough for the hostesses not to completely despair of my attendance.' He smiled at Thea. 'Good evening, Miss Winslow. May I take you to find some champagne?'

Thea blinked. As simple as that.

'Certainly, sir. That would be lovely. I'm sure his lordship will excuse me.'

Dunhaven's hand came across and settled in hard possession on Thea's fingers, clamping them to his arm. 'There is no need, Miss Winslow. I shall be happy to escort you and find you something suitable for a lady to drink. Some ratafia, I think you would prefer.'

Not the usual paralysing fear, but anger surged through her. With a sharp movement, she slid her fingers from under Dunhaven's grip. Telling her what to do was bad enough, but presuming to tell her what she would like was going entirely too far. Besides, she didn't like ratafia.

'Dunhaven! Just the man I was looking for.'

The newcomer was familiar to Thea. Tall, with jet-black hair and brilliant, deep blue eyes—surely… Shock lurched through her—yes, it was David's friend, Julian Trentham…only he had succeeded now to his father's title—Viscount Braybrook.

He smiled at her and bowed. 'Miss Winslow. Braybrook at your service. Friend of your brother's, if you recall? You won't mind if I steal Dunhaven, will you? Blakehurst here will look after you.' He glanced at Richard, 'Won't you, old chap?'

Richard's mouth twitched. 'I think that could be managed.'

Thea's gaze narrowed, despite her suddenly pounding heart. There was something wicked in Lord Braybrook's limpid blue eyes. However, she wasn't fool enough to reject a lifeline, no matter how it presented itself. 'Of…of course.' She seized the opportunity to step away from Dunhaven. Richard caught her hand and set it on his arm, anchoring it there and again that shock of awareness jolted through her at his touch. Dazed, she met Braybrook's gaze, but the bright eyes told her nothing—what would David have told him? Could he possibly know any of the truth?

'You'll excuse us, gentlemen.' Richard's clipped voice shook her back to herself, and he drew her away through the crowd.

'What the devil are you playing at?' he muttered, and nodded curtly at an acquaintance smiling at him. 'Dunhaven, of all men! He's desperate to marry again and sire an heir. He's looking for a bride! A nice, young, *fertile* bride to bear his sons!'

'He's also a friend of my father's!' said Thea, blushing scarlet at Richard's blunt assessment. 'I can't just cut him, or snub him, when—'

'Then let Almeria do it for you!' came the riposte. 'Trust me, she'll be only too happy to see him off with a flea in his ear!'

She didn't doubt that for a moment, but—

'Even Lady Arnsworth can't do that when my father has practically given his blessing to the match!' she snapped.

'*What?*' They were near an open door, and Richard whirled her through it and along a corridor. He opened another door and she found herself whisked into the library. It was empty, lit by a single lamp. Even in her annoyance she could not repress a spurt of amusement. Trust Richard to know the location of the library.

He faced her in the dim light. 'What the hell are you talking about? Dunhaven is old enough to *be* your father! You can't be serious!'

Furious that he could even think she might accept such a match, Thea glared at him. 'Perhaps you might care to mention that to Aberfield?'

'I would if I thought it would have the least effect! For God's sake, Thea! Dunhaven's a complete wart. He's so desperate to cut his brother out of the succession, it's a wonder he hasn't found a young enough widow with a couple of brats to her credit!'

The moment the words were out of his mouth he knew he'd said the wrong thing. She flinched, as though he had struck her, and the colour drained from her face.

Something white hot jolted through Richard. He caught her arm, steadying her, feeling her tremble. 'Thea! Are you all right?'

'He *couldn't!*' she whispered. 'Even Aberfield wouldn't do that to me!'

Richard slipped his arm around her waist to support her, and she shook her head very slightly as if to clear it, tensing. Ignoring her attempt to pull away, he guided her to a sofa and eased her down onto it, seating himself beside her.

'Just sit,' he told her.

Her chin came up. 'I am perfectly well, thank you.'

'Dammit, Thea—you are not all right!' he said furiously. 'You nearly fainted!'

'I did not!' she snapped. 'I was merely a little dizzy. It's…it's stuffy in here! Look, I must go back—if we're caught here together!'

There would be the very devil to pay. He'd be offering for her immediately. Surprisingly the idea didn't send the usual battle alert along his nerves.

'I can think of worse fates,' he told her. 'For both of us.'

The mere thought of Dunhaven touching her in any way at all had something growling inside him—a clawed beast with a distinctly greenish cast to its eyes.

Blue eyes snapped fire at him in the dim light. 'But you said *you* don't want to marry me, so—'

'The devil I did!' he growled. And right now, with that pink gown hinting at feminine mysteries, the delicate lace edge at her breasts that tempted a man to slide his finger beneath to tease velvet-soft flesh—he tore his mind free of its imaginings and concentrated on reality.

Reality was glaring at him. 'Yes, you did. At breakfast!'

'I never said that,' he told her bluntly. 'I told you I wouldn't marry you for your fortune. First rule of scholarship: don't tamper with the text!' Or with those silken glossy curls feathering about her brow—or the one lying against the slender, creamy column of her neck...especially not that one. His own collar itched.

A merry voice interrupted. 'Thea! I thought it was you! How naughty of you to hide away here with Mr Blakehurst. And how delightful to see you after all these years! Do you know, I quite thought you must have retired to a convent.' A slender woman stood in the doorway, several feathers nodding in her dark, elaborately coiffed hair. 'I couldn't believe it when they said you were here,' she continued, 'and then I saw you vanishing out of the door! Am I interrupting?' She stepped into the room, leaving the door open. 'Are you about to box his ears?'

Richard recognised the fashionably dressed young matron. Lady Fox-Heaton's famous smile beamed as she came across the room, holding out her hands to Thea in unaffected pleasure.

Hesitantly Thea placed her own in them and stood up. 'Diana—how well you look.' She smiled. 'You are married, of course?'

Diana Fox-Heaton flushed slightly. 'Yes. Had you not heard?'

At Thea's denial, Lady Fox-Heaton looked troubled. 'Oh, well, I...I married Francis—Francis Fox-Heaton.' She sighed. 'You will remember him, of course—he was friendly with poor Mr Lallerton.'

To Richard it seemed that Thea's expression froze.

'You married Sir Francis Fox-Heaton?' she said carefully.

Lady Fox-Heaton's smile glimmered. 'Oh, yes. And I know what you are thinking! How did I come to marry a mere baronet? We were all going to marry earls at the very least, were we not? But Sir Francis is an MP now! Such consequence!'

Richard repressed a snort. It was rumoured that Diana had

outraged her family by dismissing a marquis to marry Fox-Heaton. A love match if ever there was one.

'How lovely for you,' said Thea. But Richard could not rid himself of the impression that she thought it anything but lovely.

'Yes,' said Diana cheerfully. 'It is. But for now, we had better get you back to the party. If I saw you leave, you may be sure others did, and I must say—there are some *very* odd stories circulating anyway.' She gave Richard a severe look. 'I should have thought, Mr Blakehurst, that you had more sense than this.'

Richard choked.

'Odd stories?' Thea's query sounded casual. Too casual, thought Richard. Were she not wearing gloves, he'd swear her knuckles would be showing white.

'Very odd,' said Diana. 'I'll explain later.'

Returning to the party, Richard was hailed by a small group headed by the Marquis of Callington, wanting his opinion on the value of the late King's library, recently presented to the nation by his Majesty. More than happy to promote his belief that the value of the library was immense, he joined them, but discovered to his disgust that part of his mind remained focused on Thea. His gaze kept straying to where she stood with Diana Fox-Heaton and a number of other young matrons, and several men whom usually he considered good enough fellows, but whom right now he would have cheerfully flung through a window. Men who were far too wary to hang around most matrimonially inclined young girls and their mamas—but who might nevertheless be interested in a woman with an independent fortune...

'Well, the last thing we want is a repeat of the tragedy that you say befell the Cotton manuscripts, Ricky,' said Callington.

Richard dragged his mind back to agree with Callington's conclusion that it was of the first importance to ensure that the late King's library was well protected from fire or any other calamity. He breathed a sigh of relief to see that David Winslow had joined the little group about Thea. If Winslow was ready to carve slices out of *his* hide, then he was well able to re-educate the thinking of any other overly libidinous suitors.

Chapter Four

By the end of the evening, Thea felt as though she had been boiled up in a copper with the sheets. She was exhausted, limp, by the time Almeria summoned the carriage to return to Grosvenor Square. But she had survived. She had renewed her acquaintance with a number of women who had been brought out in the same season as herself and had been accepted back into their number.

Her public acceptance by Diana Fox-Heaton ensured that. Diana had accompanied her back to the drawing room. Several women she had known as a girl had come up to her, inviting her to various parties. She thought about Diana as the maid readied her for bed. They had not been close friends years ago, but they had liked each other. And Diana had gone out of her way to help tonight. She had warned her that rumours were circulating. Rumours that suggested Miss Winslow's long absence from society might have very little to do with mourning a lost love...

She shivered. Diana was married to Sir Francis—one of the very few people who could have any inkling of the truth. He had been a close friend of Nigel Lallerton's, that was how she had come to know Diana. They had been part of the same circle. What would he say to his wife's renewed friendship with her?

She slipped into bed and blew out the lamp. Despite her exhaustion, sleep mocked her. Diana had been quite as outspoken as Richard on the subject of Lord Dunhaven... *Francis says he simply wants a brood mare—and that no father of sense will give his consent to such a marriage. You know, there was all sorts of gossip when his wife died—but nothing could be done. No servant would ever speak out in a matter like that!*

Thea shivered. Aberfield, however, *was* willing to promote the match.

A hard-edged face slid into focus. Dark eyes that usually spoke of cool control, self-discipline—eyes that had positively blazed with some violent emotion this evening. Heat flickered, tingling inside her—Richard must really loathe Dunhaven for some reason, she told herself. She didn't think she had ever seen him so angry— except once when he was a boy, and his mother had just visited... She sighed. She hadn't much liked Richard's mother herself and she wondered what the new Lady Blakehurst was like... Richard seemed to like her, even if Lady Arnsworth didn't.

Richard walked back to Grosvenor Square in company with Braybrook. They had ended the evening in the card room, playing piquet for penny points with an added shilling for a game, and a pound a rubber. Richard had emerged ahead by a couple of pounds and half a bottle of brandy.

'The sad thing is,' said Richard, jingling the coins in his pocket, 'that if I played for larger stakes, I'd lose resoundingly!'

'Naturally,' said Braybrook. 'My father always said much the same; you only win when you can afford to lose. Pity he didn't take his own advice speculating. Here we are—Arnsworth House.'

'So it is,' said Richard, inspecting the familiar portico.

A faint scraping sound brought both of them swinging around sharply. A small dark shape detached itself from the steps leading down to the area and resolved itself into a boy.

'What the devil are you doing there?' demanded Richard.

The lad hung back. 'Would one of you be Mr Richard Blakehurst?'

'What's that to you, lad?' asked Braybrook suspiciously.

Richard shook his head. 'It's all right, Julian,' he said. 'Yes, I'm Mr Blakehurst.'

'Note for you then, guv,' said the boy, approaching. 'From a lidy,' and pushed the note into Richard's hand. He was gone in a flash, racing off along the pavement and disappearing around the corner into Upper Grosvenor Street, before either of them could stop him.

Richard stared after him with raised brows. 'Idiot boy,' he said. 'I'd have given him sixpence. Wonder who's writing me love notes?'

Braybrook raised his brows. 'Love notes, Ricky? You?'

Richard grinned, breaking the seal and opening the note. 'Do you think you and Max are the only men in London ever to—*good God!*'

He stared in disgust. Who the hell had penned this filth?

Braybrook twitched the note out of his hand and read aloud, *'How many times will you tup the gilded whore tonight?'* In an expressionless voice, he said, 'Charming, Ricky. Absolutely charming.' He handed it back.

Crumpling the note in his fist, Richard shoved it deep in the pocket of his coat. 'Quite.'

The burning question, of course, was just who was the gilded whore? He hoped, he very much hoped, that he didn't know the answer.

'Sure you won't seek lodgings, old man?' asked Braybrook.

Richard shook his head curtly and limped up the steps, refusing to acknowledge the wisdom of the suggestion.

Thea frowned at the note from Lady Chasewater, inviting her to drive her in the park the following day. Relieved that it wasn't for that afternoon, Thea managed to persuade Lady Arnsworth that a quiet hour in the back parlour would be more beneficial than more shopping.

Reluctantly, her ladyship consented. 'Very well, dear. If you are quite sure it is necessary. You do look pale. And of course you must send a note accepting Laetitia's invitation. She is very influential. And there must be no question of you not being able to attend the Montacute ball this evening, so I suppose…'

Thea assured her that with a little quiet she would be perfectly ready to attend the ball and Lady Arnsworth departed.

Telling Myles that she was not at home to anyone, Thea asked for a pot of tea to be brought to her in the parlour.

Ten minutes later she was ensconced on a sofa with her writing box and sipping her tea. Peace descended in the familiar room. Faint sounds from the street and the mews reached her, but they seemed oddly detached, as though the house hung suspended beyond the noise.

Hastily she wrote a note to Lady Chasewater, assuring her that she would be delighted to drive with her the following day. Then she summoned a footman to take the note. That done, she took out another sheet of paper to write to Aunt Maria.

For a few moments her pen scratched away. Then it stilled as her concentration wavered and she gazed about the familiar room. Little had changed since last she had been there. It was not a public room, and the furniture was rather old-fashioned and crowded. Not a crocodile leg or sphinx in sight, as though the room had been forgotten when Lady Arnsworth redecorated.

Of all the rooms in Arnsworth House, this was the one she had always known best when she visited as a child. Here Richard had spent his days after the riding accident that broke his left leg. Here, she had been introduced to him at the age of five, as a suitable chess opponent. She smiled, remembering. The twelve-year-old Richard had barely choked off the exclamation of disgust. He had, however, taught her to play chess.

She laid the pen down.

What was he really like now? She had known him as a boy, but did she know the man? Perhaps she did. No doubt he still loved dogs. And horses. The fuss there had been when he insisted on riding again after his accident! His mother and Lady Arnsworth would have kept him wrapped in cotton wool on the sofa if he hadn't been so stubborn about it. She couldn't believe *that* would have changed. Richard could make a mule look cooperative.

Which probably meant he was in no danger of being lured into a matrimonial trap with her.

And he was still kind. Protective. The thought stole through her, insensibly warming. He had been protective last night. No, that had not changed. So perhaps she did still know him. A little. Far better than he could know her.

The child who had known Richard was gone beyond recall, as if a knife had slashed the thread of her life leaving it in two utterly separate pieces. Short useless pieces that could never be woven back into the pattern.

No one knew her now. Sometimes she wished she didn't know herself. There was no point wondering about Richard Blake-hurst. He was no concern of hers. She thrust the thoughts away and went back to her letter. That was how she had learnt to manage. One thing at a time; concentrate on the task at hand.

The only sound within the parlour was the scratching of Thea's pen as she concentrated on manufacturing neat, ladylike sentences for Aunt Mary.

A light tap at the door disturbed her.

'Yes?'

The door opened and Myles came in. 'A note for you, miss.'

'Oh. Thank you, Myles.'

She took the note with a smile.

'Will that be all, miss?'

'Yes, thank you. I'll ring if I need to send a reply.'

As the door closed behind the butler, Thea looked at the note. A single sheet folded once and sealed with a plain seal. It was directed to Miss Winslow, Arnsworth House, in clumsy, ill-formed capitals. Thea frowned, broke the seal and opened the note.

Time stood still and her veins congealed as the single word slashed her hard-won peace to shreds: *SLUT.*

Who? *Who?*

How long she sat staring at the note, she had no idea, but a deep voice wrenched her out of the nightmare with a shock like icy water.

'What the deuce have you got here?'

The writing box hit the floor, accompanied by the crash of splintering glass and china as the inkpot and teacup broke. Thea found herself on her feet, every sense at full stretch, one fist clenched. Ready to fight.

Richard's shocked face steadied her. 'It's only me, Thea.' Then, 'Damn! Stay still!'

He strode towards her, his expression fiercely intent.

Despite herself, she flinched, stepping back.

'Damn it, woman! *I said to stay still!*' he roared.

She froze in sheer outrage, and he was beside her, his booted feet crunching on the ruins of the inkpot and teacup.

And gasped as she was lifted bodily with ease and dumped back on the sofa with a marked lack of ceremony.

'And *stay* there,' he growled, 'while I send for someone to clear this up. Those slippers won't protect you from a shard of glass!'

She looked down. Broken glass and china sat in the lake of spilled ink and tea soaking into the Turkey carpet. And with them the anonymous note.

Sanity flooded back in some measure, but the violence of her reaction still shook her. 'I…I didn't hear you come in.' She leaned forward and reached for the paper.

His mouth quirked. 'Obviously.' And before she could stop him, he had bent down for the note. 'Here you—' it was open, face up— 'Good God!' he exclaimed, staring at the note.

Then he looked up and Thea's stomach turned over as she met his eyes. Fury, sheer protective fury blazed there.

Oh, God! If Richard tried to find out…

For a moment the shocked silence held, then Richard spoke, scarcely recognising his own voice, soft, deadly. 'Who the devil sent you this?' He forced himself to consider the matter logically, controlling the choking rage. Last night's note had disgusted him, but this! His fingers shook in the effort not to shred the note.

He turned it over. Like his, the seal had been plain, the writing consisted of clumsy and ill-formed capitals…and directed very clearly to Thea. This piece of…of filth had been intended for her. As last night's note had been directed straight to him. His fist clenched, crushing the note. His own note he might have ignored, but if he ever found out who had sent this—he'd serve them the same way. Slowly.

'Who sent it?' he repeated.

'I don't know.' There was not the least tremor in her voice now and her eyes were steady and clear. 'Myles brought it in. It's nothing to fuss about, Richard. Just foolish spite.' She essayed a faint laugh. 'No doubt the rumours of my fortune inspired it. I'd burn it, but the fire isn't lit.'

Undoubtedly the fire was where it belonged. If he had not been watching her for a moment before he spoke and startled her, he might have believed her not to be upset. But he had seen the pallor of her face as she stared at the note, seen her hands trembling. She had been so lost in whatever emotion had gripped her that she had not even heard him enter the room. And now she was trying to hide it from him.

Surely a piece of casual spite would not strike to the heart like that? She had looked devastated. Had she heard the whispers the previous night? Should he mention his own note? Common sense said he should. But…

'Do you receive many letters like that?'

'No! Give it back, Richard. I'll burn it later.'

'I'll deal with it,' he said. 'I don't want you touching it again.' The thought of a piece of vileness like this coming anywhere near her offended him. He put the crumpled note in his pocket.

Flushing, she met his gaze. 'I thought you were out.'

As an attempt to change the subject it was pitiful. 'I came home,' he said. 'Thea, that note—'

'Please—no,' she interrupted. 'I know what you would say— that I ought to find out who sent it, but really, Richard, it doesn't matter. Just burn it for me. It's just someone…someone who doesn't like me, I suppose. Someone…very unhappy.'

'How do you work that out?' he growled.

Her eyes dropped. 'Oh, well…can you imagine a happy person sending a note like that?'

He couldn't, of course. There were times when feminine intuition was absolutely irrefutable. Only he could have sworn she meant something far more specific. Something personal. That she knew who had sent it, or at least suspected.

'Leave it, Richard,' she urged. 'There's no point making a fuss. It was horrid and I admit gave me quite a shock, but that's all.' She smiled at him, eyes steady. 'What brought you in here?'

Another attempt to change the subject.

He didn't like it. Not one little bit. Every instinct told him that Thea was deeply shaken, that her increasing calm was a façade, that if she knew of the note he had received she would be even more upset. For now he would accept her reticence. It seemed more important to distract her from the vile note. And definitely more important to distract her from wondering what he might do about it.

'What brought me in here?' He smiled. 'Myles told me you were here and he swears that Almeria is out.' The mess of ink and tea caught his eye and he reached out to ring the bell. 'So I thought it would be safe to have a game of chess without giving her any encouragement.'

'Chess? In here? Do you…do you think that's wise?' Suddenly self-conscious, she said, 'If Lady Arnsworth has some idea…that is, that we…that we—'

She broke off and Richard had to suppress a grin.

'That we might make a match of it?' he suggested helpfully. 'So she's spoken to you about it, has she?'

She flushed. 'She didn't precisely *say* anything to me. Only…'

Richard laughed. 'Didn't she? You escaped lightly. She said a great deal to me. Very precisely and in detail. You must know that Almeria has been trying to marry me off to the nearest available fortune for the past ten years!'

Something flickered in her face. Pain? This was not the moment to suggest to her that maybe they should give some thought to Almeria's matchmaking. Not when she had just stopped calling him *sir* with every second breath. Instead, he said gently, 'Thea, we need not consider it. You must know that I would never court any woman for her fortune, let alone you. We can still be friends, can we not? Despite Almeria's meddling?'

For a moment Thea hesitated. Friends…it would be safer not… Yet, unbidden, some long-buried, unrecognisable sensation unfurled within her. She nodded. 'Friends. Yes.'

He smiled. 'Good. Then leave Miss Winslow in the drawing room where she belongs.' He rose, stepped carefully over the mess of ink and broken glass and china and went over to a large, old-fashioned chest under the window. 'Now, let's see…'

Leave Miss Winslow in the drawing room…

'What do you mean?'

He shot her a glance. 'Miss Winslow is all very well for the rest of the world. But I've always been quite fond of Thea.'

He knelt down with a muttered curse and pulled out the bottom drawer. 'Ah hah! Here we are.'

Despite her confusion, Thea felt the unaccustomed smile curving her lips, warming her heart. He had found the old chess set he had taught her to play with. And there in the corner, half-hidden behind a fire screen, was the little chess table.

That sensation inside her stirred again, and this time she recognised it with shock. It was happiness. She had been so utterly determined to enjoy herself, even if she had to pretend, and here happiness had been quietly waiting within to be let out. Along with the Thea he said he was fond of? Was she waiting to escape too?

Automatically the old words of challenge rose to her lips. 'No quarter? No chivalry?'

His answering smile flashed, lighting the dark brown eyes. 'To the death!'

Together they set out the pieces, the memories of all the times they had done this stretching back and forth between them.

'You were about five when I taught you how to do this,' said Richard.

She looked up, an answering smile in her eyes. 'You must have thought I was the most frightful little pest.'

'I did. And I was furious with Almeria. I'd been enjoying my games with Myles. He kept having to rush off to do his job, so I had plenty of time to contemplate my moves. Try to work out

what he would do next. And, of course, he could actually play.
A distinct advantage.'

'Rather than having to teach me?'

He thought back, pushing out a pawn. 'You learnt fast enough.
Once you found your voice and started asking questions.'

'I was terrified your leg would fall off,' confessed Thea.

'What!' A pawn went flying as he spluttered with laughter.

She went scarlet. 'Well, from what Lady Arnsworth told
Mama, I thought your leg had been broken off and stuck back
on. And my nurse was always saying I could talk the hind leg
off a donkey, so I thought if it fell off again while I was there
everyone would blame me!' She glared at him, as though daring
him to laugh.

Laughter shook him anyway, as he righted the fallen pawn.
Amazing how one could laugh at a terror almost twenty years
old. At the time he'd still been having nightmares that he would
lose the leg after all.

'No wonder you didn't say anything,' he said with a grin.

Bit by bit, the constraint between them loosened and he found
himself telling her what he had been doing since last he'd seen
her. Learning about the land to be, in essence, Max's steward.
'Since I have now bought my own place, at least I know what
I'm doing,' he said.

'Your own place?'

And he told her about the small property just ten miles from
Blakeney over the North Downs; the sheep grazing on the
uplands and the old house and gardens nestled in their small,
hidden valley, sheltered from the worst of the storms that could
sweep up the Channel.

'Not grand,' he said, 'but it will be a home. Enough for me.'

'Sheep?' she said. 'You? I thought you would remain at Oxford.'

If Max had not inherited, he probably would have. 'Sheep,'
he informed her, 'have a long and noble history in this country.
I've been going through the Blakeney papers. Centuries they go
back, and sheep are mentioned frequently.' Odd, but he was
finding the task just as stimulating as more conventional study

at Oxford. He tried to explain that to Thea in answer to her questions, and realised that somehow he had done nothing but talk about his own concerns for over an hour.

He looked at the mantel clock. Well over an hour. 'I must be boring you rigid!' he said. 'Why on earth didn't you tell me to shut up?'

'Because you weren't boring me,' she said. 'Because I was imagining it all, and seeing how right it all is for you. It sounds wonderful, Richard. Peaceful, yet busy. Fulfilling. Something practical to fill your days, and something to occupy your mind. That was always what you needed.'

With a shock he realised that she was exactly right, that Oxford had never quite been right for him because of that. That he had given it up and come home so readily when Max asked, because deep down he had known that.

'And you?' he asked. 'What have your days held?' Too late he remembered that the question might be unwelcome, but it was gone now, and could no more be recalled than a loosed arrow.

Only in the tightening of her mouth did he see the question strike home. She didn't look up from the board, but said at last, 'Very little. After…after I was considered out of mourning I remained with Aunt Maria. She…she required a companion, and since I had—*have*—no wish to marry, it seemed the logical thing.' She moved her knight.

He didn't know what to say. She had said that yesterday—that she did not wish to marry. But surely…

'My brother thought that he would never marry,' he said. 'And I doubt that he has ever been happier than he is now.'

She did look up at that. 'I'm glad,' she said. 'Tell me about your sister-in-law. She is…expecting a baby, is she not?'

He heard the faint hesitation and ached. Was that something she had wanted, and thought now was for ever lost to her? Nevertheless, she had changed the subject, and he could only respect that. So he made his countermove, and told her a little about Max and Verity, that the baby was nearly due, and that Max was terrified. Far more so than Verity herself.

Thea did not look up again, but surveyed the board, apparently concentrating, soft pink lips very slightly pursed. But her hands, resting in her lap, shifted continually, fiddling with her cuffs, turning a small turquoise ring on her little finger.

He should be concentrating himself, predicting her likely move and its consequences. He knew what he wanted her to do, what nine people out of ten would do at this point. Only it seemed unimportant, compared to the stray curl escaping to tickle her face and make her frown. She pushed it back and his own fingers itched to capture the wisp and tuck it in safely. Or to release a few more of her softly curling tresses to twine about his fingers. He leaned forwards...

She glanced up, pushing the errant wisp out of her eyes yet again. Their eyes met, his suddenly narrowed, intent; hers wide and startled. Reality reined in his half-formed desire. What in Hades had come over him? He needed to conduct this courtship logically...and playing chess was a very rational and logical thing to do.

Dazed, he realised that in the space of two hours he'd gone from considering the possibility of a match to courtship. Thea had loved once, and was disinclined to give her heart again. Would she perhaps consider a marriage based on friendship? Mutual interests and understanding? Would that be enough for her?

She reached out and he watched, fascinated, as the slender, graceful fingers hovered over her knight. He rather thought she had seen his little trap. And the next question occurred to him: would such a marriage be enough for him?

The door opened.

'Mr Winslow,' announced Myles.

'David!' cried Thea as her brother stalked in.

Richard looked up. Winslow's eyes glinted gun metal as he took in the scene.

'Good afternoon, Winslow.' For a moment the quiet greeting hung there and then David Winslow seemed to relax infinitesimally.

'Blakehurst.' A rather reluctant smile curved his mouth. 'I remember that you were fond of chess. Am I interrupting?'

Thea glanced back at him questioningly.

'Yes. You are,' said Richard blandly. 'You will have to wait about three seconds for your sister.' He shot Thea a grin. 'It will take her about that long to mop up my king.'

Thea chuckled, an unshadowed ripple of delight that sent streamers of pleasure curling through him. A sudden movement caught his attention. About to seat himself on the sofa, David Winslow's head had jerked up, his gaze fixed on his sister, as though he had only just seen her. Startled grey eyes flickered to Richard, and then back to Thea in wonder and speculation.

'Don't let me disturb you,' he said with an odd smile.

As Richard had predicted, his king fell in short order.

'Ah, well,' he said. 'That will teach me not to underestimate you again. I'll take my revenge on another occasion, Thea.' He rose and turned to Winslow. 'I'll bid you good day and leave you with your sister.'

Winslow stood. 'As to that, Blakehurst...' He hesitated, seeming to consider something and coming to a swift decision. 'I was hoping for a word with you later.'

Richard held his gaze. 'Were you, indeed?' A challenge? A warning?

Winslow looked very slightly embarrassed. Probably not a challenge, then. 'Er, yes. Perhaps you might care to dine with me this evening at my lodgings? I'm in Jermyn Street.' He took his case out of his pocket and handed a card to Richard.

Definitely not a challenge.

Richard took the card. 'Very well, Winslow. What time?'

'Will eight suit you?'

'Of course. I shall look forward to it.' He smiled at Thea. 'Save me a dance this evening, won't you? Or even two.'

'A dance?'

'Yes, a dance.' He grinned at her look of confusion. 'You know what a dance is—something you do with your legs.'

The door closed behind him and Thea strangled the urge to scream in frustration. Curse him! She knew what a dance was— what she really wanted to know was if he envisioned dancing with her or still preferred to sit out because of his leg. Although...*something you do with your legs*...that did rather suggest that he intended to dance...

Banishing speculation, she turned to David. 'Why do you wish to speak to Richard?'

He didn't answer immediately. Just stared thoughtfully at the chess set.

'I'd forgotten how fond of you he was, Thea,' he said at last. 'I understand he stepped in for you with Dunhaven last night—' he frowned '—even if he did take you off somewhere alone.'

She saw where that was going immediately.

'No!' she said furiously, banishing the memory of the earlier look in Richard's eyes that had for a moment spoken of more than friendship. 'I mean, yes, he did—but don't read anything into it beyond his good nature! He wished to warn me about Dunhaven. Just as you did!'

Not kiss her. And even if he had, any curiosity she might have felt on what it might have been like had been well and truly extinguished years ago. She knew what a man's kisses were like.

'Thea—'

'No!' She ignored the odd little voice that whispered that she wished it could have been different, that she could share the peaceful life Richard was creating for himself. And that she was being illogical in lumping all men and their kisses in the one pile. Richard's kisses might be as different as the man himself.

There was no rule forcing fear to be logical.

Forcing that out of her mind as well, she said, 'You are perfectly right; Richard is *fond* of me. He considers me a friend. Leave it, David. I don't have so many friends that I can afford to lose one.'

'Are you so sure that you would lose a friend?'

She laughed at that. A sound without a vestige of humour. 'Ask yourself how you might react in a similar situation.'

David sighed. 'Very well. Why don't you put on a bonnet and pelisse? I'll take you to Gunther's for an ice.'

She stared. 'An ice?'

He smiled. 'Why not? You like them. Or you certainly used to. And I'm prepared to wager you haven't had one in eight years!'

Richard found Myles in the butler's pantry. This was one of those moments when action was vital. Apart from the need to do something about the letters, he needed something to occupy his mind. Something other than the queer longing that stirred in him at the memory of Thea saying he had found exactly what he needed in life. In one sense she was perfectly correct, but he had a niggling idea that something was still missing. Or if not missing, perhaps unrecognised. Some final colour or shape to complete the picture. One thread to knit the whole.

'Who sent the note, Mr Richard?' Myles looked puzzled. 'Why, I'm sure I couldn't say. Edmund must have answered the door, I believe, since he was on duty in the entrance hall. He came to me with the note, asking where Miss Winslow might be. I took it up to her.'

Richard nodded. 'Very well. Send Edmund to me in my room, please.'

Ten minutes later, Richard swore as his bedchamber door closed behind Edmund. The footman had not seen whoever had delivered the note. It had been pushed under the front door and the bell rung. He'd had a brief glimpse of a boy running off. A dead end. But perhaps he could learn something from the notes themselves.

Frowning, he found the note from last night, pulled Thea's note out of his pocket and spread the pair of them out flat on the dressing table. He'd looked at enough old documents in his life. Surely he could tell something from these?

Not much. Each had been written on the same ordinary, good-quality paper. The watermark wouldn't help. It was common enough. What about the handwriting? A contrived-looking scrawl of capitals, which he suspected was nothing like the writer's ordinary hand. A faint fragrance teased him…feminine, flowery. Frowning, he sniffed at the note. The odour seemed to cling to it…as though the writer had perhaps been wearing perfume—on her wrists, at the pulse points. It wasn't much, but it was something. He was looking for a woman.

He also had the answer he hadn't wanted the night before; the *gilded whore* referred to in his note was Thea herself. Something else from the previous evening came back to him; a woman's voice, dripping with malicious gossip about Thea—*I had the most interesting letter, my dear…* Such a simple way to start gossip if you didn't wish to be identified.

Deep inside he was conscious of fury burning with a cold intensity. When he found the culprit…

Common sense spoke up; unless the sender was foolish enough to send any more notes here to Arnsworth House, it was going to be devilishly hard to find out who she was. His jaw hardened. Difficult, perhaps, but not impossible. And there was something else; with a grim sense of resignation, Richard acknowledged that whatever the wisdom of seeking lodgings all thought of it had been abandoned—he was remaining at Arnsworth House.

Chapter Five

Richard limped up the steps of Winslow's Jermyn Street lodgings, still wondering what might have inspired the invitation. A servant led him to a snug, if rather untidy, parlour, and his host stood up with a friendly smile, which didn't quite disguise the frown in his eyes.

'Blakehurst.' Winslow held out his hand and Richard shook it.

Winslow went straight to the point as the door closed behind the servant. 'I owe you an apology. Brandy?'

Richard raised his brows. 'Oh? Yes, please.'

Winslow looked rueful, as he poured a glass of brandy and handed it to him. 'Yes. I rather leapt to conclusions the other day. Braybrook put me right.'

Richard couldn't quite suppress a snort. 'Don't refine upon it too much, Winslow,' he said. 'By now most of society has leapt to the same obvious conclusion.' Including the harpy who had penned those poisonous notes.

'So I hear.' Winslow gestured to a comfortable-looking leather chair on one side of the crackling fire.

Richard sat down and they sipped quietly for a few moments before Winslow broke the silence. 'Braybrook gave me some advice.'

Richard looked at him carefully. That sounded dangerous.

Julian's advice was frequently sound and always outrageous. 'Did he?' He managed to sound mildly interested rather than suspicious.

'Yes.' Winslow swirled the brandy in his glass, and met Richard's gaze over the rim. 'Apart from convincing me that if you were hanging out for a rich wife Lady Arnsworth would have married you off years ago—'

Despite the simmering remnants of his annoyance with Winslow, Richard laughed.

'He also said that you were in the perfect position to help Thea.'

Richard choked on his brandy.

A moment later, after a helpful bang on the back from Winslow, Richard cleared his throat.

'And just how did he come to that conclusion?' he asked.

Winslow grimaced. 'One, you aren't hanging out for a wife. Two, you're on the spot. Three…' He hesitated and then said, 'Well, I saw that for myself this afternoon. You were always kind to Thea when she was a child. She sees you as a friend. And when Braybrook told me about your run in with Dunhaven last night, he said you wouldn't ask a lot of questions I couldn't answer.'

Richard was silent for a moment, wondering just what Winslow thought he had seen that afternoon. 'Bearing in mind all those questions I am apparently too discreet to ask,' he said, with only the merest hint of irony, 'would you care to explain exactly why Thea might be supposed to require my assistance? And perhaps even what you think I can do?'

'Thea is…disinclined to marry,' began Winslow. 'After her— that is, after what happened eight years ago, she does not wish it. Unfortunately, our father sees matters quite differently. He wants her married.' Narrowed grey eyes glittered. 'I understand you share my opinion of Dunhaven as a *parti* for my sister?'

'I should think it extremely likely,' said Richard evenly. 'He's a wart.' He tried to ignore the response boiling up inside him at the idea of Thea and Dunhaven. *Over my dead body.*

'Quite.'

It took Richard a moment to realise he hadn't actually spoken that last phrase aloud; that Winslow had merely agreed with his summation of Dunhaven's charms. 'There was talk,' he said slowly, 'about the death of Dunhaven's wife.' He loathed gossip and avoided spreading it, but in this instance he'd make an exception.

Winslow said nothing. Just waited. He didn't even look surprised, so there was no point suggesting that he mention this to Aberfield. Aberfield knew and didn't care.

Hell and damnation. 'You know, Winslow, you really didn't need to ask. Did you think I'd let an excrescence like Dunhaven anywhere near her?'

'There'll be others too,' said Winslow quietly. 'He's the worst, I agree. But if she really does not wish to marry, I don't want to see our father force her into it.'

'I beg your pardon?' Richard could not quite believe what he was hearing. 'Why would—?'

'Gossip,' said Winslow savagely.

'What?' That made no sense at all.

Winslow hesitated, as though choosing his words carefully. At last he said, 'Someone let it out how much Thea's inheritance is. Our father decided to marry her off to his satisfaction before she became a target for fortune hunters.'

Richard frowned. Winslow wasn't telling him everything. But then, he hadn't told Winslow everything...

'Forgive me, Winslow, but I overheard some speculation last night—' Seeing his companion's suddenly narrowed gaze, he said irritably, 'Oh, for God's sake! Take a damper! You've asked my assistance and I'm more than willing to help, but I need to know what's going on.'

Winslow subsided and Richard continued, 'Some of the tabbies were speculating that there might have been a reason other than grief at Lallerton's death, some indiscretion, that has kept Thea in retirement.'

'Were they, indeed?' grated Winslow.

'Yes. And, no, as Julian informed me at the time, we can't call them out over it.'

Winslow gave an unwilling crack of laughter. 'We? Blakehurst, calling someone out on a woman's behalf is usually reserved for her brother or her husband! Or her betrothed.'

Richard ignored that. To his shock, the idea of calling someone out on Thea's behalf didn't feel in the least out of place. Especially if it turned out to be Dunhaven. Banishing the thought, he stuck to the point. 'It strikes me that, given it was Thea's first appearance in years, the gossip was surprisingly fast. Even for London. Which suggests that people were talking even before Thea came to town. Is that part of the reason for your father's determination to marry her off?'

Winslow's fingers drummed on the table, and again Richard had the impression that he was considering his answer.

Finally, 'Yes. He doesn't want any hint of scandal. He's being considered again for a Cabinet position.'

All perfectly reasonable. But why had the gossip started in the first place? *Who* had started it? Gossip was part of life in society, but usually it was about current events. Not a non-existent scandal that was eight years old to boot. Not unless someone had an axe to grind…

'So someone wants to block your father's Cabinet appointment.' It was the obvious solution.

Winslow looked arrested. 'What?' He caught himself hurriedly. 'Well, yes. That…that would fit.'

Except that it was so bloody obvious, Winslow shouldn't look surprised. And where did the notes fit in? And was he going to mention the notes to Winslow? Thea obviously hadn't mentioned hers. If she had, Winslow would know that he knew. Which answered his question.

'Blakehurst?'

He looked up. 'Sorry. Thinking.'

Winslow looked rueful. 'Braybrook warned me about that too. Said you wouldn't ask questions, but that wouldn't stop you thinking them. Shall I ring to have our dinner brought in?'

'By all means,' said Richard. He wouldn't mention the notes yet. The least he could do was tell Thea about his own note before telling her brother. Nor did he consider it necessary to inform Winslow that he had already decided to keep an eye on Thea. Winslow would want to know why, and he wasn't entirely sure he was ready to give that answer. But he was still curious...

Winslow tossed off the remains of his brandy and tugged on the bell pull.

Watching him narrowly, Richard asked his last question. 'Why not you? You are her brother. No one could censure you for protecting your sister from a match with Dunhaven, even if your father is mad enough to think it acceptable.'

'I am afraid, Blakehurst,' said Winslow apologetically, 'that that is one of those questions I cannot answer.'

He'd rather thought it might be. Which meant he'd have to find out by himself. And how those damned letters were connected—if they were. And there was another question he hadn't even bothered to ask—why did Aberfield think Dunhaven an acceptable match for his daughter?

Thea gazed about the rooms Lady Montacute had hired for the evening with a growing sense of confidence. The heavy perfume of hothouse flowers mingled with melting wax, noise and heat. It should have panicked her, and yet it did not.

Madame Monique had sent an exquisite ball gown in a brilliant shade of poppy muslin, trimmed with tiny sprigs of gold and gold lace. 'A bold colour per'aps,' *madame* had said. 'But you are a leetle older. There is not the need to dress *à la jeune fille*...'

She had not been convinced at the time, but now she began to understand what Lady Arnsworth had meant about feeling different with a new wardrobe. Somehow the bright gown was like armour. The young girl might be gone, but gone also was the acquiescent creature who had slowly taken her place. In her poppy-bright gown and matching headdress, she felt secure in a fortress. Of course, she thought with a spurt of amusement, the new, perfectly fitted stays might have something to do with that!

And the dainty fan of peacock feathers was the ultimate weapon in a lady's arsenal...with it one could hold the world safely at bay. And, buoying her courage was the fact that Richard had asked her to save him two dances. Not that he danced very much, Almeria told her. He preferred to sit out and chat to his partners, which suited her perfectly. It meant that she wouldn't have to waltz. She thought she could manage all the other dances, but the waltz terrified her, the thought of being held in a close embrace brushing ice down her spine.

Waving her fan negligently, she smiled at Mr Fielding. She could do this. She just hoped Richard would appear in time for the first waltz.

'No, sir, I fear that I am already engaged for both waltzes.'

Richard, entering the ballroom with Winslow, saw Thea at once and his breath jerked in. Standing beside a potted palm, with Almeria seated on a *chaise* beside her, Thea was the centre of a small group of men, all jostling and vying for position.

'Damn!' muttered Winslow. He started forward.

'Winslow! Might I have word, if you please?'

Sir Francis Fox-Heaton, tall, elegant and frowning slightly, stood just ahead of them. 'I intended to call tomorrow, but since you are here…' He cast a faint smile at Richard. 'Mr Blakehurst. You will excuse us?'

Winslow turned to Richard, his mouth a hard line. 'I'll find you later. Would you mind…?'

'You asked already, if you recall,' said Richard.

A slight relaxation of the jaw that might have been a smile. 'So I did. Thank you.' He turned. 'At your service, Fox-Heaton.'

Richard made his bow to Almeria and to Thea, exchanging friendly greetings with the various gentlemen attempting to capture Thea's attention. Most of them harmless, he forcibly reminded himself, and it occurred to him that she was not paying them a great deal of attention. He had the oddest notion that she was, in some way, not really there. That for all her smiles, and polite responses to her admirers, she was other-where, and that gently waving peacock fan had something to do with it.

He saw Dunhaven approach and the growling creature within stirred restlessly. Dunhaven was not harmless, in any way, shape or form.

'Oh, I say, Miss Winslow,' Tom Fielding was protesting. 'It's a great deal too bad! Both the waltzes, and you won't say who has been granted them, so we can—'

'Miss Winslow,' cut in Lord Dunhaven, 'will be dancing the waltz with myself, Fielding. A prior arrangement, you understand.'

The air of assured ownership had the beast sitting up snarling.

'Oh?' Thea's eyes narrowed and the fan stilled. 'A prior arrangement with whom, my lord? I fear it was not with me.'

The beast subsided very slightly. Polite, gentle Thea had just delivered a snub one of the Patronesses of Almack's might have envied.

A smile, and the resumed gentle movement of the fan, served only to hone the edge in her dulcet tones.

Almeria, chatting to Lady Hornfleet, turned her head slightly, clearly listening.

Lord Dunhaven cleared his throat and frowned at her. 'I felt that under the circumstances—I was speaking to your father this afternoon—'

'Were you, my lord?' The cutting edge glittered with frost. 'And how was he?'

'Very well, Miss Winslow.' Dunhaven bestowed an indulgent and proprietorial smile on Thea that had Richard grinding his teeth. Almeria's head snapped around and she stared at him.

Richard clenched his jaw into silence as Dunhaven continued. 'He assured me that you would be most happy—'

'How times change, my lord,' said Richard, his jaw escaping his control. 'Nowadays, whatever customs may have pertained in Lord Aberfield's youth, one solicits the lady, not her father, for a dance.' With a slight bow, he added, 'As I did earlier.' Earlier could mean a great many things, not necessarily that he had been alone with Thea in Arnsworth House that afternoon.

And not for anything would he employ Dunhaven's strategy of forcing Thea into a position where she must either dance or deal him a set-down. They had not agreed on which dances, but if she wished it...

Over the top of that lethal fan, blue eyes questioned him.

He smiled.

'Perhaps another time, my lord,' she said, stepping away from Dunhaven. 'I have indeed promised this dance to Mr Blakehurst.'

Dunhaven's eyes narrowed in dislike as he swung to look at Richard. 'Oh? I didn't realise you *danced*, Blakehurst. How very singular!'

The indrawn hiss of Thea's breath was balm to his cold fury.

'Of course my nephew dances, sir!' snapped Almeria.

'No, my lord?' Richard looked his lordship up and down with mild curiosity, and the earl reddened with annoyance. 'Ah, well, there's plenty of time yet for you to acquaint yourself with all manner of things you don't know. I do dance. Upon occasion. When I consider the effort worthwhile.' He flicked a glance at Thea. 'It's a little like culping wafers at Manton's, you know. I only bother to engage in matches with those I know can give me a halfway decent match.'

Over the peacock feather fan Thea's blue eyes glimmered with silent laughter.

She turned, saying coolly to Dunhaven, 'Perhaps a country dance, my lord. I have promised both waltzes to Mr Blakehurst.'

Richard uttered a mental malediction. He doubted that his leg would survive two waltzes in one evening.

Dunhaven nodded curtly. 'Servant, Miss Winslow.' He nodded even more curtly to Richard, turned on his heel and stalked away. Thea knew a moment's fear. Richard might be the son, and brother, of earls, but Dunhaven was a powerful man—what if he—?

'Shall we, my dear?' said Richard, offering his arm. As she permitted him to steer her through the crowd, he gave a deep laugh. 'Pompous ass,' he said.

'Richard! It's not funny!' she whispered fiercely. 'What if he—?'

'If he tries anything with you,' said Richard, in deadly quiet tones, 'I will take great pleasure in dealing with him.' All vestiges of amusement had vanished.

'I'm not worried about *me!*' she snapped. 'I'm worried about *you!*'

He blinked, patently surprised. And then a quite different sort of smile crept across his face. A tender smile, a smile that spoke of things she had long considered lost to her. Despite the warning bell clanging deep within her, a glowing sensation spread through her, and for a moment there hung between them something almost tangible. She caught her breath…if only—oh, if only!

'Where shall we sit out?' she asked.

'Sit out?' He stared at her. 'We're going to dance.'

'Dance?'

'Well, of course! Unless—' An odd look came into his eyes. 'Unless *you* would prefer to sit out?'

Shock slammed into her. He wanted to dance? Actually dance? She hadn't really believed that he could mean it.

It would be safer not to dance. This shattering awareness of him unsettled her as it was. Dancing, being held in his arms, with music a shimmering web around them, would be twice as dizzying. Like the sudden blaze in the dark eyes as he stared at her.

She had never intended to dance—she had not thought he would want it.

And yet, why should she not? What harm could there be in dancing with Richard? Of all men, he was the one she would feel most comfortable with. She summoned a smile, swallowed the last of her champagne and said, 'I would be honoured to dance with you, Richard.'

He took her empty champagne glass and handed it, along with his own, to a footman. Then, with another devastating smile, he offered her his arm. 'Our dance, I believe,' he said. He steered her on to the dance floor and swept her into the waltz.

She didn't know what she had expected. Not fear. Certainly not that. And not revulsion. Not with Richard. Never with him. But…the chill…the sense of distance she had learnt to place mentally between herself and anyone who came too close…she had felt it all evening as people jostled around her and she had held them at bay with her fan. Especially with Lord Dunhaven. And now…

Now, in Richard's arms, adjusting her steps to his uneven strides, the fan dangled unneeded from her wrist, and she felt only warmth, and an enveloping closeness. Whatever she had expected, it had not been this.

Held safely by his arms in the surging rhythm of the dance, she was wildly conscious of his strength, his sheer maleness. It brought only pleasure, a purring, purely feminine delight that he had thought her worth the effort. She felt alive, as she had not in years.

She lifted her gaze to his face. It was as if she had never truly seen him before. Strongly chiselled planes, the deep brown eyes set under dark brows. So familiar. And yet new. New lines, graven she thought, by pain. And he was simply older. More mature. To some his face might look forbidding, yet his smile denied that. And he was smiling now. At her. As though having her in his arms was a pleasure. Her breath hitched and she found herself smiling back.

It wasn't supposed to feel like this. Not as far as he could recall, anyway. And it was quite some time since he had danced at all, let alone waltzed. In fact, Thea was one of the very few women he had ever waltzed with.

His stride was as awkward and uneven as ever. That wasn't different. What shocked him was the sheer delight in having Thea's slender, supple body in his arms completely overrode the increasing ache in his leg. Worse, the delight of looking down into her soft blue eyes, seeing the delicate colour fanned on the pale cheeks, and her slightly parted lips nearly made him forget which leg ached.

And then she smiled up at him. A tentative smile, uncertain, as though unsure of its welcome. His breath caught. Never before in his life had he been conscious of an urge to sweep a dance partner out of sight and kiss her, and himself, senseless. With a shock he realised that if he gave in to the urge, he might forget all about sweeping them out of sight.

The music was like a drug, its rhythm one with their shifting bodies. Never had he been so wildly aware of a woman—as a woman. Never had every sense clamoured for more. To be closer, to breathe her soft flowery scent, to hear the soft hush of her breathing. Never had he known the urge to pull a woman closer in the dance so that her thighs shifted against his, so that her breasts touched his coat. Every muscle hardened savagely in the effort not to just do it.

He knew at once when she felt the change in him. The sudden tension in his arms as he fought not to haul her closer, the added clumsiness in his stride, which owed nothing to the ache in his leg.

'Richard?'

Somehow he met her concerned gaze.

'I knew this would hurt your leg! Do you wish to stop?'

'Not in the least,' he informed her. It wasn't his leg that was causing the problem.

'You are sure it doesn't hurt?'

'Quite sure,' he lied. 'It's, er, just a kink. Moving will ease it.' Only not the sort of moving he was doing at the moment. Or at any other moment in the foreseeable future for that matter.

By the end of the dance they were at the far end of the dance floor from the chaperons. Richard was violently aware that Thea was flushed, glowing and radiant. And that he was heated in an odd tingling way that had nothing to do with the heat of the ballroom and everything to do with the slow heat consuming him. Aware that although the dance had finished, music still sang and ached to every heavy beat of the blood in his veins.

He fought for control, reminding himself that it had been a while since he had been with a woman. Casual liaisons with discreet widows had lost their savour some time ago. Apparently with the inevitable result that desire had conducted an ambush in the most impossible, and unexpected, place imaginable. All perfectly logical, if potentially embarrassing.

She looked up at him and his breath caught as their eyes met. Good lord! What a place to realise that he desired a woman!

Especially a woman as untouchable as his aunt's protégée and goddaughter. Unthinkable.

Well, no, not unthinkable precisely, since he was thinking about it. But definitely inappropriate.

Carefully he stepped back, his mind reeling at the wave of tenderness that poured over him. At the sight of her smiling up at him, all shadows fled, just as he had wanted. This was different, somehow—more than desire. Oh, he'd always liked his partners—what was the point in going to bed and being intimate with someone you didn't like? But this shattering ache?

'More champagne, Thea?' he suggested, in as light a tone as he could muster. He'd known Thea for so long—not surprising if he felt protective towards her. She was lovely—desire was not surprising either. But this tenderness, this welling up of delight merely to see her smile…to see her smile in his arms—this was different.

'Good evening, Mr Blakehurst.'

Chill disapproval splintered in the voice.

Richard turned slowly to find Lord Aberfield watching them, his face expressionless. 'Lord Aberfield.' He acknowledged the older man with a bow. Beside him, Thea stood motionless. Silent.

The moment stretched as Richard felt the tension sing between the pair of them. He flicked a glance at Thea. No shadows, but the woman he had been dancing with was gone. In her place stood a marble statue, blue eyes frozen to arctic winter.

Then, in a voice that cut like a polar wind, she spoke. 'Good evening, my lord.'

A perfectly correct form of address…for a perfect stranger. As a young woman's greeting to her father, it was the ultimate snub. And in that icily correct voice, it was a snub with a sting in the tail.

Not surprisingly Aberfield's face turned slightly purple.

Thea continued, 'You are well again, my lord?'

'Very well,' he grated. 'A word with you, Dorothea! In private.'

Her brows lifted. 'Oh? Yes, I think that is possible.'

Aberfield's teeth grated audibly at the implication that Thea might have, if she had chosen, refused his request. 'Perhaps, *daughter,'* he said with silky emphasis, 'you would come with me, then. There is much that I wish to discuss with you. Privately.'

'Now?' Her fan flickered open with a swish, and she disappeared behind it. 'I assumed you meant to call tomorrow at Arnsworth House. Yes, that would be better. Far more scope for privacy there. What time will suit you?'

'Now would suit me!' snapped Aberfield.

Thea's smile was a naked blade. 'I am afraid, dear sir, that Lady Arnsworth would be sadly inconvenienced were I to steal her carriage and return home now. But I am perfectly happy to hold myself at your disposal tomorrow. Call at whatever time suits you. I promise you shall find me home.'

For a moment it looked as though Aberfield might explode, but he nodded and stalked away.

To say that Lady Arnsworth was unimpressed the following morning to hear that her protégée had undertaken to remain at home all day awaiting her father's convenience, would have been an understatement.

'You were to drive with Lady Chasewater, you remember?' said Lady Arnsworth.

'I sent her a note explaining,' said Thea. A very convenient added benefit she had not thought of at the time. 'I felt my father's request must take precedence.'

There was no answer to that, and Lady Arnsworth didn't attempt one, only saying, 'But he gave *no* indication of when he might call?'

Thea contrived to look repentant. 'No, ma'am. He wished to speak to me privately, and at a ball—' She spread her hands. No need to tell Lady Arnsworth that it had been her strategy to avoid leaving the safety of a crowd with Aberfield. She didn't trust him an inch.

Lady Arnsworth pursed her lips. 'Very well, my dear. There is nothing to be done. I *must* pay some calls this afternoon, and I shall drive in the park afterwards. Naturally I shall give instructions to Myles that he must admit only your father, and any female visitors you might have. No gentlemen, of course, unless your brother were to call.' A very faint smile played about her lips.

'Oh, of course,' agreed Thea.

Lady Arnsworth nodded. 'Yes. And, dear, if you play chess with Richard again, it might be for the best if you were to leave the door open.'

Thea's jaw dropped, as her ladyship continued, 'You may trust Richard, of course, as you would your own brother, but it doesn't do to give the gossips the least bit of encouragement, you know. If anyone were to call and find you together—well!' She patted Thea's hand. 'Your father wouldn't like it at all.'

Chapter Six

'Lord Aberfield is here to see you, miss,' said Myles. 'Shall I show him in here?'

Thea laid down her pen and considered the alternatives. She was in the back parlour, writing a note to accept an invitation to attend a picnic with Diana Fox-Heaton the following week. While being received in there would sting his pride, she hesitated. Somehow the back parlour of Arnsworth House was associated with happy times, with her childhood visiting the house, with Richard teaching her to play chess, with his slightly crooked smile. She did not want Aberfield anywhere within spitting distance of those memories.

'No. Show his lordship into the drawing room, please, Myles. And, Myles—?' An inner demon suggested another way she might infuriate Aberfield. 'Tell his lordship that I will be with him very shortly.'

She heard Aberfield being ushered into the next room, heard Myles offer refreshment, and heard it refused. Deliberately she completed her letter to Diana. And read it over. Then she sealed it, addressed it, rang the bell and waited for Myles.

When he came, she smiled and handed him the note with instructions to have it delivered at once. 'And bring tea to the drawing room in fifteen minutes, please, Myles.'

Then, feeling that she had made her point, Thea settled her elegant morning gown, tucked a stray curl back into place under her lace cap, assumed an indifferent expression, and strolled through the door connecting the back parlour and drawing room.

'Good afternoon, my lord. I've kept you waiting.' It could be construed as an apology. Just.

Aberfield turned and glared at her. 'Where the devil have you been, miss?' His colour was high, and the faded blue eyes glittered at her.

She granted him her most gracious smile. 'Finishing a letter, my lord. Do be seated and tell me what I may do for you.' She sat in a small chair set slightly apart, and waited.

Aberfield didn't waste time on niceties. 'You can tell me what the devil you're playing at with Blakehurst,' he snarled. 'Waltzing with *him* when Dunhaven had honoured you with an invitation to dance!'

So that had got back to him. Lord, he was a fool! Had he learned nothing from the past?

'Playing at, my lord?' she queried. 'Unlike some, I play no games. Mr Blakehurst asked me to dance with him—'

'Asked you after Dunhaven asked you!' snapped Aberfield.

'Not at all,' she said sweetly. 'He had asked me earlier.'

Aberfield looked her over. 'Think you can get him up to scratch, do you?' He snorted. 'I doubt it! Too high in the instep the Blakehursts, even if his brother *has* made a fool of himself.'

Thea froze and Aberfield continued, his voice contemptuous. 'Knew Almeria Arnsworth would try her damnedest to marry you to him, but he's dodged every other heiress she's found. Some of 'em a damn sight wealthier than you!' His lip curled. 'And they weren't some other man's leavings.'

Words, meaningless words. They can't hurt unless I permit it ...

Something Richard had said about Dunhaven slid through her mind, displacing her father's barb: *He's so desperate...it's a wonder he hasn't found a young enough widow with a couple of brats to her credit...* What had Aberfield told Dunhaven? She didn't really believe it, not quite. But if she trailed the lure ...

'One wonders,' she mused, 'what can possibly have induced Lord Dunhaven to relax his standards.'

The fish rose. 'Dunhaven needs an heir,' he told her. 'For a wealthy bride he knows can breed a brat, he's willing to overlook things.'

'I have no "brat", as you put it.'

Just aching grief and guilt over the death of a nameless child she had neither seen nor held, and the opium-hazed memory of a newborn wail.

Aberfield opened his mouth and shut it again. His gaze shifted and then he shrugged. 'Even if the whelp died, you still went full term,' he said.

Bile rose, choking and sour.

'More than his first wife ever did,' he continued. 'For that assurance and your fortune, it's worth it to him.'

She swallowed the bile, reaching for control. 'I'm sure it is,' she said. 'But tell me, my lord—was it not rather a risk for you, confiding so much in Dunhaven?'

'Why should he talk about his bride?' Cold triumph gleamed. 'No reason for him to talk if you're married. And he's willing to marry you.'

'But if I don't marry him—?'

Aberfield's fists clenched. 'You'll marry him, or I'll…I'll—!'

'You'll what, my lord?' The time for dissembling was past. She stood up, casting aside caution. 'You really have no power left, sir. Do you?' She smiled. 'You may cast me off, but in two and a half months I turn twenty-five and will have two hundred pounds a year. A pittance to you, I am sure, but I will manage very well. And just think of the gossip if you cut off my allowance now.'

Aberfield had risen as well, his face mottled. 'And this is the gratitude I receive for protecting you from your folly eight years ago!'

Thea rang the bell. 'I think there is nothing more to be said, my lord.'

'I'll see you don't get a penny of the money!' he blustered.

She laughed. 'You can't. Under the terms of the will, once I turn twenty-five there is nothing you can do to block the two hundred a year. With that I will be independent and can do as I please.'

Aberfield's colour deepened to an alarming purple. 'You mean to have Blakehurst, then?'

'That, my lord, is not your concern.'

His teeth clenched, he said, 'Make sure he understands you'll not see a penny more than the two hundred before your thirtieth birthday.'

The door opened to admit the butler.

'Ah, Myles. His lordship was just leaving.'

His face stiff with fury, Aberfield stalked out of the room without another word.

As the door closed, Thea sank on to the sofa, all the cold fury ebbing to leave her drained and shaking. But she had done it! Stood up to Aberfield and forced him to realise that he had no power over her any longer. That there was nothing he could do to force her marriage or control her actions. That knowledge had fuelled his anger. His parting shot about only receiving the two hundred per annum until she turned thirty suggested that he accepted that she would not marry Dunhaven. Which left her free to contemplate the sort of life she wanted for herself.

The future stretched out before her, not golden, but peaceful. Or it would be if she could only rid herself of the guilt and pain—the child had been an innocent, blameless of any wrongdoing. Had her actions been responsible for its death? At the very least she had been partly responsible for its unmourned, unmarked grave. *It*. That sounded so cold. So uncaring. Like Aberfield's reference to the child as a brat or whelp. As though its very life hadn't mattered. *It* again. She had no other way to think of her lost baby. A shudder racked her as she stared blindly into the empty fireplace. She was vaguely aware that the doorbell had rung. An annoyed voice echoed in the front hall, followed by the slam of the front door. It wasn't important. Her vision blurred. She didn't even know if her baby had been a boy or a girl…they had refused to tell her.

For the first time in seven years someone had spoken of her

dead baby—as proof of her fertility. Her hands clenched into fists until the nails dug into her palms as she looked back at the mess her younger self had made of everything. If only she had known…had realised in time… She swallowed hard. She could see now what she should have done…and it was far, far too late. She felt cold, cold all over, as though a void inside her had been filled with ice.

The door opened and she looked round. 'Yes, Myles?'

'Your tea, miss.' The old man looked at her kindly. 'If I may say so, Miss Thea, you look as though a nap wouldn't go astray. Why don't you go on up and I'll send one of the maids to help you?'

Heat pricked at her eyes at the kindness in his voice. What a fool she was to feel like crying because of a simple expression of kindness when her father's callous actions merely left her cold with fury.

'Thank you, Myles,' she said, forcing words past the choking lump in her throat. 'I'll do that.' She went over to the door. 'I'll leave the tea for now. I'm sorry to waste your time.'

He shook his head. 'Not to worry, Miss Thea.' He hesitated. 'Lord Dunhaven called. Just after Lord Aberfield left.'

So that was who had owned the loud, blustering voice.

'You denied me?'

Myles's mouth flickered into what in a less well-trained butler might have been a smile. 'No, Miss Thea, although her ladyship had instructed me to do so.' The smile escaped its bonds. 'Mr Blakehurst beat me to it.'

Warmth eased the aching chill within her.

'I am never at home to Lord Dunhaven,' she told him. 'Nor…' she drew a deep breath '…to Lord Aberfield, unless I have informed you of a prior appointment.'

'Very good, Miss Thea.'

She nodded and left the room.

The maid answered her summons and helped her out of her gown and stays. Clad only in her shift, Thea snuggled down under the bedclothes and closed her eyes.

When she opened them again the shadows in the room had moved. She yawned and stretched. She felt better, although she didn't think she had slept for terribly long. A glance at the clock on the mantel confirmed this. She hadn't slept for more than an hour and a half. But she felt refreshed, in spirit as much as body.

It was as though facing her father had drained a poison from her, its passage leaving her cleansed. She was a long way from happy, but there was no longer the sapping despair. Her gaze fell on a carved wooden box beside the armoire. Now there was a task she had been putting off—sorting out her collection of…of what? Rubbish? Tangible memories? Ever since she was a little girl she had kept cherished mementoes in that box. Reminders of past joy. Birthday party invitations, tickets to Astley's Amphitheatre, courtesy of a generous impulse on the part of Richard when she was ten, letters, even a few from her mother after she had been banished to Aunt Maria, despite Aberfield's orders to the contrary. David's letters. And some things that had given her pain…like the brief, factual note her father had written informing her of her mother's illness and death, after the funeral had taken place.

That had been almost the last thing she had put in apart from David's letters. For the past year or so she had not even dared to look inside, just shoving each letter in and locking the box again.

But now…now she had things to put in it again. Invitations. Notes from Diana—telling her that friendship could endure. There was a little pile of papers down in the drawer of the *escritoire* in the drawing room. She would take the box down there and sort it out. When she had glanced into it before leaving Yorkshire it had been a terrible mess. It was time to sort it all out. She rang for a maid to help her with her stays.

She found the drawing room occupied.

His back to the door, Richard was sitting near the window in one of Almeria's prized Egyptian chairs, complete with gilt crocodile arms. Not odd in itself, but the chair was placed squarely in the middle of a raft of newspaper sheets. A faint scraping sound gave her the clue, and she understood; Richard was carving. He had the tea table beside him, and on it she could see several knives, a cloth and several small wooden objects on more spread newspaper.

Silent laughter welled up. He hadn't changed at all. Except that he obviously thought of the newspaper for himself now, rather than after Lady Arnsworth scolded him for making a mess.

She cleared her throat and he glanced round, frowning.

'Ah.' The frown disappeared. 'Ring the bell.'

She did so, and then asked, 'Why?'

'Myles will bring some tea now you are awake. Did you sleep well?'

She nodded. 'Am I disturbing you?'

'Idiot. What have you got there?'

A blush heated her cheeks. 'My collection, for want of a better word.' Heavens! He'd think all this rubbish…well, rubbish!

'Collection?' He looked curious. 'I had no idea you collected something. What is it? Sea shells? Roman coins? Max and I used to find them around Blakeney when we were boys.'

'Nothing so exciting,' she told him, and explained.

To her complete surprise he wasn't in the least dismissive. 'When you're an old, old woman, your grandchildren will find that fascinating. It will tell them something about how you lived.'

She set the box down on the *escritoire*, and said dubiously, 'I suppose so.' Perhaps David's grandchildren.

He laughed. 'Would you believe the British Museum has an extensive collection of ephemera, courtesy of old Miss Banks?'

'Miss Banks?' She lifted the lid of the box.

'Sir Joseph Banks, the naturalist's, sister. After she died a few years ago her entire collection came to the museum.' He paused. 'All nineteen thousand items of it.'

Thea dropped the lid with a bang. 'Ninetee—! Good God!'

'Quite,' said Richard with a chuckle. 'Visiting cards, invitations, admission tickets, you name it—she kept it.'

Thea looked at her own collection. 'I think I need a new box.' She opened the lid again and lifted out some of the contents.

His husky laugh warmed her. 'I'll make one for you.'

'Would you?' The warmth spread, and she reached into the box again. Her fingers felt something small and hard, irregularly shaped, at the bottom. Curious she delved and drew it out— 'Ohh...'

In her hand lay a small wooden bird, rather crudely carved, its beak open, wings half-spread. Richard had made it for her, and all these years it had lain forgotten in the box, the unheard song stilled. She had thought it left behind when she went to Yorkshire.

'What have you got there?'

Blinking hard, she turned and held out the little bird on the palm of her hand.

For a moment he seemed not to understand. Then, 'You've kept it all these years?' There was an odd note in his voice.

Scarlet, she said, 'I had forgotten all about it.' Desperate to change the subject, she asked, 'What...what are you making now?'

'Something to hang over the cradle for my godson or goddaughter,' he answered. 'Max and Verity's child. Tell me what you think.'

She went over to the table and a gasp of delight escaped her. Five gaily painted little wooden horses, in various attitudes, pranced there. A sixth, as yet unpainted was in his hand. 'Not very exciting,' he said. 'I did think of dragons, but these pieces of wood insisted on being ponies. I'm just doing the finishing touches to this one before painting it.'

'They are lovely,' she said softly. 'And I think your godchild will treasure them.' She reached out and stroked the nose of one pony with her forefinger. 'They're like my box of clutter—one day your great-nephews and nieces will look at these and think of you.' Perhaps even his great-great nephews and nieces. And so on until the children no longer knew anything about the man who had carved these dancing ponies so long ago. But they would know the toy had been made with love.

Just as she had remembered the wooden bird.

Very softly, she said, 'I shall like to think of you making something like this for your own children one day, Richard.'

He went very still as her words fell into a deep silence within him.

Until a year ago he had assumed that one day he would marry. There was no reason not to, but marriage had never been compelling. He had been busy, satisfied with his life, and his role as Max's steward. Indeed, that role was still his. But ever since Max's marriage he had been increasingly aware that something was missing in his life, and that it was time to fill the void.

'Thea—' Unsure what he was going to say, only knowing that words were there, he reached for her hand.

The door opened without warning.

He slewed around in his chair.

'Damn it, Myles! What the devil do you want now?'

Myles looked severely shaken. 'Mr Richard—there…there is a magistrate in the front hall—'

There came a sharp gasp from Thea. Richard reached out and took her hand, enveloping it in his, shocked to feel her trembling.

'A *what?*' Surely Myles hadn't said—

'A magistrate, sir. Sir Giles Mason. From Bow Street. Requesting an interview with Miss Winslow.' Myles swallowed. 'I know her ladyship will not like it, but, sir, perhaps you—since her ladyship isn't here?'

Her ladyship would probably have apoplexy when she found out, reflected Richard, but he couldn't see any alternative. Thea's hand, still lost in his, was trembling, although when he looked up at her, she appeared perfectly calm.

'I'd better see him, I think,' she said. Her voice was perfectly calm too. Turning to the butler, she continued, 'Tell Sir Giles that I will see him in the dining—'

'Show Sir Giles up, Myles,' said Richard, cutting straight across Thea. He eyed her in flat-out challenge. 'If you think for one moment that I am going to permit you to see a magistrate alone, you have some more thinking to do.'

'But—'

'But nothing,' he interrupted. 'Call me a coward, but I have no intention of admitting to Almeria that I let you face this alone!'

The door shut behind Myles.

'Thea…' he caught her other hand, holding them both in a gentle clasp '…do you have any idea what this might be about?'

She shook her head, and her eyes met his unflinchingly, but a deep, slow blush mantled her cheeks … He swore mentally and let out a breath he hadn't realised he'd been holding.

'I hope,' he said grimly, 'that you can lie a great deal more convincingly for Sir Giles's benefit.'

Sir Giles was a tall, grizzled man with a slight stoop. In his late fifties, Richard judged. Shrewd green eyes looked over the top of half-moon spectacles and flickered down to a sheaf of papers he had produced from a small case.

Polite greetings over, he got straight down to business.

'Miss Winslow, I am sure this must be a shock for you, and I am very glad that you have a responsible friend to support you in this. Painful though it must be for you, I must ask you some questions about your late, er, betrothed, Mr Nigel Lallerton.'

Shock jolted through Richard. He stole a sideways glance at Thea. There was not the least hint of surprise, manufactured or otherwise.

'Yes, sir.'

Sir Giles looked at her closely. 'That doesn't surprise you?'

'Your being here at all is a surprise, Sir Giles.'

The magistrate cleared his throat. 'No doubt. Now—did anyone dislike Mr Lallerton? Have a quarrel with him?'

She hesitated, then said, 'I am sure there were many, sir.'

'Many?'

'No one is universally popular,' she said, her hands shifting restlessly in her lap, pleating her skirts.

Richard reached out and took possession of one hand; instantly the other lay utterly still.

'Hmm. I meant,' said Sir Giles, 'was there anyone in particular who might have had a grudge against Mr Laller—?'

'Would you mind informing Miss Winslow of the reason for these questions, Sir Giles?' said Richard.

The older man's mouth tightened. 'We have received information, sir, that, far from dying in a shooting accident when his gun misfired, Mr Lallerton was murdered.'

'Information? From whom?' asked Richard.

'As to that,' said Sir Giles, 'the information was anonymous.' Richard froze, but said nothing. Sir Giles continued. 'We have made some enquiries into the matter, and it would appear that further investigation is in order.'

'You take notice of anonymous information?'

Sir Giles shrugged. 'Information is information, sir. Naturally we would not hang a man on the basis of an anonymous submission, but as a starting point for investigation, it is perfectly normal. Now, Miss Winslow—on the subject of your betrothed's popularity—did you know of anyone who might have wished him ill?'

'I know of no one who wished him dead,' said Thea in a low voice. She met his eyes squarely, her face pale.

'I see. And your own feelings…' Sir Giles shifted in his seat '…were you on good terms with Mr Lallerton? Happy about your coming marriage?'

Faint colour rose in Thea's cheeks as she said, 'I was counting the days, Sir Giles.' Her hand in Richard's shook.

'And tell me, Miss Winslow—where were you when Mr Lallerton died?'

'I was at my father's principal seat in Hampshire. My mother was giving a house party.'

'At which Mr Lallerton had been a guest. I understand he left rather precipitately and returned to London?'

'That is correct, sir.'

'And he had an accident in which his gun discharged and hit him in the leg, so that he bled to death?'

The pink deepened to crimson. 'So I was told, sir.'

The green eyes were steady on her. 'You can tell me nothing more, Miss Winslow?'

'No, sir.'

The magistrate nodded. 'Very well. If you should think of anything, please send a message to Bow Street. And I must warn

you that I may question you again as the investigation proceeds.'
He rose. 'I'll bid you good day, Miss Winslow.'

His mind reeling, Richard saw Sir Giles out, accepting his
repeated apologies for the intrusion.

Closing the front door, he faced the inescapable fact that Thea
had not been in the least bit surprised by the direction of Sir Giles's
questioning. Which of itself suggested that there was something
to find out, despite her neatness at sidestepping questions. He did
not for one moment doubt that Sir Giles would return.

His mouth set grimly as he went back up to the drawing room.
Hell's teeth! If Nigel Lallerton had been murdered, how had it
been covered up? Good God! Surely his family would have
noticed if there had been anything suspicious about his death?
And how the devil was he meant to protect Thea from this if she
wouldn't confide in him?

His jaw set in a state of considerable rigidity, he stalked into
the drawing room, only to find that the bird had flown. Thea had
taken her box and gone. Probably to her bedchamber. Well, if she
thought that was going to stop him—from below came the sound
of the front door opening…then,

'*Who called?*'

Almeria's outraged shriek came up to him in perfect clarity.
He swore. Invading Thea's bedchamber and forcing some
answers from her was no longer an option. Hearing the sound of
hurrying feet on the stairs, Richard braced himself, pushing to
the back of his mind the realisation that of all the questions to
which he wanted answers, the most pressing was not directly
connected to Lallerton's death.

He dearly wanted to know exactly what Thea had meant when
she told Sir Giles that she was counting the days until her wedding.

'Richard!' Almeria hurried into the drawing room. 'What is
this that Myles tells me? What were you thinking of to permit
such a thing?'

'That admitting Mason was preferable to having him summon
Thea to Bow Street,' he told her.

'But, surely…' Almeria's voice trailed away. 'Good God! A pretty thing that would be!'

'That's what I thought,' said Richard.

Almeria sat down, frowning. 'It might be worse. Myles assures me that none of the other servants is aware of Sir Giles's identity, and of course *he* won't gossip. As long as that is the end of it.' She eyed Richard in blatant speculation. 'I understood from Myles that you remained with Dorothea—thank you, Richard. I am most grateful.'

'Not at all, Almeria.' Damn. Now she was extrapolating all sorts of things from his intervention.

'I will be attending Lady Heathcote's assembly with Dorothea this evening,' she informed him. 'After a dinner at the Rutherfords. Will you—?'

'I will join you there, if you wish it,' he assured her. He could see absolutely no need to acquaint Almeria with the fact that he had already been planning to attend whatever entertainment Thea might be gracing that evening. That would only serve to encourage her.

Breathing with careful concentration, Thea forced her hands to steady enough to remove the stopper from her ink bottle and dip the quill. Then she stared blindly at the blank paper. What should she write? If she were quick, she had enough time before she needed to bathe and dress for the dinner and assembly she was attending with Lady Arnsworth that evening.

Dearest David—a magistrate from Bow Street questioned me this afternoon and I lied faster than a fox can trot?

Or perhaps:

Dearest David—Bow Street is asking questions about Nigel Lallerton's death…

A dry little sob escaped her. There was nothing she could write that might not be construed as a warning, suspicious in itself, unless… Her quill hovered above the paper and common sense finally broke through the fog of panic. What a ninnyhammer she was being!

She wrote quickly:

Dearest David—Sir Giles Mason, a magistrate, called this afternoon. He asked some very odd questions about Nigel Lallerton's death. You will understand that I found it most distressing. I would like very much to discuss it with you at the earliest opportunity. I will not be home this evening; we are to attend Lady Heathcote's assembly.

　　Your loving sister,
　　Thea

Quite unexceptionable, really. After all, there was nothing unusual in a sister asking her brother's advice on such a matter. Ringing the bell, she summoned a footman and asked him to deliver the note to Jermyn Street immediately.

She could do nothing further.

To her relief, David approached her within ten minutes of her arrival at Lady Heathcote's assembly. He came up and greeted them politely, chatting on general topics for a few moments. Then, 'Lady Arnsworth, I wonder if I might steal my sister away from your side for a little?'

Lady Arnsworth looked a little dubious, but said, 'Of course, Mr Winslow.'

He smiled and bowed, then led Thea away, saying in a low voice, 'I received your note. We had better talk.'

'Is there somewhere we may be private?' she asked, just as softly.

'Come with me.'

He took her to a small parlour on the next floor. Closing the door, he turned to her. 'Very well—tell me.'

She did so, leaving out nothing.

He listened in shocked silence, his eyes hard. 'Hell and damnation!' he muttered. 'Where the devil did that come from?'

'David—what if you are arrested? You might hang!' That fear had been tearing at her with black claws all afternoon until she could think of nothing else.

He looked up, obviously surprised. 'Hang? Me?' He took one

look at the distress in her face and gave her a swift hug. 'Don't be a peagoose! It was a duel, not murder, and the only reason it was hushed up was to prevent your name coming into it. If it had become known that I had fought a duel with my sister's betrothed, the next question would have been—what caused it? Someone would have worked it out.' His mouth twisted cynically. 'Even old Chasewater didn't want that—some of the mud would have stuck to them as well.'

'But—'

'Thea, even if it comes out, I'm in no real danger. There are enough witnesses to prove that it was a fair duel. Yes, I might have to face a trial, but they would be unlikely to convict me. I'm safe enough, even if there is a bit of gossip.' His mouth flattened. 'What *is* of concern is the danger to you. You're the one who will be ruined if this—'

'I don't care about that!' said Thea.

'Well, I do!' he informed her. 'You said Richard Blakehurst was there—what did you tell him?'

The world rocked. 'Nothing,' said Thea.

He sighed. 'You'll have to tell him in the end, you know.'

'No,' said Thea. 'I won't.'

David's mouth tightened. 'I think Richard Blakehurst is a better man than you give him credit for.'

Thea turned away and closed her eyes. He was. And that was precisely the problem.

Richard found Almeria almost as soon as he arrived. She was seated on a *chaise longue,* chatting to Lady Jersey, making frequent use of her fan in the stuffy, overheated salon. Full battle regalia, he noted. The famous Arnsworth diamonds blazed and dripped from every conceivable vantage point. Thea was nowhere to be seen.

His stomach clenched. Walking up to Almeria in front of Sally Jersey and demanding to know where Thea might be had as much appeal as strolling naked along Piccadilly. Sally Jersey might never stop talking, but that didn't mean she wasn't as shrewd as she could hold together...

He looked round again, and saw Thea slip into the salon with Winslow. David Winslow looked calm enough, but Richard could see him scanning the room, as though looking for someone in particular. He leaned down and murmured something to Thea, who frowned and looked straight across at him.

What the devil was she frowning at *him* for?

'Evening, Ricky.'

He looked around. Braybrook stood at his elbow.

'Julian.'

'Something bothering you?'

Not for the first time, Richard cursed the blessing of a friend who knew you too damn well.

'You might say that.'

'I did,' said Braybrook drily. 'Ah, here comes Winslow with his sister.'

Sure enough, Winslow was escorting Thea straight towards them. Tall and slender, in the poppy-red muslin with gold trim.

He waited for them with Braybrook.

'Blakehurst.' Winslow greeted Richard with a quick handshake. 'Can I trouble you to escort Thea back to Lady Arnsworth? I need a word with Braybrook.'

'Of course. It's no trouble at all.' He smiled at Thea and offered his arm. Hesitantly, she took it. The light touch of her gloved hand, despite two layers of cloth, jolted through him like a lightning bolt. Some soft summery perfume laced with the sweet temptation of woman wreathed him.

And she only had her hand on his arm. He shuddered to think what the effect would be if he waltzed with her. He found himself wondering if this became less incapacitating with custom, if, after they were married, his reaction to her sheer proximity might be more manageable. Given that Max could function in a reasonably normal fashion now with Verity around, he had to assume that—shock hit him. Apparently he'd made his decision about offering for Thea without his mind being involved anywhere in the process.

'I've told David what happened,' she said.

That focused his mind very effectively. 'What did he say?'

'That I ought not to worry about it too much.'

Good God! Was Winslow insane? A ripple like this could overturn a woman's reputation in a flash. And Thea, damn it, looked as though at least part of the load was off her mind.

He flung a glance after Winslow and Julian. The pair of them were standing by themselves, conversing with their heads close. Winslow looked taut, almost feral as he gesticulated. Whatever he might have said to reassure Thea, plainly it hadn't convinced *him*. As he watched, the two of them were joined by Fox-Heaton, who looked as though he'd swallowed something unpleasant. The three of them made for the door.

He looked back at Thea. Her gaze followed Winslow and the other two as they left the room. The combination did not seem to surprise her one whit. Which was more than could be said for himself. While Winslow taking Julian into his confidence might come as no surprise, what the devil did Fox-Heaton have to do with it?

Memory supplied an unwelcome suggestion—Sir Francis had been a very close friend of Nigel Lallerton's...if Lallerton's death had *not* been an accident... Icy foreboding crawled up and down Richard's spine. Fox-Heaton was exactly the sort of fellow who would ask some very awkward questions if any rumours began to circulate. This had all the makings of a scandal *extraordinaire*.

A surge of protective fury roared through him. No matter what it took, he was going to keep Thea safe from whatever folly her brother had committed...

'Richard?' Thea's fingers tightened on his arm. 'It's Lady Chasewater.'

'Confound it!' muttered Richard, as he saw the Dowager Countess of Chasewater heading straight for them. 'Don't tell her about it. Not here.' She turned dazed eyes on him, and he laid his hand on hers, squeezing it in reassurance. 'Keep your chin up, and we'll get through.'

Arranging a polite smile on his face, he said, 'Good evening, Lady Chasewater.'

She gave him a distracted look. 'Mr Blakehurst.' She turned at once to Thea.

'Dear Dorothea! Such a dreadful thing! I must tell you before someone else does!'

Hell and the devil! Surely not?

'A magistrate, Sir Giles Mason, called on me to ask about poor Nigel,' said Lady Chasewater in tones calculated to turn heads.

Several heads did turn, but she continued regardless. 'It seems they are not after all quite happy about the way he died. There has been some suggestion that it might have been murder!'

Richard swore under his breath. No one nearby was making even a pretence of not listening, as her ladyship went on, 'Can you imagine it? Who could possibly have wanted to kill my poor boy? Why! 'Tis unthinkable!'

Not any more it wasn't. The blasted female had just made sure the entire *ton* would be thinking about it by breakfast time.

Thea's chin lifted. 'Yes, a very dreadful thing.'

'And so distressing for you, my dear!' went on Lady Chasewater, apparently oblivious to the fact that by now at least fifty people had drawn closer the better to hear what she was saying.

Richard gritted his teeth. The cat had its head out of the bag now—how the hell could he shut her up before the whole beast escaped? 'Ma'am, perhaps you would like to speak to Miss Winslow a little more privately? You might—'

'And I understand he plans to call on *you,* my dearest Dorothea.' She caught at Thea's wrist. 'Why, whatever would you be able to tell him?'

Shocked murmurs rippled outwards.

In a steady voice, Thea said, 'Very little, ma'am, I am afraid. Sir Giles called this afternoon.'

'Oh, my dear! You must let me know if I can be of the least help,' she told Thea, clutching her wrist convulsively.

Keeping your tongue still would have been a start! It was far too late now. The cat was right out of the bag and scurrying around the room, leaving murmurs and exclamations of astonishment in its wake.

Fury sang in every fibre. Damn the blasted woman! Dimly he could feel pity for her; she had lost her son, and this must be upsetting for her, but didn't she know better than to reveal the whole affair like this? Had she no discretion? All he could think was that the shock must have addled her wits.

By the time Richard left the assembly, scarcely anything else was being spoken of save the shocking news that Nigel Lallerton had apparently been brutally murdered.

'Slaughtered, they say, my dear!'

He ignored several offers for snug games of cards and a bottle of brandy and walked home.

Hell's own broth was brewing around him, and he had no idea how to get out of it. And getting out didn't matter a damn beside the far more pressing need to protect Thea.

He wasn't her brother, curse it! Winslow was the one with the right to defend her, but it seemed that Winslow was leaving it to him. Aside from her brother, there was Aberfield... Richard dismissed that idea. Any father who could view Dunhaven as a suitable husband for his daughter was worse than useless. And as for Dunhaven, who had been hovering all evening—Richard's teeth ground savagely as he trod up the steps of Arnsworth House.

The only way to circumvent Dunhaven's plans was for Thea to be married, or at the very least, betrothed. To someone else.

Someone like himself...

His latch key missed the keyhole.

He tried again, this time managing to unlock the door. Why hadn't he seen it earlier? A simple solution was often the best, and the simplest way to protect Thea from the attentions of Dunhaven, and her father's machinations, was to offer for her himself. Immediately. Otherwise, his power was limited. At least if they were betrothed he could deflect much of the inevitable gossip. And there was another thing—once they were betrothed,

Thea might confide whatever she knew about Lallerton's death to him, which would mean he could help her.

Closing the door, he acknowledged that there were other things motivating him. He liked Thea—more than liked. He *cared* about her. About the woman who had kept that badly carved little bird all these years. About the woman whose eyes spoke sometimes of a pain he could only guess at. And who could wipe him off a chessboard. He smiled as he picked up a candle from the hall table and lit it from a taper. It was the only candle there so Almeria and Thea must be in already. He blew out the taper.

Yes, the more he thought about the idea of marrying Thea, the more right it seemed. Once he could get past the idea of facing Almeria's smug gloat. *No point cutting off your nose to spite your face.* There would probably be a certain air of well-fed-cat-picking-its-teeth-with-yellow-feathers about Braybrook too. Not even that had the power to bother him.

Not beside the anticipated delight of Thea as his wife, his bride, his lover… Desire kicked sharply as he trod up the stairs. If they were married, instead of passing her room with every muscle, nerve and sinew straining at the leash, he would be opening the door and stripping quietly, before sliding into bed with her…to hold her, love her gently… His blood burned and he realised to his horror that he had actually stopped at the door.

He took a shuddering breath. Tomorrow morning he was going to propose to Thea Winslow. It might be the only way to retain his sanity.

Chapter Seven

Thea stared blindly at her teacup. A piece of toast, reduced to crumbs on her bread-and-butter plate, bore mute testament to her lack of appetite. A sleepless night had left her with a crashing headache, and a churning stomach. The Heathcote assembly had turned into a nightmare with everyone speculating on the possible truth behind Nigel Lallerton's death.

Perhaps she had been mad to admit that Sir Giles had called, but once Lady Chasewater had made the suggestion, there had seemed little point hiding anything. Aching pity stirred inside her. How hard this must be for the woman...she had adored Nigel...

'Miss?'

The footman, James, stood just inside the door of the breakfast parlour, holding a silver salver. 'Yes, James?'

'A note for you, miss. It's just been delivered.'

She set her teacup down carefully, with only the slightest of rattles. 'A...a note?' No. It couldn't be. Foolish to think it might be another note like the one the other day...what purpose could such notes possibly serve now? All the damage had been well and truly done.

'Thank you, James.'

He brought her the note and she took it, seeing instantly that it was addressed to her in the same scrawl as the last one. A chill slid through her. 'That will be all, James.' Her own voice, calm, oddly distant.

'Yes, miss.'

She put the note by her plate, refusing to look at it until the door closed. Shivering now, she picked up her cup of tea and sipped, savouring it. There was more tea in the pot, and she poured herself another cup, adding milk with careful precision.

The note sat there. Unavoidable. She didn't have to read it. There was a fire in the grate. She could drop it in there unread. That would be the sensible thing to do. Swiftly she rose, picked up the note and hurried over to the fireplace.

She stared at the dancing flames. *Drop it in. That's all you have to do.* Only she couldn't. After yesterday, and last night…what if the note contained a threat? A demand. Something that ought to be dealt with. She shivered—what if—?

With shaking fingers she broke the seal—first she would read it, just in case. Then she would burn it… Fumbling with cold, she unfolded the letter.

Did they tell you that the child was dead? Were you relieved, Slut?

The room spun around her in sickening swoops as she crushed the note. Dear God…bile rising in her throat, she bent down and placed the crumpled note on the fire. It hung there for a moment and then the edges blackened, slowly at first, and then in a consuming rush as the flames fed hungrily. It was gone in less than a minute, paper and ink reduced to ashes.

Only, it wasn't gone. Not really. Because she had been fool enough to read it. She could not consign knowledge to the flames and the words remained, branded on her soul—but what could they possibly mean? The phrasing—*Did they tell you…?* What else should they have told her? Unless…unless they had lied.

She dragged in a breath, shutting her eyes as she fought for control.

The door opened.

'Thea?'

She straightened at once and her breath caught. Richard had come in, dressed for riding, dark eyes fixed on her. Dear God…if he had read this note! Her glance flickered to the fire, half-expecting to see the accusation writhing in the flames.

'Good…good morning, Richard.'

He frowned at her as he came into the parlour. 'Did you sleep at all? You should still be abed. Are you all right?'

She forced a smile into place. 'I was…just a little cold,' she lied. Change the subject, quickly. 'Have you been riding?'

He sat down at the table. 'Yes. Thea—about last night—'

'You must be hungry then.' She rushed on. 'Shall I ring for coffee? Were you up very early?' Heavens! She was babbling like an idiot in her attempt to sound vaguely normal.

'Thank you, but Myles knows I'm in. He'll bring me some coffee, and I breakfasted before riding.' He looked across at her. 'Thea, don't pretend with me. About last night—we need to talk. Privately.'

'Oh.' Her heart gave a funny little leap. She squashed it back into place and ordered her thoughts. Very carefully she said, 'Is that wise, Richard?'

His gaze narrowed, and she flushed, remembering a comment of Diana's about how peculiar it was to see Richard in town at all, let alone attending so many parties. Diana seemed perfectly certain that there would be an announcement at any moment— and that wagers had been laid that, finally, Lady Arnsworth would succeed in her dearest ambition.

'After all, you can't wish to…raise expectations, and…and then—'

His brows lifted. 'Expectations?'

She could not quite identify the undercurrent in his voice.

'Am I raising your expectations, Thea?'

He didn't sound concerned, but then he was always in control of his thoughts and feelings.

'Not mine!' she clarified. 'Society's expectations.'

What Richard said about society had a certain eloquence to it.

'You're my friend, Thea,' he told her. 'And I don't give a

damn about anyone else's expectations,' he added, still with that odd, intent look. 'Yours would be a different matter.'

A friend. Her heart, foolish organ, glowed. Should she tell him about this note? Not because she wanted him to do something about it, but simply to tell someone. So that she did not feel quite so alone.

No. She couldn't. She could hear the conversation now.

Another note? What did this one say?

Oh, nothing much. Just…it was just nasty.

Nasty, how?

No, she couldn't tell him what it had said. The other one had looked like general spitefulness. This one was more directly aimed. He would want an explanation. Yet another explanation she couldn't give.

'Thea? Thea! Are you all right?'

To her horror she realised that he had been speaking to her, trying to gain her attention.

She flushed. 'I'm sorry, Richard. I…I was wool-gathering.'

'With a vengeance,' he agreed.

She pinned a bright smile in place. 'What did you wish to say?'

He didn't look at all convinced, but said, 'I planned to drive out towards Richmond this morning in the curricle, if you would care to join me. We do need to talk.'

'Driving…but…' Her voice died in her throat and the walls of the present dissolved, memory flooding through the breach. Another offer to drive out on a sunny day…another curricle…shame, embarrassment, and terror stretched out their tentacles, pulling her back in time …

Come, Thea, you cannot possibly believe that I mean you the least harm. Your mama is perfectly happy for me to drive you out. She wishes you to entertain me… At least you might tell me the reason for your change of mind…

'Thea? Thea? Is something wrong?'

His words made no sense. He had never asked before if anything was wrong. She tasted fear, sour in her mouth, and felt her knees buckle.

'*Thea!*'

Strong hands gripped her, lifting her, and then she felt herself being lowered, helpless—

'It's all right, Thea. Here—just lie still.'

Just lie still, you stupid girl!

No! Not this time. She *wouldn't* submit. Even as she felt the sofa beneath her, she squirmed, struggling wildly, clawing, striking out in panic.

The blackness cleared, dissolving to reveal an elegantly appointed breakfast parlour, and, instead of *him,* Richard Blakehurst bending over her, his cravat askew and a livid red mark on his left cheek.

Horror stabbed her.

'I...I—' The words dried up in her throat. There was nothing she could say in answer to the question in his shocked dark eyes. Cold flooded her from the flash of memory, and the disbelief on his face. What had she done?

Very slowly he straightened up.

'You will perhaps be more comfortable if I take my coffee in the back parlour, Thea.'

Thea sank back on the sofa, shivering. But not from the resurgence of nightmare and fear. Horror seeped through her at what she had seen in his face.

What had she done? She had insulted one of the most honourable men in London in the worst possible manner.

Richard Blakehurst was the last man on earth who would take advantage of a woman. Anywhere. Let alone in his godmother's breakfast parlour. She owed him an apology at the very least. And what could she say if he demanded an explanation?

I didn't see you. *I saw* him. *Felt his hands on me. Heard his voice, telling me to lie still...his weight crushing the breath out of me. His strength...*

She choked off the flow of memory, before it could become a nightmare. Not for years had she had a reversion of memory like that—the nightmare leaping to hellish life in her waking mind. Once the slightest unexpected touch had been enough to cast her back into hell…she had thought she was past that. Plainly she was not. But for now it could not be allowed to matter. She had to find Richard and apologise.

And when she had done that, she must decide what she was to do about this last note.

Having retreated to the back parlour, Richard pulled a letter he was writing to his sister-in-law out of the small desk he used. Unfortunately, all he could see was Thea's blanched terror, her dazed eyes.

How had he got himself into such a confounded mess? He'd thought she must be ill, that she was about to faint…dammit! She *had* fainted. If he hadn't caught her, she would have landed on the floor.

He gritted his teeth. Plainly he should have let her hit the floor and simply walked out. Apparently his chivalrous behaviour in catching her and laying her on the sofa had been interpreted as attempted ravishment!

He took another sip of coffee and reached for his pen. Putting words on paper had never been so difficult.

The soft knock on the door startled him so that the pen sputtered all over his half-written letter.

'Come in,' he called.

The door opened and Thea slipped in.

'Richard?'

He waited. He had no idea what to say anyway. Dammit! *She* had come looking for *him,* after as good as accusing him of attempting to rape her!

She looked stricken and his conscience accused him of wanting several pounds of flesh. At which point his body started speculating on which particular pounds he might start with. Banishing his fantasies forcibly, he consigned his conscience and good manners to hell, and waited, his mouth set grimly.

'I'm…I'm sorry, Richard. I would like very much to drive out with you. That is, if you still wish it.'

All the offended fury melted in the face of her distress. And something else, deep inside him that he couldn't even have put a name to, responded with a surge of tenderness.

'I think that it is for me to apologise,' he said quietly. 'I frightened you. I'm sorry, Thea.'

She shook her head. 'No, Richard. You are not to apologise. I think I'd feel better if you raged at me. It was not your fault. I know that you would never...never—' She took a shuddering breath, and said in something approaching her normal voice, 'It was just that I felt dizzy for a moment and became confused.'

He didn't believe it for one moment, but smiled and said, 'Then if you truly wish to drive out, I will order the curricle.'

'Yes, please. It would be lovely. As long as Lady Arnsworth does not object.'

He couldn't help laughing. 'Almeria? I should think you'll find her ready to hand you up into the curricle!'

She blushed.

'In half an hour, then?' he said.

'Yes. Thank you. I'll tell Lady Arnsworth now.'

Richard leaned back in his chair as Thea left the room. God help him; if Almeria knew what was in his mind, she'd be sending instructions around to Doctors' Commons within ten minutes.

Which would definitely be jumping the gun. They weren't anywhere near the point where a special licence was required. He'd intended proposing to her this morning. Suggesting that they marry quickly. Perhaps he needed to step back a little; discuss the idea with her. Point out the rational reasons for a match between them. If he could focus on them through the haze of fury that enveloped him when he thought of Dunhaven. Or the desire that tightened his loins every time he laid eyes on Thea.

Had she seen his thoughts in his eyes as she regained consciousness? If he were to be brutally honest with himself, he couldn't swear even now that he wouldn't have kissed her. He *thought* he wouldn't. He *hoped* he wouldn't! Surely he wasn't such a cad as to take advantage of an unconscious woman? But he wasn't quite sure. She'd exploded in panic before he'd been put to the test.

The worst of it was that little though he might like to admit it, the thought had been there. Oh, not to actually ravish her! But feeling her soft weight in his arms, breathing the fragrance of her hair, seeing those soft pink lips parted and vulnerable—his whole body had tightened with the urge to taste, his fingers had itched to caress her cheek and find out if it really was softer than silk. Not to mention the graceful curve of her throat.

He swore. If he kept on like this he'd be a basket case before ever they reached Richmond.

Thea was awaiting him in the hall, fashionably attired in a carriage dress of deep blue twill when he brought the curricle around to the front door. Almeria came out with her.

'Thank you, Richard,' she said, as he got down. 'A drive is just what will do Dorothea good after last night. A dreadful business. I cannot believe that Laetitia Chasewater, of all people, was so lost to all sense of decorum! And I am determined that tonight we shall attend only Lady Fairchild's *musicale*.'

'A very sensible decision, Almeria.'

He understood perfectly. It was vital that Thea continued to be seen, but at a *musicale* chatter was perforce limited. Of course there would be supper afterwards, but, knowing Lady Fairchild, it would be a small, select affair. All the better if it were.

He handed Thea up into the curricle and hid a smile to see that Almeria, even if she hadn't precisely pushed Thea into the vehicle, was reaching up to pat her on the hands.

'Enjoy your drive, dear. And a little stroll along the river. I am sure you will find it refreshing.'

She stepped back and Richard gave his horses the office, putting them into a slow trot the moment his groom, Minchin, had swung up behind.

Impossible to have any private conversation with Minchin there, so he kept the talk to indifferent topics as he threaded the curricle through the streets and out on to Piccadilly. There the traffic rendered any conversation impossible, until he was past Apsley House and the Knightsbridge Turnpike.

They trotted on, out through the village of Chelsea and on down through Walham Green to cross the river at the Putney Bridge before turning west again to go around to Petersham. It was a glorious day, sunny with a gentle breeze and with London far behind them. Thea relaxed. It seemed that every bird in England was singing for joy in the hedgerows at the fragrance of wildflowers and damp grass, driving out all fear, all memory. She pushed it away, determined, if only for this one perfect day, to live entirely in the moment and not worry about what might be around the corner, or what lay shadowed in the past. Right here, right now, she was happy.

'A penny for your thoughts.'

Richard's voice broke in on her trance-like state. She sighed. 'I was thinking that it would be lovely to live out in the country, somewhere like this, not too far from London so that one might come up easily to visit friends or go to the theatre.'

'But still live peacefully away from the crash and clatter?'

She looked at him gratefully. 'Yes, that's it exactly. I think when all this is over, after my birthday, that is what I shall do.'

'Your birthday?'

'Once I turn twenty-five, under the terms of my uncle's will, I receive two hundred pounds a year whether I marry or not, and whether Aberfield likes it or not. I can do as I please.'

'I see.'

'Do you disapprove?'

He laughed. 'Would it make any difference to you?'

She hesitated, and Richard waited, oddly aware that her answer was somehow important. At last she said, 'No. Not if I thought I was right. I should be sorry to disappoint you, but even if I make a mistake, it would be *my* mistake.'

He could hardly quarrel with that. It was his own creed— make your own mistakes and learn from them. His heart leapt in recognition. This could work. More than work.

Encouraged, he began to talk about his plans for his property, what improvements he had made in the house, how sheltered it was from the worst of the Channel storms. 'A little further from London than this,' he said, as he drew his horses up outside the inn in Petersham. 'But still close enough to come up easily for a visit.' Minchin sprang down and went to the horses' heads. 'And don't tell Almeria,' he added, 'but I've just bought a small town house.'

'Don't tell her? She'd be delighted,' said Thea.

He let himself down carefully to the road, aware that his leg had stiffened slightly. 'Not when she finds out where it is, she won't be.'

Thea looked her question.

'Bloomsbury,' he confessed.

Laughter rippled. 'Near the museum?'

'Mmm. She'll probably have palpitations.' Then, casually, 'Should you mind?'

'No, of course not.'

She looked at him oddly and he held up his hands to help her down. Time to change the subject. 'Are you hungry?' he asked. 'We could have something to eat here and then stroll along the river.'

The river slid past, deep and tranquil. They hadn't walked very far. Richard had produced a bag of old bread from the curricle. In her childhood a drive out to Richmond or Petersham with a picnic and a walk along the river to feed the ducks had been a high treat. Standing there on the bank, throwing bread to the quacking, squabbling ducks, she could almost forget her worries and how many years it had been since last she did this.

Richard's deep quiet voice drew her back. 'Has it occurred to you how similar our plans are?'

She threw a piece of bread to a duck. 'Standing beside the Thames feeding greedy ducks?'

He laughed. 'No. Although that's part of it. Neither of us wants any sort of public life—we both plan to live in the country, at not too great a remove from town.'

A swan moved in, its grace belied by its quickness in lunging for a scrap of bread.

'A quiet life,' he continued.

She threw bread to the swan. 'I'm not planning to run an estate and breed sheep,' she said.

'You could learn to help, though,' he said. 'And I'd enjoy teaching you.'

Shock hummed through her as she began to see where this was leading.

'Richard—you…you can't possibly be suggesting that—you said I could have twice the fortune, and—'

'Dammit, woman! I'm proposing to *you!* Not your blasted fortune! I'm asking you to marry me. Share my life.'

Share my life.

Those simple heartfelt words tore at her like a twisting knife. Share his life…and what did she have to share in return? A sordid secret in her past? And the way things were developing, a sordid and far-from-secret scandal here in the present.

'No,' she said.

Richard's heart landed with a thump in his boots. Owing to the extravagant poke of Thea's bonnet, gauging her expression was impossible, but a glance at her gloved hands showed them clenched together. No doubt the knuckles were stark white.

That was it? No?

He supposed it had the merit of being succinct. None of that nonsense about being honoured by his proposal, and—

So much for being rational. There was a moment's silence, in which he had an eternity to curse himself for the clumsiness of his address.

'This is not because of those silly notes? You do not feel that you must offer for me because of that?'

'Of course not! Lord, every mama in the *ton* would be sending anonymous letters in that case!' He dragged in a breath. 'Thea— I'm offering because I wish to marry you.'

The quacking of the ducks fell into the well of silence that had opened up between them.

'I am very sorry, Richard, but I cannot possibly marry you.'

He held back all the things he wanted to say. All the far-from-rational things that were burning a hole deep inside him. Somehow, he realised, it had not really occurred to him that she might refuse.

'Will you tell me why you cannot?' He flicked a glance at her, but she was staring straight ahead, her face hidden again by the poke of her bonnet. 'After all, we have always been good friends, you must know that I don't give a damn about your fortune, and—'

'Of course I know that!' She turned to him in obvious surprise, and he saw the pain in her eyes. 'It's nothing to do with that. It's just…just that I cannot…it never occurred to me that you could want to marry me!'

He waited, but she fell silent and looked ahead again.

'I frightened you this morning, did I not, Thea?' he asked quietly.

'No!' She faced him again, her face absolutely white. 'The truth is, Richard—' She stopped. He saw the convulsive movement of her throat before she turned away again. Her voice came again, utterly devoid of expression, 'Yes. I was frightened. But it was *not* because of you! Only because I did not realise that it was you.' Her mouth twisted. 'I know that sounds foolish and I…I cannot explain, but I do thank you for your offer. No one who knows you could possibly imagine you would offer because of my fortune.'

'Don't delude yourself, love.' The endearment hung between them, alive and shimmering. *Love.* He had called women that before, of course. One did in bed. It had been a meaningless endearment. But when had he ever really heard himself say it? When had it ever rung like a bell?

She looked up at him, soft lips curved in a trembling smile. 'They do not know you then, do they?' she said quietly. 'I said anyone who knows you, Richard. Would your brother, or Lord Braybrook, make that mistake?'

No. Not even if he lied. They would know. And apparently Thea knew…

'Are you sure, Thea?' he asked gently. 'Ungentlemanly of me to press, I know, but—'

'Quite sure,' she whispered, looking straight ahead again. 'It…it is not possible…if it were…that is…' Her breath came raggedly, as though she breathed glass. Her voice when it came was utterly steady and expressionless. 'I have no intention of marrying. Ever.'

Had she loved the fellow so deeply? She had only been sixteen when they were betrothed; seventeen when Lallerton died, and he had always assumed the match had been arranged by Aberfield and Chasewater, but…perhaps it was time to resurrect his rational proposal.

'Thea,' he said carefully, 'I quite understand how you must feel, but surely after seven years—' He felt her stiffen beside him and altered tack slightly. 'Have you considered that one may marry for friendship, as well as love? We have always been good friends. And this would solve your problem—I may not be a brilliant catch like Dunhaven in your father's estimation, but I'm perfectly eligible.' Only half-joking, he added, 'You wouldn't have to bother with toads like that any more, at least!'

Thea swallowed hard. She knew he would protect her. And it was tempting, so tempting… No! She didn't dare. To marry Richard, she would have to tell him the truth. 'I cannot, Richard,' she whispered. 'Please, will you take me back now?'

'Of course.'

They walked back along the path in silence. In the silence of her mind she railed at fate that had brought her here to this moment and mocked her with his proposal.

As they arrived back at the inn, he said quietly, 'Thea, just because you have refused my offer of marriage does not mean that we cannot continue friends, does it?'

She flinched, and, to her horror, tears sprang to her eyes. Forcing them back, she stared fixedly ahead, not trusting her voice. It would shake like her gloved hands, locked in front of her.

'Thea?'

'Friends—of course, Richard.' Her voice did wobble. Despicably. Friends told each other the truth. Trusted each other. She hated that she was deceiving him so deeply.

You could tell him the truth.

No. She could not. Not to save her life could she tell him that. It would be worse than death to see the pitying contempt in his eyes. And what if he didn't believe her? No one else ever had, save David. And perhaps David had believed her partly because he had disliked Nigel so much.

She shut her eyes. It would be better if David had not believed her either. If he had not, he would not be in such danger now. It would also be better if she did not have to see Richard again. Especially now. Now when she wasn't even sure that *she* knew the whole truth. *Did they tell you that the child was dead?*

With Minchin up behind them during the drive back, any further private conversation was impossible. Thea did not know whether to be glad or sorry. Richard was very quiet, speaking only to point out landmarks, or comment on the state of the roads.

Only when they reached Grosvenor Square and he escorted her up the front steps of Arnsworth House did he refer again to what lay between them.

'Lallerton was a very lucky man for you to have loved him so deeply.'

Not the slightest hint of bitterness. No anger. Just the kindest understanding of the lie that she and her family had cultivated to screen the truth. So easy simply to nod. To accept what he had said and agree. It stuck in her throat. Even if she dared not tell Richard the truth, she would not lie to him. Not in any way.

She turned to face him fully. 'I did not love Nigel Lallerton. Ever. Not then. Not now.'

And she opened the front door and fled into the house.

Richard stared after her, stunned. She *hadn't* loved Lallerton? Then why in Hades had she remained in seclusion for seven years? Why had she set herself so flatly against marriage?

There was something odd here. She had *said* simply that she hadn't loved Lallerton. But her tone of voice had said a great deal more...

Her perfect day was over. Thea sat with a smile of polite interest plastered to her face as she listened to the violinist Lady Fairchild had engaged for the evening. She should be enjoying this, but as the violin sang and soared, her thoughts spun wildly between doubt and searing conviction. Richard had not attended and Lord Dunhaven's presence beside her served only to increase her distraction.

Could they have lied about her child's death? Yes. Easily. And why, oh, why had she been fool enough to tell Richard that she hadn't loved Lallerton?

Had Lord Dunhaven moved his chair slightly? He was too close, especially in the overheated room. Her temples began to throb.

His lordship leaned closer, murmuring something about how much he enjoyed Mozart.

'Haydn,' she told him, and had the dubious pleasure of seeing him turn a dull brick-red. Dunhaven hated being contradicted— especially when he was wrong.

Would they have lied?

Over something like that? With the honour of the family involved? With David at risk? Oh, yes. They would have lied. In a moment.

The accusation of that morning's note hung before her in letters of fire: *Did they tell you that the child was dead? Were you relieved ...?*

The sonata ended and the audience applauded with well-bred enthusiasm.

Yes. She had been relieved. For a moment. A day. And then the grief had come. The grief she had not been allowed to show. And the guilt.

But what if her child had survived? How could she find out?

Chapter Eight

She came down to breakfast the following morning to discover Richard already there. He had plainly finished his bacon and eggs and progressed to the toast-and-coffee stage.

Richard smiled at her over his paper. 'Good morning.'

Was it her imagination, or did he look somehow careworn? 'Good morning,' she replied.

'Shall I bring some more toast, Miss Thea?' asked Myles.

'Yes. Yes, please,' she said. She doubted that she could face eggs.

Myles disappeared.

Richard said, 'Thea—about yesterday—'

Myles burst back into the parlour.

'Mr Richard!'

Richard dropped the paper into his toast.

'Yes?'

Myles was holding out a letter. 'A messenger brought this. From Blakeney, sir. His lordship's writing—'

Richard had shoved his chair back, leapt to his feet and was breaking the seal with fumbling fingers before Myles had finished speaking. Thea stared, dumbfounded. He looked…he looked frightened, his eyes dark in a white face, his mouth a hard, set line as he scanned the letter. Then—

'YES!'

Thea's tea sloshed into the saucer as Richard's howl of triumphant delight rent the air. Then, the letter floating to the table, Richard seized Myles and practically waltzed around the room, his face alive and brimming with joy.

'Mr Richard! What is it?'

With which breathless question Thea heartily concurred.

'A boy, Myles! It's a boy! I'm an uncle. And her ladyship is perfectly well! She's come through safely, *thank God!*'

Her heart contracted. His sister-in-law, Lady Blakehurst, had come safely through the birth of her child. A small hidden corner of her soul echoed his words: Thank God.

She shook her head, refusing to acknowledge the memories pouring through her. They came anyway, relentless, raking her painfully. She forced them away, concentrating on the unknown countess, Richard's sister-in-law, Verity. What was it like to hold your child at the end, to see it after the months of waiting, of feeling it kick and wriggle inside? To rejoice in the *birth* of your child, rather than...

Strong, lean hands plucked her from her nightmare and out of her seat.

'Thea! Did you hear? I'm an uncle!' He whirled her around, laughing, alight with joy. His strength startled her; he seemed to hold her effortlessly, spinning her around so that her feet left the floor. She clutched at his shoulders, feeling hard muscles surge under the superfine of his coat, wildly aware of his hands on her waist, spanning her ribcage.

Her heart pounded, her mouth dried and his eyes laughed into hers as he set her down. 'I'm an uncle. And—' he cleared his throat '—about to be a godfather.'

He still had his hands on her waist, not gripping now, just resting there, as though...as though they belonged there. Intimate. Possessive.

'That's...that's wonderful, Richard,' she faltered, gazing up at him. He was close, so close. Sensation splintered through her, leaving her dizzy and breathless.

The laughter faded from his eyes as he stared back at her,

stared as though he saw her for the first time, his mouth suddenly hard. His hands tightened slightly at her waist, fingers shifting in a way that sent heat flying through her. It reached her cheeks in a fiery blush as she realised the intimacy of his hold, that her breasts were nearly brushing against him. That they ached. And then, to her utter shock, that she wanted to lean forward, to press the ache against him. That did frighten her.

Richard knew instantly; saw the moment her eyes widened, heard the sudden startled breath as she realised how close they were.

He forced his fingers to relax, his hands to drop to his sides. But his body remained taut with the tension that had exploded when he felt the softness of her body in his hands, saw the delicate flush on her cheeks as he swung her around. Hell! He wasn't supposed to feel like this!

Like what?

As though he wanted to take her back into his arms and kiss her until they were both breathless, until her mouth and body melted under his, and…

Stop right there! This was insane. Surely he couldn't possibly be standing here—in his godmother's breakfast parlour, no less!—struggling against the urge to kiss Thea Winslow sense-less? After she had categorically refused his offer of marriage the previous day? Apparently he was. And no matter what honour, not to mention common sense, thought of the idea, his body was making its opinion strongly felt. Visible too. *He* certainly didn't need to look and he hoped to heaven that Thea *wouldn't.*

She was still standing there, her hands resting on his chest. Why the hell wasn't she using them to push him away? And why was she looking up at him like that, with that wide-eyed look of disbelief, when she should have dealt him a ringing slap and kicked him in the shins?

He could, of course, step back himself. He did so, feeling as though part of him had been ripped away to leave weeping raw flesh. As if his retreat had broken a spell, Thea backed up too, her face scarlet.

And just in time.

Almeria walked in, a letter in her hand.

'Richard! Have you heard? Did Max write to you—oh!' She saw the letter on the table. 'You know already.'

Richard smiled. 'Yes. Wonderful news, is it not?'

Almeria cleared her throat. 'Naturally one must be glad that Max's wife has come through the ordeal, and write a letter of congratulations,' she said stiffly. 'Very obliging of Max to inform me.' She sniffed. 'If it can be called a letter! I could scarcely read it!'

Richard laughed. 'Yes, mine is a trifle incoherent as well. I'm not sure if it mentions the baby's name. If it doesn't no doubt he'll tell me when I see him.'

'See him? Will you be going to Blakeney?' asked Almeria.

He hesitated. He didn't want to leave town right now, but—

'You should go, Richard,' said Thea gently.

Almeria frowned. 'Of course you will have to go down, Richard. Whatever his failings…' she sniffed '…Blakehurst is your brother. I am sure that Dorothea and I can manage for a day or two.' She turned to Thea. 'I thought to visit Bond Street this morning, my dear, and would like you to accompany me.'

'Of course, ma'am, if you wish it,' said Thea.

Refolding her letter, Lady Arnsworth tucked it away in a pocket.

'Almeria, Max mentions in his letter that he has asked you to stand as godmother to the baby,' said Richard.

Lady Arnsworth flushed. 'Yes, his letter to me mentions something of the sort, but of course I cannot accept. Impossible to leave town at the moment with Dorothea to chaperon. It would be most remiss of me. No, I am afraid it is not to be thought of. I shall write to Blakehurst presently and inform him. Although I doubt that he can really want me to attend!'

Turning to Thea, she said, 'I shall be ready to go out in half an hour, dear.' And sailed from the room, leaving a thunderous silence behind her. It held for a moment and then detonated as Richard said several things that Thea had never heard before. Given the shaking fury in his voice, she rather thought she ought to be blushing.

'Damn it!' he went on, slightly more moderately. 'She knows

quite well what the gossip will be like if she *doesn't* attend the christening!'

'But why should there be gossip?'

Richard sighed. 'Because, to put it mildly, there was quite a bit of scandal attached to Max's marriage one way or another. The most popular version was that Verity trapped him. Almeria has even openly wondered if the child is *his*.' His jaw seemed to turn into solid stone.

'But—'

'Don't worry,' he said shortly. 'It is. Verity…well, you'll understand when you meet her.' His face softened. 'She is the best thing that could possibly have happened to Max. And she suffered enough with her own family. Max will never overlook a slight to her from Almeria.'

'I'm sorry—'

He stared. 'Why should you apologise? Oh. That nonsense about being your chaperon? No. That was an excuse so that I could not rip up at her. Nothing to do with you.'

But he was frowning as he took his leave, and Thea could not but see that she was a confounded nuisance one way or another.

Richard retreated to the back parlour upstairs, shaken by the near cracking of his control. Having Thea in his arms like that…he wanted her. Had wanted to tip her face up and kiss her until she had forgotten whatever reasons she had for not marrying.

He forced his mind back to Max's letter. Almeria had actually taken the fell tidings much better than he had antici- pated. He suspected that she was feeling rather small and foolish after her behaviour towards Max's bride, that she did not wish to climb down for a generous serving of humble pie. He thanked God that Max had actually written to her directly, rather than relying on him to make the announcement. Perhaps in a day or so she would be a little more resigned over the birth of… He frowned, attempting to decipher a little more of his brother's scrawled letter…ah, William Richard. He grinned. As long as Almeria could be persuaded to attend the christening, all would be well.

A discreet cough interrupted his thoughts.

'Mr Blakehurst, sir?'

He turned and looked at the young footman standing in the doorway. 'Yes, Edmund?'

The young man shifted from one foot to the other, as though unsure of himself.

'I've a note here for Miss Winslow.'

'She is still in the breakfast parlour, I believe.'

'Yes, sir. It's just, well, after that one t'other day—you asked me about who brought it, and I think this might be another from the same person.' He proffered the note to Richard. 'An' from what James says, there was another one for Miss Thea.'

Damn. He should have told Edmund to alert James, but what excuse could he possibly have given for checking Thea's correspondence?

'Thank you, Edmund. I'll take it.'

The same excuse he was going to give now—none.

But what the hell was he to do with it once he'd opened it? Hand it over to Thea? Richard stared at the sealed note, his gaze narrowed. It looked like the same scrawl as on the first notes. The seal a plain blob of wax. And Thea had received another…which she hadn't mentioned to him. Why not?

'When did the other note come for Miss Winslow?' he asked slowly.

'Yesterday, James said,' answered Edmund. 'He reckons he gave it to Miss Thea at breakfast.'

Yesterday at breakfast? His stomach lurched. And Thea had fainted. Damn it! She'd been upset by one of these blasted notes. No wonder she'd been upset and confused.

But why hadn't she told him about the note? He already knew about the first one, so—? He'd wanted to find out who it was, and stop it. Thea hadn't wanted that. Why? Good God! Did she imagine he'd believe the sort of person who would pen filth like that? And was he really going to hand more of this filth to Thea? The hell he was!

His decision made, he broke the seal and opened the note. The ugly words slashed across the paper: *SLUT! How many times did he have you, you filthy little trollop?*

Searing rage gripped him. Bad enough that his own note had accused him of bedding Thea, but to fling the muck at her—something akin to a snarl escaped him.

'Sir?'

'Pushed under the door again, was it?' It was all he could do to keep his voice calm. He wanted to smash things.

'Yes, sir.' Edmund hesitated, then said, 'Only this time I saw him, sir. I was coming back from taking a note for her ladyship an' saw him at the door.'

'You did? Do you know him?'

'No, sir. Not to say *know*,' said Edmund. 'No livery. But I've seen him about. Often holds a horse for a penny. Anyway, I hope I've not done the wrong thing, sir, but I've taken him round to the mews.'

'You've done *what?*'

Edmund looked uncertain. 'You did want to speak to him, didn't you, sir?'

'Oh, yes. I definitely want to speak to him,' answered Richard, crushing the note and shoving it in his pocket.

He was going to deal with this before leaving for Blakeney. Thea might have refused his offer of marriage, but she was going to have his protection and help whether she liked it or not.

The boy, who laid claim to the name of Jacob, stared at up at Richard from his seat on an upturned bucket in mute confusion.

'Dunno, sir.'

Richard tried again. 'Well, a man or a woman?'

The lad's brow cleared. 'Oh. A *lidy*, sir. A *real* lidy,' he added. His gaze wandered around the stable yard, and became openly admiring as Richard's chestnuts were led out of their stalls.

Richard waited with scant patience as the boy cast a worshipful eye over the horses. 'And can you describe her?' he prompted at last.

The boy jerked his attention away from the horses with obvious reluctance.

'Wore black,' he said. 'Black dress, black hat, and one of

them veils. Real heavy one it were. Couldn't see her face hardly at all. Gloves too.'

Richard frowned. 'So you couldn't tell me if she was old or young?'

'Oldish, I think, sir,' said the boy hesitantly. 'It's her voice. Dunno why, sir, but she sounds older now I think on't.'

Richard suppressed a curse, mindful of the boy's wide-eyed gaze.

That did narrow the field somewhat, but not enough. Which of the ton's tabbies would have something to gain from destroying Thea's reputation? And the letters were not aimed at Thea's reputation, but directly at Thea herself. Did it have something to do with this bizarre tale that had sprung up about Lallerton being murdered?

'I can show you where she lives, if you like, sir.'

'You can—' Richard stared at the boy. Children were like that, he reminded himself. They answered the question asked. He hadn't thought to ask about where she lived…

Twenty minutes later Richard gazed disbelievingly up at a small house in Half Moon Street.

'*Who* did you say lives there?'

The hurrying footman he had stopped obligingly repeated himself and then went on his way.

The house seemed to gaze back benignly—the epitome of discreet elegance. Impossible. There was no reason—surely! Yet…the connection was there…

He looked down at the boy who had brought him here. 'Are you certain, Jacob?'

The boy bristled at his dubious tone. 'Aye. *Told* you; I followed her.'

Perhaps there was a strange logic to it after all, albeit twisted and bitter. Which shouldn't surprise him, given the content of the letters. He grimaced. Indeed, a very ugly pattern was beginning to emerge.

'Very well.' It couldn't be coincidence that Jacob had led him here. He handed him a half-crown. 'There you are. Take care of it. And remember what I said; don't hang about here for a while and if you see her again, keep clear.'

The boy rushed off with a wave of thanks, and Richard trod up the steps to the front door to tug on the doorbell. He waited, bracing himself for what promised to be a most unpleasant interview.

A footman answered the door.

Richard handed him his card. 'Inform Lady Chasewater that Mr Richard Blakehurst has called.'

He was shown into the hall. 'Please to wait here, sir, while I see if her ladyship is at home.'

'Thank you.'

He supposed he could understand Lady Chasewater feeling bitter about her son's death, but why take it out on Thea? Could the woman resent that her son's chosen bride was alive and well? Was she perhaps a little mad?

A moment later the footman was back. 'You are to come up, sir. Her ladyship will see you.'

He was ushered into a dimly lit drawing room. Lady Chasewater was seated on a sofa beside the fire. Clad in black, spine ramrod straight, her mittened hand rested on the top of a jewelled cane. She inclined her head. 'Mr Blakehurst. Do, please, be seated. To what do I owe this pleasure?'

He met her gaze levelly. 'I doubt that *pleasure* is quite the word to use, and I think I shall remain standing. This is not a friendly visit.'

He brought the three notes out of his pocket. 'Do you have some explanation for this filth, ma'am? Beyond sheer vindictive cruelty, that is. What did you think to achieve?'

A cold smile twisted her mouth. 'Ah. Miss Winslow worked it out at last, did she? And ran to you, begging you to stop me. I expected the brother, you know.'

His fist clenched. 'Miss Winslow worked it out when she saw your first note, ma'am. And all she said was that the person who had sent it was unhappy.'

A muscle twitched in the sunken cheek.

Richard continued. 'She did not, however, identify you, and to the best of my knowledge, her brother knows nothing of the notes. I should also tell you that she has not, and will not, see this one. I repeat, Lady Chasewater—what did you think to achieve?'

She ignored the question. 'If Miss Winslow didn't tell you, what made you think of me?'

He'd thought of this. Lying seemed contemptible, but the last thing he wanted was this vindictive old woman going after the boy. 'I set someone on to watch the boy you used. You were seen handing the note to him this morning.' All true enough, but slightly expurgated.

'I wore a veil.'

'And came back here.'

A harsh laugh escaped her. 'As easy as that. Well, no matter. I suppose you are here to tell me not to send any more letters? Very well. You may rest easy on that head.'

Suspicion flickered. That had been too easy.

'And may one assume—'

'You may assume whatever you please, Mr Blakehurst, but there will be no more letters. I've tastier fish to fry.' She reached out and rang the bell. 'I think we have nothing more to say to each other, Mr Blakehurst, save perhaps that I think you are a fool. Good day, sir.'

Anger seared every vein, all the hotter for being impotent.

'You hide behind your sex, madam,' he said coldly. 'I assure you that only that, not your age, saves you from a direct challenge. But understand this—if you distress Miss Winslow by any other means, I will find a way to strike at you.'

A cold smile played about her mouth. 'Then, Mr Blakehurst, we shall see what manner of fool you are. A chivalrous one, or an ignorant one.'

'Of course, I won't be attending this…this christening party!' announced Lady Arnsworth as she stepped into the barouche for the planned visit to Bond Street. 'Really, I cannot think why Blakehurst has asked me to stand as godmother. He must have known what my response would be. And it is not as though he wishes me to do so. He has asked only because he feels obliged!'

Catching a glimpse of the footman's unconvincingly stolid face as he put up the steps and closed the door on this announcement, Thea winced. Lady Arnsworth never seemed to make the connection between gossip and talking unguardedly in front of her servants. Then again, perhaps she did. She looked a little self-conscious. 'You will not repeat that to Richard, will you? He has some ridiculous idea that Max's marriage is a good thing. Even though he is disinherited!'

She wouldn't need to. From the footman to Richard's groom, to Richard? He'd have heard about it before he left London.

'But, surely Richard never expected to inherit the earldom?' queried Thea. Perhaps another, disinterested voice might make itself heard?

'Certainly not,' said Lady Arnsworth. 'And neither did Max, but after Frederick's death—why, it was *clearly* understood that Max would remain unwed for Richard's sake.'

Judging by Richard's support of his twin's marriage and delight at the birth of the child who had supplanted him, Thea took leave to doubt that Richard had been counting on this at all. She cast a nervous glance at the coachman's very rigid back. A wonder that his ears weren't visibly flapping.

'And anyway, I wouldn't dream of leaving town at the moment with this dreadful story flying about,' said Lady Arnsworth. 'No, no. It is not to be thought of. Having undertaken to chaperon you, I must not be thinking of my own pleasure!' She leaned over and patted Thea on the knee. Drat! Richard was right. Lady Arnsworth was going to hide behind her chaperonage of Thea as an excuse. But people would know... Thea felt a jolt of sympathy for the unknown countess. Richard liked her. Richard was determined that his aunt should attend the christening, not simply because of potential damage to the family name and status, but because he was fond of his sister-in-law and didn't want her hurt.

But what could she do to help? It would take a very strong motive to shift Lady Arnsworth from London to Kent... Thea gulped. The reason that occurred was devious if not downright shabby. It might, however, take the trick.

What had Richard said of his sister-in-law? *Verity suffered enough with her own family.*

No matter the shabbiness of the stratagem, Lady Arnsworth must not refuse to attend. The gossip if she did so would be horrific.

'I have always heard that Blakeney is very lovely,' said Thea thoughtfully. 'I wonder if Rich—er, Mr Blakehurst, will return before the christening? I understand he has been asked to stand as godfather. He seems very happy about it.' She heaved an audible sigh. 'I dare say *you* will very much miss having him about the house.'

She found that she was holding her breath. Would the bait be snapped up? Or had she overdone it?

Lady Arnsworth was looking at her in a very startled fashion. 'Ah, yes. Yes. Of course.' A slight pause. 'You know, dear—Blakeney *is* very lovely at this time of the year. A shame to miss it.'

'I should so much like to see Blakeney one day,' said Thea, injecting a tone of wistfulness into her voice.

'Oh. Well, I suppose…of course…' Her ladyship's expression gave new layers of meaning to the word *smug*. 'Richard grew up there, you know.'

'Yes,' murmured Thea.

'And his own estate is not so far off.'

'Richard—I mean, Mr Blakehurst mentioned that he had purchased an estate,' said Thea.

Lady Arnsworth waved dismissively. 'Only a small one.' She sniffed. 'And after all my hopes! He bought it last year, after Max married. He said he had meant to buy his own place for quite some time, but really, there was no need until—' She pursed her lips and gave Thea a considering glance. 'You know, my dear, I do think you must stop calling me Lady Arnsworth and call me Almeria. As Richard does. After all—' She broke off and then started again. 'Ah, yes. Where was I? You know, I dare say that if I were to write and explain the *circumstances,* Blakehurst would be more than happy for you to come to Blakeney. So sad for Richard to be cut out, but one must make the best of it! And I shall depend upon you to choose a suitable christening gift for me. So difficult to know what to buy a boy. For a girl, of course, a gift of jewellery is most appropriate.' She beamed at Thea, and changed the subject. 'I think, dear, that a pretty travelling dress would be in order. So important to make a good first impression. And you ought to take a nap this afternoon. We must have you looking your best, must we not? Yes—a little nap will freshen the colour in your cheeks. You have been looking positively wan the past few days. I am sure Richard has noticed, my dear!'

Clenching her teeth at the grating archness, Thea accepted what she had done—namely, encouraged Lady Arnsworth's...damn! *Almeria*'s...expectations that she and Richard would make a match of it. She shuddered to imagine precisely what circumstances Almeria would explain to Lord Blakehurst.

She sighed. Apparently she was going to attend a house party. Complete with a christening. Which meant that she too had better purchase a christening gift. A thought occurred to her—she would have to tell Richard what she had done to assure Almeria's attendance. She could only hope he would deem the game worthy of the candle. The bitter irony of the fact that she might indeed have been attending the christening as Richard's betrothed seared her like a brand.

A christening. A celebration for the birth of a longed-for child. Lucky child. Pain welled up within her. Somehow, before she left town, she had to find out the truth about her own baby. There had to be a way.

Chapter Nine

Lady Chasewater's ambiguous capitulation exercised Richard's mind all the way down to Blakeney the following day. What other fish did Lady Chasewater have to fry? Had she stirred up the trouble with Bow Street? He pushed the horses hard, changing at each stage, using the horses Max kept stabled between London and Blakeney, and arrived in the early evening.

He walked up from the stables through the gardens to the terrace outside the library. Mellow lamplight poured out of the French doors to spill gold on the stone flags. The doors were closed against the cool evening and he looked in to see Max at his desk, writing. He grinned and rapped on the glass. Max's head jerked up and there was a flurry of barking from the pair of spaniels who had been dozing at his feet.

Max leapt up and strode to the door in the spaniels' wake. He opened it and the dogs shot out, leaping up at Richard, barking in delight.

'Get off, you idiots,' he said, bending to pat them. 'Calm down.'

'Speaking of idiots,' said his twin, 'what in Hades are you doing here?' The huge grin on his face belied the words.

Richard laughed. 'Don't gammon me, Max. You knew damned well I'd be down. Congratulations. When am I allowed to see my godson?'

Max gripped his hand. 'As soon as you like. We were expecting you. In fact you've lost me a wager with Verity. She would have it that you'd be down by tonight—*I* credited you with more sense and bet on tomorrow.'

Ten minutes later Richard was staring down into a carved wooden cradle at a ridiculously small swathed bundle with a shock of black hair. A watchful nurse sat knitting by the fire surrounded by racks of drying cloths.

'He's tiny,' he said, awed.

'Eight and a half pounds is not tiny,' Max informed him drily.

Richard shook his head in wonderment at the sleeping baby. 'And Verity? She is well, your letter said.'

'Yes. Exhausted, but well. She's sleeping now. That's why I was down in the library.' The relief in Max's voice hinted at the knife edge of recent fear. Max reached into the cradle and lifted his son out very carefully. 'Would you care to hold him? He was fed not long ago, so he's unlikely to wake.'

Richard took the child with shattering care. So little, so light. Ridiculously long, dark lashes lay on red cheeks. A tiny hand, with nails like pale pink shells, peeped out of the top of the wrappings. Inside him some strange new emotion swelled and burst in benediction. His nephew, hopefully only the first of a string of nephews and nieces who would add to Max and Verity's joy. For the first time in his life, he felt envy for what his twin had. No. Not envy—a bitter, poisonous draught, that. There had never been envy between them. No, this was a longing, a yearning to experience the same deep joy and peace he could see in Max's face.

He looked up to find Max watching him, wry amusement glinting in the amber eyes. 'It's a bit like that, isn't it?' said Max. 'I may become accustomed to it some time in the next ten years or so.'

Richard looked from his brother to his nephew and back. 'Or not?' he suggested.

Max laughed. 'Or not,' he agreed.

* * *

Thea tossed restlessly in her bed, haunted by the memory of Richard's joy at the birth of his nephew. Folly! she berated herself, to lose sleep over a dream, a might-have-been. She had a far more pressing problem—how to discover the truth about her baby and not alert Aberfield to her suspicions. This was reality and only she could face it and resolve it. Imperceptibly pallid grey light banished the darkness, bringing cold counsel with the dawn. The only person who would know the whole truth now was her father. And Aberfield would never tell her. He would lie without hesitation if it suited him. Somehow she needed to find out for herself.

Lord Aberfield's butler opened the door to her and stared in surprise.

'Miss Thea!' Carnely said. 'Are you come to visit his lord-ship? I am afraid he has just left.'

Since Thea, watching from the drawing-room window of Arnsworth House across the square, had seen her father not ten minutes ago leaving in his curricle, this did not come as a surprise.

'Oh, dear,' she said mendaciously. 'Will he be long?'

Carnely looked genuinely sorry. 'He's gone out to Richmond for two nights, Miss Thea. I can send one of the grooms if it's urgent.'

Thea shook her head. 'No need for that, Carnely. I shall leave him a note to find when he returns. I'm sure there must be pen and ink in the library.'

'Of course,' said Carnely. 'I shall send some tea and cakes to the library.'

Curse the fellow! Why did he have to be so beastly well trained? How on earth did anyone ever manage to burgle a fash-ionable residence with servants dripping from the chandeliers, offering cake and cups of tea at every turn?

'No, thank you, Carnely. I'll just write the note. That will be all.'

'Very good, Miss Thea.'

Once inside the library she closed the door, turned the key and stared around the well-remembered room. How she *hated* it!

She could almost feel Aberfield's presence in the ordered rows of books, the painfully tidy desk, not a paper out of place. Controlled. Disapproving. As though it knew what she was doing. She steadied her nerves. It was only a room. It could neither know, nor betray her purpose.

Her conscience informed her in no uncertain terms that what she intended went well beyond shabby this time and into the realm of the utterly dishonourable. She gave her conscience short shrift, consigning it to oblivion. Not terribly successfully, but an occasional twinge wasn't going to stop her now.

Where should she look first? What was she looking for?

She looked at the *bureau plat* with loathing. Everything perfectly ordered, the standish set just so. Aberfield was the sort of man who never spilt the inkpot and whose pen never sputtered. Methodical, organised… Her eye fell on a ledger placed neatly in the centre of his desk. She opened it…it was his accounts book, detailing expenditure… Her mind raced. If Aberfield were supporting an illegitimate child there would be expenses at regular intervals…the quarter days. She checked the date on the book. Yes. This was the book for this year, 1823. So…swallowing hard, she turned the pages, forcing herself to read the entries and dates…here it was, March 25th, Lady Day. Her entire body felt cold, frozen to the marrow, despite the fact that a fire still crackled in the grate and the room was warm… Her finger ran down the list of quarterly expenses: bills, servants wages…her own allowance, David's allowance, and—a payment to Miss Dale's Seminary for the Daughters of Gentlemen. The cold inside her spread further, leaching out from the dark. A quarter's fees for SG. So; she knew something already—the child was a daughter, with initials SG.

There were other explanations. The child need not be hers. It could be David's. Or even Aberfield's. She clutched at the frail hope. Yes, that would be the answer. David's child. No. David would look after his own child. More likely Aberfield himself. She needed more information. This ledger only had the current year's expenses.

She found the ledgers for previous years easily enough in a neat row in a bookcase near the desk. Pulling out the last one, she discovered that sure enough, it was for the previous year. A quick glance at the quarter days revealed payments to Miss Dale's Seminary for SG at Christmas and Michaelmas.

At the midsummer quarter day there was a change in the pattern. A final payment, together with an extra amount noted as a bonus was paid to a Mistress Kate Parsons for… 'the succour and housing of SG'. And something else '…monies paid for the removal of SG from…' her eyes widened '…Kelfield to Bath.'

Ice condensed in her stomach, a hard painful lump. Kelfield was only a few miles from Wistow, where she had lived with Aunt Maria. No. It was not possible. They had *told* her…

Shaking, mired in disbelief, Thea took down more ledgers. She had to trace those payments to their beginning. If they went back too far…or not far enough…either way she would have her answer. Year by year she traced the payments back through the ledgers until she could find no more. Fear, nausea, shuddered through her as she confirmed the dates in the last ledger. It couldn't be. Perhaps he had missed a couple of quarters… Frantically she checked the ledger for 1815. Nothing. The payments began at the end of March 1816…seven years ago.

Seven years ago. Within days, *days* of… She choked off the memory. *NO!* She wouldn't believe it! She couldn't, mustn't think about it. Fear rose up, choking her. And with it, the memory of pain. Terrible, racking, rhythmic agony, laced with shame…and Aunt Maria's cold voice reminding her of the wages of sin… And later, when she recovered consciousness, the rector, reading her that passage from Exodus about the iniquities of the fathers being visited upon the children…and the child of David and Bathsheba—struck down for his parents' sin…

Shaking, she checked another date in the 1816 ledger…back and forth in the adjacent pages, until she found something…monies paid to Aunt Maria for engaging the services of a midwife…she shivered, remembering…a doctor…and the rector? Why would the rector of the parish need to be paid if the baby had died without baptism? She looked again at the detailed amounts: twenty pounds to the midwife, fifty pounds to the doctor and another fifty pounds to the rector. The amounts were staggering for the services rendered. Unless they were bribes … Aberfield would have paid well to hide the family's shame.

With clumsy, shaking hands she replaced the ledgers, making sure they went back in the correct order. Where to look next? Her numbed brain moved slowly. Where did he keep letters, correspondence?

A row of deed boxes on top of the bookshelves caught her gaze. Squinting up, she moved along the bottom of the bookshelves. They were all clearly labelled. Swiftly she scanned them…SG. Shifting the ladder was the work of a moment and she had the box in her hands.

She sat down at the desk and stared at the box.

A quiet, eminently reasonable voice whispered to her: *Do you really want to know? You could put it back. No one need know.*

But if she put it back…she might never have another chance to slip in here. And she already knew the truth…there was no possible explanation beyond the one pounding in her brain.

Why does it matter anyway? What can you possibly do?

She recognised the calm, reasonable little voice: cowardice, pure and simple.

The box was locked.

For a wild moment Thea contemplated breaking the lock. Madness. Someone might hear it. And even if she got away with it now, the box wasn't dusty. Plainly the maids dusted up there regularly; even if they didn't, Aberfield would discover it the moment he needed that box.

Footsteps in the hall panicked her. Her heart slammed against her ribs. If she were caught with the ledgers and Aberfield found out…if he realised that she knew… Shaking, she scrambled back up the ladder, replacing the box exactly as it had been. She had still to write some sort of note to explain her having been in here.

She frowned, pulling paper and the standish towards her. Dipping the pen in the ink, she pondered…something plausible…some concern about the unpleasant rumour that Nigel Lallerton's death had not after all been an accident. She scratched away busily for a moment. Did he know anything of the matter? What else? Ah, yes…the information that she was to be invited to a house party—that would round it out nicely. Swiftly she sprinkled sand on the note and glanced around. Was everything in place? Nothing to suggest she had done anything but write a note to him? Nervously she adjusted the position of the current ledger to the exact centre of the desk. Folly! If he did note anything a trifle out of place he'd think it had been bumped when the maid dusted.

She sealed the note and left it propped against the standish, addressed simply: Aberfield.

Richard spent two full days at Blakeney, leaving after an early breakfast on the third morning.

'Why not stay down longer, Ricky?' urged Max over a final cup of coffee. 'You know you are welcome here, and your house is nearly ready, I understand. No need to go back.'

Richard shook his head. 'I've a few things left undone.' An understatement if ever there was one—something about his brief encounter with Lady Chasewater had left him very suspicious of what her next move might be. Quite apart from that, he wouldn't care to wager that Almeria would accept her christening invitation if he wasn't there to bring her up to scratch—which begged the question of where Thea was to go.

He took a deep breath. 'When I return with Almeria for the christening, would you mind very much if her other house-guest came too?'

The suspicion of a smile played about Max's mouth. 'Miss Winslow—Almeria's latest candidate for the position of Mrs Richard Blakehurst? Not at all, since the suggestion comes from you. At least she's found a candidate who can give you a good game of chess this time.'

Richard finished his coffee and stood up, conscious of heat on his cheekbones. There was absolutely nothing in the fact that someone, probably Braybrook, had kept Max informed. Nor that Max had remembered Thea's liking for chess...but that faint, amused smile was unnerving...he resisted the urge to tell Max there was nothing in it, or at least not much. And definitely not as much as he wanted there to be in it.

Richard arrived back in Grosvenor Square that evening to discover that Almeria and Thea had already left for a ball at Monteith House.

'And that was just delivered, Mr Richard,' said Myles, indicating a note on the hall table. 'For Miss Thea and marked urgent, it is. Her brother's man brought it around. Very distressed, he was.'

'Distressed? What about?'

'He wouldn't say. Just that I was to see Miss Thea received the note.' Myles looked uncertain. 'I did wonder if I ought to send the note around to Monteith House, but if it's bad news—' He left the sentence unfinished.

Richard frowned. 'I'll take it. I'll go up and change. Have some hot water sent up.'

He arrived at Monteith House to find the ball in full flight. Judging by the cacophony, everyone who was anyone was in attendance. Weaving his way through the crowded rooms and halls, he exchanged brief greetings with several acquaintances.

'Excellent news, old man!' said one friend, clapping him on the back.

'Er, yes. I'm delighted,' said Richard, wondering how Barnstable had heard about the baby. Almeria must have talked, he supposed.

Another voice broke in. 'Richard! Richard Blakehurst! How delightful! Congratulations, dear boy. And, of course, dear Almeria is in *alt!*'

Every nerve and instinct suggested that now would be a good time to bolt as he politely acknowledged the Dowager Lady Whinlatter. 'Good evening, ma'am. I am afraid, though, that I have not the least idea why I am to be congratulated.'

She laughed. An arch, tinkling sound that made Richard wonder if Whinlatter had cocked up his toes merely to escape it.

'Now, Richard! You must not think to pull wool over my old eyes! Such an old friend of Almeria's as I am! And I am *sure* Lady Chasewater must be mistaken, and that Miss Winslow is everything delightful…'

He only just managed to choke his natural response into submission. Instead, 'I *beg* your pardon?'

Her conspiratorial smile broadened. 'Well, of course I know nothing is *settled,* Richard,' she said, tapping his arm with her fan. 'And naturally, Almeria did not precisely *say* anything, even to me, but of course one *understood!*'

He dragged in a breath—prepared to deny everything categorically—and let it go again. What was he supposed to deny, without adding fuel to the gossip that was doubtless burning unchecked? What the *devil* was Almeria about? Not to mention Lady Chasewater. Extricating himself from Lady Whinlatter's fulsome delight without actually committing himself took several minutes of tact and diplomacy, but he was finally free and headed for the ballroom, smiling at people as he slipped past, but not stopping for so much as a 'good evening'.

He was a trifle late. From the top of the stairs leading down to the ballroom, he could see that the dancing was already underway. He needed to find Thea. His eyes found her almost immediately. Waltzing. With Dunhaven. He went cold all over and could only thank God it wasn't a waltz.

'Ah, Richard. Congratulations, old chap.'

Richard turned, reminding himself that punching Tom Fielding on the nose would not only create a scandal, but would be highly unfair.

'For what?' he asked irritably, looking back at Thea. Even at this distance her pallor struck to the heart. Nothing else betrayed her—just that balanced, expressionless mask.

Aberfield stood waiting nearby, watching them. The chill of warning intensified. Something was afoot here…he had to get to her.

'Er, your betrothal?' His attention snapped back to Fielding. 'What!'

Fielding gave the impression of backing up without actually moving an inch. 'Charming girl and all that.'

'And who told you I was betrothed?'

Fielding visibly relaxed. 'Oh, secret, was it? Well, everyone's talking about it. And although Lady Chasewater's sayin' no man of honour would have Miss Winslow for double the money—no one's takin' her seriously, mind you.'

'I see,' he said, his brain working furiously. This, then, must be what Lady Chasewater had meant by having tastier fish to fry. Hell and damnation. If she was now openly destroying Thea's character between sips of ratafia, to deny a betrothal would be tantamount to pouring oil on the blaze. He had to say enough to avoid committing himself, yet not so much that he gave the least credence to Lady Chasewater's attack on Thea.

'Yes, well, this is all rather premature, Tom,' he said calmly.

'What? Oh, yes—no announcement yet? I take you.' Fielding grinned comfortably. 'M'mother knows, of course. Well, I had to have some reason for not pursuing the woman! A trifle put out that I've let another eligible bride slip past, but never mind. Always another one.' He looked at Richard carefully. 'Something the matter with your teeth, old chap?'

To his horror, Richard realised that the loud crunching noise just happened to be his own teeth grinding. 'One infers, then, that your interest in Miss Winslow was purely pecuniary, Fielding?'

'What? Oh, lord, yes! Nothing personal, take my word for it. Charming girl, but not quite my style. And seeing you smitten—'

'Seeing me *what?*'

'Er, is that—yes, it is! Excuse me, old fellow. Have to dash.' He gave Richard a clap on the shoulder. 'Chappie over there I simply must see! Do hope Miss Winslow enjoys her stay at Blakeney, and m'mother says to congratulate you!'

And with that, Fielding hurled himself into the crowd.

Leaving Richard in a state of total confusion. How the hell did Fielding know about Thea's prospective visit to Blakeney?

And what the devil had been going on to give so many the impression that a betrothal was imminent?

By the time the dance ended, several more people had offered oblique congratulations to him and it was only the glimpse of Lady Chasewater, seated on a chaise at the side of the room, that had prevented Richard from denying the betrothal. Loudly. The old woman's eyes were blazing with triumph.

'Thank God, you're back!' came a relieved voice and he turned to find Julian Braybrook at his elbow. 'There's been a most unfortunate development.'

'Oh, really?' That was one way of putting it.

'Winslow was arrested earlier for the murder of Lallerton.'

Richard went cold all over. The note burning in his pocket was explained if Winslow had been arrested, and every instinct urged him to find Thea. Fast. He knew now what fish Lady Chasewater had been frying.

The end of the dance came at last, and Thea, every nerve raw, stepped back out of Lord Dunhaven's arms.

He reacted swiftly, imprisoning her hand and clamping it on his arm. 'You will honour me with your company at supper, of course,' he said. 'I believe your father plans to join us.'

Nausea churned. Somehow she had maintained her self-control during the dance, but she had reached her limit. Forcing calmness and a smile, she said, 'How lovely. But if your lordship might excuse me for a few moments? I…I need to retire. I will join you as soon as I can.'

He looked at her consideringly. 'Of course, my dear,' he said at last, and released her.

Quickly, she slipped away through the crowd, making for the supper room.

Monteith House was huge, but Thea had visited there often as a child and knew it well enough to find her way out into the garden from the library. With a sigh of relief, she leaned against the wall of the house and breathed the soft fragrance of the garden. The roar of the gathering inside was strangely muted.

Just a few moments and she would go back.

'What a charming spot you have found, my dear.'

Thea's blood congealed at the soft purr, as she realised too late what a fool she had been to come out here.

He was between her and the door back inside.

'Lord Dunhaven,' she infused her tone with ice, 'this is most improper. You should not have followed me out here.'

He shrugged. 'What does it matter? We are to be married, are we not? Your father has given me his blessing. All that remains, my dear, is to decide the wedding date.'

His arrogance stiffened her, banishing fear and replacing it with coruscating fury. Controlling it, she said lightly, 'I think there is something you have omitted, my lord. Is it not traditional to ask the woman if she wishes to marry you?'

'If you wish, but we both know you have little choice. Very few men would be prepared to overlook your…state, shall we say?' His voice mocked. 'So, my dear; will you make me the happiest of men and consent to be my wife?'

'No, my lord. I will not. Now if you will excuse me—'

'I think not, Miss Winslow,' he said. 'Perhaps you have failed to understand your situation. You have obviously not heard the news? Such a tragedy it will be for your family if someone with the right connections does not step in.' His smile was all teeth and triumph.

Thea fiddled with her reticule. 'What news is this?'

'Why, your brother, my dear,' he said. 'Such a hurried note I received from Aberfield this evening—of course, if we act quickly it will all come to naught, but naturally I could not possibly have cause to intervene at Bow Street without a *family* connection.'

'Bow Street?' She summoned indifference to cover the frantic pounding of her heart, the chill fear that clogged her brain. 'And what has that to do with me?'

'Oh, not you, my dear,' he told her. 'Your brother—arrested early this evening for the murder of Nigel Lallerton, and it would be so unfortunate if *your* little indiscretion with Lallerton were to leak out. Such a powerful motive for murder, is it not?'

'What are you suggesting?' Her lips felt cold and stiff.

He shrugged. 'It's simple enough; your father and I have agreed on the match, and that is precisely what is going to happen. You have no choice. Naturally, as your betrothed I will use my influence at Bow Street on your brother's behalf.' He smirked. 'For which service your father is disposed to be *most* generous in the marriage settlements.'

Thea sucked in a breath. It was just possible that he was lying, but not likely. Could she get away with agreeing to a betrothal, and then jilting him once David was safe? She shuddered. Too risky. He would sue for breach of promise and take half her fortune. She couldn't risk that. Not now. There was the child to provide for.

'You will understand, sir,' she said carefully, backing away and trying to ease around towards the house, 'that I would prefer to discuss this with you at a more appropriate time.'

'No doubt,' he said, closing the distance. 'Your father warned me about that though, so my preference is for here and now.' He lunged for her just as she dodged. Her foot slipped and she found her wrist caught in a brutal grip.

'We'll settle this now,' he told her, hauling her close.

She fought him, kicking and scratching as he tried to force her away from the house, further into the garden. His odour nearly overwhelmed her; rank and sour, it was worse than during the dance, and the light from the library gleamed on a trickle of sweat at his temple.

She bit his hand savagely as he tried to clamp it over her mouth, and, twisting to face him, brought her knee up hard. She missed, striking his thigh, but he jerked back.

'*Bitch!*'

His grip loosened and she tore free, whirling to run.

He caught her again, but, even as she dragged in her breath to scream, a voice sheathed in ice lashed through the night.

'*Take your hands off her, Dunhaven.*'

Framed in the glow from the library two tall figures stood. One came forward, his steps slightly uneven.

'What the hell's it to you, Blakehurst?' snarled Dunhaven, but his hand dropped from Thea's wrist.

She cradled it, and saw the flare of rage in Richard's face. Saw the lines of his face harden to steel.

He came forward and without hesitation she went to him. 'Are you all right?' His voice was harsh, raw, strangely at odds with the gentle, shaking touch of his fingers on her cheek.

She nodded. 'Yes, but he says David has been arrested. He—'

'Tried to use it as a lever?'

She nodded again and Richard realised that his control hung by a single, burning thread, stretched to breaking point. He reminded himself that calling Dunhaven out would inflame the rumours already circulating. That the news of Winslow's arrest would just about blow the lid off an already bubbling pot.

'Obviously the word "gentleman" has not the least resonance for you, Dunhaven,' said Richard. 'I suggest you get out of here before I lose my temper.'

'Does the fact that I have her father's permission—?'

'Not unless you have hers, Dunhaven,' said Richard coldly. 'And in my understanding, when a woman uses that last trick, her permission is unlikely to be granted.'

'A whore's trick!' spat Dunhaven. 'Used by a soiled little dove, who's already been—'

The rest of Dunhaven's vitriol was lost as Richard's fist slammed into his jaw, sending him staggering backwards against the balustrade.

Swearing sulphurously, Dunhaven struggled up, his fists clenched, an ugly look on his face.

Braybrook stepped in. 'That will be enough for now. Dunhaven—you will accompany me back into the house.'

'The hell he will,' said Richard softly. 'Take Miss Winslow back inside, please, Braybrook.'

Thea's eyes widened at his voice. Deathly quiet, it rang with suppressed violence.

Terror shot through her as she realised where this was going. No! Not Richard too. She couldn't let him!

She dragged in a breath, but Lord Braybrook spoke first.

'No, Ricky. Leave it! It will cause even more gossip if she's seen coming back in with me!' He turned to Dunhaven. 'After you, Dunhaven.' He spoke quietly, but his voice held the ring of cold, tempered steel.

Breathing heavily, Dunhaven obeyed, cradling his fast-swelling jaw.

Relief sighed out of Thea. They were going to let it drop, thank God!

Richard's voice lashed out. 'Don't think you've heard the last of this, Dunhaven.'

His meaning ripped into Thea; he still intended to call Dunhaven out.

His lordship looked around. 'If you think it worthwhile, Blakehurst,' he spat out. 'I assure you, I wouldn't.'

He turned and strode back inside.

Braybrook glanced back. 'Don't stay out too long, Ricky,' he said, and followed Dunhaven.

Shaking, Thea turned to face Richard, her breath catching as though on powdered glass at the thought of the whole tragedy unfolding again. Whatever the cost, she had to stop this now.

She was safe. Richard felt some of the riptide ebb. Then he looked at Thea properly and it surged again. Even in the poor light he could see that she was blanched, her eyes huge and strained in her pale face. Her gown, although not torn, was dishevelled. Carefully, refusing to let himself dwell on what he was doing, he began to put it to rights with deft, gentle touches. She stood quite still, her eyes on his face. He could feel her gaze even as he concentrated on his task. Feel the fear and panic leaving her, as he fought the instinct to gather her into his arms and just hold her.

At last, he said, 'That's better. And now—' He dragged in a ragged breath. 'What the devil were you thinking?' he growled. 'To come out here with a loose screw like Dunhaven!'

'I didn't come out with him,' she said. 'I came out alone. I…I didn't feel well, so I slipped away. I don't know how he found me.'

'The same way we found him, no doubt,' said Richard savagely. 'Asked a servant. Are you sure you're all right?'

She nodded. 'Yes. Just…cold.' Her voice shook.

Stifling the urge to take her in his arms and warm her, he said curtly, 'Then we had best go back inside.' He couldn't answer for his own control if he touched her again.

'Richard?'

'Yes?'

'Please don't call him out. Please. It's not worth it. Promise me.'

'Forget about it, Thea,' he said gently. 'No challenge has been issued.' .

She came to him then, laying her gloved hand on his arm. He stiffened, the light touch, muffled by kid gloves and his coat and shirt, searing bone-deep. Even as his blood leapt, her other hand lifted hesitantly to his chest.

'Thea,' he whispered. Just that—her name breathed over soft fragrant curls as he covered the trembling hand with his, holding it captive over his pounding heart. He abandoned the struggle and his other arm went around her, instinctively drawing her into his warmth, cradling her against his aching body.

'Richard, please don't call him out.'

He didn't answer the plea. Holding her was so sweet. He gathered her closer, resting his cheek on her hair.

'Richard—promise me!' Her voice broke on a sob.

He took a very careful breath, cursing himself for being such a fool as to make his intentions plain in front of her. Now she was frightened for him.

'Give me one good reason why I shouldn't,' he said grimly.

He felt her go utterly still, every fibre of her being frozen in his arms. Then came a shuddering breath.

'One good reason?' she asked, her voice a mere thread. 'Just one? And if I give it to you, will you swear to let this drop? That you'll not challenge him?'

'That would depend on the reason,' he answered. There was no answer that he could think of that would change his mind.

She pulled away and reluctantly he let her go. The soft curve of her mouth trembled, making him long to drag her back and cover her lips with his own, kissing her senseless until she agreed to be his.

She took another ragged breath, that pierced him to the core.

'It is the same as the reason why I cannot possibly marry you,' she said steadily. 'Or any other man like you.'

He went very still. 'Like me?'

Her gaze never wavered as she said, 'A man of honour.' Her voice sounded dead, bereft of all expression. 'Lord Dunhaven spoke only the truth when he called me a…a soiled little dove, Richard.'

Chapter Ten

She stepped back, drawing away from him, and, totally confused, he let her go.

Now her gaze did falter. She looked away and said simply, 'I am not a virgin, Richard. That is why I have never married and why I refused your offer.'

Shock slammed into him. Of all the reasons she might have given for not marrying him, that one had never even crossed his mind. What the hell was he supposed to say? By every tenet of society, unless he took a widow to wife, he had every right to expect that his wife would come to him untouched.

His brain whirled. So much now made sense. Her unwillingness to marry. Lady Chasewater's bitterness…Winslow's arrest. God! What a coil! Of course at the time it would not have seemed such a terrible thing. The betrothal had been announced—the marriage imminent. It probably happened more often than one would think. Only this time it had gone horribly wrong, because David Winslow had found out and quarrelled with Lallerton over it.

According to society's rules, his reaction was laid out for him…

A little voice murmured in a corner of his mind: *Thou shalt not be found out.* Society's unspoken, immutable law.

He glanced across at Thea. She looked white, her underlip

gripped firmly between her teeth. His heart clenched. He forced himself to look at the situation logically.

He wasn't a virgin himself. And no one jumped up and down about his lack of chastity. Except Almeria, of course, and even she had only ever glared daggers at whichever of society's widows he happened to be bedding at any time. More, he suspected, because she had feared he might one day offer marriage to one of them.

What the hell should he say? She had been honest with him. Brutally honest. She could have accepted his offer and said nothing. Instead, she had refused it because her honour demanded it. And she had only told him now to stop him issuing a challenge to a man who had insulted her.

He looked at her again and his heart ached as he saw the glistening silver track on her cheek. Just one, where a single tear had escaped. She expected him to condemn her for a single misstep in her youth? When he had made the same step over and over?

What should he say? There was only one thing he could say in all fairness. He went to her and reached out to wipe away another tear.

'Neither am I, Thea.'

She flinched slightly at his touch, but then turned to face him and he saw the pain in her eyes. And confusion.

'I…I beg your pardon? Neither are you what?'

'A virgin,' he said. He managed a smile. 'Thea, it was Lallerton?'

She nodded wordlessly.

'And this is why you have never married?'

Again she nodded.

'We had better return to the house,' he said quietly. What was the point of averting one scandal, only to cause another, if they were caught out here? His brain had numbed anyway, refusing to think at all, let alone rationally.

Carefully he asked, 'Were you aware, by the way, that the news of our betrothal is the latest item of gossip?'

'*What?* But we aren't!'

'So far three people have congratulated me on it,' he told her. 'Apart from this coil, what the devil have you been up to?'

'Almeria,' she whispered. 'But it's all *my* fault.'

Sick understanding washed through her. She had allowed their godmother to believe that there was an understanding between them. Almeria had doubtless told just one or two of her dearest friends—in strictest confidence, of course. And, equally of course, no doubt with many an arch smile and discreetly fluttering fan, the story had been wafted on its way, to be further enlivened by Lady Chasewater's innuendoes.

'Just what did you do?' The tone of bland enquiry did little to disguise the steel behind the question.

She met Richard's eyes. 'I…I gave Almeria to understand that I…that I would miss you when you left for Blakeney—that I had heard how lovely Blakeney is, how much I would like to see it one day, and…and…I think…she believed that—' In the face of his patent disbelief, she burst out, 'Damn you, Richard! I was trying to find a way of persuading her to attend your nephew's christening, and that was all I could think of! Some way to give her an excuse to go so that she wouldn't lose face over it!'

'I beg your pardon?' Tone and expression were unreadable.

'I'm sorry, Richard. I never imagined this would happen. She must have told people, and—'

'You have persuaded Almeria to go to Blakeney?'

She nodded.

'Why?'

Fellow feeling for your sister-in-law. She thrust that response back into the shadows.

'You were worried about the Countess and the potential gossip if Almeria refused to attend. How it would hurt *her*—not how it would affect your brother's standing, or the family—'

'Just how it would hurt Verity,' said Richard softly. 'But why should *you* care? You've never even met her, Thea.'

Thea shook her head. 'No, but you like her. Don't you?'

He smiled. 'Yes. I'm very fond of Verity.'

She went on, 'And you once said she had borne enough from her own family…so, I…I just wanted to help. I'm sorry, Richard.'

He shook his head. 'No. Don't be sorry, Thea. Getting Almeria to Blakeney is a major victory. Worth any amount of embarrassment.' He frowned. 'To me, anyway. But you, Thea—this rumour—we can deny it, but it's bound to be damaging. To you more than to me.'

She shrugged. 'If I don't care, why should you?'

His glare was a revelation. 'Because you, or I, would be labelled a jilt. Probably you, since Lady Chasewater is doing her best to ruin you! Can't you just hear them? *Running true to form…* And I do care about that!'

Her hands were taken in a strong grip, and she found herself moving towards him again. Close enough that the sharpness of his cologne breathed about her with the scents drifting up from the garden, close enough that she felt surrounded, enveloped by his presence, by his sheer caring. It was a potent spell, woven of moonlight, fragrance and the gentle pressure of his fingers, and bound together by the ache in her heart that longed to sink into it.

Her mind fought free of the spell. He shouldn't care! Not like that. Not as though he cared about *her,* rather than the likely damage to his own reputation. Safer if he didn't care, if he read her a lecture on the dangers of…of deceit and…and loss of reputation, rather than looking and sounding as though he cared about Thea Winslow, who was not at all the sort of female he should care about.

And he certainly shouldn't be holding her hands like this and leaning forward…and nor should she be simply standing here, waiting, waiting for his lips to brush hers. Not just waiting, but yearning…

'*My goodness me!* Oh! Oh, good heavens! Oh, it's you, Richard.'

Hell's teeth! Instinctively Richard stepped across Thea, sheltering her from view with his body. And realised that he had effectually taken her into his arms—in front of Lady Jersey, who looked as if she had been granted a high treat.

'Really, I couldn't quite make out what Lord Dunhaven was saying,' said Lady Jersey, her bright gaze flickering between them. 'Which might have had something to do with his jaw—it did look a trifle swollen.' Briefly her glance touched Richard's grazed knuckles. 'He seemed to feel there was some impropriety, but since you and Miss Winslow—' She waved airily, 'Well, it's no bread and butter of mine!'

Resisting the temptation to swear loud and long, Richard placed Thea's hand on his arm and said to Lady Jersey, 'I fear Miss Winslow has just received some very disquieting news, ma'am. You will understand she did not feel capable of discussing it in the ballroom.'

Lady Jersey looked intrigued. 'Oh? I am so sorry, Miss Winslow. Shall we all stroll back together? And, of course, I must wish you happy!'

Thea's fingers tightened on his arm, and he brought his other hand across to cover them. Whether the gesture was one of affection or protectiveness, he had no idea. All he knew was that it felt right. That the shocking idea that he was betrothed to Thea, like it or not, felt anything but shocking. And why should it? He had asked her to marry him days ago. Only, he had not quite intended a public announcement of this nature.

Lady Jersey kept up a flow of chatter as they made their way back through the house towards the ballroom. Richard suppressed with difficulty the instinct to throttle her. Better if they did look to have been chaperoned, and from the sound of her chatter the countess was disposed to be lenient with this breach of propriety. But he had that damned note in his pocket—somehow he had to give it to Thea.

They stepped into the ballroom and there, just inside, stood Lord Aberfield. Bitter resignation stood in the faded eyes, and scorn curled the thin lips.

'My congratulations, Mr Blakehurst.' His voice cut through the murmuring to an expectant silence. 'Of course, in my day it was considered polite to ask a father's consent. Which Lord Dunhaven had obtained.'

Banked fury leapt to blazing life. Richard fought it down and said in tones of cool courtesy, 'So I understand, my lord. He forgot the most important thing, however—the lady's consent. An offer of marriage is just that: an offer. It suggests that a refusal is possible.'

Almeria hurried up. 'Dorothea! I have just heard the news about poor David! Dreadful! But I understand Lord Braybrook and Sir Francis have the matter in hand—oh! Good evening, Lord Aberfield. Such a shocking thing—but I am quite persuaded it is a simple misunderstanding—naturally my *other* nephew, Earl Blakehurst, will look into it also should it become necessary.'

Aberfield's teeth grated. 'I assure you, I'm counting on it, ma'am.' He did not look as though the promised interest of that particular earl afforded him the least satisfaction.

In the quiet of her bedchamber, Thea looked back on the utterly disastrous evening. David had been arrested and society believed her to be betrothed to Richard Blakehurst. A rumour her father had deliberately confirmed. She understood why—Earl Blakehurst's influence was far-reaching. He was unlikely to sit back and twiddle his thumbs while a potential scandal threatened to wash over his family.

Only she wasn't family. Nor had she the least claim on Richard beyond this insane false betrothal.

False from her perspective, that is.

She knew his sense of honour well enough to realise that, as far as he was concerned, the betrothal would stand. He had made that quite plain in the few moments he had taken with her in the hall after Almeria bid them goodnight—in the sort of absent-minded tone that suggested she was already planning the nuptials.

'Thea—it is not so bad as all that. You must know that for me to draw back would seriously damage you. We can sort it out, away from prying eyes, at Blakeney.'

He had held her hand for a moment and said, 'Promise me that you will not repudiate the betrothal yet, Thea. Let us discuss it rationally down at Blakeney. You already know that I wish to marry you. That I am not standing by this betrothal out of duty.' And when she hesitated, 'Come—would I really be that terrible a husband?'

Mutely, she shook her head.

'Then, I have your promise?'

He was still asking, assuming, forcing nothing. Except what he perceived to be for her own safety.

'V...very well.' It was all she could get out.

His smile was the sort that ought to have been outlawed. Relief, tenderness, and comfort tore at her heart.

'You honour me with your trust, sweetheart,' he said quietly.

Before she could answer, he had feathered a gentle kiss over her cheek and left her.

Even now her fingers stole over the place his lips had brushed. *Sweetheart.* How could such a simple endearment shred all her defences and leave her longing for nothing more than to hear him say it again?

He had given her that note from David, too, apologising for not giving it to her sooner. Her fingers closed on it convulsively.

Aberfield. He considered the matter closed. He thought that her money would be enough for any gentleman to overlook the fact that he was receiving *soiled goods*. Maybe to some men the money would be sufficient—but she didn't want a man like that. Blinking back tears, she acknowledged what she did want—someone who would believe her, someone willing to accept her as she was. Someone who loved her.

The tears leaked from beneath her tightly closed eyelids. She wanted Richard, who was probably resigned to the marriage because he was fond of her and needed a wife. But what if in the end, despite his kindness and tolerance, he came to resent her? There was no point even wondering. What she planned to do in the morning would see to that. The final words in David's brief note were seared into her...

On no account, Thea, are you to do anything foolish. I am perfectly safe and this will all blow over soon enough. You are to remain out of it...

But what if it didn't blow over? She could not take that risk.

She slipped into bed, blowing out the candle. Past three, and sleep seemed impossible. Her mind lurched back to the struggle with Dunhaven. Sweat broke out on her body and nausea roiled her stomach, as though she could still smell his breath, feel his hand fumbling at her breast, taste his foul breath as he forced her mouth open. Forcing her memories open...

If Richard had not come...but he had come. She was safe. Safe as long as she remained awake.

Her eyelids felt heavy...she drifted on the verge of sleep... and jerked herself back. She mustn't sleep. Not now. Not tonight. She didn't dare. Despite her body aching with exhaustion, she forced herself to keep thinking, putting off the moment when she must sleep...

Nightmare raked her with black claws, draining her of strength. She fought it, struggling for her voice, choking on her terror...

'*Thea...Thea!*'

Loud knocking punctuated the harsh voice. She sat up, flinging off the clinging shreds of fear, aware that she was sweating, her heart beating frantically.

The knocking came again.

'Y...yes?'

The door opened and Richard, in his nightrail and dressing robe, came in bearing a candle. Swiftly he closed the door behind him. She stared. He was out of breath, as though he had been running, and came across the room with a quick, uneven stride. Perhaps Almeria was unwell?

She clutched the bedclothes to her. 'Is something wrong, Richard?'

He blinked at her as he set the candle down on her bedside table. 'Wrong? Thea, you were screaming. What happened?'

She had been screaming? Shame, embarrassment, flooded her. 'I...I must have had a bad dream.'

He frowned. 'You don't remember?'

She never did. Not really. The details always faded when she woke, leaving only strangling terror. But then, she didn't need to remember the dream. She *knew*. What her dream memory lost, waking memory could supply in endless detail.

Richard's mouth tightened. 'It's all right, sweetheart. Here.' He swept up her dressing gown from a chair and came towards her. Before she could protest, he was wrapping it around her, and pulling up the counterpane to snuggle it securely around her shoulders.

She still felt cold, clammy from the nightmare. She had not dreamed like this for several years, waking terrified, sometimes crying, but with no real memory of the dream beyond paralysing fear.

Richard was sitting beside her on the bed, one arm cradling her. 'Shh. You're safe.' Shocked, she realised that she was still shivering, her breath shuddering through her. Ashamed, she fought for control, trying to still the shaking. 'It's all right, Thea. Just breathe deeply. Come, relax. There's no need to fight it. Nothing can harm you.'

She barely heard the words, just felt the deep, soothing voice, easing her, banishing fear. The strength of the arm holding her against his shoulder. And his hand, stroking her hair, pushing back the tangled, sweaty locks in a gentle hypnotic rhythm. Somewhere at the back of her mind a warning sounded: impropriety. She dismissed it. No one would ever know. And it felt so good, so right, to be held and cared for. Richard's limp and his spare frame, she vaguely realised, were utterly deceptive. One did not expect his strength. On the heels of this realisation came another; that it was not only his physical strength that one tended to overlook—his quietness masked the fierce strength of his will. Men like Dunhaven overlooked him.

Slowly the shaking stopped. Yet he still held her. His own warmth infused her, body and soul. With a shock, she knew that she had not felt this safe for years. That she had become so used to the inner tension of the guard she set on herself that she had forgotten it was there. Until now when, twice in one evening, Richard's arms had banished it to the shadows along with fear.

'Better now?' His voice sounded husky, very close to her ear. His cheek, she realised, was resting on her hair.

'Yes.' It wasn't precisely a lie. She did feel much better. And it was hardly Richard's fault if in her foolishness she wished they could remain like this for longer.

'Good.' He released her and settled her back against the pillows. 'Stay there. I'll be back very soon.'

Her eyes widened. 'Back?'

He smiled. 'Yes. With something to help you sleep.' Gentle fingers brushed her cheek. 'I'll be as quick as I can.'

The door opened and closed behind him.

How had he known? How *could* he know that sometimes after a bad dream sleep would evade her? Her mind churned with questions as she wriggled down further into the feathers. No doubt he had gone to fetch a glass of brandy, or possibly laudanum. She shivered. She ought to have told him that she hated the stuff. The last time anyone had given her laudanum... She pushed the thought away. No doubt Aunt Maria had thought she was helping.

He returned about twenty minutes later with a glass in his hand.

She sat up. 'I don't want laudanum,' she said immediately, as he closed the door.

He raised his brows. 'That's good. I wasn't going to give you any.'

'Oh.' She subsided. Now she thought of it, he wouldn't take this long to pour a couple of drops into a glass of water. Or to pour a glass of brandy. So what ...?

He came to her and sat down on the bed again.

'Hot milk,' he said blandly, holding it out to her. 'I invaded the kitchen.'

'Hot milk?' Instinctively she accepted the glass, feeling its warmth seep into her fingers.

'Hot milk,' he confirmed. 'Much better for you than laudanum.'

'I suppose you dose yourself on hot milk when you can't sleep?' she suggested, between sips.

A husky chuckle greeted this. 'A gentleman, Thea, is supposed to dose himself with brandy.'

She flickered a glance at him. 'You ought not to be here, Richard. If anyone came in...'

He sighed. 'No. I ought not. But never fear; that innocent little glass of milk is our chaperon.'

'*Chaperon?*'

'There's an echo in here somewhere,' he teased. 'Yes, chaperon. Name me just one self-respecting seducer who offers his victim a glass of hot milk! I have it on the best authority that hot milk is considered most unseductive. Now, had I been foolish enough to give you brandy, or laudanum—! As it is, no one will ever believe that I came in with the intent of ravishing you.'

Laughter welled up in Thea, warming her even more effectively than the milk. Except for that tiny jolt of disappointment—that he had *not* wished to ravish her... She swallowed. Where had *that* thought come from? She couldn't possibly *want* him to ravish her. That warmth, unfurling within, wreathed around her certainty, dispelling it.

'That's much better,' said Richard. He stood up carefully. 'Don't forget to brush your teeth again,' he said, further dispelling any idea that there might have been anything more than brotherly concern in his care of her.

'I'm not a child!'

At her outrage his smile deepened. 'I'd noticed. A friendly word of advice, that's all,' he said. 'If you don't, your mouth will feel like the bottom of a birdcage in the morning.'

She had to laugh.

'Is that the voice of experience?'

He grinned. 'Bitter experience, I'm afraid. Only not gained with anything quite so innocent as a glass of hot milk. Goodnight.'

'Goodnight,' she whispered. She would be quite all right now. So why was she holding out her hand to him? Why did she want to cry out, begging him to stay? To hold her again. She was perfectly all right now. She didn't need comfort. Yet it had felt so good in his arms. Warm, cherishing.

A large hand enveloped hers with gentle strength. 'Thea?' As though her unspoken longing had found an answer within him.

She forced her voice to function. 'Thank you, for...for everything.' *For being here. For being you.* But he had to leave. If he were found here, it would trap him.

He bent down. Surprise sang through her. Surprise, but not

fear, as long fingers slid into her hair, tilting her face up to his. Breathless, eyes closed, she waited for his kiss. And it came: warm, firm lips brushing lightly over her temple and brow, and finally, finally, a gentle feathering over her lips. Heat shot through her and she gasped, her lips softening, parting... His hand holding hers shook, she felt the backs of his fingers caress her cheek, her throat. Then he straightened and stood back. Her eyes opened and she saw him watching her, a queer taut expression on his face.

'No more, Thea. This is not...wise.' His voice sounded odd, too. Strained.

But he was right. This was not wise. It was madness.

'Goodnight, Richard.'

He turned to go. Then swung back. 'Thea—I should not have kissed you. I hope that you will not—'

She cut him off. 'I quite understand, Richard, that your offer of marriage is no longer open. You need not fear that I will misconstrue anything.'

His jaw seemed like to crack for a moment. Then, very carefully, 'What I wished to say was that I hoped you would not think I kissed you because what you told me had altered my view of you! Or that I intended to take advantage of it!' He glared at her. 'You have a remarkably unflattering notion of my character!'

He swung around, stalked to the door and left, closing the door behind him with commendable control for a man in what looked to be a considerable temper.

Damn, damn and double damn! A rare bumblebroth he'd made of that.

Richard removed himself and his aching erection from Thea's chamber, after a surreptitious glance into the corridor. He resisted the urge to bang the door. The last thing he needed was to be caught coming out of there dressed in his nightrail and dressing gown. In that sort of situation Almeria wouldn't accept the company of saints as sufficient chaperonage, let alone a glass of hot milk. She'd have them fronting the altar before the ink had dried on the special licence. And God help him if she'd caught him kissing Thea! What in Hades had possessed him?

He reached his own room, dropped his dressing gown on a chair and got back into bed.

He swore and thumped the pillow. He knew what had possessed him: desire, burning like a brand in his gut. He could only thank a merciful God that Thea had been far too upset by her dream to notice the state he was in.

It had been all he could do not to *really* kiss her. And he'd wanted to. Like hell burning. And he'd wanted other things—soft sighs, a silken body shifting beneath him... The violent pain of his arousal pointed out that his desire was not even slightly in the past tense. He still wanted her.

And she, apparently, had not had the least idea of the effect she was having on him. With another curse he leaned out of bed to blow out the candle on the bedside table. Just as well she hadn't realised. After Dunhaven—had that been why she'd dreamed? He grimaced. Having a lecher like Dunhaven sniffing around would be enough to give anyone bad dreams.

Hell's teeth! Just how far had the oily brute been willing to go to force the marriage?

At best, he'd simply been trying to compromise Thea technically. Ruining her reputation in order to give her no choice.

At worst...the thought sickened him, but there were other ways to force an unwilling woman into marriage and Thea would not be the first woman coerced like that. The surge of fury, of sheer primitive rage, that roared through him came as a complete shock. He lay there, shaken, waiting for it to subside. It did. To a steady rolling boil. Ready to erupt again at the least provocation. Thinking about Dunhaven coercing Thea into marriage was more than provocation—it was incendiary.

He forced himself to think of other things...Winslow's arrest...the magistrate's visit the other day. No wonder Thea had been upset. Had she suspected this might happen? Did that mean Winslow *had* killed Lallerton? Or simply that Thea believed he had done so? But why? Why kill his sister's betrothed?

He rolled on to his back and stared up into the darkness. Sleep was going to be a long time coming, he realised. Not that he was any stranger to sleepless nights; over the years his leg had given him quite a few. His leg ached a little right now, but that wasn't the reason sleep eluded him—seared on his memory was Thea's white face as she told him why he need not challenge Dunhaven. She had told him for one reason only—to save him. And she expected him to despise her for what she had done.

Thea felt battered as she faced Lady Arnsworth and Diana Fox-Heaton in the drawing room the next morning. The events of the previous evening, coupled with far too little sleep, had left her drained, but deep within a vein of determination beat a steady, sustaining rhythm. It flowed through her. The worst was over; she had told Richard the truth. Beyond securing David's safety, nothing else mattered now.

Richard stood by the mantelpiece in silence, his face grim, set in hard lines, with the dark eyes shuttered. Pain stabbed her. He'd had time to think, to realise what a lucky escape he'd had...and as she had always known it would, his rejection left the world grey and bereft, as though the sun had abandoned it.

Diana Fox-Heaton was speaking. 'Sir Francis believes that this meeting with the magistrate is vital,' she said. 'He thinks that Sir Giles wishes to ascertain whether or not a trial would have any chance of success, that it is possible the case might be dropped if Sir Giles is of the opinion Mr Winslow would be acquitted.'

Thea's breath jerked in, but Richard might have turned to stone. Not by so much as a flicker did he react to Diana Fox-Heaton's message.

Lady Arnsworth was not so restrained.

'Really! This is most improper, Diana!' she fussed. 'Dorothea cannot possibly appear at Bow Street!' She glared at Diana Fox-Heaton in a way that suggested that Diana was running the gauntlet of all the risks associated with being the bearer of bad tidings. 'Surely this is all a mistake and Mr Winslow will be released anyway.' When no one answered she demanded, 'Why *does* Sir Francis think her presence necessary?'

Diana shook her head. 'He didn't say, ma'am. You know what men are. Explanations are not a strength, unless one insists, and he *was* in a hurry. All he said was that if Thea knew anything that might assist her brother's case, she should attend.'

Thea waited, her hands linked carefully in her lap. In an odd way she felt completely detached from the situation. This discussion could not make the least difference to her course. She already knew what she had to do. She had known since finding out about David's arrest the previous night, but she had neither energy nor inclination to argue with Lady Arnsworth. Nor did she look again at Richard, still standing silently by the mantelpiece. There was a measure of peace in having her decision so clearly laid out for her this time—a calm certainty that she was doing the right thing.

'Richard!' said Lady Arnsworth. 'Surely you must see the impropriety of this!'

At that, Thea turned to look at him. The dark gaze was focused on her, still shuttered.

'Thea?' was all he said.

Shock burned through her. He was not going to attempt to influence her one way or the other. This decision, for good or ill, was hers and he knew it.

'I have to go,' she said.

'Dorothea!'

'Enough, Almeria!' Richard moved then, coming to stand beside and slightly behind Thea's chair. 'This is her decision to make. Winslow's life is slightly more important than matters of propriety.'

Lady Arnsworth favoured him with a polar glare. 'And you *approve?*'

From the corner of her eye, Thea saw tension take him.

'It is not my place to approve or disapprove,' he said gently. 'But whether Thea likes it or not, I will go with her to Bow Street.' She turned to stare up at him and his hand, warm and strong, gripped her shoulder. 'As a friend,' he added.

Heat stung and burned her eyelids. He had come to her last night, comforted her. It seemed that he refused to judge her, despite what she had told him. And now he would stand her friend. If there had been any judging, it had been done by herself.

She had completely *mis*judged the depth of his loyalty. And now he would discover the rest of the truth. She did not think she stood a chance of persuading him to remain outside Sir Giles's chamber.

The cab rattled over the cobbles towards Bloomsbury. Richard had thought it better not to advertise their visit to the entire world by using a crested carriage. Thea sat spear-straight beside him, her face hidden by the poke of her bonnet and a veil. Almeria had insisted on the veil. Thea had agreed, but not, Richard thought, because she thought it a good idea. He didn't think she cared one way or another. Her whole being was focused on what was to come.

As they swung around into Bow Street, he asked himself yet again if, in supporting her decision, he was doing the right thing. Telling the magistrate the truth handed him an iron-clad reason to send David Winslow for trial. Duelling—he assumed it would have been a duel—was frowned upon; the magistrates wanted to crack down on it. If it were decided to make an example of Winslow…he bit his lip. Thea would never forgive herself.

They drew up outside Number Three, Bow Street, and Thea turned to him and spoke for the first time since she had thanked him for handing her into the cab.

'Will you forgive me, Richard?' She reached out and her hand hovered over his.

He captured it swiftly. 'Forgive you? For what?'

She bit her lip. 'For not telling you quite everything. Please believe that it was not because I did not trust you. Just that…I have to tell Sir Giles…' She swallowed and her fingers trembled. 'But this is not something I can talk about easily.'

'Of course not,' he said quietly. 'There is nothing to forgive.'

He opened the door and stepped down to pay off the jarvey before handing Thea down.

She took a deep breath and squared her shoulders. Exactly, thought Richard, as one might imagine a person would face a firing squad.

They were ushered into Sir Giles's private chamber and found Winslow, Sir Francis Fox-Heaton and Lord Braybrook already there.

Winslow's mouth went white as he saw Thea.

'Damn you, Blakehurst!' he said. 'This is no fit place for her! Why didn't you stop her?'

'With what authority?' asked Richard.

'It was my choice, David,' said Thea. 'Good day, Sir Giles. I hope we have not kept you waiting.'

The magistrate rose. 'Not at all, Miss Winslow. Thank you for your message.'

'Message?' She looked puzzled.

Richard intervened. 'I sent a groom.'

The glare Winslow shot him was lethal. 'Thought of everything, didn't you?'

Ignoring this, Sir Giles said, 'Miss Winslow, this is a very serious matter. As you know, we received information that Mr Nigel Lallerton, to whom you were betrothed, was murdered. That initial information suggested that you might be able to shed light on the matter. Since then, more information has been provided, directly accusing your brother of cold-bloodedly murdering Mr Lallerton.' He paused. 'I must ask you, Miss Winslow,' he continued, a steely bite in his voice, 'if you know of any reason your brother might have had to murder your betrothed?'

'Leave her out of this!' snapped Winslow. 'Yes, I killed him, but it wasn't murder! It was a duel, properly conducted according the Code of Honour. Will that satisfy you?'

'I will remind you, Mr Winslow,' said Sir Giles, 'that duelling is now illegal, no matter how properly conducted, and that my question was directed to your sister. I want the whole truth. Miss Winslow?'

She glanced at Winslow. 'It's better this way, David.'

'Thea—!'

Something in her gaze quelled his protest and he fell silent. Richard swallowed as Thea turned to Sir Giles. If it had taken courage to tell him the truth, how much more must it take to confess here?

'It was my fault, sir. I ask you to remember that I was not quite seventeen at the time—'

'Dammit, Thea!' snarled Winslow, shaking off Braybrook's restraining hand as he surged to his feet. 'It was not your fault that the bastard raped you!' He turned on Sir Giles, naked fury in his face. 'That's what happened—now are you satisfied ?'

Chapter Eleven

Shocked silence hung there thickly. For a moment no one moved. Sir Giles's shrewd eyes rested on Thea, who met the searching gaze unflinchingly.

Richard felt as though an avalanche had swept over him, as odd little things tumbled into place...

'Is that true, Miss Winslow?'

Something about Sir Giles's voice had changed. There was a gentleness in it that had not been there earlier. But the underlying steel remained. The sword might have been sheathed, but it remained a sword.

'Yes, sir. That is the truth.'

Her soft reply lacerated Richard as though he had swallowed powdered glass. Why hadn't he seen it? She had *told* him that she had never loved Lallerton...her dazed terror the other day when she had fainted and come to on the sofa and found him leaning over her...even her reluctance to marry might stem from a fear far more elemental than worry over a bridegroom's reaction to her lost virginity... Hell's teeth! If Lallerton weren't already dead... His fists clenched involuntarily. A pistol would be too quick.

Movement drew him back.

Sir Giles had risen to his feet and gone over to a small side table that held a decanter and glasses. He poured something into a glass and came back, placing the glass gently in Thea's hand.

'Brandy. Miss Winslow, I understand that this must be distressing for you. If you can bring yourself to speak of this...I can make no promises, but it may help your brother.'

She looked up and nodded. 'Yes, sir. I...I know.'

'You *were* betrothed to Mr Lallerton, were you not?'

She hesitated. Then, 'Yes, Nigel Lallerton and I were betrothed—that is, our fathers had arranged the match. I...I was not entirely happy about it and had expressed my doubts to my father. I asked for more time to...to become better acquainted with Mr Lallerton.' Richard saw her swallow. 'Instead, my father announced the betrothal and an early date for the wedding.'

Sir Giles's hand shifted on the desk. 'Go on.'

'I panicked and told Mr Lallerton that I did not wish to marry him. He...he appeared to accept my refusal, but asked me to drive out with him. There was a storm, and we were forced to shelter at an inn for the night...'

Not caring what anyone thought, Richard reached out and took one clenched hand from her lap, cradling it protectively.

'Damn it, Mason!' he snarled. 'Hasn't this gone far enough?'

Shrewd green eyes met his furious gaze. 'I think so,' said the magistrate quietly. 'Miss Winslow, if it were necessary, would you be prepared to tell me the rest? Even in open court?'

Richard felt the hand in his tremble, and protested, 'For God's sake! You cannot mean to make her go through such a confession in court!'

Sir Giles shook his head. 'I am not asking that of you at the moment, Miss Winslow—but if it were necessary, would you give that evidence?'

She dragged in an audible breath. 'Yes.' Firm and clear, although her face was blanched and she was visibly shaking.

He nodded, turning to Winslow. 'Very well. It seems you had sufficient motive to challenge Lallerton, Mr Winslow.'

'The hell I did!' snapped Winslow. 'Lallerton had exactly

what he wanted—my sister in a position where she had no choice but to marry him. How the hell could I challenge him?'

'I beg your pardon?' Fury seared through Richard. His jaw felt as though it might crack.

Winslow turned on him. 'What the devil was I supposed to do, Blakehurst? Think about it! And believe me, I had every intention of being the brother-in-law from hell!'

'Are you saying that you did not issue the actual challenge, then, Winslow?' asked Sir Giles.

Winslow's teeth grated. 'I did not. Lallerton had been staying with my family in the country up to that point. Everyone was in an uproar over them being out all night, and he returned to town.' He glanced at Thea. 'At first my sister said nothing. Literally. Until our father said that he had told Lallerton to return with a special licence, that she had no choice now. She ran from the room. I followed to try to make her see sense.' He broke off and swallowed.

'That was when she told you about the rape?' asked Sir Giles.

Winslow nodded. 'More or less. I noticed bruising on her wrists, one on her cheek.'

A savage growl escaped Richard.

Winslow glanced at him. 'Precisely.'

'And what then did you do?' pressed Sir Giles.

A mirthless smile curved Winslow's lips. 'I followed him up to town with the intention of beating him to a pulp! When I reached town, Lallerton was not at his lodgings—his man told me that he was dining with Fox-Heaton, so I went round there.'

The magistrate turned to Sir Francis. 'Can you confirm or deny this?'

Sir Francis nodded. 'Certainly. Winslow arrived at my rooms in a rage and forced his way in past my servant. There was a fight in which Lallerton sustained a black eye and lost several teeth.'

Richard failed to suppress an approving mutter, and the magistrate gave him a quelling glare.

'Did Mr Winslow give any indication of what the quarrel was about?'

'He did not,' said Sir Francis. 'And nor did Lallerton. He told

Winslow in very offensive terms that he would meet him and that was that. Winslow told him not to be a damned fool, and—'

'I beg your pardon?' interrupted Sir Giles. 'What did you say?'

'Winslow told him not to be a damned fool?'

'Yes—that. Very well. Go on.'

Sir Francis shrugged. 'There's very little more to say. Lallerton accused him of not having the stomach for a duel and Winslow then agreed to the challenge in even more offensive terms and told me that his second would call on me.' He nodded at Lord Braybrook. 'Braybrook called the following morning. Neither principal was prepared to back down, the duel went ahead and Lallerton was killed. Both Lord Aberfield and Lord Chasewater decided to hush the matter up.' He hesitated, then said, 'In fact, although I had my suspicions, I was never sure, until just now, what had occasioned the quarrel between Winslow and Lallerton.'

'And you, Lord Braybrook? What can you add to the story?' Sir Giles's voice was non-committal, but Richard could see a muscle flickering at the corner of his mouth.

Braybrook shrugged. 'What can I add? Very little, sir. Winslow called on me early the following morning to request that I act for him in the affair. He told me that he would not under any circumstances apologise and to make sure we arranged a surgeon.' He glanced at Thea, and said, 'Like Fox-Heaton, I had my suspicions about the cause of the quarrel—especially when Miss Winslow vanished so completely from society. I did not communicate these suspicions to anyone.' He shot an apologetic look at Richard.

Richard nodded in acknowledgment. He could hardly fault Julian for that.

Braybrook continued. 'As Fox-Heaton told you, we arranged the meeting. Both combatants fired at almost the same instant— Winslow was hit in the left arm and Lallerton high in the leg, severing an artery. The surgeon was unable to stop the bleeding.'

There was a moment's silence. 'Mr Lallerton did not delope? He shot to kill?' asked Sir Giles. He sounded shocked.

Braybrook exchanged a glance with Sir Francis. 'That would

be my opinion. Left side, on a level with the heart—yes. He only missed by a few inches. Fox-Heaton?'

'Agreed,' said Sir Francis shortly. 'He had an ungovernable temper at times and this was one of them. I will say that I did my best to dissuade him from the duel, fearing that he meant to kill Winslow. He would not listen, so I dealt with Braybrook accordingly.'

'And you, Winslow—had Lallerton retracted his challenge and…apologised…?'

Sir Giles watched Winslow closely.

Winslow bit his lip. 'What choice would I have had? Had he withdrawn, I must have accepted it—faced with his challenge, I had no choice but to shoot. To wound.' Bitterly he added, 'Whether or not it helped my sister is another matter.'

Silence fell, broken only by the drumming of Sir Giles's fingers on the desk, as a deepening frown creased his brow. 'If this had come before a court,' he said at last, 'the most likely result, Winslow, is that you would have been acquitted. Duelling may be illegal, but there is very little chance that you would have been convicted, especially given the particular provocation—' he glanced at Thea '—and considering the fact that the challenge was not actually yours. Therefore one must conclude that the main reason it was covered up was to protect Miss Winslow's reputation. Am I correct?'

Winslow nodded. 'Yes, sir. My father feared that even if it were possible to keep my sister's name out of it, the attendant speculation would ruin her and the family. Chasewater agreed.' His lip curled. 'He too feared the scandal if any of it came out. It did not paint his son in a flattering light.'

Sir Giles continued, 'Under the circumstances, while I am far from approving of such an affair, I can see little benefit in proceeding any further. To bring you to trial when you would almost certainly be acquitted would serve only to ruin your sister.'

He looked at Thea kindly. 'Miss Winslow, I can only honour you for having the courage to come here today and tell me this. Given that neither Sir Francis nor Lord Braybrook have breathed a word of their suspicions in the past eight years, I think you may be assured of their continuing discretion. For myself, I can promise that no word of what has been said in this hearing will ever pass my lips.'

'Then…David is free to go?' she asked dazedly.

Sir Giles nodded. 'Quite free.'

Except for Lord Braybrook, who had ridden, they all squeezed into Sir Francis's carriage to return to Mayfair. Conversation was sporadic. Thea felt incapable of speaking.

Sir Francis handed her down and bowed over her hand. 'I understand you are going down to Blakeney soon, Miss Winslow.'

'Yes, sir.' No doubt he would be relieved that she was unlikely to see much more of Diana.

He smiled. 'Enjoy your stay. Perhaps you might dine with Diana and myself when you return?'

Her jaw dropped. 'Sir?'

'Let Diana know when you return to town. Good day.'

Descending from the carriage with her as well as Richard, David held out his hand to Sir Francis. 'Thank you, Fox-Heaton.'

Fox-Heaton shook his hand. 'Not at all, Winslow. That affair has bothered me for years. I'm glad to have it settled at last.'

The carriage rolled away, and Richard, David and Thea looked at each other. David let out a breath. 'I had best go and relieve Father's concern that his heir is about either to dance a hempen jig or take up permanent residence on the continent.' He enveloped Thea in a hug. 'You never should have put yourself through that for me.'

She shook her head. 'How could I not?'

He looked awkward. 'Yes, well.' He turned to Richard. 'I'll leave her with you. Thank you, Blakehurst. For everything. And I suggest you hone your authority!'

He strode off around the square towards Aberfield House, and Richard escorted her inside.

'That's it then,' he said. 'Your brother is safe thanks to your courage. You can rest easy now.'

She did not contradict him. Yes, David was safe. But there was still something left that she must face.

Half an hour later, Thea gave a hastily written letter to Almeria's footman. 'You will deliver this to the lawyers, Sydenham and Beckett, in Lincoln's Inn Fields. You will make sure that it is delivered directly to Mr Sydenham and you will await a reply.'

'Yes, miss.'

She gave him money for a cab and a little extra. 'The reply is to be given directly to me, James. It is understood?'

'Yes, miss.'

She nodded. 'Thank you. You may go.'

She sat back with a sigh as he left the drawing room. It was all she could think of. Somehow she had to discover the truth about her child. Was she safe? Happy? She only hoped that she could set it all in motion before she had to travel into Kent. Which reminded her; she had yet to buy a christening gift… Her heart faltered. A gift for a baby. Had anyone bought her baby a christening gift?

She didn't even know the child's name. An innocent life, blighted because she had been too frightened…

Shivering, she remembered her father's reaction: *Damned missish behaviour. Of course the marriage must go ahead! As fast as possible from the sounds of it! What the devil did you* think *happened? Nothing happened that wouldn't have happened in the marriage bed! You'll marry Lallerton and there's an end of it!*

The end of it had been that she had threatened to refuse her vows at the altar and state her reasons. Publicly. Even now, the memory of her father's fury and her mother's disbelief…*but, dearest! He's so suitable*…remained a gaping wound.

Only David had truly understood and believed her. The only one prepared to defend her… He had been in exile on the continent by the time her pregnancy was realised—by the time she realised how reckless she had been in refusing the marriage. The definition of a Pyrrhic victory.

If David had never known the truth, would she have married Lallerton? Probably. Her soul shuddered in horror at the idea, at the memory…yet an innocent child had been condemned as a result of her decision…she didn't know. She just didn't know… Hindsight, she thought bitterly, was a two-edged sword.

No one had ever suggested to the terrified sixteen-year-old girl that she might be pregnant. Would she have listened? Would she listen now? Condemn herself to the hell of marriage with a man who would force an innocent girl? Would she give that advice to another? She still didn't know.

Had they lied about the child to spare her shame? Or because Aunt Maria had found her that day, not long before the birth, her hand on her distended belly, feeling the baby's squirming, watching it through the fabric stretched over the mound of her pregnancy. Through her fear and humiliation there had been wonder that a life was blossoming within her. She could feel no hatred for that life, only wonder…curiosity to meet it. Had Aunt Maria seen that? She had certainly read her errant niece a savage lecture on the fruits of sin…and Aunt Maria had tipped that dose of laudanum down her throat after the delivery. Yes. It was more than possible. But did she have the courage to find out? What would she do with the knowledge? Would it be better not to know any more? Even now it was possible to back away. When Sydenham's letter came, she could write that she had changed her mind, no longer needed…

A very quiet voice spoke behind her. 'Thea? I thought you would be resting.'

Richard.

'Are you quite all right?' There was a world of gentleness and concern in his voice.

Determinedly, she turned, daring the tears to fall. She saw his mouth twist, saw his hand stretch out to her and stepped back, lifting her chin. If he held her, it would all come spilling out, all the pain, the guilt, the terrified confusion…

She summoned a smile. 'I…I was just wondering, thinking about a christening gift for your godson. Do you…do you think something for a baby would be acceptable or ought I to choose something for the future?'

His hand dropped to his side and she rushed on, covering the stab of pain. 'Of course, a girl would be far simpler; jewellery, you know. Although I dare say it would be sadly dated, by the time—'

'Are you feeling quite the thing?' he asked, cutting into her babble. 'Thea—if you are thinking that because I wish our betrothal to stand—you must know I would never force anything upon you, no matter how much the idea of marrying you might tempt me—'

He stopped, an odd, taut expression in his eyes.

'Of course I know that,' she assured him. 'It…it is as I said—the christening gift. Indeed, once I have made my decision I planned to summon a maid to accompany me out to buy the present.'

'Consider me summoned,' he said with a wrenching smile.

'You! But you're not—'

'Not a maid. No.' He heaved a lugubrious and wholly spurious sigh. 'I suppose it is rather obvious, but I did hope you wouldn't hold it against me.'

'But—'

That smile—the one that a merciful providence should outlaw—demolished all her defences, all the cogent reasons why she should not accept his escort. Like the fact that it would give further credence to the belief that they were on the verge of announcing their betrothal. Although after last night accepting his escort was a mere bagatelle. Richard had publicly nailed his colours to her mast last night and this morning. And she would have to tear them down. Just as publicly.

'What do you think I should buy?' She gulped. Why on earth had she asked that? Thinking about babies and all the might-have-beens in connection with Richard was guaranteed to shred the remaining rags of her peace.

He smiled. 'Well, I made those little horses to hang above the cradle. What about something to hang with them?'

She remembered the little bird she had found in The Box. If things had been different, would she have given it to her child?

The child she had condemned…perhaps wilfully. Would God have been more merciful if not for her foolish pride and fear? Could she simply alleviate the lot of *SG* without ever seeing her…a child was a child after all…perhaps helping her lost baby anonymously would ease that pain so long denied…?

She forced the pain back, back into its dark corner, and faced Richard. 'I could buy some bells to hang above the cradle with them.'

His smile reached deep. 'A wonderful idea. Shall we go now?'

Thea blinked. 'But where?' For the life of her she couldn't think where one might go in London to buy such a thing.

Richard raised his brows. 'Weren't you ever taken to see the beasts at the Exeter 'Change when you were little? And then per-mitted to spend your pin money at the stalls downstairs after-wards? It's exactly the sort of place to find bells.' He grinned. 'Unless you had something more ambitious in mind and planned to steal them from St Paul's belfry?'

'The Exeter 'Change will do very well,' she told him primly. 'Shall we walk or do you prefer to take a hackney? I know you won't wish to keep your horses standing.'

'Walk, if you would like,' said Richard. 'We can always take a hackney home.'

A funny little spurt of pleasure buoyed her: walking meant more time spent with him. Quietly. With no one to disturb their friendship. She bit her lip, banishing a flicker of hope that their friendship might be something more. For both of them.

She could not in honour encourage his suit. But still that little voice whispered: *Why should he ever know?*

Chapter Twelve

They found the bells easily enough as it turned out, at a fascinating stall in the Exeter 'Change on the Strand. Richard watched Thea surreptitiously as they strolled around the stalls afterwards. She appeared perfectly in command of herself, but he could not banish the memory of her eyes when she turned to him in the drawing room. For an instant, before she began babbling about christening gifts, he had felt that he was gazing into a well of utter despair. For a moment her guard had been down and he had seen a pain she hid from everyone. Even from him.

The instinct to go to her, to hold her, had been nearly overwhelming, but the memory of her terrified reaction the other day had held him back. That day she had scarcely seemed to know where she was, let alone who he was. As if she had been flung into a waking nightmare…and the horror in her eyes when she realised that it was him… He swallowed—that haunted him.

He had held her since then, of course, but today had been like that day—as though she had looked into a living hell. All that babble about a christening gift! Had she thought to throw dust in his eyes? Or simply to hold herself together after what she had been through already that day? Lord, her courage shamed him.

'Shall we leave now, Richard?'

He looked down at her and smiled. A little sadly. He had

enjoyed just being with her like this. Quietly. But she looked tired, her eyes shadowy.

'Did you sleep again last night, Thea?'

'Of course,' she said.

There was no 'of course' about it. Except possibly that, of course, she was lying.

He gave her a considering sort of look and her eyes fell before it.

'Hmm. You do know that you are a terrible liar, don't you? We'll take a hackney.'

Her gloved hand tightened on his arm. 'Please, couldn't we walk a little of the way back?'

'You are tired, Thea—' he began.

'Yes,' she said honestly. 'But I have so enjoyed this. And if you are…are not returning to town from Blakeney, we will not be able to do this again, so…' her voice trailed off.

The idea that she was enjoying her time with him had a warm glow spreading right through him.

'Then we can walk,' he said.

They could walk together at Blakeney too. It would do her good to have some gentle walks and rides on the Downs in the fresh air. Come to think of it, he wouldn't take it amiss either.

'Thea, about last night, my offer of marriage—even before I knew…before you told Sir Giles what had happened—'

She looked up swiftly as they left the building. 'No. Please. I know what you would say. But there is not the least need for you to make me another offer. It is not such a disaster. I do not wish to be married.' She bit her bottom lip. 'Least of all because you feel obliged to rescue me. So, we will go to Blakeney and no doubt when I return to town there will be some other scandal to amuse people. They will forget soon enough.'

He should, of course, have been heartily relieved. No man wanted to find himself compelled by scandal to take a bride. So why did he feel so completely bereft that she would not consider marriage as a solution? His body made a very definite suggestion, which he promptly quelled. Leaving his body's disgraceful urgings out of the question—difficult with the object of his urgings strolling beside him—his feelings were in a complete tangle, pulling him in several different directions at once. But right now, only one predominated: somehow he had to find a way to protect Thea from the scandal. Whatever it took, he would do it—short of forcing her into marriage.

He couldn't bear the idea of Thea being forced into anything…she deserved better than that after what that bastard Lallerton had done to her.

And he definitely didn't like the idea of Thea returning to town after the visit to Blakeney. But she would have to when Almeria returned… Unless Verity were to invite her to stay on… Verity would do it if he asked. In her own way, Verity was as eager to see him married as Almeria, but her interest never bothered him. Probably because she wouldn't have dreamt of throwing an heiress at him, even if she knew one.

Yes, that was it. Ask Verity to invite Thea to stay on. He would only be a few miles away… He blinked a little at the suddenly violent need surging through him to remain close to her, not to let her slip away.

He set his jaw, firmly ignoring what his body was telling him. He was fond of Thea—and she was in trouble. As for this extremely inconvenient urge he had to sweep her into his arms and kiss her senseless—that was completely irrelevant. Or ought to be.

If he wanted Thea like that, he'd have to persuade her to marry him. Preferably before he disgraced himself and seduced her. Because…?

Because he loved her…

His mind came to a complete halt, as he discovered that, almost without realising it, he had come to an understanding, or acceptance, of what he felt for Thea.

He loved her. Thea Winslow—an heiress? Good God!

The small, irritatingly logical part of his brain left functioning pointed out that Thea was a woman, before she was an heiress. That his body was not responding to Thea's fortune. That he was worried about *Thea;* Thea sleeping badly, Thea in distress because of the visit to Bow Street. It wasn't her damned fortune cutting up his peace—except, of course, the worry about other men courting her for it. He felt as though he'd been hit with a brick. Could love creep up on one like this? With a woman one had known for years? Without one even realising it?

He thought about his twin. Love had hit Max like a thunderbolt. There'd been no creeping about it. It had been obvious to everyone.

Everyone except Max, of course.

Oh, rot! Maybe Max hadn't noticed, but he was far more rational than Max! Surely he'd have noticed if he was falling in love!

A sudden scuffle on the pavement ahead drew him back to reality. Two mongrel dogs, sniffing in the gutters, had disagreed over territory and were circling, stiff-legged. A black horse, hitched to a waiting gig, shifted restlessly, flinging his head up and down, plainly unsettled by the snarling dogs.

Watching them all closely, Richard hurried Thea past, placing himself between her and the dogs.

She cast a surprised look up at him. He returned it with raised brows.

'Thank you,' she said simply.

He managed a smile. This couldn't be happening. He couldn't have fallen *in* love. Could he? All the way in love?

Behind them the volley of snarls exploded into outright battle.

Richard would have walked on, a dogfight was a dogfight, and well behind them now. But Thea stopped and glanced back, as the scream of a frightened horse combined with a sudden clatter of hooves and wheels to mask her sudden gasp.

He swung around, every nerve taut.

Frightened, as the snarling dogs rolled into the roadway under its hooves, the restless black hitched to the gig reared up snorting, jerking the reins from the boy holding them. Taken by surprise, he lost his grip on the bridle and stumbled in the gutter, startling the horse even more. With a rattle of hooves and wheels the horse leapt forward, swerving to avoid a carriage going the opposite way; the near-side wheel mounted the pavement, scattering goods and yelling pedestrians.

No time. He had no time. The horse was bearing down on them and there was no doorway to dodge into. Seizing Thea, he crushed her against the nearest wall, holding her there with his full weight, his arms wrapped over her head.

He shut his eyes…the clatter of hooves bearing down…if it struck them… He pressed her into the wall, using his entire weight to keep her there. A glancing blow ripped him away, sending him spinning…a brief vision of the wheel flashed past as he hit the pavement and rolled, the impact slamming all the air out of his body.

'Richard!' The scream burst from Thea's throat as she felt the blow from the gig shudder through his body, protecting hers, and felt him torn away, saw him spin like a rag doll and hit the ground.

For a heart-stopping eternity she saw him lying motionless on the dusty pavement, his eyes closed, his hat sitting nearby.

No. Not Richard. Not him. God, why did you let him…?

Terror, agony, fury all swept through her as she flung herself away from the wall and dropped to his side.

His eyes still closed, a totally blasphemous and, she suspected, quite graphic phrase escaped his lips. They were the sweetest words she had ever heard, uttered in a voice that reeked of annoyance and discomfort rather than anything worse.

The brown eyes opened and he tried to sit up. She helped him, unable to control the shaking of her hands as they carefully dusted him down. The gathering crowd barely existed, the excited cries and mutterings a meaningless blur.

'Are you…are you hurt?' she managed. 'Your leg…'

'My leg is perfectly well,' he lied. It pained him like the very devil. 'And I'm not hurt in the least,' he said reassuringly. 'Or not in places I'm meant to talk about,' he added with a wince. 'Let's just say that I'm going to be stiff and I might not sit down too comfortably for a few days.'

Relief breathed through her, loosening terror's icy claws. There was a smudge of dirt on his cheekbone. With shaking fingers she pulled off her gloves to brush at it uselessly. And realised that the dirt was an excuse, she needed to touch him;

needed to touch the warm, living flesh, to reassure herself that he was alive, that he hadn't been taken from her.

Barely conscious of what she did, she felt the slight scratchiness of his cheek under her wondering fingertips, the hard line of his jaw…and then the touch of firm, warm lips. Her breathing shattered; he had turned his head to kiss her fingers… The sensation rippled through her…such a simple innocent caress, to release a flood of heat and pent-up longing.

She drew her hand back, gently, her gaze never leaving his.

Experimentally, Richard began to get up. A dozen hands, apart from Thea's, appeared to assist him. He ignored them all. Without explanation, or apology, in the full view of the crowd he put his arms around Thea and held her.

'And you? You're not hurt?' His voice was husky. Shaken, as she had never heard it.

'No. Thanks to you.' He had saved her. At the risk of his own life. Protecting her with his own body. And now he still sheltered her with his body, comforting the fading fear, the trembling that she could not control. Not fear for herself, but the fear she had felt in that dreadful moment she had thought him dead. His death at her door.

She felt safe, completely and utterly safe, here in his arms. Better than safe. The closeness of his hard body was a delight, a bone-melting joy she had never imagined. And the memory of that body crushing her against the wall, his full weight on her…heat pooled, deep and mysterious inside her.

The glorious sensation of holding, and being held by, another human being flooded her. She did not think she would ever be able to let go again.

But she must. Of course she must.

Richard felt the beginnings of tension in the soft body pressed against him. What the hell was he doing, embracing Thea Winslow in the middle of a public street? Rebellion screaming in every fibre, he released her. Well, sort of released her. He kept one arm about her, assuring himself that it was mere chivalry. Not the wild conviction that to release her was to lose her for ever.

Losing Thea…his stomach churned.

A burly jarvey came forward from the gathered crowd and held out his hand. Automatically Richard accepted it.

'Ye're a ruddy hero, lad,' said the jarvey. 'You 'op up into my cab and me an' the old nag'll get ye both safe 'ome. An' I won't take a penny, s'welp me. Can't let the lass walk 'ome after that.'

His sentiments exactly.

Thea put up no protest at all about being bundled into the cab. A phenomenon Richard unhesitatingly ascribed to her concern about him. He was well enough, although bruised and rapidly stiffening, but the dazed look in Thea's eyes…shock. A cup of tea and a biscuit were what she needed.

Someone handed him his very dusty and battered hat, and he stepped into the cab and closed the door. After checking that they were comfortable, the jarvey mounted the box and they set off.

Safe. She was safe. The thought that he might have lost her pounded through him, along with the memory of her body pressed between his and the wall…to lose her and never know the sweet joy of holding her again, of making slow, aching love to her, of feeling her response…and knowing that she was his for ever… The truth of his feelings swirled through him now with all the violence he could possibly have wished or expected: he truly did love Thea Winslow. He'd probably always loved her, since he couldn't think when his feelings had changed. Just like Max, he hadn't noticed himself falling in love.

He was definitely noticing now.

He *wanted* to marry Thea. Just that. He wanted her. And he also wanted to spend the rest of his life with her. Two desires which added up to marriage.

Shaken, he faced the truth: he loved her. Deeply, irrevocably.

Beyond helping himself, he found his hand seeking Thea's, needing to touch her. For a moment her hand lay still, and then, in a gesture whose sweetness stole his breath, her hand turned into his, slim fingers sliding between his, clinging, as though she too needed the comfort of touch.

He leaned back against the seat, closing his eyes to banish the

vision of soft, pink lips, slightly parted; gritting his teeth against
the urge to haul her into his arms and possess those lips, taking
her mouth as he longed to take her, body and soul. Too soon. It
was too soon to propose again. And he dared not give rein to his
need until she had agreed to marry him.

She trusted him, cared for him. Now he must teach her to
desire him.

Thea retired to her bedchamber when they reached Grosvenor Square. Her mind refused to function, lost somewhere
between the terror she had felt and the shattering memory of
Richard's body holding her trapped and safe, the feel of her own
body rioting in shock, his lips on her fingers, his hand reaching
out in comfort on the way home. Madness. He would have protected any woman. It was not that she was special in any way.

That didn't help at all. Knowing that he was the sort of chivalrous idiot who would risk his life without question for another
was not exactly a discouraging thought.

He was an honourable man. He probably would have flattened
Lady Jersey or a scullery maid against that wall if the situation
had arisen.

Would he have kissed her fingers?

Stupid question. Neither Lady Jersey nor the scullery maid
would have been fondling his cheek, and nor should she have
done so. Richard was kind. They had both been shaken. There
was nothing more to his tenderness than that. There was
nothing to fear...

No. Thea stripped off her pelisse. She did not fear Richard.
What she feared was not having the strength to refuse if he really
offered for her again.

He wouldn't. He'd made it clear that her fortune held no
interest for him. And men didn't fall in love with childhood
friends with reputations for jilting suitors.

Just as well. For she could never marry him.

A tap on the door was followed by the entry of a maid. 'Oh,
miss! Mr Blakehurst was after telling us what happened. A tea-

tray will be up in a moment. And her ladyship sent her smell-ing salts!'

Thea eyed the proffered vinaigrette with considerable suspicion. She hated the things. Still…she took it gingerly. 'Do thank her ladyship and assure her I shall be perfectly recovered after a cup of tea.'

'Yes, miss. There's this too. Just come while you were out.' She produced a letter from the pocket of her apron and held it out.

Her fingers suddenly unsteady again, Thea took the letter. The familiar, precise writing leapt out at her: Mr Sydenham.

'Thank you, Becky. That will be all.'

'Yes, Miss.' Becky bobbed a curtsy and went out.

Thea ripped open the letter and quickly scanned the contents. The little lawyer's disapproval dripped from every clipped sentence, but he had done as she asked. The meeting was arranged for two days hence. Just in time. She would be off to Blakeney two days after that.

With a shock, Thea realised that all her indecision was gone. Not her misgivings, just the indecision. She must know the truth. This afternoon she had nearly been killed. If not for Richard, she would likely now be dead and cold in the street.

Mortality brushed past, ruffling her skirts, leaving her chilled to the soul.

If she had a child, then she must provide for it. She must make a will, and to do that she must know the child's name. Her mind refused to go any further, refused to dwell on the forming thought that to know the child's name might be dangerous, might bring her perilously close to wanting more…

Chapter Thirteen

'Miss Winslow.' Mr Sydenham appeared from his office to greet her. 'You received my note, I see. Ma'am, all the arrangements are made. The individual you requested is here, but really! This is all most irregular! If you would give me your instructions, I could pass them on without you having to demean yourself, and—'

She cut him short. 'Sir—I asked you to find the most reliable, discreet man available. You have done so?'

'Well, yes, but it is not fitting that a *lady* should involve herself with such—'

'My business is private, sir. I need not reiterate that if I find word of this has reached Lord Aberfield, I will be searching for a new man of affairs when I attain control of my fortune.'

'No, ma'am. But surely his lordship would be the most fitting person—'

'No. You will conduct me to this gentleman and leave us.'

Mr Sydenham looked thoroughly disapproving, but obeyed, ushering her into an office occupied by a burly man with small, shrewd eyes.

He arose as she entered the room.

Sydenham floundered, his respectable soul evidently harrowed by the situation. 'Er, Rufton, this is, ah…'

Thea took pity on Mr Sydenham's mortification and stepped

forward. 'I am Miss Winslow, Mr Rufton. I understand you may be able to help me.' To the little lawyer, she said simply, 'Thank you, Mr Sydenham. You may leave us.'

As the door closed behind him, she said, 'Do sit down, Mr Rufton.'

He did so and said, 'Thank you, ma'am. But as to helping you, I couldn't rightly say. Mr Sydenham refused to tell me what it is you want. All I've been told is that someone wanted to hire me. Privately.'

'That,' said Thea, 'would be because Mr Sydenham has no idea what it is that I require of you. And I wish it to remain that way. All I told him was that I wished to hire a Bow Street runner, and that the man must be utterly honest, reliable and discreet.'

Mr Rufton looked gratified. 'A private matter, would it be, ma'am?'

'Very private,' she assured him.

He nodded. 'Well, then, there's one or two things you need to know first. One: I won't step outside the law. Two: if I find something that does step outside the law, I'm duty bound to report it. Three: any foreseeable expenses, travel and suchlike, need to be paid upfront. Begging your pardon, ma'am, but I've got my family to think of.'

She nodded. 'Very well. I accept your conditions. My conditions are simply that you are to say nothing of this to anyone. You will report your findings to me in writing.'

He looked at her keenly. 'One thing, ma'am—be very sure you want to know whatever it is.'

'I've thought of that, Mr Rufton.' She took a very deep breath. 'I wish you to trace a child for me. A…a girl.'

He flung up a hand. 'Ma'am—no matter if it's inside or outside the law—I'm a married man with childer of my own. I won't be party to anything that brings hurt to a child!'

At that moment the last of Thea's doubts about what she was doing melted. This was a man she could trust.

'Good,' she said. 'I shall explain what I require and you shall be the judge. She is currently a pupil at Miss Dale's Seminary for the Daughters of Gentlemen in Bath. I believe her to be about seven years old with a birthday in…late March.' Her heart contracted. She knew the date. None better, but it was possible it had been changed to avoid questions.

'A name?' asked Rufton quietly.

'Her initials are SG,' said Thea. 'I wish you to discover as much as you can. I believe she was brought up at Kelfield in Yorkshire by a Mistress Kate Parsons, but I wish you to check. Find out, if you can, where she was born and if…' the words backed up in her throat '…if she is happy.' *If she is my daughter…* She couldn't say that. Surely Rufton would be able to discover enough for her to know. One way or the other.

'It is *Miss* Winslow?' said Rufton slowly.

She nodded. 'What has that to say to anything?'

He looked at her gravely. 'Wouldn't be the first time a monied lady wanted to find out about something on the quiet like this. Like I said, I won't be party to anything that might bring hurt to a child. Ain't the child's fault her father had no proper respect. No more it mightn't have been the mother's fault neither.'

Thea shuddered. 'Mr Rufton—I wish to be assured of the child's welfare above all. I give you my word. I…I wish to know if…if there is anything…anything I can do to help her.'

After the near accident the previous day she could not take the risk. Mortality had breathed an icy warning. Only Richard's courage and swift response had stood between her and death. If her child were alive, then she must know it and make a will…one worded beyond all fear of challenge.

For a long moment he stared at her, as if summing her up, weighing her in the balance of his mind. She felt the colour surging in her cheeks, as if he read all her secrets with those shrewd eyes. Proudly, she held his gaze.

Finally he nodded. 'I'll take it on then.'

Her sigh of relief shocked even her. She had not realised that she was holding her breath. 'Very well. You will please to take this money for your expenses. It is a generous sum, but if I have not allowed enough, you must tell me. Here also are three names—a midwife, a doctor and the rector at Wistow, near Kelfield.' She handed him a sealed note. 'They may perhaps have information. Naturally your travelling expenses there would be defrayed if you needed to go there.'

Rufton took the purse she held out and the list of names. 'I'll be needing an address, ma'am.'

'Send the report here,' she said. 'Mr Sydenham will have it sent on. I shall also instruct him to pay whatever you are owed. One thing—'

'Ma'am?'

'The money in that purse—that is separate to your fee. You will render that in full and separately. If any of the expenses money is left, you may keep it with my goodwill.'

'Now, ma'am—'

'Keep it, sir. You will buy something for your wife and children. I shall like to think of that.'

His eyes bored into her. 'Ma'am, you are sure?'

He did not, Thea knew, refer to the money.

She lifted her chin a notch. 'Quite sure, Mr Rufton.'

She stepped out of the dimness of the chambers to find it drizzling and looked around for the hackney before descending the few steps to the pavement. It stood a few yards away on the opposite side of the road. The horse had a nosebag on and was munching rhythmically while the jarvey consumed his own lunch. She breathed a sigh of relief that he was still there as she adjusted her veil. Not that she was likely to meet anyone, but... Scarcely had she framed the thought when she saw a tall, very familiar figure strolling along the pavement towards her.

In the shadow of the veil her eyes widened, as she froze halfway down the steps. What on earth was Richard doing here? He'd said something at breakfast about being at the museum this morning. She did a mental calculation—the museum wasn't all that far. Obviously he'd had some business. Thank God she had decided to put the veil down inside. He'd never recognise her like this—probably wouldn't even look her way. Why should he?

At that moment Richard, seeing the hackney waiting for her,

stepped across to it. The jarvey shook his head and to her utter horror she heard him say, 'Sorry, guv'nor. The lady there asked me to wait. Bound to be someone along in a mo' for yeh.'

Richard turned to look at her. She stopped dead. At this distance he couldn't possibly recognise her... Yes, he was turning away, nodding to the jarvey in acceptance of the situation. Without hurrying, she started across the pavement—and Richard's gaze snapped back to her. His jaw dropped.

Then he was striding across to her, staring intently.

How on earth? He couldn't have recognised her. He couldn't!

He stopped in front of her, still staring.

The best defence...

'Good morning, Richard. Whatever brings you here?' she asked.

He blinked. 'It is you! What brings me—? Some papers to sign for my house. And what about you? You know quite well that you shouldn't be here unescorted.'

She lifted her chin. 'I was visiting my own solicitors and my business was private.'

'You should still have brought an escort,' he told her.

To her shock she realised that he was handing her into the cab.

'The lady and I are acquainted,' he told the driver. 'Grosvenor Square, if you please.' And stepped in after her.

'Richard—'

He shut the door. '*I* didn't ask *you* anything about your business,' he pointed out gently. 'Only why you were here unescorted.'

She bit her lip. 'I'm sorry...'

A large hand enveloped hers as the cab pulled away from the curb. 'No. There's no need. I've not the least right to question your actions. Have I?'

Regret echoed in his voice and her fingers clung to his instinctively as she forced herself to give the answer she must. 'No,' she whispered. But, oh, how she wished he had! That it was not so impossible...

He sighed and released her hand. She felt utterly bereft and was grateful for the screen of her veil for what she had to say next.

'Richard—I'm not going straight home. Please ask the driver

to take me to Half Moon Street before taking you on to Grosvenor Square.'

Shock sliced into Richard, but he put his head out and called the change of destination up to the driver.

'Right y'are, guv.'

'Half Moon Street, Thea?'

Beside him, she nodded. 'Yes. I must.'

'Thea—'

'No, Richard!' she burst out. 'Don't tell me I can't, or ask me to let you deal with it. This…this is something I have to do. For myself as well as David. Alone. I have to try and ensure she never does this again.'

She turned to him and raised her hands to the veil. As he watched, she lifted it and put it back over her bonnet. Resolution was steady in the blue eyes, in the lift of her chin and set of her mouth.

'Alone?' Couldn't she understand how he felt? That he wanted to stand between her and the whole world? Between her and anything that might harm her, be it a runaway horse or Lady Chasewater. By now the woman must know that her attempt to ruin Winslow and Thea had failed. He told himself that Lady Chasewater could hardly hurt Thea, whether he was there or not. It was just…just that he could not bear the thought of her facing the old dragon by herself, facing more of Lady Chasewater's bitterness and rancour. He looked at her again, and remembered…there were things, some things that one had to face—

'Alone,' she repeated, finishing his thought. And shyly she reached out to touch his hand. Swiftly he caught it in a gentle grip.

'I owe her that much at least,' she said in a low voice.

Anger stirred. 'You owe her nothing!' he said savagely, his grip tightening. 'It is she who owes you—an apology amongst other things!'

She shook her head. 'No, Richard. None of this has been her fault, although it is not completely mine. Or David's. But none of it is hers.'

Her hand returned his clasp, and he fought the urge to haul her into his arms and kiss her resistance, her scruples into oblivion.

'You're asking me to let you walk into the lion's den alone?'

It was important to her. He understood that. That fierce drive to stand unbeholden and independent—only, that didn't have to mean alone.

She nodded. 'Not because I do not trust you. It is just one of those things, that—'

'—one has to do for one's self,' he finished for her. 'Thea, I have not the least right to ask this, but would you mind if I came in with you…' He saw the denial forming. 'No,' he said quickly, 'not to see her. Just let me wait downstairs for you. Whatever you have to say to her will remain between the two of you, I'm not asking for an accounting afterwards—' he smiled at her wryly '—you neither owe me one, nor do I require it. Whatever you are doing will be the right thing—just let me wait. As a friend. No more.'

He could not know how that simple request affected her.

'As a friend?' she whispered. He was asking nothing. Except that she allow him again to stand her friend. In some odd way— her second. It was her battle, all the way.

Richard held her back slightly as she made to descend from the cab in Half Moon Street.

'Your veil, Thea.'

She gave him back a straight look. 'I don't need it now.'

Because of you. She left that unspoken. She didn't understand it herself. She had intended entering Lady Chasewater's house veiled. Quite why she could not now remember. There was no reason to hide this visit. There never had been beyond her own cowardice.

She knew as she trod up the front steps at his side and rang the bell that she did not need the veil now. Not because Richard was coming in with her. But because his unswerving trust had shown her that there was no need to sneak into Lady Chasewater's house in secrecy. She would discharge this obligation openly; if Lady Chasewater refused to receive her, then she could do so—openly.

As the door opened, she took a deep breath and said very clearly to the butler, 'Miss Winslow. To see Lady Chasewater.'

* * *

She was ushered into the drawing room.

'Miss Winslow, my lady.'

The door was shut behind her.

Lady Chasewater was seated upon a sofa with a small black pug, which leapt yapping from its place and rushed growling at the visitor. Thea stood still and waited until the little dog reached her and sniffed around her skirts. Then she bent down and offered a lightly closed fist. The pug sniffed, bared its teeth and then scampered back to its mistress.

'He doesn't like you,' observed Lady Chasewater coldly.

'He doesn't have to, Lady Chasewater,' said Thea. 'And neither do you.'

The old eyes narrowed in their nests of wrinkles. 'No. I don't. Like you, that is. Whether I have to or not.' Bitterness curved the thin lips. 'And there are plenty to tell me that there are fifty thousand very good reasons why I should like you. Or at least tolerate you. What have you done with young Blakehurst? I take it that it is he who came with you? Is he not coming up to threaten me again?'

'Again?'

'Didn't tell you that, did he? Oh, he came. Warning me off as though you were a perfect nosegay of all the virtues. But you and I know better, don't we, Miss Winslow? He'll soon know the truth.'

'This is nothing to do with him,' said Thea, drawing off her gloves. 'For what it's worth, Richard Blakehurst already knows the truth, but this is for you and me to settle.'

Lady Chasewater stared at her. 'For God's sake, sit down, girl!' she snapped. 'I've no need for a stiff neck staring up at you! No. Wait.' She lowered her voice. 'Give the door a good hard thump. With your fist. Just about the keyhole.'

A little puzzled, Thea complied. The muffled grunt on the other side and retreating footsteps spoke volumes for Lady Chasewater's acumen. Thea stared at her unwilling hostess, reluctant amusement bubbling within.

'I've no idea what Almeria Arnsworth's servants are like, but mine are a pack of busybodies!' said Lady Chasewater disgustedly.

The amusement deepened, entwined with regret. Under other circumstances she would have liked this outspoken old woman.

'You may sit over there.' Lady Chasewater indicated an open-armed chair at least three yards from her own sofa. 'And then you may tell me the reason that you have demanded to see me. And why this is none of Richard Blakehurst's business.'

Thea seated herself and gave the old lady back stare for stare. 'I made no demand, Lady Chasewater. I have merely called upon you because there is something I wish to explain to you. And Mr Blakehurst accompanied me as a friend.'

The old woman gave a harsh bark of laughter. 'A friend! And you make no demand, eh? There is merely something you wish to explain.' Her lip curled. 'How you can imagine anything you might say would influence my opinion of you is beyond me!'

'You mistake, ma'am. I could not care less whatever your opinion of me may be. You are welcome to think of me as you will.'

'Then what the devil do you want of me?' flashed the old woman.

'I want you to listen to the truth.'

Cold eyes bored into Thea. 'And you think this will alter my opinion of you?'

Thea shook her head. 'No. You think as my father does. His opinion has not altered in eight years. Like you, he has fifty thousand reasons to acknowledge me. The truth is not one of them.'

'I don't imagine it is!' mocked Lady Chasewater. 'Very well then, girl: what is this "truth" that you would tell me?'

'Eight years ago when...' She swallowed and tried again. 'Eight years ago, your son, with the approval of my father and his, offered me marriage. I was not quite seventeen.'

Lady Chasewater snorted. 'If you think youth excuses—'

'I did not initially refuse him.' Reminding herself that the old lady had been Lallerton's mother, she said quietly, 'But I was uncertain about marrying him. He was very much older, and I asked for time to think. To come to know him. Just that.'

'At sixteen you should have accepted that your father knew what was best for you and thanked God for a respectable match!' snapped Lady Chasewater.

Thea gritted her teeth. That was the view many people would take. She had expected nothing more. 'As you know, my father and Lord Chasewater were determined that the match should go ahead; my father told me that the match was settled.'

'As it should have been! Does it make you proud to know that *your* intransigence caused the death of my son?'

Thea continued. 'He also told your son that the match was a settled thing. That I would be brought to see reason. A day or so later, your son invited me out driving. Since I had requested the opportunity to come to know him better, I went. Your son drove some miles, it was late afternoon, a storm was coming on, and although I kept telling him we were too far from home and should turn back, he ignored me and we ended up seeking shelter at an inn. There was no choice but to remain there for the night.'

'So you were compromised.' Lady Chasewater's voice spat contempt.

'So he told me.' Thea hung on to her composure, her coldness, the icy armour that was her only defence against the searing humiliation and choking terror. It had happened to someone else, a girl who no longer existed, a stranger. She was telling someone else's tale.

'Perhaps foolishly, I told him that I would not marry him, that if he had engineered the situation to force my consent, it would not work. I retired to my bedchamber for the night with one of the maidservants. In that way, I thought, the worst of the scandal could be averted.'

'Thought of everything, didn't you?'

'Everything except your son bribing the girl to leave the chamber in the middle of the night—'

'What rubbish!'

'He admitted it, ma'am. Proudly. As though he had done something clever. Straight after he raped me.'

She had said it aloud. For the first time ever, she had said it aloud to someone. Always before she had shied from the actual word. Even in the silence of her own mind, she had flinched from the ugliness of that particular word. No longer.

'You were betrothed,' said Lady Chasewater with a shrug. 'No doubt he should have waited, but with your father sanctioning the match, what right had you to—?'

'I refused him.' Thea forced her voice to remain cold. Steady. Unflinching. 'I had refused his suit and when I realised…when I woke up to find him in my bed, I refused…I refused—'

She broke off. Shutting out the memories that rose black and monstrous to engulf her. The heavy body, crushing her struggles, the hand stifling her screams, his triumphant grunt as her thighs were forced apart…and the pain and terrified humiliation as he violated her body, swiftly and completely. She forced the memories away. Back behind the icy wall that must contain them.

'Oh, good God, girl! What do you imagine happened that would not have happened on your wedding night?' The words, the impatience, echoed Aberfield. 'Do you think this changes my opinion of you for the better? Little fool! Having lost your virtue to Nigel, you had much better have married him!' Her lip curled. 'No one else would have had you, knowing the truth, and if you think to sway my opinion of you with this tale, you have missed your mark.'

'Ma'am, as I said at the outset, your opinion of me is irrelevant.'

'Then state your purpose in coming and have done.'

'Ask yourself this question, ma'am: how would you expect any man of honour to respond on hearing that his sister had been raped?'

Lady Chasewater's mouth opened. And shut again. Her lips thinned.

'I see. You expect me, then, to accept your interpretation of Nigel's behaviour, and—'

'No,' Thea cut in. 'I do not expect that. Nor do I wish it. You may think as you please of me. You may believe that it was not rape. But do you have the imagination to accept that David believed me? That my brother believed that I had been raped, and acted accordingly? I ask you again: how should a man of honour respond? You have a daughter—how would your son have behaved if the positions had been reversed?'

Bitter silence cried out between them as the ravaged old face hardened.

'What do you want of me?'

'Very little. Sir Giles Mason has dismissed the case against my brother. You, however, can still ruin him by innuendo and gossip. If you were to let it be known that it was all a mistake, a misunderstanding—'

'You must be mad!'

Thea took a deep breath. 'Then I will have no choice but to tell people the reason for the quarrel—whether or not I am fully believed, the scandal will ruin you.'

'And you too,' said Lady Chasewater. Yet she sounded uncertain, shaken.

'But I don't care,' said Thea. 'And your son's name will be smeared. You have a daughter to establish.'

There was a long silence.

Then, 'Your brother behaved as a man of honour, and I will do what I can to stem the gossip. Does that satisfy you?'

'Yes.'

'Then let me tell you this: you disgraced your name, your family, your birth. In refusing to let my son make an honest woman of you, you disgraced your sex. You were not worthy of my son's regard! Nor of your brother's!'

Thea rose. 'There is one further thing. In one of your letters you mentioned a child. A...a daughter—'

Thea broke off as Lady Chasewater's eyes blazed.

'You admit it, do you?'

Pain banded around her heart. 'I was told the child died, but now I have made it my business to find out the truth. I believe that she is alive, and once that is confirmed and I have all the particulars, I will make a will in her favour.'

'Pah!' spat Lady Chasewater. 'What good will that do? Your marriage to Blakehurst will invalidate a will; betrothed to him, you can make no legally binding disposition of your property!'

She had considered that. It had been the final death blow to her unborn hopes. If the child in Bath was hers...

'There is no betrothal. Nor will there be. That was a misunderstanding. There is nothing to prevent me making such a disposition.'

Lady Chasewater stared. 'No betrothal? He is awaiting you downstairs.' Her mouth curled in a sneer.

'No,' said Thea quietly. 'There will be no marriage.'

Lady Chasewater stared at her, and Thea swallowed. There was pain, aching, grieving pain in the old eyes.

'I see.' Lady Chasewater's throat worked and her hands tightened in her lap. 'I dare say that I have no right to ask it, but perhaps you might send me news of the child…from time to time. If you visit her, that is.'

'I…I could do that,' said Thea, dazed. Then, not quite knowing why, she asked, 'Do you wish to see her?' Seeing shock in the older woman's face, she added hurriedly, 'Not to acknowledge her, but just to see her—if it could be arranged discreetly?'

There was a long silence, stretching, breaching the gulf between them. At last Lady Chasewater said, 'I'll think about it. Good day.'

Accepting her dismissal, Thea turned to go.

As she reached for the door, Lady Chasewater spoke again. 'Does Aberfield know yet of your intention?'

Thea looked back. 'Not yet. I'll tell him when I have all the information. I wish to give him no chance to hide the child again.'

A harsh laugh broke from the old woman. 'Very wise. I only knew of her existence after my husband's death. I found a letter from Aberfield, but he refused to give me any information. You will tell me if he causes any difficulty. Now go!'

The door shut behind her. She began to shake uncontrollably as the enormity of what she had done hit her. It was over. David would be safe now. Lady Chasewater had accepted that David had acted in all honour. She forced herself to breathe deeply, willing the shivering to stop. And, slowly, it did. Because she had said it must.

And not only was David safe, but there seemed now to be a queer, tacit understanding between herself and Lady Chasewater. She looked back to the bitter, frightened woman who had arrived in London a few weeks ago. Could that woman have walked into Lady Chasewater's drawing room, spoken the truth and forged this resolution?

She didn't think so. That woman had found it difficult enough just to hold herself together behind her façade. Somehow, somewhere, she had discovered her strength. And the courage to use it. Twinkling dark eyes and a crooked smile formed in her thoughts. Richard. He would never know how much he had helped—simply by being her friend.

He was waiting in the front hall, seated exactly where she had left him. As she came down the stairs he looked up and stood swiftly. His eyes seemed to search her, inside and out, for the least trace of harm. Then he smiled.

'Dragon slain?'

She shook her head. 'Not exactly.' Unless it had been within herself, nothing had needed slaying. Accepting his offered arm, she said, 'Understanding seemed better.'

The dark brows lifted. 'It often is. Come. I'll walk you home.'

The walk was just what she needed to order her thoughts. Richard didn't speak, but she was aware of his quiet strength beside her, somehow surrounding her while not being in the least overwhelming. A friend. And more, something much more that could not be acknowledged.

'You are leaving for Blakeney tomorrow?' she asked as they turned into Grosvenor Square.

'Yes.' Wry amusement touched his voice as he said, 'According to Max, my godson will be making all sorts of amazing progress that I simply must see.'

A strangled laugh escaped her. 'Of course.' Inside she bled, thinking of the child in Bath whom no one had wanted. The only thought at her birth had been to hide her. Even from her own mother.

'And you and Almeria will come down the day after. I'll look forward to that,' he told her. Gently, he said, 'Stop worrying, Thea. We can sort it out it. Talk it through.'

It would be so easy to accept what he offered—surely he would understand her desire to provide for the child first?

If you visit her… Lady Chasewater's words haunted her. She had thought only to ensure the child's safety. Children needed more than that. Her own father had kept *her* safe—according to his code of conduct he had done his duty by her—and more. Many fathers would have simply flung her out. He had at least provided for her.

Safety and security—but no love.

Didn't her own child need more than that? If she accepted Richard's offer, would he permit more than that?

Chapter Fourteen

Richard relaxed back in his chair by the French doors in the library at Blakeney, Max's spaniels at his feet. It was a glorious evening and the doors onto the terrace were open. All the sounds of the dusk drifted in, the cry of an owl, a faint whinnying and stamping from the stables. Scent wafted up from the garden, lavender, rosemary. It had been a warm day and the fragrances lingered on the air with a promise of the coming summer. He always felt at ease here, at home. This house, this room particularly, had been home all his life. Not any more. Oh, he still felt perfectly at ease, with the familiarity of long acquaintance. The room had still its welcome for him, as did the house.

But it was no longer home, much as he loved the place and always would. He had known that for some time. His brain had known it from the day Max announced his imminent marriage to Verity. His heart had known it from the moment he had realised the reality of his brother's marriage.

This house might hold his past. Another must hold his future. Everything was in readiness over at Tarring House.

Not that Verity or Max had shown the least eagerness for him to leave. On the contrary—they were delighted for him to remain. Verity especially had been upset, worried that he might have thought *she* wanted him gone.

He smiled, remembering her worry.

Verity, you goose! I need my own place. This is what I should have done years before the gudgeon met you.

That had been the truth. Max had seemed to see it. Only Max-like, he had decided it was all his fault.

I suppose I have been selfish keeping you here so long.

He hadn't called Max a goose. It had been a good bit more direct than that.

Max came back into the room. He had been upstairs with Verity, seeing little William Richard safely into his crib.

'All tucked up?' asked Richard gravely. Lord! Who would ever have thought to see Max such a doting father! As for the sudden ache in his stomach, and pricking behind his eyes, when Verity had placed his godson in his arms this evening—well, he just wasn't going to think about that. Thank God Max hadn't seen.

'Oh, shut up, Ricky,' said Max without the least rancour. 'Don't think I didn't notice how dewy-eyed *you* were over your godson when Verity gave him to you!'

'Dewy-eyed?' Richard protested. 'Damn it! You make me sound like some feather-brained débutante!' Good God, had it been that obvious?

His twin chuckled and said, 'Speaking of which, are you betrothed or are you not?'

'Thea Winslow,' said Richard, with a tolerable assumption of diffidence, 'is not a feather-brained débutante.'

Strolling over to a side table, Max said, 'Drink?' And proceeded to pour two very large brandies without waiting for a response.

He gave one to Richard and continued, 'I'd be surprised if she was. I seem to recall that by the age of ten she could give you a damn good game of chess.'

Richard smiled. 'That hasn't changed.' He sipped the brandy. 'This is good. The "Gentlemen", one assumes?'

Max gave a wry grimace at this reference to the local smuggling gang, as he lowered his large frame into a chair across from Richard. 'Who else? They keep on leaving the curst stuff right behind the stables, despite any number of messages I've sent that it really isn't necessary. They must know by now that no self-respecting Blakehurst would inform on them. The other day they left scent and a length of lace too!'

Richard grinned and raised his tumbler. 'To tradition!'

Max snorted. 'I understand that there's a barrel or two awaiting your arrival at Tarring House, by the way.'

Richard burst out laughing. 'Is there, indeed?'

'Apparently so. And no doubt if you play your cards properly the lace and scent will follow in due course. Now stop changing the subject, and tell me about this betrothal of yours.'

Richard sighed. 'It's not exactly a betrothal. If you must know, it's hell's own mess.'

Max's black brows rose and the amber eyes glinted with amusement. 'So I gathered from the somewhat incoherent letter I received from Almeria telling me that she would be delighted to come to Will's christening, that she had a houseguest—to wit, Dorothea Winslow—and it would be most unfortunate if we all missed such a splendid opportunity to secure your lasting happiness, and, er—dare I say it?'

'Fortune?' suggested Richard.

'In a word. I was all for telling Almeria to go to the devil at that point, but since I'd already told you Miss Winslow would be welcome…' He shot Richard an amused look. 'I received the impression from Almeria's letter that Miss Winslow was positively yearning to see the beauties of Blakeney.' He shook his head. 'However it came about, I'm relieved that Almeria is putting aside her disapproval to come.'

'That, twin, is one of the reasons Thea is coming to visit,' said Richard and explained what Thea had done.

When Max had stopped laughing, or at least had subsided to an unholy grin, and occasional chuckles, Richard went on, 'Not being perfectly *au fait* with the extent of Almeria's obsession with seeing me married to the largest available fortune—' he waited patiently while Max regained some semblance of self-control '—she didn't realise that our mutual godmother would consider the whole thing as settled,' he finished ruefully.

'Either of you could have denied it,' Max pointed out, swirling the brandy around his glass and inhaling beatifically.

'No,' said Richard shortly. 'At least, I couldn't. Not at that point. And I persuaded Thea not to.'

'No, I suppose not,' said Max. He ventured nothing further. Julian Braybrook's last letter had given him the gist of the massive scandal that hovered over Thea and David Winslow. He was sure there was more to it than Winslow's arrest and subsequent release, but hesitated to probe as to the reason *why* Winslow had ended up in a duel with Lallerton. Richard would tell him in his own good time if he could.

And there was that earlier letter from Julian…

Of course, without you in town to distract her, Lady Arnsworth is interfering in Ricky's non-existent matrimonial plans—flinging heiresses at him hither and yon. But oddly enough, this time she seems to have got it exactly right. For all the wrong reasons, one might add. Fifty thousand of them, in fact. In the face of which, one can only pray that the almost terminal stubbornness of the Blakehursts will not blind the gudgeon to what is as plain as day to the rest of us…

Leaving aside that quite unwarranted jibe about the infamous Blakehurst stubbornness, apparently Braybrook thought Miss Winslow had something to offer Ricky beyond her fortune. And observing Ricky's abstraction since his arrival that afternoon, Max had a sneaking suspicion that Julian could be right.

Never before had he seen Ricky so silent, or so preoccupied. At least, he had, of course, but only over his books. Never about a woman. And on the occasions when Richard had struck up a liaison with a woman, never had his emotions been engaged.

If indeed they were now. Verity said Richard was in love. Max did not pretend to know *how* she divined that from the simple fact that while letters from half their acquaintance had mentioned Ricky's interest in Miss Winslow, Ricky himself had not so much as mentioned her once in any of his letters. But Verity was sure. And Max was inclined to agree.

One thing in particular convinced him: never in all their lives had Richard been loath to offer a confidence to his twin. He stretched out his legs, sipped his brandy and silently wished the half-remembered Miss Winslow luck. He looked forward to renewing his acquaintance with her on the morrow. They would all arrive then. Almeria was coming post with Miss Winslow, and Julian was driving himself down. The christening was set for the following week.

He wondered if it would be tactful to thank Miss Winslow for her efforts. Without the lure of marrying Ricky off, he suspected that either Almeria wouldn't have come at all, or her visit would have been of the most fleeting. As it was, she planned to remain for at least a week. He laughed suddenly.

Ricky's gaze narrowed over his brandy. 'Yes?'

'Nothing. I was just thinking—it's not surprising that Miss Winslow can still give you a good game of chess, if she manoeuvred Almeria that neatly.'

Not entirely to Max's surprise, his twin let that one pass.

Thea stepped out of the chaise the following afternoon, smiled her thanks at the footman who had let down the step, and heaved a sigh of relief. Not just for the physical relief of being able to stretch her legs, which were tired and cramped from the journey, but for the mental relief of no longer having to sit in the same space as Almeria.

Listening to her godmother casually enumerate all the best silk mercers and warehouses for brideclothes had imposed enough of a strain on her self-control. The musings on whether or not Princess Charlotte's example, some seven years earlier, of silver brocade must be considered a trifle outmoded, had tried her even higher.

She had acidly pointed out that Her Royal Highness's death in childbed the following year was not a good omen.

Very true, my dear. Not a lucky bride at all.

But the monologue between Canterbury and Blakeney on the advantages of being married in the cathedral, as opposed to St George's Hanover Square, interspersed with reflections upon the advisability of employing a wet-nurse, had nearly broken her restraint. Never mind counting chickens before the eggs were hatched, Almeria Arnsworth hadn't even managed to get the rooster into the hen-run.

Almeria stepped out behind her, leaning heavily upon the hapless footman.

'Really! One would think that Max would at least—oh.'

She broke off at the sight of her nephew coming out of the front door.

Thea blinked. She had forgotten how alike the Blakehurst twins were. Not identical by any means, but the resemblance was still a shock.

Earl Blakehurst came down the steps with a lithe grace, a delighted smile on his face.

'Here you are, then. I've just given orders for tea to be served in the library.' He took Almeria's hands and bent to kiss her cheek. 'We're delighted you could come, Almeria. Verity will be down in a moment, I am sure. She was having a rest, but insisted I send a maid to awaken her as soon as you arrived.'

Under Thea's fascinated eye, Almeria thawed visibly. 'Well, I'm sure I would not wish to be disturbing her rest.'

Blakehurst chuckled. 'If you don't, I can assure you that our son will do it anyway! Come along in.' He turned to Thea. 'Miss Winslow. I'm delighted to renew our acquaintance. Welcome to Blakeney.'

'Thank you, my lord. It looks beautiful.'

It did. The house, a rambling Tudor mansion standing in extensive flower gardens, seemed to have sprung out of the landscape.

His smile reminded her of Richard's. 'Thank you, Miss Winslow. Please come in. Ricky is about somewhere and Braybrook arrived a couple of hours ago. I trust you have been enjoying your Season.'

Almeria said primly, 'It is very good of you to invite us, Blakehurst. While I continue to deplore the notoriety that accompanied your marriage last year, one can only be grateful to Verity that marriage has curbed some of your more obnoxious habits.'

Thea didn't know where to look. She knew exactly what

Almeria meant by obnoxious habits, but it was not at all the sort of knowledge she was meant to betray. On the whole she thought an expression of blank uninterest might be best.

Blakehurst ruined that.

'Oh? Which habits would they be, Almeria?'

Thea stifled a choke of laughter and Almeria favoured Lord Blakehurst with a quelling glare. 'You know perfectly well to which habits I refer, Max!'

'Ah! *Those* habits,' said his lordship urbanely. Gesturing for Almeria to precede him, he offered Thea his arm. 'Come and meet Lady Blakehurst, Miss Winslow. She has been looking forward to your visit very much.'

Thea's assumption that the countess's eagerness to meet her was a polite fabrication on the part of Lord Blakehurst died in the face of Lady Blakehurst's very genuine delight and pleasure when she came into the library to find Almeria and Thea already fortifying themselves with cups of tea.

The countess was utterly lovely, thought Thea, with her dark hair and deep grey eyes. Small and slender, she still looked rather pale and Lord Blakehurst leapt to his feet, hurrying over to hand her to a chair.

'You slept well?' he asked, before she could say a word.

An ache spread through Thea at the concerned tenderness in his voice, the fleeting caress of his fingers on his wife's hand as he led her to a chair. This was how it should be.

'Yes, thank you, Max,' said the countess. 'Good afternoon, Aunt Almeria. How nice to see you here again.' Her voice was lovely too. Husky and musical. Finding Lord Blakehurst putting her into a chair, she ventured a protest. 'But I should be greeting our guests properly, not languishing in a chair!' She made to get up, but was firmly held back by her husband.

'You may greet them from there,' he said. 'You know perfectly well I think you ought still to be in bed! Verity, this is Almeria's goddaughter, Miss Winslow. Miss Winslow, this is my wife, Lady Blakehurst.'

'He's a tyrant, you know,' said Lady Blakehurst with a perfectly straight face. 'I was never so glad of anything when Richard went up to town because he was almost as bad! I have never been so fussed over or cosseted in my life! How do you do, Miss Winslow? I am so happy to meet you.'

Thea curtsied. 'Thank you, Lady Blakehurst. I am honoured.'

'Blakehurst,' opined Almeria, 'shows a very proper concern and regard for your health, Verity. I congratulate you on the birth of The Heir.'

Lord Blakehurst smiled. 'A secondary concern from my point of view, I assure you, Almeria. Speaking for myself, I was delighted with the birth of my child.'

'A sentiment which does you great credit, Max,' allowed Almeria. 'But naturally you must have been relieved that it was a son.'

Another voice broke in from the open doors onto the terrace. 'Actually, I don't think he was, Almeria.'

Richard strolled in with Lord Braybrook. 'Judging by the letter he sent me, anyway. All the first three paragraphs said was that a baby had been born and that Verity was perfectly all right. The baby's sex was almost an afterthought!'

To Thea's delight, Blakehurst reddened. 'Oh, go to the devil, Ricky! Wait until your turn and see how *you* like it.'

Lord Braybrook chuckled. 'Ignore them, Miss Winslow. Sometimes they are worse than this. Servant, Lady Arnsworth. Miss Winslow. I trust you had a comfortable journey down?'

'Most comfortable, thank you, Lord Braybrook,' said Almeria. 'And when, Verity, may we see—William, is it not?'

Lady Blakehurst smiled. 'Very soon, Aunt. He woke up about half an hour ago. I fed him and Nurse said she would change him and bring him down.'

Almeria's jaw dropped. 'You feed him yourself? My dear Verity, this is most unnecessary—a wet-nurse is far more—'

'I prefer it, Aunt,' said Verity quietly. 'It was my decision.'

Lord Blakehurst, still standing beside his wife's chair, laid his hand on her shoulder, saying, 'And one which I fully endorse.'

Much to Thea's surprise, given the very decided views on the subject aired in the chaise, Almeria subsided at once. 'Naturally, Max, if you approve, then there is no more to be said.' Then, rather diffidently, she added, 'As long as it does not tire Verity unduly.'

Thea rather thought that Lord Braybrook looked distinctly relieved that the subject was to be shelved. Even Richard looked to have relaxed somewhat. Although that might be more due to his worry about this meeting. His glance flickered back and forth between his brother, Almeria and the countess.

Then, without warning, his gaze rested on her and his heart-stopping smile dawned, lighting the dark eyes from within. His lips moved silently as he lifted his teacup in unspoken salute.

Thank you.

All Thea's defences shook to their foundations, to the very core of her being. And if he ever suspected what she felt for him... Somehow she managed to smile back. Brightly. *Happy to have helped.* As though it meant nothing.

The door opening to admit the nurse with a small, shawl-wrapped bundle, was akin to a relieving troop of cavalry approaching a citadel under siege.

Lord Blakehurst strode across the room and the nurse, with a suspiciously primmed mouth, delivered the bundle into his arms.

'Thank you, Nurse. We'll let you know when he is back in the nursery.'

'Yes, m'lord.' She curtsied and went out.

The reason for the nurse's suppressed amusement was not far to seek. When Lord Blakehurst turned back to his guests, the expression of undisguised, tender pride on his face stabbed into Thea with undiluted pain, tearing at wounds she had thought healed and forgotten.

No one had ever looked at her child like that.

The countess spoke. 'Perhaps...perhaps Aunt Almeria might like to hold him, Max?'

Slowly, his lordship turned to his aunt. 'Almeria?'

'I...I should like that very much, Max.' Her voice, utterly expressionless, fell into a breathless hush.

Lord Blakehurst bent down, carefully depositing the babe in her arms. 'His...his head needs support, you know—'

'Max—I have held a baby before,' said Almeria with asperity. 'You, for one.' She shot a glance at Braybrook. 'Even you. In fact—' she settled the baby in her arms and drew back the shawls a little '—the only one of you here that I did *not* hold as a babe would be Verity.'

Silence fell as Almeria examined the baby. A very careful, elegant finger stroked gently, and a corner of the severe mouth flickered.

The knife twisting inside Thea dug a little deeper. No one had rejoiced at the birth of her daughter. Not even reluctantly. She had been hidden away, her very existence denied. She clenched her hands in her lap, willing the hurt to subside, forcing her face to remain calm, politely interested as they waited for Almeria to say something.

Then, 'Thank you, Max. I do not know how it may be, but the title Great Aunt seems far more ageing than that of Grandmother.'

Lord Blakehurst grinned. 'It must be the "Great", Almeria. Shall I take him again?'

'You may.'

He bent down and scooped up the little bundle effortlessly.

'That,' pronounced Almeria, 'is a very healthy and well-developed child, Max.' She turned to the countess. 'You have done very well, Verity. Very well, indeed.'

'Thank you, Aunt,' said the countess.

Almeria frowned. 'Verity, it is time and more that you ceased to call me "Aunt", if you please.' The frown deepened. 'I dare say that I have been very foolish in the past year. I hope that—'

'Almeria,' said Lord Blakehurst quietly, 'your presence here is a great pleasure to us. No more needs to be said.'

Almeria looked even more pokered up. 'You are generous, Max. Thank you.'

For an instant time stood still and Thea knew that, although doubtless there would be disagreements and Almeria might never fully approve of Lady Blakehurst, there was healing and acceptance, that the family was no longer split.

Involuntarily she met Richard's gaze. Quiet pride, gratitude and, oh, God—that something else that she dared not acknowledge.

Lord Blakehurst broke the spell. 'Miss Winslow, would you care to hold him?'

Hold the baby? Panic assaulted her. She couldn't—not a baby. Bad enough looking at every small child and wondering, endlessly wondering what her child might have been like…tall, fair? Mischievous, obedient? But to actually hold a baby… Only, that was *her* voice, saying politely how much she would like to hold the child, and Lord Blakehurst was already bending down and there was the weight in her arms, the weight she had never felt before, only imagined.

Such a tiny weight.

She was holding Richard's nephew and godson-to-be and all she could feel was rage. And pain. Rage that this had been stolen from her, that—no.

She would not feel bitterness. Not with a child in her arms. Not with the sweet, milky scent wreathing through her. There could be pain, yes. But not the bitterness of envy. This little one had done nothing to deserve that. She forced herself to focus on the tiny face. A small fist was stuffed into his mouth and she found herself smiling into the sleepy unfocused eyes blinking up at her.

Joy swept her, lighting the darkest corners, burning away all else in its path. Instinctively she found herself rocking gently, patting in the same rhythm, and before her wondering eyes, the child fell asleep, still with his fist stuffed in his mouth.

Richard saw the wonder take her, the amazement, the awe. In that instant he saw everything he wanted for himself. And for her. The knowledge shook him to the very foundations of his being and he knew what he had to do. He had to convince Thea that he wanted her. He had to convince her that his offer of marriage, when he made it again, had nothing to do with honour and chivalry, and everything to do with love.

A swift movement drew his attention. He glanced sideways,

to catch Almeria dabbing moisture from her eyes. She caught his gaze and glared, stuffing—the only word for it—her lacy handkerchief into her reticule.

'There must be something drifting in from the garden,' she said defiantly, 'or perhaps those flowers on Max's desk!'

'Of course, Almeria,' he agreed gravely, not daring to look at Max.

He looked back at Thea, her head still bent over the baby, her arms and hands cradling the bundle in absolute safety. And the tenderness in her expression—as though she held her own child.

The thought of her holding her child, *their* child, hit him in a rush of possessive desire. Every muscle in his body turned to steel as he hardened. It was all he could do to remain in his chair. He wanted her. In his arms, his bed. His life.

She looked up, as if he had spoken her name. Her expression was dazed, shocked. He thought he knew exactly how she felt; as though her world had turned upside down, and quite possibly inside out.

An odd sound from Max recalled him to his surroundings. Tearing his gaze from Thea, he met his twin's eyes. Amused understanding glinted in the amber.

'Always such a shock,' murmured Max.

Lord William Blakehurst having been duly christened and welcomed into the church, and having yelled his lungs out the whole time, his relatives and well-wishers removed themselves from the church in a laughing, joyous crowd.

Lord Braybrook, holding his squalling godson, appeared more than marginally harassed. 'Lady Blakehurst, I swear, it's nothing *I'm* doing!'

The countess smiled. 'Here. I'll—'

'Give him to me,' said Max and took his son, who immediately yelled louder.

'It's the baptism,' said Richard, trying not to laugh as they strolled across the churchyard. 'I'm sure I have heard somewhere that if they yell, it means the devil is leaving them.'

'Which begs the question why Max yelled and you didn't on the occasion of your joint baptism,' said Almeria very drily.

Richard choked and turned instinctively to share the joke with Thea, whose soft blue eyes were indeed full of laughter. For an instant the corner of her mouth lilted in the beginnings of a smile, a smile that caught at his heart, that brought every suppressed longing raging to the surface. She immediately looked away.

As she had done for the past week.

Ever since that moment in the library when their eyes had locked over the baby in her arms, she had avoided him. Oh, not completely, but she had made quite sure that they were never alone together, never paired except in the most general way.

She had been the most charming and delightful of guests, leading several of Max's neighbours to comment that the rumours that had reached them from London must have been greatly exaggerated.

Even now she was chatting sensibly to old Lady Aldicott, a stickler if ever there was one. The old lady caught his gaze on them and smiled knowingly. 'And you're staying on at Blakeney, then, after Almeria returns to town?'

Thea denied it quietly, although colour rushed to her cheeks.

Not for the first time Richard cursed Almeria's not-entirely-accidental indiscretion in London. How to tell if Thea truly did not wish to marry him, or simply wished not to see him obliged to marry her out of duty?

His jaw hardened. All week he had held back, and she had slipped further and further away. It was, he understood, difficult for a woman to wear her heart on her sleeve if she were not quite certain of a man's affections. And for Thea, perhaps, impossible.

Screwing his courage to the sticking place, he strolled over to Thea and Lady Aldicott.

The old lady smirked. 'Well! And about time too that a new generation of Blakehursts came along to plague us!' She poked Richard with her walking stick. 'I'll look forward to seeing you do your bit.' Heat flared on his cheeks as the old she-devil nodded to Thea. 'I'm pleased to have met you, my dear. I'll look forward to continuing our chat some time. I'm off home now. My old bones need a rest. Good day to you both.'

She stumped off, and Richard turned to Thea. 'We need to talk,' he said. 'Quietly, privately and honestly. You know I won't lie, and that I won't force either of us into an unwanted marriage—'

'Richard—'

'We need to talk,' he repeated. 'Before you return to London. That is all I ask.'

'Very well,' she said. 'Now?'

Now? In the middle of a christening party? 'After dinner,' he said.

Chapter Fifteen

When the gentlemen joined the ladies in the library after dinner, Thea was not there. Richard frowned as he glanced round. She had looked very pale during the meal. Perhaps she had retired already.

Verity glanced up, smiling, from her conversation with Almeria and the rector's wife. 'Are you looking for Miss Winslow, Richard? She is on the terrace. I think she has the headache a little.'

Almeria shot him a severe glance. 'I dare say a little fresh air will not go amiss, Richard. I know that I can trust you to take Dorothea for a gentle walk in the gardens.'

An excellent idea—if only he could extend to himself the same trust!

Sure enough, he found her just outside, gazing out over the velvety darkness of the gardens from the balustrade. Mingled scents of flowers and newly cut grass came up to them, twining with the rippling song of a fountain. Such a fragile peace.

She looked up at him as he came up beside her. 'It is lovely here, is it not?'

'Beautiful,' he agreed. 'Should you care to come for a walk with me?' What they needed was a little privacy. Somewhere they did not have to worry about being interrupted and he could tell her…tell her—his heart felt as though steel bands were tightening around it—he needed to tell her that he loved her.

She did not answer immediately and a shaft of foreboding stabbed into him. Surely, surely he had not been wrong about this—

'Sir…that is, Richard—I do not think that would be advisable, you see—'

He laid his hand over hers on the balustrade, felt the fine tremor and the tension. 'Thea, we need to talk.'

'There is not the least need, Richard. And indeed it is not wise. Almeria will find it hard enough to believe when our supposed betrothal comes to naught.'

His heart clenched. 'Must it come to naught, my dear?'

It was all he could do to keep his voice light, and his hands still when every instinct urged him to drag her into his arms and kiss her until she knew the truth he knew—that she was *his*. He forced himself to remain still. After what had happened to her, Thea was the last woman in the world to be won over in that way.

She bit her lip. 'Yes. This…this is not what I want…to be manipulated and forced into marriage to satisfy society.'

Put like that… If Thea felt that she was being constrained— his throat tightened around the aching loss. More fool him. He had thought that beyond the impossible situation in which they found themselves, beyond the affection he knew she felt for him, that there had been something else, the possibility of something more.

Could she believe that he was offering a marriage without love?

'Thea…in marrying you, I would not be bowing to the dictates of society—'

She flinched, tugged her hand from under his. 'Please, Richard. No more. I…I cannot marry you. It is not possible.'

He could not mistake her determination. Nor that his suit distressed her. Her eyes were bright with unshed tears, yet she was facing him squarely, proudly.

She smiled, a wobbly travesty of a smile, but still a smile. 'Your wife, Richard, will the luckiest of women. But it cannot be me. We are dear friends—let it remain that way.'

Resolutely he faced the truth: that *his* truth might not be hers. That if he truly loved her, he would not bind her to him.

From somewhere he dredged up a semblance of a smile.
'Then we must wish each other well?'

Thea nodded, her eyes full of pain.

Somewhere deep inside him there was pain also. Pain he
thought he might carry for the rest of his life. Unable to help
himself, he reached out his hand, lifting it to her face. This must
be the last time. He would not touch her again. Gently he traced
her jaw, memorising the silky softness, the delicate whorls of her
ear and the line of her brow. Desire, longing, flooded him. It
would be so easy to take her in his arms and kiss her. He must
not. Slowly, carefully, he brushed over the curve of her mouth
with his fingertips…never again…never…and it should not be
happening now.

He forced his hand to drop, seemingly relaxed.

'So be it,' he said quietly. And left her.

With his departure, Thea released the death grip she had kept
on herself. She had never imagined that it could be this painful.
Or that the hurt she saw in his eyes would threaten her resolution far more than the knife twisting in her own heart.

The following day brought Thea a letter from Aberfield. She
stared at it for several minutes before slipping out into the garden
and finding a quiet corner in which to open it. Her fingers
trembled as she smoothed out the folds and read.

It wasn't all bad. The news that Lady Chasewater had spoken
to David in public with every appearance of civility sent a jolt
of relief through her. Thea could only imagine what that had cost
her. But then she came to the part that concerned her directly.

*I cannot but feel that, in leaving town before sending the
notice of your betrothal to the* Gazette, *Mr Blakehurst has been
unwise. I say nothing of his failure to obtain my consent. You have
been at pains to make it clear this means little to you. I dare say
he has taken that as his cue.*

*In any case, such a marriage will be convenient in many
ways. As a younger son, without the family honour to uphold, one
may assume that he will be somewhat more lenient in certain*

*areas and your earlier indiscretion need not be considered. He
is a sensible man, and will no doubt accept this as the price of
an alliance otherwise beyond his expectations. I have no doubt
that you will deal well together.*

There was more, but she could not bear to read it all. The
brutal assumptions chilled her to the bone. Her marriage to
Richard would have been a convenience to Aberfield, settling
the problem of how to manage her fortune, scotch any remaining scandal. It suited Aberfield; oh, and in marriage to a younger
son, her—how did he put it? She glanced again at the letter—
*your earlier indiscretion need not be considered…you will deal
well together.*

She walked on, through the gentle fragrance and humming
bees of the knot garden, the letter crumpled to a ball in her hand.

Marriage to Richard. Aberfield's reasoning sickened her, but
in a way he was right: Richard was the one man to whom she
could have given herself.

And now she knew what she would have wanted in marriage
to Richard. Love. The sort of love that blazed between Max and
Verity. That was what her heart had been trying to tell her about
Richard. A shiver went through her. Her heart and her body had
both tried to warn her.

Carefully she smoothed out the letter and folded it back into
the original creases, tucking it into her reticule. She had chosen
her course. No good could possibly come from mourning over
a might-have-been. Even if Richard had come to care for her in
that way, it was impossible. She knew now, had known from the
moment she held Richard's nephew in her arms, what she had
to do. And doing it would cut her off from Richard for ever.

It was not something she had any choice about. It simply was.
Her decision was made, and there could be no going back from
it. Not if she wished to live at peace with herself. She went into
the house by a side door and made her way towards the library.
Verity was usually to be found there often with little William.

At first the library seemed empty, but then voices drifted in
through the open doors from the terrace. Smiling, Thea went

towards them. And then, in the doorway, she froze to utter still-ness. A comfortable-looking *chaise* had been placed in a shady corner of the terrace. Verity was there and Lord Blakehurst, who held his son cradled in one arm. The other encircled Verity as he kissed her, so tenderly it brought tears to Thea's eyes. Blinking, she stepped back behind the curtains. Back from the incarnation of all she could never have. All she would have most desired.

Impossible now to remember the way she had felt when she returned to London, wanting nothing more than her freedom and peace. That had been a safer ambition. One she could achieve. Now…she could never have what she now desired.

She was about to slip away when male voices floated up from the garden. Richard. And from the sounds of it, Lord Braybrook. Returned from their ride.

Booted feet sounded on the terrace steps, one set uneven. She sighed. There was no reason now to walk away.

'Hullo, Max.' Lord Braybrook's light baritone. 'Servant, Lady Blakehurst. Sorry to be so long. Ricky dragged me off to see his house.'

'Oh, did you like it?' Verity's soft tones.

Thea stepped out of the shadow into the open French door.

'Just the thing for Ricky, I should think,' said Braybrook. 'Sort of place that even had *me* thinking of marriage and families.'

'Julian?' That was Richard.

'Yes?'

'Stubble it.'

'Well, it's true,' averred Braybrook. 'It did. Gave me quite a turn, I assure you! I shall have to offer for Miss Winslow and—'

Thea froze in place, her wits whirling.

'Ah, Julian—' Earl Blakehurst's bright amber gaze was on her, his mouth twitching. Thea pulled herself together.

'Be refused?' she suggested, taking her cue and stepping out onto the terrace.

Lord Blakehurst gave a muffled crack of laughter. 'Very sensible, Miss Winslow. Do come and join us.' He rose to his feet, still cradling his son, and came forward to greet her.

His smile gave not the least hint that he and his wife had been interrupted, that he might be wishing his guests at the devil.

'I wanted to see you. I understand that Almeria intends returning to town the day after tomorrow. There is not the least need for you to leave at the same time. I, that is, *we* would be most happy if you chose to extend your stay.'

A queer sound escaped from Richard. She glanced at him and found him staring at his twin with a totally disbelieving expression on his face. Outraged, even.

Despite knowing that she could not stay, pain slashed through her to know that the thought of her staying did not endear itself to Richard at all. Probably he'd heard quite enough speculation on the subject of their non-existent betrothal by now. Not that Lord Blakehurst would have made that mistake. He must know his brother better than that.

'Thank you, my lord. I will give that some thought.' Best to be non-committal.

'Do come and sit down, Thea,' said Verity. 'There is plenty of room here on the *chaise*.'

'Actually, I thought I might go for a walk,' she said. 'Up on to the Downs. It is such a beautiful day. Is there a path I could follow?'

Lord Blakehurst frowned. 'There is, but you were not thinking of going alone, were you?'

Thea flushed. 'I…I don't want to inconvenience anyone. Surely—'

Lord Blakehurst grinned. 'I can assure you that I will be more than inconvenienced when Almeria hears that we let her precious charge wander unescorted over the Downs!'

'Dear Miss Winslow,' said Braybrook. 'Behold your escort. No—don't demur. It will give me a chance to propose in private and you a chance to—'

'But you promised that you would play piquet with me!' protested Verity in some indignation. 'Richard may take Thea.' She turned to her brother-in-law with a ravishing smile. 'Won't you, Richard? You could take her up through the beech woods. It will be lovely up there today.'

Richard, Thea swiftly realised, was in as impossible a situation as she was herself. He could scarcely refuse without the appearance of rudeness, and, having said she wished to go for a walk, *she* could not now draw back. Not without publicly rejecting Richard's escort.

Meeting his gaze, she saw wry amusement there, and resignation. He rose to his feet. 'If we are to go up on to the Downs, Thea, you will need to change your shoes. And find a bonnet that ties on securely. It will be windy up there.'

Thea bowed to the inevitable.

By tacit consent they talked very little on the walk up through the woods. Indeed, Thea scarcely had breath by the time they reached the top of the valley and left the trees behind. Up and up they climbed, until Thea's legs ached and her lungs burned. Just ahead she could see the crest of the hill…only a little further… She took a deep breath before the wind could whip it away, and pushed on to the top.

Once there the view snatched away the remnant of her breath. Around them spread the Downs. Above them swung the blue arc of the sky. In the distance the Channel shifted and glimmered in the late afternoon light.

'We should turn back,' said Richard, coming up with her, not sounding in the least winded, although his limp was slightly more apparent. Her own lungs were burning at the climb and she felt utterly exhausted. Her face must be scarlet and her legs felt as though they might actually drop off.

But the view was worth it. Blue and green and limitless. Up here it was almost possible to believe that if one only spread one's arms and leaned on the wind one could fly. Up here all the problems and trivialities of the world fell away. Oh, they still existed, but they could not *touch* you up here.

She sighed. 'Yes. But I needed this. Needed to get out. Feel space around me. London—' She broke off, not quite sure how to express herself.

'Cabined, cribbed, confined?' he suggested.

She nodded. 'Yes. This—' she gestured wildly '—this is beautiful. You can be alone without being lonely.' She knew he would understand. He always did.

A faint smile curved his mouth. 'It's called solitude. At least that's what I call it. My mother didn't like it at all. She hated Blakeney. Said it was too isolated. She spent as much time as she could away from it.'

Thea remembered the late Lady Blakehurst. And thought of the present Lady Blakehurst.

'I don't think Lady Blakehurst minds.'

'Verity?' Richard smiled. 'I doubt she'd mind where she was, as long as Max was somewhere nearby. But, yes. She loves Blakeney.'

Slowly they descended, following the faint path down until they reached the beech woods. The cool green shade welcomed them, the light breeze sighing, rippling above. Caressing. Gentle. The way Lord Blakehurst had kissed Verity.

She pushed the thought away. And then faced it. Yes. That was how a kiss could, *should,* be. The new-found knowledge ached inside her. This was something she would only ever be able to guess at. Something she could never know for herself. But at least she now knew that with the right man, there was nothing to fear. Richard had taught her that.

She tripped on the thought. She really ought to thank him. But how? What to say? To Richard of all men.

And there was the rub. Richard. The man she loved. The man she would always love, so deeply that he seemed a part of herself. Even if he never knew it. She shut her eyes against the prickling tears. He must never know it.

But somehow she must thank him for what he had taught her. For what he had forced her to see. Here, still high above the world, she could see what she had known deep down for weeks. The day he had swung her out of the path of the gig, holding her afterwards as if he would never release her; the night he had come to her during her nightmare and comforted her; his protective fury when he rescued her from Dunhaven; the day he had swung her around in joy at the news of Verity's safe delivery. Above all, he had accepted her as she was; he had stood by her. He had not judged. Oh, yes; she had been in love with him for weeks, yet, held prisoner in the darkness of her own fears, she had been too cowardly to acknowledge it.

But now in the sunlight, she knew: with Richard there would have been nothing to fear. The world misted and she blinked furiously. It was impossible. She had made her choice—and yet…

The woods were thinning. Soon the house would be in sight and this was the sort of thing that she would much prefer to say very privately indeed.

'Richard?'

'Mmm?'

'The other day—when you asked me to marry you…' She hesitated, struggling to give words to her thoughts. 'Even though I can't possibly marry you—I wanted to thank you, for…for believing me, and even before that…for not judging me.'

His smile tore her heart from her breast, deepened, reaching places within her that she had thought lost. Dazed, she realised that he had taken her hands, that he was bending towards her, that he was going to…

His lips brushed across hers in the gentlest of featherlight caresses. Her whole being leapt and surged unbidden as he straightened and drew back. She felt as though a flame leapt and burned within her, dancing in joy.

He had kissed her. Just.

And her whole being yearned for him to kiss her again. Properly.

He said in an odd, tight sort of voice, 'We had better keep moving.'

Automatically she followed him, shockingly aware that her lips felt bereft, incomplete, that she was like a moth dancing around a lamp. Certain to be singed, but dancing all the same and yearning for the touch of flame on its wings just once more.

Would he mind? Just to show her? It would be utterly shameless, of course, but what did she have to lose? Her virtue?

'Richard?'

'Yes?' Very curt.

Perhaps he *would* mind. Nevertheless Thea took a deep breath and asked huskily, 'Would you kiss me again?'

He stopped dead in his tracks.

'I beg your pardon?'

Stubbornly she met his disbelieving gaze. 'Please…if you wouldn't mind…would you kiss me again. P…p…properly this time.'

He was having difficulty just breathing, but he managed to say, 'I think I might just about be able to cope.' Dear God in heaven—what the hell did she mean by *properly?* Unfortunately, the way—*all* the ways—he wanted to kiss Thea Winslow came under the heading *im*proper. Extremely improper. Now was probably not the right moment to point out that he'd been wanting to kiss her properly for some time. And it certainly wasn't the right moment to lose all control. She had refused even to listen to his last offer of marriage. So why in Hades did she want him to kiss her?

'Here?' he suggested, keeping his voice very neutral. At least his voice was under control. It was about the only part of him that was. Apparently the shreds of his control had been used up keeping that last kiss within the bounds of propriety.

She looked about. 'Y…yes. Here would be nice.'

Nice? Richard took a shuddering breath. *Here* would be perfect. He suspected that *here,* in the sun-dappled green of the beech woods, was about to become the most wonderful place on earth. Slowly, he raised a hand and brushed his fingers along the elegant line of her throat and jaw. So soft. So silky. He couldn't remember any woman's skin ever being that soft. He couldn't remember any other woman at all for that matter. She, and only she, filled his memories, his heart, his soul. And she had asked him to kiss her. Just kiss her. If anyone had ever offered him anything sweeter, he didn't remember that, either. Carefully he cradled her jaw, smoothing his thumb over her lips. They parted on a soft gasp and heat shot through him.

Just a kiss, he reminded himself.

Thea waited, shivering in wonder at his touch, her mind reeling with shock, that she had actually done something so outrageous as to ask a gentleman to kiss her. Properly. Only...having asked him to kiss her, she now had absolutely no idea what the next move should be. She didn't even know what *properly* involved. Fortunately it was obvious that Richard *did* know.

His fingers, light and caressing, drew tingling magic from deep within her, melting her shyness in the warmth of his tenderness. Gentle, featherlight kisses caressed her temples, her closed eyes. Controlled strength drew her closer, nestling her against his body as that teasing mouth brushed fire along the line of her jaw, until, in sudden frustration, she turned, clumsily capturing his lips with her own.

A moment's stillness as their mouths met, then his lips moved in a heart-shaking entreaty, the silky heat of his tongue tasting, teasing her own lips open. So different, a melding this, and she responded to the heat spreading within her, parting her lips, opening her mouth in acceptance.

His tongue slid deep, stroking, and heat burst inside her as she felt the aching pulse deep within, echoing the possessive surge and retreat of his tongue.

He took, but he also gave. And she could sense his restraint. In the taut strength of his arms, cradling her so tenderly. In the low groan deep in his throat as she tentatively returned his kiss, tasting, probing with her own tongue.

Her bones melted. Every fibre softened in delight and she clung, pressing against him, closer than sunlight, feeling joy and love pour through her, illuminating every dark corner, flinging back the shadows.

Finally, far too soon, he drew back, releasing her mouth and settling her cheek against his chest. She could hear his heart hammering. Beating to the same wild, burning rhythm as her own. His hand stroked her hair, soothing, gentle.

His voice came, utterly calm. 'Was that what you meant by properly?'

Her heart steadied slightly.

'I...yes...I think so. Yes.'

Her own voice wobbled despicably. Properly? Yes, oh, yes! If properly mean shot with fire and life and a promise that could never be fulfilled.

She took a careful breath, forcing it past the aching lump in her throat. 'Thank you, Richard.' At least the wobble was gone from her voice. She wished she could say the same for her knees. Regardless she pushed gently against his chest, asking wordlessly to be released. She could stand alone.

She would have to.

He released her the moment he felt her desire to be freed, and wondered if some part of him had ripped free of its moorings, for ever to swing rudderless. He had known that he desired her. Hell! He had even known that he loved her.

But he had not put the two together. He had not realised what it would be like to kiss her in the full knowledge of how deeply he loved her. To hold her in his arms and feel the wild sweetness of her response to him. To feel the tenderness restraining his own wild ardour.

And then to release her, knowing that it might be for ever.

She had asked him to kiss her. She had wanted to know.

Knowledge. Not possession.

His soul flared in rebellion: not yet, he promised himself. But it was a start. That kiss had allayed his greatest fear: that Thea's refusal to marry him might spring from fear. Fear and distaste for what would happen in the marriage bed. Believing that, he had resolved not to press her, but surely now she could not deny what lay between them, and her own response to it, any more than he could. And he could as soon deny his own breath.

He wanted her. Wanted to see her in his home. *Their* home. He wanted to see their children growing around them. If he could tell her that...or better, show her. He thought he understood what was holding her back. Doubt and fear. Doubt that he could possibly want her. A fear that his offer sprang from chivalry and pity, that he might one day come to resent her.

The idea slipped into place very simply. He needed to show

her. Show her that she lay at the heart of what he wanted. And then, perhaps, he might be able to find the words to say what was in his heart.

Tucking her hand into his arm, he began walking again. He didn't have long. Almeria had finally decided to return to town.

'Thea, would you ride with me tomorrow afternoon?' he asked.

'Ride?'

'Yes, echo! Ride with me.' He took a deep breath. 'If Almeria intends to return to town the day after tomorrow… A last outing? Just the two of us?'

Chapter Sixteen

'Where are we going, Richard?' asked Thea, pushing her mare into a trot to keep up.

He grinned across at her. 'You'll see. How do you like Fidget's paces?'

'Very nice,' she said. 'What else would I expect from an earl's favourite mare? Don't change the subject! Where are you taking me?'

'Over the hills and far away?' he suggested. 'I'll tell you when we get there.'

Thea sighed. She ought not to have agreed to this ride. Being alone with Richard again like this was not wise. Not wise at all. Her treacherous heart sang and danced in joy that he wanted to be with her, had leapt wildly at the thought of riding out with him this afternoon. Even his teasing refusal to tell her their destination only added to her delight.

It was so long since anyone had arranged a surprise for her.

They cantered on in companionable silence over the Downs, past the great flocks of sheep, hearing the calls of larks riding the wind high above and further away the crash and roar of the sea boiling around the cliffs.

They came over the brow of a hill and Richard flung up his hand.

'Here we are,' he called, as they reined in.

He pointed down. Thea looked. There below in the valley, nestled in a beech wood, stood a house. An old rambling manor house; over the years it had been added to until it appeared to have simply grown there along with the trees and gardens. Smoke curled up from a chimney.

'Who lives here?' she asked. It felt familiar, yet she was sure she had never been there before.

He flashed her a smile. 'You'll see. Come along. And mind the track down. It's a little steep here. This is the back way in. Much faster than coming round by the roads.'

She followed him, letting the mare have her head, but prepared to gather her up in event of a stumble. At the bottom she found that they were in an orchard. Gnarled old apple trees were laden with blossom. She gazed around in delight as the mare followed Richard's gelding. They clattered into a cobbled stable yard and an old man came out, blinking.

'There yeh be, Mester Richard,' he said, without the least evidence of surprise, taking the bridle of Richard's horse as he dismounted.

'Good afternoon, Sam. This is Miss Thea. Thea, may I present Sam Decks?'

Thea smiled, masking her puzzlement.

'How do you do, Mr Decks?'

He touched his cap. 'Nicely, ma'am. Nicely.' Jerking his thumb over his shoulder, he said, 'Ye'll find the missus inside, sir. Been like a pea on a griddle, expectin' yeh this last hour.'

Richard's eyes twinkled. 'I'd better not keep her waiting any longer then.' He came over and Thea's heart and stomach pirouetted in a mad waltz as he set his hands to her waist and prepared to lift her down.

'Richard! I...your leg!'

He grinned. 'These are my arms, Thea. Nothing wrong with them.'

Memory stirred...his arms...remembered delight rippled through her—no, there was nothing wrong with them at all.

A wheezy laugh from the old groom drew her back, and she

was being lifted to the ground in a gentle, inescapable grip. For a fleeting instant she met his eyes. Heat, wild and unbidden, leapt within her at their expression. Dark, intent. Breathless, she dropped her gaze. To his mouth. To the firm lips that had swept away the world and replaced it with a new one.

One in which she could not dwell.

Mercilessly she fought back the urge to lean against him, refused to believe that the strong, tender hands had lingered on her waist, that the withdrawing fingers seemed to trace and caress the curves.

No. It was impossible.

'What…who are we visiting?' she asked, wishing she didn't sound so breathless.

Richard didn't appear to have heard. He was leading her across the cobbles and out of the stable yard.

'We'd better go around to the front. Mrs Decks will skin me if I bring you through the kitchens this time.'

'Richard! Who is Mrs Decks?'

And what was so special about this time?

His smile was half-guilty. 'Well, she was my nanny. Mine and Max's, that is. Now she's my housekeeper.'

The world seemed to contract around her to utter stillness, even though she was still moving, following him along a flagged path around the house and its flowerbeds. Bees hummed, a black-bird flashed past them. At the front of the house a rather weedy carriage drive swept up to the front door. No wonder it felt familiar—it was exactly as he had described it. But why in the world had he brought her here?

'It's a trifle neglected,' said Richard ruefully. 'But it's gradually coming into order. I'll be moving in this week. All the staff will be here tomorrow, but today it's still just Sam Decks and his wife.'

The front door stood open and with a smile and bow, he ushered her over the threshold into a dim, flagged hallway, then called out, 'Nell?'

Firm steps were heard and an elderly woman came bustling into the hall.

'Well and surely! 'Tis about time, Master Richard.'

Bright eyes looked Thea over and Richard said, 'Nell, this is Miss Thea. She came down from London with Lady Arnsworth for the christening. I thought she would like to see the house.'

He turned to Thea. 'Thea, may I present Mrs Decks. She ruled Max and myself with a rod of iron. Terrorised us, I give you my word!'

Mrs Decks went scarlet. 'Oh, you and your nonsense! Pleased to meet you, I'm sure, miss. Enough to turn your hair grey, this one and his lordship. Looks like you just missed the rain and all. Setting in it is, Sam reckoned.'

Richard frowned. 'Hmm. Not precisely what I wanted. We might have to make a very quick tour and head back earlier than I planned. If it really blows in…'

Thea supplied the rest mentally—they would be in for a very wet ride back to Blakeney.

Turning to her, Richard said, 'Come and see the house, Thea. Then we can have a cup of tea and, if I know Nell, she will have baked a cake.'

Mrs Decks smiled fondly. 'I'll bring it all to the parlour in half an hour then, Mr Richard.'

Richard's house.

Thea followed him around, listening.

'I bought it a few months ago, but it needed work, so I stayed at Blakeney while it was done. There's quite a bit of land attached. Enough to keep me occupied. In fact, some of those sheep we saw on the way were mine.'

'Oh.' It felt so right for Richard. She could see him here, managing his land, reading his books…but—this was a house for a family. Gazing out the window of one of the bedchambers, she could almost see and hear children racing through the garden…wicked, dark-haired little boys who spent more time in mischief than out…one could have a swing under that big oak, and Richard's dogs would love it…he'd always had dogs. And the stables, now empty but for their mounts, would be full of horses. The whole place would be alive, brimming with joy, echoing with noise.

She bit her lip.

'Thea?'

'It's...it's lovely, Richard. I'm sure you will be very happy here.'

He smiled and came to her. 'Will I, Thea?'

She backed away. 'Yes. I am sure you will. Goodness! Just look at that sky! Positively threatening! Perhaps we should keep moving?'

Richard glanced out of the window, saw the clouds piling up in dark masses, and frowned. 'Damn. It does look murky. We'll have to gulp our tea and go.'

Mrs Decks had laid out a meal in the parlour, cakes, biscuits, bread and butter. A fire crackled in the grate, casting its golden dance about the room so that shadows shifted and played.

Richard watched as Thea poured tea. The light caught in her soft, coiled, tawny tresses, so that he longed to reach out and scatter her hairpins and release her hair and the light to tumble around her shoulders. He forced the thought down. Seducing Thea was not an option. She looked so...so *right* here. Somehow he had to convince *her* of that. Convince her that she belonged. Not *to* him. But here—*with* him. There was a slight rattle of the teacup in its saucer as she handed it to him and their fingers brushed.

Her eyes were wide, questioning. Lord! If the eyes were truly the window to the soul and she could see what was pouring through him, surging at the constraints of honour, she'd flee. At least with the tea table between them, she wouldn't see any more tangible evidence of the direction of his thoughts.

Thanking God for whoever had invented tea tables, he eased in his chair just as the rain began to patter fitfully against the window. Standing up again, he went to look out.

One glance at the sky settled his decision. Black clouds were piling in from the Channel. Even as he watched there was a distant flash, followed by a rumble of thunder. It wasn't going to be a gentle spring shower. This one meant business. Already gusts of wind were flinging the rain harder against the window panes.

'Richard?'

He turned to her. 'I'm sorry, Thea, but I rather think we're caught.'

'Caught?'

He nodded. 'There's no riding home in that, and I've no carriage here yet. It's going to blow, and blow hard. It's too exposed to take the short way over the Downs and if we go around by the roads it will take hours. I doubt the rain will let up much before morning.'

Another roll of thunder, closer this time, drove home his point.

Her face was white. '*Morning?* But…Richard, if we don't go home…I…we…' Her voice trailed off.

He didn't need the problem spelt out. Her reputation. Hell and damnation! This was the last thing he had wanted, for Thea, when he offered for her again, to have the least reason to think he offered out of the promptings of honour. Or worse, that she had been tricked because he wanted her fortune.

Very carefully he said, 'You know, it's not as bad as it looks at first sight, my dear. Nell is here. She can sleep with you. That should preserve the proprieties. And the only people likely to hear about the whole thing are those at Blakeney and I really can't see Braybrook, let alone Max and Verity, making an issue of it!'

'And Almeria?'

Yes, well. There was the rub. Almeria would be practically dancing a jig at the thought of a marriage between the pair of them.

'I can handle Almeria,' he lied. As long as he could make her see that delivering a long-winded discourse on duty and propriety would be just the thing to have Thea digging her heels in.

Judging by her raised brows, Thea didn't believe him.

He temporised. 'Very well, of course Almeria would do everything possible to force a marriage between us. And yes, she will see our non-return tonight as a blessing from heaven.' He smiled wryly. 'She'll be in alt! Thinking that I will be obliged to offer for you and that you will be forced to accept. And all the while she will be having a marvellous time deploring the moral turpitude of our generation in general and Max and myself in particular.'

'What a charming evening for your brother and sister,' said Thea, trying not to laugh.

Richard grinned. 'That's better! They won't mind. Make a pleasant change, I shouldn't wonder, to hear Almeria condemning *my* morals instead of Max's.'

Good. She was distracted.

'Then you won't be making another formal offer for my hand in the morning?'

That brought him up short. Obviously she wasn't distracted enough, confound it. He had every intention of making an offer for her hand the next morning. Not necessarily particularly formal, though. Kissing properly was one thing, but he wasn't sure how to kiss formally. This required some out-and-out duplicity. He summoned up his best glare. 'Thea Winslow, do you, or do you not, trust me?'

She glared back. 'Well, of *course* I trust you!'

Thank God for that!

'Then you may trust me when I say that I will make another offer of marriage to you, when I have fallen tail over top in love with you, and not before!'

'And...and you're not going to do that?'

Was there just the faintest hint of disappointment there?

'No,' he said firmly. 'I am not going to do that.'

But only because he'd already done it. Although he wouldn't like to swear that he mightn't fall even deeper into love with her. On his current record the whole thing seemed to become more overwhelming by the minute.

She met his gaze. 'I...very well, then. Should we—should *you* inform Mrs Decks?'

Yes. He most definitely should inform Nell. And warn her not to open her budget to Thea. Warn her that he hadn't offered yet, so that she didn't accidentally put her foot in it. One thing, he knew he could rely on Nell to keep her own mouth shut, along with keeping Sam's shut for him.

* * *

Nell, of course, thought it all highly romantic when he found her in the kitchen and explained matters.

Her face beamed. 'Well, of course I can dress a dinner for you. There's a chicken can be killed and don't you worry about a thing. What's that? Sleep with Miss Winslow?' Her eyes twinkled. 'No, we won't have any nasty gossip. Never you fear. I'll get on now and make up the rooms. And when will the pair of you be moving in for good?'

'Nell!'

'Oh, go on with you!' she said crossly. 'Think I can't see you're nutty on her? I won't say a word to your young lady, but don't you think to pull wool over my old eyes!'

Never before had Thea realised how dangerous a room could be. The parlour they retired to after dinner was full of temptation of the worst sort. The curtains had been drawn against the storming darkness, muffling the blattering of the rain. Mellow candlelight lit the room and a fire danced in the grate. Even the shadows were friendly in this cosy, intimate chamber.

That was the danger. The intimacy. Oh, not that she believed for one moment that Richard had designs on her non-existent virtue! But she felt so comfortable here. So at home. She had a dreadful feeling that through all the years ahead, the memory of this room would stand for all she had lost and could never regain.

Angrily she shook herself mentally as she sat down. That sounded remarkably like self-pity. Better to think of this room with joy. Not the bitterness of regret. It would be good to be able to picture Richard here. To know that he was happy.

'A game of chess? Or piquet?' offered Richard.

'Yes, please.' Anything to take her mind off what she really wanted—for him to kiss her again. She knew Richard's sense of honour. If he believed that his behaviour had in any way compromised her, the promise he had made earlier would be swept aside in what he would view as the greater obligation to her.

Ironic. The one man she could have given herself to joyfully was the one man from whom she must, at all costs, avoid an offer.

So, chess.

Except that she found herself distracted; watching him surreptitiously as he considered his moves, loving the concentration on his face, the half-frown as he watched her moves; nearly breathless as the long fingers took hold of a piece and she remembered the way he had touched her face, the tingling magic flickering in their wake.

Even the memory had warmth unfurling inside her, an ache of unbearable longing. Her fingers trembled as she reached for her queen and knocked several hapless pawns and Richard's bishop flying.

Flushing with embarrassment, she began to pick up the pieces, fumbling as she did so. A gentle hand closed over hers, stilling it, and every nerve quivered to life.

His large warm hand enveloped hers, his thumb caressing. Unconsciously her fingers clung as she lifted her gaze to his face. Dark need burned in his eyes, in the hard line of his mouth, in the fierce tension she sensed in his body. It should have terrified her, not awakened an answering need in her own body. Yet his hand held hers so gently.

Knowledge came to her then; she could stand up, leave the room and he would not make a single move to stop her. Indeed, he would open the door, summon Mrs Decks and bid her a goodnight.

If only…her heart cried out within her.

'I must have been mad,' he whispered, as he stood up, releasing her hand.

'Why?' she asked softly.

He came around the table to her and drew her to her feet.

'This.' He took her in his arms, brushing his cheek lightly over her brow. 'It's no good,' he said huskily. 'I've tried, but—if you will look at me like that…'

He broke off, drawing her against his hard body, soft curves fitting as though they belonged. She should stop him; this way lay madness. She knew that. But her heart and body were at odds with her common sense. There would be time later for sanity. A whole lifetime.

She could spare a few moments for madness.

Madness was a gentle mouth, caressing and possessing hers; steely arms supporting and cradling her body, tightening instantly as she melted against him. Madness was the joy of his hands, trembling as he released her curls in a pattering of hairpins and tangled his fingers in the thick coils that tumbled around her shoulders. Madness was her own response; her arms reaching up to pull him closer to her own, hot twisting need, her fingers sliding into his hair, her mouth and tongue answering the temptation of his.

Her name was a groan in his throat as he deepened the kiss, sending streamers of heat rippling through her core. She should stop him. She knew that. But she could no longer recall the reason.

He should stop. He knew that. But soft fingers brushed over his jaw in wondering tenderness, banishing the knowledge to oblivion. Such a simple touch to set the fire inside him blazing higher. He wasn't quite sure how they had ended up on the sofa together. A remaining particle of sanity and honour raised a feeble protest in some corner of his brain. He ignored it, heart and body intent on the same thing—the loving, intoxicating response of the woman in his arms. All fire and burning sweetness, she returned his kisses with a trust that consumed him.

He definitely ought not to be unbuttoning the bodice of her riding habit. But his fingers had other ideas and continued regardless. Shaking, he pushed the halves of her bodice apart, reaching in to cup a soft, full breast through the fine muslin of her shirt. The nipple sprang to life in his palm and every muscle in his body tightened in response.

He'd never known it could be like this. Desire, yes. He knew about that. But this was not merely desire. This was need, burning him alive as he clumsily unbuttoned her shirt, and sought the drawstring of her chemise. One tug dealt with that, and his fingers met silky, yielding flesh.

Her response was a sigh of pleasure that his mouth absorbed, and a shift of her body that pushed her breast more firmly into his hand. With an aching groan he released her mouth. Soft husky cries spilled from her lips as he slowly kissed his way down her throat and over the creamy curve of her breast. He should stop. He knew that. He even knew there was a reason. He just couldn't recall what it might be. Shuddering with need, he closed his mouth over the taut nipple and sucked gently.

Her whole body stiffened in shock. Not resistance. Simply shock.

It was enough. Honour won.

And not just honour. Love. And the need to protect her. Especially from himself.

She had not struggled. Nor had she protested. His conscience informed him pithily that she should not need to. With a wrenching effort, he forced himself to stop. For a moment he fought for control, for breath. This was Thea. His Thea. His love. He had sworn not to compromise her. And he was willing to swear that, despite all, she knew very little of the passion between a man and a woman.

Swearing mentally, he lifted from her.

'Richard?' Her voice was ragged, husky. Breathless.

'No more, sweetheart,' he said hoarsely. 'We mustn't. Not like this.'

She deserved a bed. Or at the very least his wedding ring on her finger. He wouldn't answer for making it as far as the bed-chamber with her.

Her dazed eyes gradually focused. He saw the moment when control, and understanding, returned.

'I...I'm sorry,' she whispered. 'This...I never meant to make you do something you would regret...'

Regret?

'You didn't.' Every muscle locked with restraint, he leaned over and kissed her gently. 'But if I hadn't stopped—' his body roared a protest just thinking about it '—if I hadn't stopped, then we would have been anticipating our wedding vows.'

The moment the words were out, he realised his mistake, even before the look of shock hit her face and she began to struggle with the buttons of her bodice as she sat up.

'But—you promised! You said we wouldn't be compromised!'

'Dammit, Thea! That was before I kissed you!'

Slight understatement there, but there was no need to go into details. She knew perfectly well what he'd done.

'But, no one has to know you…kissed me!'

The blush on her face as she said it, her hesitation, nearly undid him.

'I'd know,' he said simply. 'But that's not the point.'

'And the point is?' She managed to do up two more buttons.

She was going to make him spell it out? Did she think he normally went about kissing innocents like that?

'The point is that I want to do it again!' he said shamelessly. Her blush deepened. He eyed it appreciatively, adding, 'And next time I don't want to have to stop!'

Her eyes widened and he took advantage of her shock to say, 'No more now, Thea.' He reached for the bell pull by the chimneypiece. 'I'll ring for Nell and you can go up with her. But let us have one thing straight: my offering marriage has nothing to do with our situation tonight, and everything to do with what just took place on that sofa! And why it took place.' He ran his hands through his hair. 'Think about it. Why do you imagine I brought you here to show you my home?'

He took one step towards her and stopped at the look of horror in her eyes. It cut him to his core.

'Sweetheart?'

Sweetheart. She swallowed convulsively, still fighting with her buttons. No. Not this. Not with him. The knife twisted relentlessly in her soul, slicing it open, as she saw the truth in his eyes.

Denial leapt, useless, to her lips.

'No, Richard. No. You can't!'

He smiled. A smile to tear a woman's heart from her breast. 'Oh, yes, I can. I do. I love you, Thea. That's why I brought you here. To see my home. To convince you that I love you. That you belong here. I was planning to ask you again to marry me tomorrow. Spending the night here was *not* part of my plan! I never wanted you to feel coerced.'

No. She knew that. Richard neither wanted nor needed her fortune. And even if he had needed it, he would never have coerced her into marriage. It was worse than that.

Richard had been all too convincing. He wanted *her*. Thea Winslow. Because he loved her.

In silence she finished setting her clothes to rights, then she drew a ragged, slicing breath.

'Richard—'

A gentle tap on the door announced the arrival of Mrs Decks, who bustled in cheerily.

In the morning. She would tell him everything on the way home, including the decision she had made. After which she supposed she would never see him again.

Never before had Richard felt like banging a door in Nell's face. All he could do was bid Thea goodnight and wonder what in Hades he had set loose. She couldn't, *couldn't* believe he'd trapped her for her fortune! And she certainly couldn't believe that if he had been frightened of compromising her further, that he would have been fool enough to touch her, let alone…kiss her. All right, let alone nearly bed her on the sofa!

So, why? *Why* was she still so dead set against marriage to him? That had been another refusal quivering on her lips. If Nell had not walked in just then—

He cursed. Given Thea's response, he refused to believe she didn't care. She was not the sort of woman to give herself lightly. Could it be that she still doubted *his* love? That she believed he would in the end resent her lost virginity? Would cast it up at her?

He could think of nothing else. Taking a deep breath, he looked around for a brandy decanter. And realised there wasn't one. It was definitely going to be a very long night.

Chapter Seventeen

The storm had largely blown itself out by the following morning. Heavy clouds still scudded overhead, but there was little rain, and Sam Decks, when consulted, gave it as his expert opinion that there would be little in the time it would take Mester Richard and his young lady to ride back to Blakeney.

'Better set out sharpish,' he opined. 'His lordship'll have a search party out by now, like as not. If so be as he don't come hisself. Be in a right tizzy with you not comin' back lars' night.'

Richard stared. And realised the truth of this statement. In fact, he wouldn't put it past Max to be saddling a horse right now, if he wasn't already halfway across the Downs.

He swore, eliciting a shocked look from old Sam, and strode back to the house. They had to start early. He had a very great deal to say to Miss Dorothea Winslow for which he most definitely did not desire an audience.

Thea went down to breakfast conscious of a headache, scratchy eyes and the sort of roiling stomach to be expected after a largely sleepless night.

Little beyond the commonplace was said over breakfast. With Mrs Decks coming in and out to see that they had everything they needed, it was impossible. For which she could only thank God.

No doubt he would open the subject of their marriage the moment they were out of the stable yard and she would have to tell him why she couldn't marry him. She thought he would understand even if he couldn't accept it. In the end, it didn't matter. On this she had to follow her conscience—that still, quiet voice that had lead her to this decision.

It was a lovely morning. Everything looked fresh and damp. Thea breathed it in deeply as she followed Richard around to the stable yard. Raindrops glistened and sparkled on flowers, turned cobwebs into nets of enchantment.

An illusion only. The enchantment was not for her.

Richard said nothing as they trotted out of the stable yard and back through the orchard and the tension gripping Thea tightened. She concentrated on the skittish mare, keeping her well up to her bit and curbing her early morning freshness.

Despite her edginess and longing to have the whole thing over with, she was grateful for Richard's silence as they rode up the now slippery track out of the valley to the Downs. But once on top she could put it off no longer.

'Richard, you must understand that I cannot possibly marry you,' she began quietly. If only he would accept that.

He nodded. 'Mmm. So you said last night. Or words to that effect. What you haven't explained is why.'

Her throat tightened.

He went on. 'You know perfectly well that I never intended to trap you into a compromising situation, do you not?'

She swallowed and nodded. It was unthinkable that she should take that way out.

'And after last night…' his voice softened to a caress '…you would be wasting your breath trying to convince me that you don't love me.'

'You can't know that,' she whispered.

His smile deepened. 'I can know that, Thea. Last night…if you didn't care for me, you would have stopped me.'

'It's partly because I care for you that I cannot marry you,' she said. Her cheeks burned. 'Richard—you cannot possibly want me. One day you would come to resent me. It would always lie between us. Perhaps even now you are wondering if…if my response to you last night was that of a…a wanton.'

She looked away. Surely that was enough. She stared straight ahead between the mare's ears and kept riding through the silence that stretched between them. Outside the silence a falcon screamed high overhead. Away on the Downs a flock of sheep grazed, the bleating of lambs drifting to them on the wind. And always the distant hushing of the sea around the cliffs.

Eventually he would say something. She bit her lip, conscious of the heat pressing behind her eyes, the choking sensation in her throat. Now, more than ever, she regretted last night's descent into madness. She felt cold all over, as though the sun had been put out.

'Thea Winslow,' he said fiercely, 'if you *ever* refer to yourself in that way again, I swear I'll put you over my knee and spank you! Who the hell put all that filth into your head? Your father? Your aunt?' He dragged in a breath. 'All last night tells me is that you love me.' He released the breath. 'You can't possibly think that I would condemn your behaviour when mine was exactly the same.' He grimaced. 'Worse! I was the one doing the actual seducing!'

'You can't know that I love you!' she flashed, quelling the agonising flare of hope. 'I…I might behave like that with every man who kisses me!'

'Then you wouldn't be telling me so now. And you wouldn't have told me the truth to stop me challenging Dunhaven.'

'This…this is impossible,' she whispered.

'No, it's not,' he said. 'Thea, I love you. Come, sweetheart. Can you not trust me a little bit further?'

In all her nightmares Thea had never imagined this—that Richard would accept her lost innocence so completely. That he would still be prepared to marry her. She *couldn't* accept. Not yet. Not now. There was the child…she had to make sure that her child was safe, provided for. Once she accepted Richard's offer, she could no longer make any disposition of her own property…and if he did not agree, there would be nothing she could do, except break the betrothal.

A yell brought her head up. Galloping towards them were two horsemen.

'Damn!' muttered Richard. 'Max and Julian. We can't talk about this now, Thea. When we are back at Blakeney. But understand this—I am not holding to my offer of marriage out of some idiotic notion of chivalry or pity or whatever other excuse you can dream up. I'm offering because I love you!'

'How can you?'

His answer nearly destroyed her.

'How? God knows. Why does anyone fall in love? Why does Max love Verity? He'd tell you all the wonderful things about her. Her courage, her loyalty, her honesty.' He grinned. 'Her temper. All things which I can see and love in her. But I am not *in* love with her. So, no, Thea. I cannot tell you why I have fallen in love with you. Only that I have. But you gave me the truth. You could have simply refused me. Or if you wished to marry, you could have said nothing.' He flushed. 'Sometimes…sometimes these things are not obvious, you know. I certainly would never have suspected.'

He met her eyes. 'But that never occurred to you, did it? Instead you told me the truth because you foolishly thought that would stop me challenging Dunhaven. It didn't. What stopped me was the knowledge that doing so would worsen any scandal for you. Thea—what happened eight years ago is done. Past. It wasn't your fault. Leave it there, sweetheart, and we can have the future.'

Lord Blakehurst and Lord Braybrook had reined into a trot and brought their mounts around in a wide circle to join them.

'Blast you, Ricky,' called Lord Blakehurst as he came up. 'Do you have any idea of how worried Verity was last night when you didn't come home?'

'Verity?' scoffed Lord Braybrook. 'It wasn't *Verity* talking about saddling a horse and coming out to look for them. At midnight, no less!'

'Oh, shut up, Julian!'

Richard grinned. 'We were safe enough. We were still at Tarring when the storm hit. Nell Decks looked after us.'

'Well, I thought that would be the case,' said Blakehurst, looking slightly embarrassed, 'But still…oh, very well! I was concerned! But only about Miss Winslow and my mare!'

Despite her pain, Thea laughed. Lord Blakehurst didn't fool her for one instant. Of course he had been worried about his brother. The link between them was almost palpable. Pain slashed at her; he would be even more worried if he knew what sort of woman his brother wanted to marry.

Lord Braybrook grinned. 'Nell Decks? Your old nanny?' His expression became mournful. 'Poor Lady Arnsworth. At least half the pleasure of her evening has been cut up!' He continued, 'Naturally she started out by condemning your carelessness, Ricky, not to mention your morals! I must say I was astonished at the details of your life that she seemed to know. You really ought to be more discreet. Anyway, by the time the tea-tray was brought in—and I do suspect Lady Blakehurst of ordering it early!—she was planning the wedding.' He cocked a brow at Richard. 'Obviously with Nanny Decks to play gooseberry, there's not the least need?'

'None,' said Richard flatly. 'At least not on that head.'

'Oh?' Lord Braybrook looked intrigued.

Richard's mouth tightened.

'Julian?'

'Hmm?'

'Shut up.'

Lord Blakehurst broke in. 'Before you call each other out and have to decide which of you has me as a second—there's something I have to tell Miss Winslow.'

She turned to him with relief.

He smiled. 'Ignore them. Especially Richard. What I have to tell you is that a letter arrived for you shortly after you left yesterday. An express.'

Thea's stomach clenched and chills washed through her. Only one person would have sent her an express. Rufton. He must have completed his investigation and sent in his report. And Almeria's butler had sent it on.

'Might I suggest we pick up the pace a trifle?' said Lord

Blakehurst. 'If Miss Winslow is agreeable, of course. It is just that Verity was a trifle concerned about you both.' His mouth twitched. 'And Almeria, of course.'

'Certainly, sir,' said Thea, forcing herself to appear calm. The sooner she knew the contents of that report, the better.

The child was called Sophie Grey. *Sophie*—her own middle name.

Numb, Thea stared at Rufton's report. And found the words blurring before her eyes. It didn't matter. Their accusation was seared into her heart. The child's age—they had not, after all, altered the birth date... The village where she had been raised— not five miles from Aunt Maria—by the daughter of the midwife who had attended the birth. And then an unknown benefactor had sent her to Miss Dale's Seminary in Bath last year. It all fitted.

All these years... They had lied to her, all of them. Even the doctor and rector. For her own good, no doubt. And she had believed the lies without ever bothering to question.

Sophie.

The rector's cold comfort echoed... *God has been merciful. 'Twas better that the child died rather than being born into such sin. Indeed, 'tis possible that the child's death is punishment for the sin of its parents. The Good Book tells us that it must be so: the sins of the fathers shall be visited upon the children unto the last generation...*

A child's life and death seen as an instrument of punishment. And used as a lie. Her mouth tasted sour with bile and her unspoken hopes crumbled to ashes. The nausea intensified.

Sophie. Her child's name was Sophie...

She was as guilty as the rector, guilty in that she had hoped, *prayed,* that her suspicions were unfounded, that the child was indeed her father's bastard. In doing so, she too had wished the death of her own child.

She could not sleep. She had dozed in the afternoon and dined on a tray in her bedchamber. Now, long after midnight, she knelt at her window sill, staring out into the dark of a moonless night. Only it was not truly dark. Above, the heavens sang with cold light. Not enough light to see by, but a reminder that the light was there. Beyond her reach.

It had always been beyond her reach, that particular light.

Or was it? She did have a choice. The letter did not mean that she had to act. It had given her the truth. At the start that was all she had wanted. Only she had not reckoned on the fact that truth was not inanimate. It had its own life and demands. It could not compel her. But it could destroy her. She understood now what Rufton had meant when he warned her to be quite sure she wanted the truth.

She had sought out the truth and now she must live with it. If she did not, she would have to live with her own conscience instead.

She closed her eyes, exhausted, leaning on the sill. Sounds came to her; the bark of a fox, the wind sighing in the beech woods, just as it must be over at Tarring House. It was all so lovely. And it would remain so, despite her own pain. Yet she could not find it in her to regret what had passed.

He truly loved her. Her heart ached in joy as she permitted her mind to drift. For the first time in years memory was not a nightmare beast dragging her into horror; it took her only as far as the previous night, when Richard had shown her what might have been. If only, she dreamed, if only he had not stopped. She wished, oh, how she wished... Her head slipped and she jerked awake as her brow bumped the sill. She had nearly fallen asleep, she realised. Stiffly she rose to her feet. Lady Arnsworth was returning to London in the morning. She would return with her.

There was, after all, only one choice that she could make. And it was not a choice that any honourable man would be able to countenance.

'Are you sure, Thea?' asked Verity, worry clouding her grey eyes. 'You need not go simply because Almeria must return. If there was a reason...I mean, if you wished to stay, we would all—' she broke off, catching herself up '—that is, Lord Blake-hurst and I would be delighted for you to remain.'

Thea bit her lip. This was dreadful. She had raised expectations and they were all expecting her to stay on. And she could not.

'I am sure, Verity. I must go. There…there is something I must do.'

Verity brightened. 'Is that all? Well then, you may come back afterwards. It is only a few hours' travel. I'll send the carriage up for you.'

Disappointing Verity was nearly as hard as hurting Richard. She shook her head. 'I'm sorry, Verity. For everything. There will be no going back.'

Verity blinked. 'Thea, what are you talking—?' She broke off and heaved a sigh of relief. 'Here he is! Richard—do come and talk some sense into Thea. She is insisting that she must return to London.'

Thea faced Richard. His face was weary, as though he had slept as little as she these past two nights.

'Perhaps you would walk with me in the garden first, Thea,' he suggested. 'Almeria is unlikely to depart for another hour at least.' He turned to his sister-in-law. 'If you will excuse us, Verity?'

She smiled. 'Of course. I must go upstairs to the nursery and see to Will. You will not let Thea go without saying goodbye?'

He shook his head. 'No. Off with you. I'll take care of Thea.'

He meant that in every sense of the phrase. He wanted to take care of her. Always. But he could see in the lift of her chin, in the set of her mouth, that her decision was made. But why? She knew he loved her, and he no longer held the least doubt that she loved him. So it must be fear that he could not truly accept her, that he would resent her past…

The fragrance of the gardens breathed around them in the soft sunshine. He took her to the knot garden, dreamy and pungent with herbs, its low lavender hedges weaving about the rainbow-filled fountain at its heart.

Sitting on a wooden bench, she told him without preamble,

truth like a slashing knife cutting across the song of the water. His brain froze with shock and for a moment he was utterly speechless as he grappled with it.

Finally, 'A *child?*'

She nodded.

Numbed, he took a very deep breath and waited for the knowledge to sink in, to feel something. Anything. He did not know *how* he felt. Anger, perhaps. Confusion, certainly.

'Why did you not mention this earlier?'

'I…I did not know.'

'A little hard to miss, I would have thought.' For the life of him he could not prevent the sarcasm slicing through. He saw her flinch, knew that it had cut deep, but still he could feel nothing. Until she lifted her eyes and he saw her pain.

And even then, he did not know what the emotion was that he felt. Only that it was likely to tear him apart.

'When I…when the baby was born…I…they gave me laudanum…straight after the delivery. Before I even held the…her. I *didn't* hold her. When I woke up finally, it was the next day…and they told me—'

Her voice cracked and before he could think, he was kneeling beside her, enveloping her cold hands in his, knowing only that she was hurting, that she had never told anyone this.

She dragged in a breath and continued in a hard little voice. 'They told me the baby had died. Had died and was buried. They would not even tell me the child's sex. They said…they said it was better not to know. When I asked about the grave…they said *it* died without baptism, that the grave was unmarked.'

'And you did not know this yesterday?'

'Not…not definitely,' she whispered.

Understanding flared then. 'The letter?'

She nodded. 'Yes. One of Lady Chasewater's notes had made me wonder. Apparently she discovered after Lord Chasewater's death that the child lived.' She shuddered. 'I did not wish to believe her, but I knew my father could have covered it up, so—'

'You asked him?'

A savage laugh ripped from her. 'Asked him? No. He would have lied. I searched his study for information. When I had it, I hired a runner to find her for me. I knew the school she was, *is*, placed at. And her initials. At first I merely wished to ensure that she was safe, and happy. But now—'

Struggling to cope with the enormity of what she had told him, Richard held her hands gently, feeling her tension. There was more. He knew that.

'What now?' he asked quietly.

'You must see, Richard...I cannot leave it like that. Apparently my father has provided for her all this time, but—'

'Of course,' he said. Typical of Thea. She wished to support the child herself. He could understand that. 'We can arrange to have all her expenses met. Set aside some of your fortune as a dowry so that she can make a respectable marriage. You can make enquiries about the school. If you are not happy, she can be moved. This need make no difference—'

'It makes every difference,' said Thea. 'She needs a family...a mother, at least, so—'

'*No!*' Denial burst from him. 'Dammit, Thea! It's too much! No man would stand for it! If you really wish it, then you may visit your child occasionally. Anonymously. You cannot ask me to accept the child of the man who raped you!'

'I have not asked that of you, Richard,' she said steadily. 'And I will not.'

He took a ragged breath. 'I...I beg your pardon, if I misunderstood.'

She shook her head. 'No, you have not. Only that I am not asking you to accept Sophie.'

'Sophie?'

'That is my daughter's name.'

'Then—'

'Richard, I cannot marry you—'

'You are refusing my suit because I will not—*cannot!*—accept your...your child?'

'No. I am refusing your suit because *I* will not ask you, or any man, to accept my base-born daughter. She is mine. And her illegitimacy is at least partially my fault.'

He could hear the pain. Feel it. Hers as well as his. And, steady despite the pain, he could hear her determination.

'*Your* fault?'

She nodded. 'Yes. Had I not let David know the truth, I think I would have been too frightened not to marry—she would have been legitimate.'

Conflicting emotions stormed inside him. He couldn't name even one of them. All he could think was that he had lost her, that her decision was made and that there would be no turning her back from it.

'Thea, I need to think,' he said very softly. 'I am sorry if—'

Thea's breaking heart stilled. He was going to apologise.

'No!' she said vehemently. 'You will *not* apologise!' Tears stood in her eyes. She held them back, refusing to let them fall. 'You are such a *good* man! You offered so much more than I had any right to expect, but…it is just, there are some things…'

Some things that one's conscience cannot bear. Some things that one cannot negotiate on. She left the words unspoken. She had said enough. Had she still doubted that Richard loved her, his shattered eyes and white face would have convinced her.

He turned away. His voice harsh, he said again, 'I need to think.'

She could not speak for the choking grief in her throat, could barely see him for the tears crowding, spilling over in silent loss. He walked away towards the house and the rainbows shimmering in fleeting loveliness in the fountain dissolved in mist as she whispered, 'God bless you, Richard.' She would not see him again and force him to say the words.

An hour later she was in the chaise travelling back to London with Lady Arnsworth. Verity and Lord Blakehurst had farewelled them. Richard was nowhere to be seen.

After an appalling journey, during which Lady Arnsworth progressed from reasonably subtle hints about the supposed forthcoming nuptials between Thea and Richard, to outright demands to know why in heaven's name Thea had not leapt at the chance to re-establish herself fully, Thea found herself back in Grosvenor Square late in the afternoon, facing Lord Aberfield. His shock was palpable as he read the report she had given him.

'You…you hired a Bow Street *runner?*' He seemed unable to believe it, his eyes wide with disbelief.

She shrugged, determined to seem unmoved. 'It seemed the obvious way to discover the truth.' She had not given him a chance to deny it all, simply flinging the report at him and demanding to know why he had lied to her.

Suddenly he seemed an old man as he sank down into a chair. 'Dorothea—you didn't think to ask me?'

Disbelief lashed her. 'Ask *you?* You *lied* to me. All these years I believed that she had died! Who arranged that?'

At that he seemed to recover slightly. 'We were trying to protect you!' he said angrily. 'Good God! It would have been better if the child *had* died! As it is, I have paid for her education and seen to her future. You need not concern yourself. She will remain at the school and be trained as a governess—'

'Have you ever seen her?'

'*Seen* her?' Had she suddenly grown three heads he could not have looked more shocked.

'Visited her,' said Thea evenly. 'Does she know that she has a family?'

Lord Aberfield frowned. 'This is excessive sensibility, Dorothea. Most ill judged. It is unnecessary to see the child. Indeed it would be most improper! One does not visit a child of *that* sort. Better that she remains in ignorance of her background. To regard her as a member of the family—impossible! To visit would only breed a…a spirit of resentment.' He shook his head. 'That is not how these things are done. If you wish, you may see Miss Dale's reports—'

'Does she think that Sophie Grey is *your* daughter?'

Aberfield's lips thinned. 'Very likely. I merely entered the child as my ward. I did not consider her parentage to be any of Miss Dale's concern.'

'Very well. Then you will write a letter to Miss Dale, asking her to release Sophie Grey into my custody, *as her mother*.'

'*What?*'

Thea faced him squarely. 'She is my daughter and I am well able to provide for her.'

'She is already provided for! For God's sake, girl! Think! Do you believe that Blakehurst will countenance this? He will never marry you—'

'There is no betrothal, nor has there ever been. We are agreed that we shall not suit.'

'*What?* Almeria Arnsworth assured me before you left London that—'

'She was mistaken, my lord,' she said quietly. 'There is no more to be said. The child is mine. You will write that letter. After which you need never see me again.'

'Dorothea—there is no need for this. I take it you told Blakehurst the truth, that you are not…that you…' He wiped his brow. 'Naturally he would not accept your, er…*explanation,* but I could still see him. After all, the match is still very much to his advantage, so I could—'

'Explain that you had given Lallerton permission to address me and he interpreted that as permission to rape me?'

'For God's sake, girl! All this talk of rape! You were betrothed! Naturally I would have preferred that he waited until you were married before bedding you, but it was not *rape!*'

Her stomach churned. 'Of course, you would know, my lord,' she said with savage irony. 'You were the one being held down, begging him to stop.'

He flinched. 'Dorothea—think!' he said. 'Years it's taken me to win back the position I lost when you refused Lallerton in a fit of missishness. And now it will be known that my daughter has a bastard!'

'No,' she said quietly. 'I am willing to use another name. No one need know. Unless you refuse to write that letter to the school. And you will also write a declaration that the child is mine. To be witnessed and held by my lawyer.'

'Damned if I will!'

She shrugged. 'No. Damned if you don't, my lord. And damned if you don't release enough of my money for me to live on comfortably. Because I will make the whole thing public.' Remembering something, she added, 'With Lady Chasewater's help.'

She watched with calm interest as his eyes bulged. It might take a few moments for him to realise, but he had no room to manoeuvre. The risk of scandal was too great. Without a word she strolled over to the chair by the window and sat down.

'What do you think you're doing?' he barked.

'Waiting for you to come to your senses and write the letter to Miss Dale,' she replied. 'You really have no choice.'

'And what about this other document?' he snapped.

She frowned thoughtfully. 'I shall speak to my lawyer and have it properly drawn up and brought to you for signing. There must be no doubt that you acknowledge the child to be mine and in my sole custody. For now the letter to the school will suffice.'

'And you promise to stay away from us and use another name?'

'You have my word. I do not wish to cause trouble. All I want is my daughter.'

Thin lipped, he stalked to his desk and began to write, the scratching of the pen the only sound. Finally he stopped writing and looked up.

'Do you wish to read it before I seal it?'

She shook her head. 'It should not be necessary. You cannot possibly desire a scandal over this. And there will be one if you have attempted to trick me.'

Silently he reached for the pounce box, sprinkled sand on the letter, then sealed it and held it out.

She stood up and drew on her gloves and went to receive the letter, tucking it into her reticule. 'Thank you, sir. My lawyers will draw up the other document as soon as possible. If you should wish to contact me at any stage, you may direct your request to them. I dare say we will not meet again.'

'Damn it, girl! You can't disown your family for a bastard child you didn't even know existed!'

She smiled then. 'Yes, sir, I can. As easily as you disowned your daughter for a sin she did not commit. Goodbye, my lord.'

Her interview with David the following morning was worse. She could no longer feel anything with Aberfield. But David...

'For God's sake, Thea!' he implored. 'Where will you live? Under what name? You realise you will have to pretend to be a widow? And what of Richard Blakehurst? I had hoped—' He broke. 'Thea?'

Pain streaked through her, all the hurt and misery that she had refused to feel.

'It is at an end.'

Not that she blamed Richard. It was not his fault. She had never expected him to accept her child. No man would be prepared to do such a thing. She had known that when she had made her decision.

David came to her and took her hands gently 'Are you sure this is necessary? I understand the child has been well provided for. She will be safe enough. For once in his life, perhaps the old man is right. Would it not be wiser—?'

'To leave her without a family?' asked Thea quietly.

'Damn it, Thea! That was not your fault!'

She shook her head. 'Yes, it was, David. Had I not been such a naïve little fool and realised that I might be with child, I would have agreed to the marriage. There would have been no other choice. And she would not now be a bastard. That bit in the Bible...about the "sins of the fathers"? I've always hated it. I can't condemn my own child for her father's crime.'

'Thea, must you—?'

'She needs a family, David. Even if it is only me.'

'You will permit me to visit you?'

Her heart leapt. 'You would do that?'

'I would do that. I shall like having a niece.' Bitterly he said, 'Blakehurst is a fool!'

Sudden fear consumed her. 'No. He is not. You will give me your promise, David, that you will not quarrel with him over this.'

'Dash it, Thea! I—'

'Your promise, David!' If he were to challenge Richard... Her heart lurched in terror at the thought.

He swore under his breath. 'Very well,' he went on. 'You have it.' He looked at her narrowly. 'You love him, do you not?'

'Yes. I returned his love.'

David stared. 'You returned—? And yet he will—'

She flung up her hand. 'Ask yourself: what would you do in his position?'

His eyes fell.

She smiled sadly. 'Precisely.'

Chapter Eighteen

The chaise rocked on its way and Thea sat huddled in the corner, staring out at the passing countryside, scarcely seeing it. All she could see was Richard's set face, the dark eyes resigned, full of pain. Pain that she had caused.

Maybe this was for the best. He deserved better than to be caught in a trap of his own decency. As perhaps he had been. She did not think she could have borne it if they had married and he had come to regret it or to resent her. His pain would pass. She had to believe that, and accept that one day he would find another woman to love.

Just as she had to accept that in comparison to her daughter's need, her own pain and despair could not be allowed to matter. There would be no one else for her.

She forced herself to think of Sophie Grey. The child she had borne; who had been taken away, brought up without knowing anything about her parents, believing herself unwanted.

Shame seared her. The memory of her initial relief when they told her the child had died—memory took her further back, remorseless. The day she had first felt the baby moving, an intangible fluttering within her and had realised it as a physical presence for the first time. Had realised that an innocent was condemned to bastardy.

Almost against her will, she had begun to wonder if it might be possible to keep the baby—and then the terror would take her, the fear choking her in nightmares that came each night, dreams when she relived what had been done to her. Feeling the child kick inside her then had terrified her.

She had been relieved when Aunt Maria told her that the babe had died. It had never occurred to her to doubt the lie. Why should she? Her parents and Aunt Maria had already settled it between them that the baby was to be fostered—she had been so dazed and panic-stricken at events that she had not so much as murmured a protest. All the protest had been shocked out of her. Yet in the end they had lied and told her the child was dead. Perhaps they had even meant it kindly, thinking to spare her.

And, yes, she had been relieved at first. And then had come more shame, more guilt, that she could have felt relief at the death of one who had been totally and utterly innocent of everything. Relief at the death of a baby who had been given no chance for life at all.

And now? Now she had the chance to put it at least partially right. She could give her daughter at least some part of the life that should have been hers.

If it was not too late.

Seven years. Seven years for Sophie to know herself unwanted by her family, an object of disgrace. Seven years knowing little but resentment. What if the child hated her?

A shudder racked her—what if her daughter resembled Lallerton? What if *she* could not look on her daughter without being reminded…no! She would not allow that to weigh with her!

She had made the right choice, the only choice, but the memory of Richard's hurt, and the knowledge of what she had lost, left an aching void within her.

Richard sat staring into the fire. He had not bothered to light the lamps. It was still light outside, but he had drawn the curtains early against the chill of the evening. A book lay abandoned on the wine table beside him. He didn't feel like reading—for once in his life the solace of the printed word had failed utterly.

Around him, Tarring felt empty, echoing. Which was patently ridiculous. He had moved in today and knew for a fact that it was full of people, his staff, all of them hell-bent on making him far more comfortable than he had any right to be. But in two days since Thea's return to London the whole world had felt like a sunless wasteland. He'd left Blakeney without a word to either Max or Verity, leaving a brief message. He'd needed to think, not talk. But now…

What in Hades was he to do, all by himself, in a house like this that had been intended for a family? The question had not occurred to him when he had bought the estate. He had vaguely thought that one day, he would marry, bring his bride here and set up his nursery. It had been a pleasant thought, something to look forward to in a comfortable sort of way.

That was before he had met Thea again. Before he had fallen in love. And before he had lost her. Now the house echoed drearily, where before its quietness had seemed to wait in anticipation. Now all the improvements he had planned seemed futile, a way to fill time that stretched out relentlessly.

She would never forgive him.

God in heaven, what a damned fool he'd been. What a blind, stupid, insensitive fool.

He took a sip of his brandy, and swallowed, watching the flicker of firelight in the amber liquid.

The door opened.

He didn't bother to look up. He knew who it would be.

'His lordship, sir.'

'Thank you, Minchin. I won't need you again tonight.'

'No, sir. Good night, sir.'

The door shut and Max said, 'For God's sake, Ricky. It's like a tomb in here. I received your message.' The bright eyes narrowed. 'What's amiss?' Then, urgently, 'Ricky, are you all right? Your betrothal—'

Trust Max to see straight to the heart of the disaster.

'Is off,' said Richard. Not that it was going to be off for long if he had anything to say about it, but at this moment that was the literal truth. It might remain the truth; it was entirely possible that Thea would tell him to go to the devil when he caught up with her.

'What the devil d'you mean?' rapped out Max.

Richard sighed wearily. 'Have a brandy…' he waved at the decanters on a side table '…and let me tell you a story.'

Max poured himself a glass of brandy, and sat down in the wingchair on the opposite side of the fireplace. 'Something tells me I'll be needing this.'

Richard avoided his eyes. The worried frown shamed him. Once Max knew…

Quietly, he told the story, as it had been revealed to him, leaving nothing out. Max sat listening, occasionally sipping his brandy. At the end he tossed off the rest and went to pour himself another. Richard waited.

'She refused to marry you for the sake of a child she had thought dead? A child most sensible women would be only too glad to ignore.' Max's voice was quiet, non-committal.

Richard nodded. A mother who would not abandon her child, regardless of the cost to herself. Exactly what he had wanted.

'She chose her child's happiness and safety over her own?'

Still Richard could only nod, his heart aching. Max had seen it immediately, as Richard had known he would. Why the hell had it taken *him* so long to see it? Was he so caught up in his own self-importance that he had not seen her courage? Her integrity?

'It won't be easy, Ricky,' said Max quietly. 'People will realise the truth. There will be some who'll never accept her. Are you willing to live with that?'

Yes. It made no difference to him.

He looked straight at Max. 'Will you support me?'

Max stared at him, jaw sagging, as if in utter disbelief. 'Confound it, Ricky! Did you have to ask? And would it make any difference?'

Richard's lips twitched at the outrage evident on his twin's face. 'Not the least. But I had to tell you. My mind is made up and there will be no hiding the truth. I don't give a damn what anyone says. Not even you. I'm going to marry Thea Winslow and her daughter will be accepted as my own.'

If Thea will have me now. If I haven't ruined everything with my stupid pride.

Max smiled at him. 'Good. I shall enjoy having a niece to spoil until Verity does her duty and provides me with a daughter or two.'

'A niece?' Did Max mean what he thought he meant? He had known that Max would accept his decision, would publicly support him, but…

Reading his mind, Max answered the unvoiced question. 'Your daughter will bear the name Blakehurst, will she not, Ricky?' He smiled. 'As such she will be my niece. Tell Miss Winslow that. Tell her that I will be proud to stand up for you. And to act as godfather to your *next* child.'

Calmly he tossed off his brandy and rose. 'I'm going home to Verity. No doubt you'll be making an early start tomorrow? I suggest that you bring them back to Blakeney before the wedding. It will take a couple of days to get the licence—shall we say, Friday week? That gives you ten days. I'll tell the rector.'

That was a bit much. Richard gave him a frosty look. 'D'you know, I think I can just about manage to get married without your advice, brother.'

Max raised a brow and grinned. 'Oh? The same way I managed to sort out my marriage?'

Richard laughed. '*Touché.* Lunacy must run in the family.'

Max snorted. 'Ah, well. At least we're doing our damnedest to breed it out. Congratulations, Ricky.'

Richard stood up. 'You haven't said it yet, Max.'

'Said what?' asked Max. 'Oh—that you're a damned idiot? It would be a case of the pot speaking to the kettle. Besides, you know it already.' He frowned and said slowly, 'There is one thing that occurs to me, though.'

'What?'

Max frowned. 'Stubble it…I'm thinking.'

Richard waited. Max's frown had deepened as he stared out of the darkening window.

'You know,' he said at last, 'society is really very hypocriti-cal about these things.'

'Fancy that,' said Richard drily.

'Yes, they are,' continued Max. 'No one would turn a hair if you had an illegitimate child—except to mutter that they'd always known you couldn't possibly be as sober living as everyone thought.'

'Pardon?'

'And gloating over what a complete scoundrel you were to make up to Miss Winslow, convince her to marry you, and *then* foist your bastard daughter on her.'

All Richard could do was stare in disbelief at his twin, who grinned and said, 'I believe you pointed out to me last year that love had completely addled my wits? Welcome aboard, Ricky!'

Making an early start the following morning, Richard drove through the Knightsbridge Turnpike as dusk was falling. Care-fully he guided his horses through the streets to Grosvenor Square, drawing up outside Arnsworth House.

He got down, passing the ribbons to his groom. 'Take them around to the stables here. Her ladyship won't mind. Have a fresh pair in the shafts first thing in the morning, I'll be making an early start.'

'Yessir.'

Richard stared across the Square. He'd sent a messenger ahead. Aberfield should be expecting him. Hoping that his self-discipline was up to the interview ahead, he walked around to Aberfield House.

Aberfield received him in the library, rising from his desk as Richard limped past the butler, still wearing his greatcoat, hat and driving gloves.

'Your coat and hat, sir?' asked the butler.

Richard shook his head. 'I won't be here long enough for you to trouble.' He jerked his head at the door. 'Out.'

'How dare you dismiss my servant, sir!' blustered Aberfield, coming around the desk towards him.

Richard raised his brows. 'I do beg your pardon, Aberfield.' He turned to the butler. 'You had better stay and listen, then.'

'That will be all, Carnely!'

Aberfield glared at Richard.

He waited only until the door closed behind the butler. 'You should be horsewhipped, Aberfield,' he said softly. 'What the hell did you think you were doing?'

The older man paled and took a step back reaching for the bell pull.

'I wouldn't,' said Richard, in conversational tones. 'You really don't want your staff speculating on the reason for my visit, do you?'

'For God's sake, man! There was no intent to deceive. Had you applied properly for Dorothea's hand, you would have been apprised—'

'Apprised? Apprised of what, Aberfield?' asked Richard, his voice a silken whip. 'What do you imagine to be the cause of my quarrel with you?'

'You feel deceived, naturally, now that Dorothea has confessed her lack of virtue.'

Richard's hands balled into fists. 'Her lack of virtue,' he repeated. 'I see.'

'You would have been told!' snapped Aberfield. 'Ask Dunhaven, if you doubt me! *He* was told!'

With difficulty Richard restrained the urge to step forward and plant his right fist in the man's face.

'Really? You told Dunhaven that you had attempted to constrain your sixteen-year-old daughter into an unwelcome marriage and condoned Lallerton's actions when he raped her to force her consent.'

'Rape? Missish nonsense!'

Banked rage surged in every vein. 'And you told Dunhaven. You handed him a weapon so that he could coerce her! Do you call yourself a father? God help you, do you call yourself a man?'

'What the hell do you want, Blakehurst?' demanded Aberfield. 'You have declined to marry Doro—'

He broke off at the sound of the door opening.

'The hell I have!' snapped Richard, ignoring the door. 'What I want from you is the address of her daughter's school in Bath.'

'Why would you want to know that, Blakehurst?' came a cool voice from behind him.

Swinging around, Richard discovered David Winslow standing just inside the door, the grey eyes glittering.

'It's obvious, isn't it?' Richard said.

'Not entirely,' said Winslow, strolling over to the fireplace and leaning indolently against it. 'Spell it out.'

'I intend to marry her,' said Richard. 'What the devil did you think? That I would take her as my mistress?'

Winslow shook his head. 'You might have more success.' An expression of regret crossed his face. 'She seems quite determined not to marry you.'

Aberfield broke in. 'She's taken a foolish notion to raise the brat herself.'

Richard inclined his head. 'So I understand. Naturally I will acknowledge the child as mine.'

Shocked silence fell in the room.

Winslow straightened. 'You care that much?' His voice was oddly expressionless.

Richard didn't bother to reply. He was watching Aberfield, who had turned grey.

'You can't!' he whispered.

With a harsh laugh, Richard said, 'I've no desire to find out how thin your blood is, Aberfield, but I'm a Blakehurst. I can.'

'Damn your eyes, Blakehurst!' lashed Aberfield. 'You really must want that fifty thousand to counten—'

He broke off, backing away as Richard took a single step towards him.

With the speed of a panther Winslow got between them.

'Better not, Blakehurst,' he said, his voice tinged with regret. 'Much as he might deserve it, we can't afford the scandal if the servants get wind of anything.'

'Hah! There'll be scandal aplenty if he's fool enough to take the brat!' snarled Aberfield. 'From the reports I've had, the whelp's the spit of all the Winslows! Blue eyes, fair hair—you think people won't remember and put two and two together?'

Winslow swore softly, his hard gaze coming back to Richard.

Keeping his expression impassive, Richard said, 'You'd better hope they don't.' His voice hardened. 'Otherwise I'd have little choice but to let the entire story be known. And you wouldn't make a pretty showing, would you?'

It could only be a last resort. Unthinkable for the child to have the truth forced on her.

Something must have showed on his face, because Aberfield said with renewed confidence, 'Gives you to think, doesn't Blakehurst?' His expression became cunning. 'You persuade the girl to give up this ill-judged start and I'll arrange to release her money. No need to have it too carefully tied up.'

Richard opened his mouth to make an explicit and blasphemous recommendation about where Aberfield could go and what he could do with his offer when he got there.

Winslow's cool voice forestalled him. 'Not an insurmountable problem, sir.' He shot a steely glance at Aberfield, and turned to Richard. 'If I might make a suggestion?'

Richard nodded curtly.

A cynical glint in his eyes, Winslow said, 'What I propose, Blakehurst…'

Thea stepped out of the chaise and stared up at the narrow house. A shiver passed through her at the forbidding aspect.

The entrance hall was grey. Grey and respectable. A pall of silence hung over the house. She waited impatiently while the maid who had admitted her took her card to the headmistress. Eventually the study door opened and the maid returned, dropping another curtsy.

'Miss Dale will see you now, ma'am.'

Steeling herself, Thea entered. This woman's opinion did not matter to her, could not harm her. She did not care what the woman thought.

Miss Dale rose. 'Miss Winslow? I understand from your letter that you are come to remove Sophie Grey.'

Thea nodded. 'That is correct.'

'You understand that she is under the guardianship of...' The woman hesitated, plainly unwilling to divulge the child's guardian. She primmed her mouth. 'I cannot simply hand her over.'

Thea took a deep breath. She would not shirk any of this. Easy to hand over Aberfield's letter, which merely told Miss Dale that Sophie Grey was to be given into the charge of the bearer, Miss Winslow, but she *would* not. Sophie should be acknowledged as her daughter.

'She has been under the guardianship of Lord Aberfield. Here is his letter resigning the charge to me. I am Sophie's mother.'

A frown creased Miss Dale's brow as she took the proffered letter. It deepened as she read it. When finally she looked up, her eyes were cold. 'I see. Very well, there is nothing more to say. I will have the child sent for and a maid shall pack her belongings.'

She rose. 'You will excuse me, I am sure, *Miss* Winslow.'

'Certainly,' said Thea. 'There is one thing—Sophie will not be told who awaits her, just that she is to be taken away to a home of her own. You will leave it to me to explain who I am.'

A chilly nod was the only reply and Thea could have sworn the woman drew her skirts aside as she passed.

She waited, fear creeping through her tiredness. What if the child disliked her? What if she looked like her father? What was she to do if she could not love the child? Sophie; her name was Sophie. She was not 'the child' any more. She was a little girl with a name, and soon there would be a face with the name, a personality...it was not possible to hate a child of seven, no matter what her father had done.

The door opened and the maid came in. 'Miss Sophie.' Then, over her shoulder, 'Come along now, do. She's not about to bite you. In you go.'

A small child came through the door with obvious reluctance, her eyes huge in a pale face.

The maid gave her a kindly push over the threshold. 'There

you are then, lass. Don't be shy. The lady's come to take you to a real home.'

For a moment Thea simply stared as the maid closed the door. The soft fair curls were familiar, blue eyes gazed back as a small hand crept to the mouth.

'Sophie?'

A nod. Nothing more.

'Did they tell you anything? Who I am?'

The head shook faintly.

'No, ma'am. Just that…just that you are taking me away…to your home.'

At the wobble in the child's voice, Thea's heart shook. Would she hate being taken away from here, from her friends?

'Shall you mind that? Living with me?'

A vigorous shake this time. 'No, ma'am. Is it true? Will I have a real home like Lucy said? Not just here?'

'Yes, Sophie. Your own home.'

'With you?'

'Yes.' Her throat had developed a choking lump. There were things that must be said; but how to say them when her throat ached and her eyes stung viciously?

'Why?'

And there it was. The question that could not be fudged, and certainly could not be put off.

And in the end, the words came easily enough past the choking lump, breaking, but clear. 'Because…I am your mama.'

The child, Sophie, took two hesitant steps forward. And one back. The eyes were shuttered, suspicious. 'I don't have a mama. At least, not one who wants me. That's what they said.'

'No, Sophie,' said Thea, blinking back tears. 'That is not true. I do want you. But I didn't know about you until a few days ago. They told me you had died.'

'But I didn't,' said Sophie, plainly puzzled.

'No. And I do want you.'

'Are you really my mama?'

Thea shut her eyes, trying to hold back the tears.

'Yes. I really am.'

Sophie nodded solemnly. 'Am I allowed to call you Mama?'

No name had ever sounded sweeter, ever pierced so deeply.
'Of course, Sophie.'

Two more steps forward. And two more. And a small, sticky, inky
hand reached for hers, clutched tightly. Gently Thea drew her
daughter into her arms for the first time; held her safely for the first
time since the child had left the sanctuary of her body. This was
right. Completely and utterly right. Feeling, looking at the soft curls
tucked beneath her chin, the small, warm body pressed against her,
she knew, deep in her heart, that there could have been no other way.

For a moment there was a gentle silence, an aching regret for
all the lost years, the lost achievements, the first smile, the first
steps, the first words. And then came a fierce joy in this first
meeting, in all the achievements to come. There would be other
firsts to balance those which were gone beyond recall.

'Will I have a papa, too?' asked Sophie, lifting her head from
Thea's shoulder.

Thea breathed deeply. She had known this question must
come. For now at least, a half-truth must suffice—that her
father had died...

She began carefully. 'Your father—'

'Is disgracefully late,' chimed in a familiar deep voice from
the open door. 'For which I beg your pardon most humbly.'

Dazed, the world and certainties she had built up so diligently
on the journey shattering about her, Thea stared at Richard
limping towards them.

Sophie took a step backward, pressing into the shelter of
Thea's body.

'Is this...Mama, is this my papa?'

There were no words. Not for the questions, nor to express
her confusion, and no words to lead her through the morass of
uncertainty. She could only stare at Richard, his eyes suspiciously bright as he knelt down beside them. Sophie's small
hand clutched hers, hard.

He made no move except to hold out his hand to Sophie.

The child repeated her question, this time to Richard. 'Are you my papa?'

He smiled, his dear crooked smile that melted glaciers and made her heart turn over. 'Yes, sweetheart. If you will have me. And if your mama will have me. We have a home in Kent just waiting for the three of us and I suspect by now that there is a pony in the stable waiting for you.'

And finally Thea understood. Understood the depth of his love. The depth of her love. And the depth of understanding that had brought him to her. To them. There were no more questions. Only his arms reaching out to encircle them. And hers, also encircling her daughter—no, *their* daughter at the centre.

An hour later in the chaise, Sophie lay sound asleep in Thea's arms, lulled by the rocking and worn out by excitement.

'Is she heavy?' asked Richard. He sat back in the opposite corner, long legs stretched out.

Thea nodded. 'Yes, but I don't mind.'

He smiled. 'No, but when your arm starts to mind, let me know.'

She finally gave voice to the question that had been plaguing her. 'Richard?'

'Yes, love?'

'Where are we going?'

He looked a bit surprised. 'Well, home, of course. But first we are going to Blakeney.'

Several more certainties came crashing down. '*Blakeney?* But, your brother—surely—'

'Is, and I quote, looking forward to having a niece to spoil, and acting as godfather to my *next* child.' He leaned forward and possessed himself of one hand. 'In the meantime, he has professed himself content to be my groomsman and Verity is more than happy to be your matron of honour.'

'But—'

'But we're Blakehursts,' he said with a faint grin. 'If you ask me, Max is so disgusted that anyone could have a worse scandal than a Blakehurst scandal, he thought it my duty to marry it into the family.' His smile deepened and he reached out to caress her cheek.

'Richard, no one else will ever accept Sophie, you will be ostracised!'

'For what? Acknowledging my daughter?' he asked, smiling.

'*Your* daughter?' A glimmer of understanding came to her then, telling her just how far he was prepared to go.

'My daughter,' he confirmed. 'As Max pointed out, society is very usefully hypocritical over this sort of thing. While condemning *me* for a heartless libertine, they'll be turning *you* into an angel for accepting my daughter so graciously.'

For a split second joy sang through her. And then she saw the hitch. 'It won't work, Richard. Look at her! She is the image of—'

'The Winslow family,' agreed Richard. 'So at the same time as I acknowledge Sophie there will be an even more scurrilous rumour making the rounds: that Sophie is actually neither your, nor mine, but your brother's child and that by taking her in we have both behaved like saints. A bit embarrassing for your brother, but it *was* his idea. Apparently he has supported the child and her mother, but with the mother recently dead, he was at a loss.'

Her silence terrified him. 'Thea, I understand that you want her to be yours, but this way she is safe—even with the rumor about your brother, officially acknowledged as my daughter she will be more readily accepted.'

'You would do that for me?' she whispered.

He went to her then, taking her into his arms, settling her where she belonged. It felt as though the jagged edges of a wound had come together and were knitting. There was still pain, but it was the pain of healing.

'That and more,' he told her. A man had betrayed her in the worst possible way and yet…he touched the soft cheek of the sleeping child with careful fingers. Soft, silken, utterly innocent…

'There you sit,' he said huskily, 'with his child in your arms. You would have sacrificed everything for her.'

'She had nothing,' said Thea. 'Nothing except shame and the

knowledge that her family didn't want her. I could not knowingly
abandon her to that.'

'No,' he said, his arms tightening, 'you could not. And when
I understood that, I knew what a fool I had been to hesitate.' His
sigh trembled through him.

'I cannot think of her as his,' said Thea softly. 'She is mine
and …' She hesitated, a tension he could feel creeping into her

'Mine,' he affirmed. 'Yes, love. I meant it. Not just legally, but
in every way. That little girl in your arms is Sophie Blakehurst
Our daughter.'

He cradled them both in his arms, his heart full as he lowered
his head to brush his mouth across hers. Hesitant, trembling, her
lips parted, accepting his caress, offering her own. Joy singing,
burning within, he took and gave in equal measure.

'Who giveth this woman to be married to this man?'

Thea smiled shakily up at David as he gave her into the
keeping of the rector. He smiled back tenderly as Richard took
her hand. Then he stepped back with a little nod of approval.

'I, Richard Alexander, take thee, Dorothea Sophie, to my
wedded wife, to have and to hold, from this day forward, for
better or for worse…'

Behind her, Thea was aware of Verity holding Sophie's
hand, and beyond Richard, Max, standing proudly at his
brother's side. And Richard himself, his voice deep and firm,
pledging himself to her '…to love and to cherish, until death
do us part…'

She could not help the tears sliding down her cheeks. They
blurred her vision and choked her when it came to her turn to
repeat her vows. In her heart the vows had already been made.
Yet here in this old church, the words rang out, alive, burning
between them, perhaps given more strength by being spoken
and received.

Richard slid the ring onto her finger and held it there as he
spoke the final vow. 'With this ring, I thee wed, with my body,
I thee worship, and with all my worldly goods, I thee endow…'

* * *

The wedding breakfast was over, the farewells said. David had put the new Mrs Richard Blakehurst into her husband's carriage with a hug and a kiss. Together with Sophie they had come to Tarring House for their wedding night. Verity had offered to keep Sophie for the night, but Richard and Thea had both thought the child better with them. It was all so new to her and confusing, that she clung to Thea as if afraid that her new life would vanish if she let go.

Their wedding night… Richard stood at the window of their bedchamber, waiting. Thea had gone to settle Sophie for the night and tell her a story. When she came back… His body tightened. He wanted her. Wanted her until it was a fire in his blood.

He had wanted women before. But not like this. Love changed everything. And beyond that was the knowledge of how deeply she loved him, how deeply she trusted him to give herself. He stared out at the darkening sky, at the stars leaping to life one by one.

There had been so little chance to speak to her in these days before their wedding. She had remained at Blakeney, of course, and he had been here. Was she afraid of what was to come?

The door opened and he swung around. Thea stood there in the doorway, plainly hesitant. His heart contracted. Shyness? Or fear? She had been a long time with Sophie…

She came further into the room, which was lit only by the flickering dance of the fire and a branch of candles on the chimneypiece. Warm, laced with intimate shadows.

'I…I am sorry to be so long. She wanted me to stay for a little. It was all so strange for her. I waited until she slept.'

His own fears, for they had been fears, vanished. He held out his hand and she came to him at once.

He drew her into his arms. 'Our wedding night,' he said softly, one hand teasing the hollow of her spine as the other removed hairpins, freeing the silken curls to tangle around his fingers.

'Yes.'

'You are sure then? You do not wish to wait?'

'Quite sure,' she whispered. 'What would I wait for? To love you more? To...to *want* you more?'

His breath caught. 'You want me?'

Her smile tore at his heart. 'Richard—that night when we were here and you nearly seduced me in the parlour, you knew then that I wanted you. Nothing has changed. I still want you.'

His heart nearly shattered with love. For a moment it was all he could do to breathe, then she whispered, 'Richard—if *you* do not want this...'

There was only one answer.

He took her hand very gently and raised it to his lips, tenderly brushing kisses over her suddenly trembling fingers. Then slowly, his touch light, he guided her hand down his hard, aching body. Even through the heavy silk of his dressing gown the touch of her hand set fires under his skin. Finally her hand rested on his thigh, inches from the taut flesh that screamed his need.

The next move must be wholly hers.

His voice harsh with restraint, he said, 'Men can lie about nearly everything, Thea. But not this. Touch me. See, *feel*, how much I want you.'

An instant's hesitation. He felt the flaring shock in the sudden tension in her body and prepared to draw back. Then a gossamer touch through the silk. A single, curious finger trailed over the aching length of his need. He shuddered at the fierce leap of desire, trying desperately to curb the response of his flesh under that delicate touch.

He didn't succeed and heard a soft gasp from Thea.

Fighting the urge to tip her face up to his and kiss her senseless, he reached for her hand, covering it, drawing it away. 'It's all right, sweetheart,' he managed. 'You don't have to—'

The touch of her lips silenced him, trailing along his jaw until he turned his head and captured them. She gave her lips willingly, sweetly and took his in return. He opened his mouth, tracing her lips with his tongue, licking delicately until they parted on a sigh. With a shuddering groan he deepened the kiss, sinking into the heat and taste of her.

She pulled her hand from his and touched him again, still lightly, still hesitant. Pleasure that was nearly pain sang through him, beating in his blood to an ancient rhythm. He had to touch her.

His fingers shaking, he tugged at the ribbon holding the bodice of her nightgown together. It gave, exposing the soft, creamy breasts.

Thea barely noticed, so entranced was she by the feel of him. Through the silk, the hot surge of flesh and blood under her exploring fingers held her enthralled. His mouth, possessing hers so deeply, told her of the other way he needed to possess her and heat swirled through her own body in response.

Gentle fingers on her breasts, tantalising, caressing, releasing fire that spread from his touch. More. She wanted more—a firmer touch—and instinctively arched her back, pushing her breast more fully into his hand. She felt his smile through their kiss as he cupped the tender offering and rubbed his thumb over the aching crest. Delight pierced her and she cried out, the sound captured by their kiss. He released her mouth and murmured, 'You like that?'

'Yes, oh, yes,' she whispered, scarcely able to speak for the hot pleasure flooding her. And not just her breasts, but aching and pooling lower, in her belly, between her thighs. She arched again, pleading for more.

He feathered kisses over her face, her jaw, tracing the curves of her ear, breathing gently so that she melted, her knees shaking until she would have fallen if not for the steely arms cradling her. She clung to him, all her fears gone, her world remade in the joy of their embrace.

'One more promise, Thea,' he whispered, drawing back a little.

'I promise,' she gasped, not wishing him to stop, not caring what promise he wanted.

'Look at me,' he insisted.

Somehow she opened her eyes to meet his gaze.

He stepped back, holding her at arm's length and said, very softly, 'There is never a moment, Thea, when you cannot ask me to stop. I will have your promise that if I do something, anything at all, to frighten you, anything you do not wish, you will stop me.'

She stared, dazed. She could feel his need, the urgency of his desire. And she could see something else too. In his eyes. Love, tenderness, all that. And with it, fear. The fear that in possessing her, he might lose her. If she had needed any further proof that he loved her, this was it.

'Only if I have the reciprocal promise,' she whispered, smiling up at him as she reached for the sash of his dressing gown.

He caught her hand. 'And that would be?'

She tugged at one end of the sash. 'That you don't stop again otherwise.'

His dressing gown fell open and she gazed speechless at the lean, hard strength of him, etched in shadow and firelight.

His heart hammering, heat pounding in every vein, he said, 'I think I can safely make that promise.' And led her to the bed.

She had not known that it could be like this. Sweet and wild, his strength and weight exciting. She had not known all the hot textures and tastes of a man. Never imagined that desire could sing, a deep, aching beat in her body. Fierce, open-mouthed kisses blazing over her throat and lower, until with lips and tongue he circled her nipple, teasing and biting gently. Her body melted and she sobbed, writhing against him, her fingers sliding through the dark locks, pressing him closer, wanting more and not knowing what *more* might be, until with a groan of pleasure he drew her nipple deep into his mouth and suckled.

A cry of shocked pleasure burst from her and her fingers clutched at his head, holding him to her.

His hand slid lower, over her belly, the long fingers caressing and exploring, telling her with each touch how lovely she was. Further, until he reached the soft curls nestled in the apex of her thighs.

He took her mouth again and she opened for him as he deepened the kiss, his tongue moving slowly, rhythmically…his hand on her thigh stroking to the same rhythm. The same rhythm as the throbbing emptiness within her. So that it seemed the most natural thing in the world to open her thighs to his tender urging.

His fingers shifted, seeking the aching heat and emptiness,

teasing, parting soft folds. Liquid pleasure welled up and she cried out in shock as it spilt over, his fingers now sliding easily…

'Richard?'

'Beautiful,' he whispered hoarsely. And his touch told her again. Endlessly seeking and loving. Her body was no longer hers to control. It had melted, softening into delight as he discovered a place where every nerve in her body seemed centred, ready to explode in fire and light. A choked cry escaped her as he pressed lightly and stars shattered about her.

'More?' His voice was a husky breath against her lips. She couldn't speak, only lift against him in frantic entreaty as he teased, circling her softness. Then…a gentle pressure and one long finger slid within, a tender invasion of her body's secrets. Slowly, so slowly he stroked as thought fled, leaving only sensation and shattering emotion as the heat of desire and need swept her body.

Shuddering need raked its claws through Richard as he felt her surrender. Felt it in the molten liquid welcome of her body, sensed it in the utter trust of her surrender, knew it in the delight of her giving.

He could take her now. She was ready. Soft, wet, her body trembling on the point of release. And his body was screaming for it, aching to be sheathed in her clinging heat and feel her shatter around him. Shaking with need, he withdrew from her sweetness and nudged her thighs further apart.

Desire hammered in his blood with every heartbeat, redoubling at every breath. But—a queer realisation came to him—this was, in some strange way, her first time. Lallerton had taken her by force, stripping her of her virginity. She had never had a lover. Only violence and betrayal.

And she lay now in his arms willingly, giving herself without reservation, trusting him utterly—her lover. Her only lover. Her husband.

Pushing himself up on one elbow, he looked down at her, continuing to stroke gently. At her body, flushed and ready for his possession, lifting to his touch. At her face, eyes closed, her trembling mouth, swollen with his kisses. As he watched, her eyes fluttered open.

'Now?' she whispered, and he felt it, the slightest tension in her body.

'So impatient?' he murmured, bending to kiss her breasts again, trailing lower over the damp heated skin of her belly, nuzzling into the soft curls. He slid between her thighs, holding them apart with his shoulders.

Shock held her speechless as she felt the hot caress of his breath and realised what he intended. No. She had to be wrong. He couldn't...

He did; and she nearly died at the fiery delight that speared her, the intimacy of his mouth and tongue. Tender, teasing and demanding. A fierce giving and a wild taking she could never have imagined. Gentle hands holding her in a tender vice for his loving. His worship. And she burned, helplessly, in wanton abandon, pleasure and need pulsing through her.

She was frantic, her body afire before he surged over her and she felt the hot seeking of his body, pushing into her hungry flesh. Not enough. Not nearly enough. She needed to feel him within, deep inside where she ached to hold him.

'Thea?'

'Yes. Please. Now.'

The naked plea nearly broke what was left of Richard's control. He hung on, his jaw cracking with strain as he fought the urge to ravish her, to sink deep.

He came a little further, stretching her, giving himself with a slow penetration. She gasped, lifting against him in a silken surge, taking more of him. He groaned. She was so tight that he feared hurting her. He withdrew a little and she cried out, wrapping her legs around his hips.

His control snapped and his loins surged, sheathing himself to the hilt in her soft depths.

Deep. He was so deep. Her softness shivered around him in the sweetest caress, yet she lay so still, her eyes closed.

'Are you all right?' His voice was harsh, shaking. He pushed a lock of hair from her eyes with trembling fingers, spreading it out on the pillow, framing her face with his hands. If he had hurt her… He ignored the hammering of his blood, the pounding urge to have her utterly, and held still.

Her eyes opened slowly and her fingers slid into his hair.

'Yes,' she breathed. 'You promised not to stop.'

Her hips shifted against him, seeking, pleading.

'I love you,' he whispered, brushing his mouth over hers.

He moved then, deep within her, taking her mouth as he took her body, gently, completely. Soft moans punctuated each stroke, mingling with his own huskier voice. Loving her with every fibre of his being until her breath fractured into desperate need and her body tightened around him in urgency. Loving her slowly, thoroughly, holding deep and still as her release shattered around him and his own consummation welled up in an explosion of love and joy.

Thea awakened in the dawn. Pale streamers of light gilded the room and the bed where she lay entangled with her husband. She was cradled in his arms, her cheek pillowed against him, one thigh nestled between his. Contentment held her. Every fibre hummed with relaxed pleasure. She snuggled closer, pressing a kiss on his shoulder, and felt his arms tighten.

'Awake?'

It was a soft murmur. Not enough to disturb her if she had been asleep.

'And if I'm not?'

He chuckled. 'I'll have to wait a little longer.' A brief pause. 'Or wake you up.'

He'd awakened her in the night, invading her dreams with tender passion… She smiled against his chest. 'I'm asleep then.'

She felt the laughter deep inside him as he eased himself around and began to wake her. To life, to joy and to the bright world that lay before them.

Epilogue

~~~~~~~~~~~~~~~~~~~~~~~~

The clatter of hooves on the carriage drive roused Thea from her doze in the shade of the oak tree. Blinking sleepily she looked up and saw Sophie trotting towards her, Richard a length or so behind.

'Mama! Papa taught me how to jump a log! And Uncle Max said it was an excellent jump.'

The child drew the pony to a halt beside the chair. The pony promptly dropped her head in Thea's lap and blew noisily, demanding largesse.

Laughing, Thea rubbed the velvety nose. 'And what did Papa say?'

Richard dismounted. 'Papa says that his daughter is an unconscionable baggage who has her uncle Max twisted around her little finger.'

His daughter. Her heart swelled in joy at the love in his voice. The complete acceptance. Not even the birth of little Davy six months ago had changed that, except perhaps to deepen the ties binding all of them.

He bent to kiss her gently. 'And how is Davy?'

Thea glanced fondly into the baby carriage beside her chair. 'Asleep. I just fed him. Did you ride as far as Blakeney? How is Verity?'

'We didn't go to Blakeney,' said Sophie as she dismounted.

'Uncle Max was out by himself. He says Aunt Verity isn't allowed to ride at the moment and she doesn't want to go in the carriage because it makes her sick.'

Thea stared up at Richard, who grinned at her unspoken question.

'Yes,' he said, a wicked twinkle in his eye. 'Max informed me that I'm going to be an uncle again. I think he's determined to catch up. Actually accused me of cheating!'

Thea smothered a chuckle. 'Oh, how lovely,' she said. 'What a marvellous idea. Perhaps we should do a little bit more cheating?'

He kissed her again. 'Another baggage. I'm surrounded by them.'

Sophie looked up from an inspection of her baby brother. 'He sleeps a lot, doesn't he?'

'He's growing,' said Thea, smiling at her daughter. 'Just like you. Why don't you run inside and ask Nell for some milk and cake?'

Sophie bent a stern look on her. 'I have to take Astra to the stables first,' she said firmly. 'Papa says always to see to my pony first.'

'Good girl,' said Richard. 'Off you go and have your milk and cake afterwards.'

Sophie led her pony away as Thea and Richard watched fondly.

'She is so happy, Richard,' said Thea softly. 'Thank you.'

He smiled down at her. 'For what? Having the good sense to marry the woman I love and gain a daughter?'

'For being you,' she said simply. 'And for having sense, if you must put it like that!'

'I'll find another way to put it later on,' he promised her, dark eyes full of wicked, smiling promise. He reached down and pulled her out of the chair, sitting down in it himself and settling her in his lap. With a deep sigh of contentment, he untied her cap and dropped the lace-edged confection on the grass, to bury his face in soft tawny tresses.

'Sometimes,' he said, kissing her ear, 'I can't believe you actually forgave me for being stupid enough to hesitate.' It still horrified him that he had come so close to failing her.

She twisted in his arms to nestle closer. 'That,' she told him, 'was *my* good sense.'

His arms tightened. He'd thought to find contentment in marriage, and he had. But this deep, aching joy that spread through everything, even backwards so that everything that had led to this moment, and this woman in his arms, was somehow a preparatory blessing. Heaven, he supposed, just might be retroactive.

* * * * *

For a sneak preview of Marie Ferrarella's
DOCTOR IN THE HOUSE,
coming to NEXT in September,
please turn the page.

He didn't look like an unholy terror.

But maybe that reputation was exaggerated, Bailey DelMonico thought as she turned in her chair to look toward the doorway.

The man didn't seem scary at all.

Dr. Munro, or Ivan the Terrible, was tall, with an athletic build and wide shoulders. The cheekbones beneath what she estimated to be day-old stubble were prominent. His hair was light brown and just this side of unruly. Munro's hair looked as if he used his fingers for a comb and didn't care who knew it.

The eyes were brown, almost black as they were aimed at her. There was no other word for it. Aimed. As if he was debating whether or not to fire at point-blank range.

Somewhere in the back of her mind, a line from a B movie, "Be afraid—be very afraid…" whispered along the perimeter of her brain. Warning her. Almost against her will, it caused her to brace her shoulders. Bailey had to remind herself to breathe in and out like a normal person.

The chief of staff, Dr. Bennett, had tried his level best to put her at ease and had almost succeeded. But an air of tension had entered with Munro. She wondered if Dr. Bennett was bracing himself, as well, bracing for some kind of disaster or explosion.

"Ah, here he is now," Harold Bennett announced needlessly. The smile on his lips was slightly forced, and the look in his gray, kindly eyes held a warning as he looked at his chief neurosurgeon. "We were just talking about you, Dr. Munro."

"Can't imagine why," Ivan replied dryly.

Harold cleared his throat, as if that would cover the less than friendly tone of voice Ivan had just displayed. "Dr. Munro, this is the young woman I was telling you about yesterday."

Now his eyes dissected her. Bailey felt as if she were undergoing a scalpel-less autopsy right then and there. "Ah yes, the Stanford Special."

He made her sound like something that was listed at the top of a third-rate diner menu. There was enough contempt in his voice to offend an entire delegation from the UN.

Summoning the bravado that her parents always claimed had been infused in her since the moment she first drew breath, Bailey put out her hand. "Hello. I'm Dr. Bailey DelMonico."

Ivan made no effort to take the hand offered to him. Instead, he slid his long, lanky form bonelessly into the chair beside her. He proceeded to move the chair ever so slightly so that there was even more space between them. Ivan faced the chief of staff, but the words he spoke were addressed to her.

"You're a doctor, DelMonico, when I say you're a doctor," he informed her coldly, sparing her only one frosty glance to punctuate the end of his statement.

Harold stifled a sigh. "Dr. Munro is going to take over your education. Dr. Munro—" he fixed Ivan with a steely gaze that had been known to send lesser doctors running for their antacids, but, as always, seemed to have no effect on the chief neurosurgeon "—I want you to award her every consideration. From now on, Dr. DelMonico is to be your shadow, your sponge and your assistant." He emphasized the last word as his eyes locked with Ivan's. "Do I make myself clear?"

For his part, Ivan seemed completely unfazed. He merely nodded, his eyes and expression unreadable. "Perfectly."

His hand was on the doorknob. Bailey sprang to her feet. Her chair made a scraping noise as she moved it back and then quickly joined the neurosurgeon before he could leave the office.

Closing the door behind him, Ivan leaned over and whispered into her ear, "Just so you know, I'm going to be your worst nightmare."

Bailey DelMonico has finally
gotten her life on track, and is
passionate about her recent career
change. Nothing will stand in the way
of her becoming a doctor...that is,
until she's paired with the sharp-tongued
Dr. Ivan Munro.

Watch the sparks fly in

Doctor in the House

by *USA TODAY* Bestselling Author

Marie Ferrarella

Available September 2007

Intrigued? Read more at
TheNextNovel.com

Mediterranean NIGHTS™

*Sail aboard the luxurious Alexandra's Dream and
experience glamour, romance, mystery and revenge!*

Coming in October 2007...

AN AFFAIR TO REMEMBER

by

Karen Kendall

When Captain Nikolas Pappas first fell in love with
Helena Stamos, he was a penniless deckhand and she
was the daughter of a shipping magnate. But he's
never forgiven himself for the way he left her—and
fifteen years later, he's determined to win her back.

Though the attraction is still there, Helena is hesitant
to get involved. Nick left her once...what's to stop
him from doing it again?

HARLEQUIN
Romance.

New York Times bestselling author

DIANA PALMER

Handsome, eligible ranch owner Stuart York knew Ivy Conley was too young for him, so he closed his heart to her and sent her away—despite the fireworks between them. Now, years later, Ivy is determined not to be treated like a little girl anymore...but for some reason, Stuart is always fighting her battles for her. And safe in Stuart's arms makes Ivy feel like a woman...his woman.

Winter Roses

Available November.

REQUEST YOUR FREE BOOKS!

Harlequin® Historical
Historical Romantic Adventure!

2 FREE NOVELS PLUS 2 FREE GIFTS!

YES! Please send me 2 FREE Harlequin® Historical novels and my 2 FREE gifts. After receiving them, if I don't wish to receive any more books, I can return the shipping statement marked "cancel." If I don't cancel, I will receive 6 brand-new novels every month and be billed just $4.69 per book in the U.S., or $5.24 per book in Canada, plus 25¢ shipping and handling per book and applicable taxes, if any*. That's a savings of close to 15% off the cover price! I understand that accepting the 2 free books and gifts places me under no obligation to buy anything. I can always return a shipment and cancel at any time. Even if I never buy another book from Harlequin, the two free books and gifts are mine to keep forever.

246 HDN EEWW   349 HDN EEW9

Name _____ (PLEASE PRINT)

Address _____ Apt. # _____

City _____ State/Prov. _____ Zip/Postal Code _____

Signature (if under 18, a parent or guardian must sign)

Mail to the Harlequin Reader Service®:
IN U.S.A.: P.O. Box 1867, Buffalo, NY 14240-1867
IN CANADA: P.O. Box 609, Fort Erie, Ontario L2A 5X3

Not valid to current Harlequin Historical subscribers.

Want to try two free books from another line?
Call 1-800-873-8635 or visit www.morefreebooks.com.

* Terms and prices subject to change without notice. NY residents add applicable sales tax. Canadian residents will be charged applicable provincial taxes and GST. This offer is limited to one order per household. All orders subject to approval. Credit or debit balances in a customer's account(s) may be offset by any other outstanding balance owed by or to the customer. Please allow 4 to 6 weeks for delivery.

Your Privacy: Harlequin is committed to protecting your privacy. Our Privacy Policy is available online at www.eHarlequin.com or upon request from the Reader Service. From time to time we make our lists of customers available to reputable firms who may have a product or service of interest to you. If you would prefer we not share your name and address, please check here. ☐

HH07

COMING NEXT MONTH FROM
HARLEQUIN®
HISTORICAL

- **CHRISTMAS WEDDING BELLES**
  by **Nicola Cornick, Margaret McPhee and Miranda Jarrett**
  (Regency)
  Enjoy all the fun of the Regency festive season as three Society
  brides tame their dashingly handsome rakes!

- **BODINE'S BOUNTY**
  by **Charlene Sands**
  (Western)
  He's a hard-bitten bounty hunter with no time for love. But when
  Bodine meets the woman he's sworn to guard, she might just
  change his life....

- **WICKED PLEASURES**
  by **Helen Dickson**
  (Victorian)
  Betrothed against her will, Adeline had been resigned to a loveless
  marriage. Can Christmas work its magic and lead to pleasures
  Adeline thought impossible?

- **BEDDED BY HER LORD**
  by **Denise Lynn**
  (Medieval)
  Guy of Hartford has returned from the dead—to claim his wife!
  Now Elizabeth must welcome an almost-stranger back into her
  life...and her bed!